Barb

SKYCHILD

Also by Suzanne Morris

GALVESTON
KEEPING SECRETS

SKYCHILD

A NOVEL BY

SUZANNE MORRIS

1981   DOUBLEDAY & COMPANY, INC.,
Garden City, New York

Library of Congress Cataloging in Publication Data

Morris, Suzanne.
Skychild.

I. Title.
PS3563.O87448S59   813'.54

· ISBN: 0-385-15305-8
Library of Congress Catalog Card Number 80-2752
Copyright © 1981 by Suzanne Morris

For my son
Quentin Phillip Morris;

for the Gessner family,
and in loving memory of Ernest

I want to express my special
thanks to Dr. Spyros Catechis
and Mrs. Darla Miller, for their
kindness and help in the conception
of this novel, and to Karen Giesen,
for her friendship and help in
proofing the manuscript.

SUZANNE MORRIS

*Genius, in truth, means little
more than the faculty of perceiving
in an unhabitual way.*

WILLIAM JAMES

CHAPTER 1

On the day she learned the Wellman place on Galveston Bay had been sold, Monica pulled out the unfinished painting of the pier with the small boat roped alongside. It struck her now as odd, there was little more than a sketch in front of her; surely she had gotten farther along than that. Yet it was not there: the loneliness and silence she meant to capture, the feeling that the pier stretched out into oblivion; all of this was still locked in her mind. What she saw was a primitive assortment of shapes and stark lines against a blank, white background. Just as well.

She shoved it back into the closet, where it had gathered dust for two years, but she could not dismiss the Wellman place from her mind. It stood in silhouette above the sloping lawn down to the bay, dark where light should have been, figures moving where they would not be.

Buzz Wellman would not be readying the place for its season of isolation. He would not be checking the pier for cross members that might have come loose in a storm, or untying the boat and bringing it around to the storage house across the alley in back. He would not be nailing the shutters closed while Hetty polished linoleum and washed up towels and bed linens for the final time of the year, and emptied the cupboards and the Frigidaire of perishable foods. For in fact (as best she knew; she heard little about the Wellmans anymore), they had not returned since the tragic summer of two years ago.

And now some new family would anxiously await the arrival of their first summer at the bay. Probably they didn't know why the house had been put on the market, and if so, wouldn't much care. Nor would they keep it for thirty years as the Wellmans did. People don't hold on to things the way they used to. . . .

Through the morning and afternoon Monica's thoughts remained in proportion, controlled as the brush with which she stroked lifelike images across the canvas in her studio. But in the early evening, just before dark, her thoughts became frightful, haunting invasions. She sat alone and thought of that summer again. She could see the small, wet face, the outstretched arms, and hear the plea that went unheeded.

Ian Maguire came into the world a beautiful child. After the swelling and pucker were gone, and his eyes lost the squinting look of the newborn, he began to resemble his parents. His hair was red like Monica's, though a shade lighter. His skin was fair and freckled like hers. From his father, Forrest, he took the curls, and the soft, vulnerable expression from deep-set eyes and small mouth, which Forrest had never lost, not for all the ups and downs of his success.

They saw themselves mirrored perfectly in Ian's image, and congratulated themselves. Soon after his second birthday Monica wrote to the three leading primary schools in Houston to place him on the long waiting lists.

Like Forrest, she took pride in the fact Ian showed signs of being bright. His inquisitiveness was such that he hardly had time to stop and languish in her embrace. He did not, in fact, seem to need her much at all.

In the absence of his warmth she sensed now and then that he regarded her as a tool, which he had found useful in time of need, but not entirely trustworthy. When she thought about this, she would say to herself: he is too smart for this world, Forrest is right. But she would not say this to anyone else, not even to Forrest. She did not like to think Ian might turn out like her husband's father, living the life of an eccentric recluse. She wanted her son to be well-rounded and happy; what mother did not? Surely, she would discover that key to his happiness which he kept well hidden.

He seemed to exist on the periphery, spending much of his time first crawling and later skipping along the walls, his slender, taller-than-average figure casting long shadows as he lightly fingered the white textured surface, as though to assure himself the wall was there, unchanged and unmoved. He seemed to be often in motion: walking, running, skipping, or rocking back and forth. Only during storms would she notice him still for long periods: face and hands against the window, his reflection one of thoughtfulness, rather than awe. Though thunder and lightning might give him a start, he recovered at once and pressed again and looked harder. Often a sudden crack of thunder would polarize Monica, and send her running to him, concerned the child's natural fear of storms would overtake him. It never did. He did not need the comfort of her waiting arms, or welcome it.

Once, out of curiosity, she put paper in front of him and placed a crayon in his hand as the sun shone and he left the window. He drew a long jagged line all the way

across. He then picked up the paper and stared at the
mark closely, finally reversing it to stare at the blank side.
She felt embarrassed that she, an artist, could make nothing of his action though certainly it was creative, or unusual. She told no one.

Nor did she admit that he hid things: a balloon from
the zoo which had long since lost its helium; a set of little
magnetized dogs left at their house by an older child;
burned-out light bulbs when he could get them, to be
kept until she discovered and got rid of them; his father's
watch; her car keys. She made no more sense of his collection than of his art work; if she questioned him he
looked at her blankly. But more than that: as a painter
she had studied facial expressions endlessly. His was a determined blankness, not a vacancy. She wondered why,
but by nature kept these matters to herself.

CHAPTER 2

Sometimes Ian caught her watching him. He understood
she was in charge of him here because she was with him
more than the others that came and went around her
when she wasn't behind the big closed door. She could be
looked to for getting his food sometimes, putting on his
clothes, and stopping a hurt on his arm or leg if she was
near at the time. But that was all. She would not help him

get back to the place where he belonged, and getting back was Ian's only concern.

He was uncertain when first he realized he was not like the others and did not belong in their place. He wondered for a while if they knew. When they left him alone in the crib, he used his time to figure out answers. He could remember things that gave him clues about what he needed to know but could not learn from the others because he could not ask. For a long time none of them expected him to speak; then, once they did, he found the words would seldom come and, when mixed with sound, were not the same as they were in his head. He found this failure to match sound with words distressing at first. But after a while, after he learned to fear the others, he would use his inability to speak to his advantage.

He liked his crib because of its close borders and cloud-soft bottom. He took comfort in rocking there, imitating the senses and sounds of the dark warm place where he belonged, for he sadly wished to be in his place again, where the borders were close and defined, and could be trusted not to move from his reach, and the slow thumpings . . . long short . . . long short . . . were even and consistent. There he had lived in wonderful peace and safety until a short time before he was suddenly wrenched loose from his place and forced to begin the long and torturous journey into the bigger alien space with blinding lights and faces cut off under the eyes. The first of the others.

He was passed from one to another, until one day he awoke from a sleep to find himself close to a different face, one with a nose and a mouth. The mouth opened wide and screamed out something he did not understand. This frightened him. He cried. Then he felt himself lifted closer to the nose and the mouth. He did not fit right in

that place. He could see no borders at all, and was afraid
he would fall, and keep falling and falling, for there
would be nothing to stop him. He cried some more,
louder. He felt something thumping his back, very fast,
and could hear a quick beating sound under him. The
voice from the new face murmured sounds he did not understand. He cried some more. Then, all at once, he felt
himself being thrust away and handed again to one of the
others without a nose or a mouth, and carried away. And
there were more sounds coming from both faces. But he
could not understand what they were.

He did not yet know his face would have a mouth and
a nose, and that everything else about him would be like
the others, except smaller. Later he knew there were still
more things to remember about that first big space, but
they would not come to him all at once. As time passed,
he would remember more. He would also come to realize
that the new space was inside an even bigger space that
the others called *outdoors*.

Soon after his journey into the strange place he was
certain his natural home was of the sky, where patterns
were consistent and logical, and where it was surely
warm and soft with puffy clouds that would hold all
things in gentle and loving safety, and was, regardless of
its varying patterns, beautiful to see. He wondered why
he should have been sent away from it. He thought at
first he was one of the others and they had all been sent
away from the sky. It was his inability to match the words
in his head with the sounds in his mouth that helped convince him otherwise.

One day he discovered a clue to the reason for the mistake which brought him here, in a clear bubble filled with
colored balls. He awoke to find it fastened to the rails of
his crib. The one who called herself Mommy, but was

called by the others Monica, put his hands into little grips on either side of the bubble and showed him how to raise himself up while holding it. But he was not interested in this. He was fascinated by the bubble. He began spinning it and watching the balls go round and round inside in a blur of color, and he studied this motion for a long time. He noticed that when the bubble was spinning, the balls would cling to its borders. If the bubble stopped, the balls fell.

He decided that the sky was a round space where he had belonged, like the balls in the clear bubble, and that his dark home had been a ball attached inside the borders of the sky. The spinning course of the sky had been stopped by a sudden crack, and the ball in which he lived fell through.

He believed if he studied the spinning motion long enough, he might find the solution of how to get back to his place inside the sky. He was convinced the ball in which he lived still hung among the soft clouds, awaiting his return, though he had not been sure of this until he watched the repeating patterns of the sky. He knew the ball continued to move, slowly, because he saw it in certain places at certain times, and now and then he could not see it, as when the sky changed from blue to gray and it cracked, and water fell from it. But then he learned it would return and no longer feared, as he had at first, that when it disappeared it would not return again, ever. The others called his ball the sun, or the moon, depending upon whether the sky was blue or black. He did not know why the color changed, but accepted its consistency.

The sky, he knew, was a place of almost perfect rhythm, and that was why his ball was always on the other side when the cracks occurred. If not, the ball may have re-entered the sky through a crack, leaving him forever behind. There were mistakes, even in his place: one resulted in his being sent to this space where the others lived, which seemed to him a very strange place in many frightening ways.

Another mistake was in something that happened shortly before he was sent out of his place and into this one. The warmth in his home became gradually warmer, and warmer still, until finally it was a hot cell and he was strangling. The thumping sound grew faster and faster, frenzied and loud, as a hammer banging at him over and over, and soon he could not get his breath. Just as he reached the point he could stand no more, he suddenly slept. He did not know for how long; the measure of time meant nothing to him then; it was a deep sleep which closed out even the rhythmic sound he knew so well, and when he awoke it was not as hot, and became cooler until he felt right again. He could hear the sound, slow and even, as he was used to. Since the scary episode happened so near the time of the journey from his place, he thought it was probably part of the whole mistake. If mistake it was; if he had not been sent away for another reason.

Yet he did not believe it would happen again, once he returned, for in all the time he had been here among the others, not another ball had fallen from the cracks. He watched all thunderstorms closely, to be sure, and the sky patterns had remained consistent. The soft clouds might form in different shapes, and move, might even change in color, but they always returned to the basic sameness and, surely, he believed, the same texture. Not like the ground, which could not be depended upon to hold to a pattern or texture or set of colors.

He did not often see the sky at night, when his ball was made to seem cool white against the blackness, throwing off specks of light which were called stars. Monica put

him into the crib when darkness came and since he had
learned early to be careful of the ground below, especially in the dark, he would not get out until she returned
in the morning to pick him up. There was a window in
the room with his crib, but the window showed the wall
of another house.

He leaned long hours against the crib rail and rocked
and thought. He'd tried so many ways to get back, from
the time he figured out where he belonged. None had
worked. Once he tried to rise with a balloon from the zoo,
but it would not pull him with it. Nevertheless, he kept
the balloon in case he could figure out another way to use
it. But soon even it would not rise anymore. Once he had
seen a rocket launching on the television. Forrest was
there and talked to Monica about it. He listened, and
watched, and decided his way might be to go on a rocket,
for it seemed to be headed in the right direction. Yet
Monica told him the rocket was going into outer space
and this did not seem to him the place he wanted to be at
all. Outer space, in fact, seemed to be where he already
was.

If he could get close enough, would the spinning motion of the sky be like that of the bubble, and pull him the
rest of the way, until he was inside his ball and safe? The
trouble was that the sky was much farther away than he
had been able to judge. And also, it was logical he would
first have to get inside his ball and wait for a crack to let
the ball back inside the spinning sky. If he could judge by
the bubble in his crib, then it was inside the sky he would
find the pull, not outside. It was all so confusing. It made
his head hurt. Once he saw two little toy dogs that stuck
together if they got close. He felt there might be a clue in
them. But while he hid them away and pulled them out

from time to time to study, this had come to nothing so far.

One day before they moved from the condominium, he did some figuring. He could by then count to fifty. He heard Monica say they lived on the seventh floor. He could see the distance between the floor and the ceiling of their rooms, and he tried to imagine this distance seven times. It seemed to him it must be very high. So he climbed upon the balcony ledge between the pot plants and stood on both feet. He felt a thrill charge his whole body as he looked toward the sky; he must be very close, and his ball seemed within reach. But then, as he stepped forward, she grabbed him from behind and pulled him back inside, and spoke to him in the loud, erratic tones which frightened him. Then Forrest came. He came and went without pattern. He spoke to Monica, then came to Ian and carried him again to the ledge. He forced him to look down, to see how far it was to the ground. Ian tried to explain he was headed up, not down, but he could not make the words come out right, he never could, and Monica said he could be killed if he tried to jump again, and would have to be buried under the ground forever.

Ian didn't know what Monica meant by being killed. He had heard the word used many times, but it did not seem to always mean the same thing. He did, however, understand what it meant to be buried in the ground. He had seen one of the others buried in the television, and he had been afraid to look but afraid not to look, so he stared. Monica was there, and turned the knob to change the picture, so Ian never found out whether the person buried could get back out of the ground again. She told him that a television did not have little people living inside it, but pictures of real people doing things and records of their talking like the records on the player in the living room. He paid little attention to the television pictures. But for the others it seemed to be a way of studying. The television was to them what his spinning bubble was to him.

He could not close out the voices, however, and that was how he learned many of their words. Only once in a while did a picture interest him, such as the one of the person being buried. So when Monica said that he might be buried under the ground forever, he was terrified. He would not be able to see the sky from under there and, worse still, should his opportunity come of getting back, he would not know it. He rocked and rocked in his crib that night, and was afraid to fall asleep.

Eventually they moved from the condominium to the new place called the house. It was very short, and did not have an elevator for riding up and down between the different floors; nor did it have stairs. However, there were more rooms inside it, and it seemed much bigger, so Ian wished at first they would not have moved. He had not felt sure of his legs holding him up until near the end of the time they lived in the condominium and he found that, when the others learned he could stand up and walk, they would no longer carry him from room to room. He soon learned he could not find his way around the seventh-floor rooms—nothing seemed as close as it had before, when they carried him—so he walked only to the room with his crib, the big living room by the kitchen, and the bathroom in between.

In the new house he was even more worried about getting lost because the borders were different and bigger. He learned to get from his room to the bathroom next to it, and into the room they called the den, with the kitchen nearby, and that was as far as he would go. If one of them asked him to go to a room that he could not find, he

would pretend not to hear. To his disappointment, there
was not a place he dared go to look at the sky. He wondered if Monica had put his crib in a room where the window looked out on another wall on purpose, so he could
not see his home. As time went by, he became more certain this was the case.

He grew more and more unhappy as his studies of the
round bubble full of colored balls showed him nothing
further than the original clue. Then he noticed one summer day, as he watched Monica peering into a small mirror in a brown frame outdoors, that the mirror caught the
brilliance of his ball and held it. He had been almost
ready to begin screaming because it was getting too hot
outside, and since the great heat in his ball home, he always feared if he became too hot he would not be able to
breathe. But then he saw the mirror in her hand, and forgot everything else.

He grabbed the mirror to look for himself, and discovered a link he had not known. He felt a wonderful sense
of closeness, almost a touching, with his home, and a reassurance he had not been forgotten and there would be a
way of getting back if only he could figure it out.

He kept the mirror positioned in his hand so that it
continued to hold the brilliance, then moved it away and
back again, just to be sure it would work a second time. It
winked at him. Excited now, he swept it in a wide circle
and back again. Again, the brilliance was captured, and
he sensed this was a holding on to his whole world, however far away it might be, from which comfort and
strength would come until he found his way back again.
He had heard the others say "world" before, and use it in
many ways. Now he understood its meaning. His world
had reached a hand out to him and he felt warm in its

clasp. He was very happy then, and jumped up and down, laughing with joy.

Suddenly Monica said, "You've seen the mirror now. Let me have it back, please. We need to get back in the house." When he tried to hide it behind him, Monica frowned and grabbed it from him. He could not put words with sound quickly enough to show his desperation. Garbled phrases came from him; he hated their imperfection. He hated the way she looked at him. She reached again. He became rigid and screamed with all his might, until she agreed to let him keep the mirror. He would not allow it to be taken from him by any of them again, even the ones at the place called *center* and *school,* where he often had to fight very hard to keep it. He learned from this and other experiences the most effective way to get what he needed was to scream. They usually understood that. And if they still did not, he knew that trying was futile because what he wanted was beyond their powers of understanding. Or so he thought.

That was before they began to play tricks on him, and to group themselves to win against him. And now they were on their way to a place called *the bay.* He had hidden Monica's car keys this morning, to stall her and get more information, for he was distrustful of new places. But all she said as she went looking in one corner and another for the keys was that it was a long drive and that they were "expected" by a word he had not heard before, and that she could not understand why he always pulled this foolishness. She did not say if there were doctors or teachers or children or long halls and many doors at the bay. Finally she lifted her other set of keys from the hook high up in the kitchen and said, "Like it or not, you are going."

He screamed all the way as she pulled him to the car.

CHAPTER 3

How hard he fought, how loudly he protested when taken places he did not want to go, places which frightened him. And Monica never listened then, never once considered that he might have some inner sense about himself that he could tell no one. On that bright afternoon in June as they drove to the bay, the harder he screamed, the more determined she became that he would see she knew best. At last he sat huddled in his car seat, whimpering and spent, gazing out the window.

His screaming was such a part of their existence she'd grown to expect it and to wait as patiently as possible until the confrontation was over and she had won, thinking always that the victory would be his in the end, that this step, or this, or this, would be the right one, the key to Ian's behavior problems.

The doctors had claimed her son was, at the least, psychotic. Even that word, not the worst to be applied to him, was open-ended, full of possible horrors, hard, strange, and cold as a steel door on an icehouse. This summer she was out to prove them wrong or to fend them off as she worked to change him. Still, she could not forget their doleful expressions, their case folders slapping shut and sealing Ian's fate. And through it all, Forrest insisted Ian was a genius and the "shrinks," as he referred to them, were the crazy ones.

It was a long drive to the bay. She laid a hand over Ian's arm and began to talk to him softly. Sometimes this seemed to soothe him; sometimes not. She told him she had come to Galveston Bay as a little girl, and that she had loved the water. She told him they would play and have lots of fun. He whimpered a few moments longer, then sighed. His red-sandaled feet remained together, straight as a soldier's at attention. His right hand clasped the mirror with the tortoise-shell frame which he had seized at the age of two, nearly two years ago. Lately he seemed to be gripping objects more tightly, but with her he was ever more distant and withdrawn. Monica's instincts told her the months of probing by doctors and technicians, of being led into one unrealistic situation after another in order to be "observed," brought him to this.

It seemed there was never a time she had not worried about him. As an infant he cried incessantly for no reason anyone could name, and after the pediatrician Dr. Winters ruled out colic, ear infection, and all the rest, he advised her to keep Ian near her during the day as much as possible. She moved his playpen into her studio when she was at work, but still he cried. So she moved him out because she could not concentrate. Eventually she learned to tune him out (Forrest never did, and she often suspected he overcame the stress this put upon him by working later and later hours), and Ian took long naps during the day, no doubt from exhaustion of the effort expended by his lungs. But it became a regular joke among the people they knew—he was always crying when someone came to visit—that Ian wished he'd never come into the world and wasn't going to let anyone forget it.

Later, the crying spells subsided and when he was four months old she and Forrest considered putting Ian into a day care center. There were a few around who took infants, though not many. By that time her paintings were being sold with some regularity—she had one showing in Houston, one in Dallas, and had even participated in the big annual art festival in Atlanta, which gave her some good contacts in the East. She had also accepted a teaching fellowship at the university, which kept her away two afternoons a week. Though Forrest understood her work no better than she understood his, he didn't try to stop her. His only complaint was that the smell of her studio, with all the art supplies, was enough to make a person gag, which suited her fine because she didn't want him or anyone else in there. And she ignored his disapproval of her "uniform": old jeans, pullovers, and tennies during the day, her long, heavy hair pulled straight back and held fast by a big barrette.

He didn't mind her having help with Ian, though she suspected his attitude stemmed not from a willingness to support her in her career, but rather to show he could afford child care as well as a cleaning lady once a week. Neither of them liked the idea of placing Ian in a day care center, where they could not be sure he would be provided everything he needed, where his diapers might go unchanged for hours and he might be allowed to pick food off the floor and eat it. (Forrest, the more fastidious, worried over this more than she did.) He suggested Monica's mother. "Amy would probably jump at the chance. She hasn't had enough to do since your dad passed away."

"I don't want Mother meddling in my business," Monica said.

He shrugged. "You know that, next to my old man, your mother's a princess. But have it your way."

So they found a woman named Dixie, who boasted the highest references and twenty years' experience with small children, both in church nurseries and in private homes. She was fifty-nine years old, in good health, and, with all her own children grown, was probably dependable.

This arrangement worked well for a while, yet by the time Ian was two years old Monica was convinced Dixie was letting him fall behind in certain skills. She spoiled him. She insisted upon feeding him, though Monica suggested he learn to feed himself. She also had such a fetish about keeping Ian antiseptically clean that she seldom took him outside to play, and was a little put out if a neighbor suggested Ian play with her children. Soon people stopped asking. And as Monica had no friends with children of Ian's age who still lived in Houston, aside from the neighbors on the block with whom she had nothing else in common, Ian simply went without playmates. He seemed content with the situation, or almost.

One night Monica opened the subject with Forrest. "I think Dixie has done too much for him. Look how late he walked—fifteen months old—and he still makes no attempt at talking. He can't even feed himself like other kids his age."

Forrest looked up from the *Wall Street Journal.* "We said we weren't going to worry about what other kids did." He regarded Dixie as a better mother than Monica.

"I know, but he just seems . . . I don't know. Sometimes I think he is lonely. I mean . . . it's really just a feeling. He plays well alone. But he looks . . . somehow . . . a little lost."

"How can you tell what he's feeling?"

"I just can . . . call it instinct."

"Well, he's walking now, so I don't see as it matters when he started. And he can always teach himself to eat, if we make him. Maybe he isn't coordinated enough yet.

And as to talking, you spoil him as much as Dixie does. Besides, you stay cooped up in that room all day and he needs to be watched. I work almost all the time, so I can't help much."

She resented his remark because it minimized the value of her own work while overemphasizing the importance of his, and this attitude served as a handy excuse for putting the burden of parenting on her shoulders. Surely all the engineers at Amalgamated didn't put in the overtime Forrest did.

"Do you really have to work so hard?" she asked suddenly, and was sorry before the words were fully uttered. She was almost thankful when he turned away without replying.

CHAPTER 4

Forrest's work had been a touchy subject for years. Monica felt he showed great courage when he chose to shelve a summa cum laude degree in engineering and strike out into the competitive world of marketing. She was proud of him when he landed a job with the small but growing Bradford Oil Tool Company, where two or three months of missed sales quotas were automatic grounds for dismissal. She understood this was Forrest's way of saying to his father: I am good and I am smart. Watch me succeed.

And succeed he had, far more quickly than she did with her painting, which, she then felt, was as it should be in a marriage. While she contented herself with such free-lance assignments as illustrating garden books and small greeting-card lines, he quickly rose to the post of sales manager of the firm. Over the next five years he worked Bradford right into the spotlight of *Forbes* magazine.

She praised him to the hilt on the night he pointed out his name and title in bold print, but then was amazed to see his mood change before her eyes from one of expansiveness to something close to pouting. He switched the subject from business to babies and said with regret, "It looks like we'll never have one."

"Why do you say that?"

"A man gets tired of waiting, that's all."

"Odd you should mention it. I didn't know it was on your mind," she replied evenly.

"Well, usually a woman . . ."

"A woman what?"

"Has a maternal instinct. You don't seem to . . ."

"I hadn't really thought about it, that's all. I do want children . . . someday."

"When?"

"I don't know," she faltered.

"You'll soon be thirty."

"Well, I'm not quite there yet," she argued, meaning she was neither quite thirty nor quite ready for a baby.

"What do we have?" he asked her. "I work hard, but what for? If we had a child, it would give our life together some meaning."

"Oh? I didn't realize our life together was so empty."

He shook his head. "I didn't mean that. We do have a good life together . . . now . . . but what about the fu-

ture? We agreed before we married that we'd have kids
one day. I think we've waited long enough, and if we're
going to have more than one, that makes it important we
begin soon."

"You sound like someone getting ready to enter poli-
tics."

He looked suddenly hurt, and she was sorry for her
crassness, and apologized.

"It's just that I was so lonely as a child. And especially
after Mother died . . ."

Whether or not he meant to, he could always touch her
with talk about his desolate childhood. In the Maguire
photo album there was a certain snapshot that caught her
eye, and that seemed to epitomize the life of her husband's family. The three of them stood together, outside
on a bleak winter day. Forrest, at the age of seven or
eight, bundled up in a heavy coat and gloves with a cap
pulled down over his ears and dark hair, stood on the end
next to his father. Professor Maguire held an arm around
his wife's waist, as though to warm her. The other arm
hung free at his side. Forrest stood a bit apart, as though
not quite accepted, an acquaintance but not a member of
the family group. Only the photos of Forrest alone
with his mother showed tenderness and affection: hands
clasped, arms entwined, confidence on the child's face.
After the death of Mrs. Maguire, the photos stopped.
Empty black pages filled the balance of the album.

Now as they talked, Forrest looked as much like that
child in the photos as ever he had. It occurred to Monica
there was no reason to put off a family any longer. Her
sister Jane always said it was like this . . . that all of a
sudden you simply knew it was time for having a baby,
regardless of finances, number of other children, age, or
anything else.

She approached him from behind and put both arms around his neck. "I'm due for a Pap smear next month. I'll talk to the doctor to see if I need anything special . . . like a thermometer and a temperature chart."

Several months later Forrest learned the article in *Forbes* had gained for Bradford a good bit more attention than he wanted. A giant conglomerate called Amalgamated Engineering and Tool had taken notice and made moves to acquire the firm. Forrest had the option of joining a competitor of Bradford's. His talents were widely recognized in the industry, and several firms were interested. Amalgamated, too, courted Forrest as he had once courted customers. They built him up; they made him promises; they offered him twice his previous earnings to do what his college education had prepared him for: working with statistics, charts, and graphs.

Monica felt he wanted to accept one of the other, more challenging jobs, some with risks and heavy travel demands. She said nothing, although waiting for him to make up his mind put her in something of a predicament. Her suspicions that she was pregnant had proven true. She knew this fact might influence his decision about a job, and she didn't want it to. So she kept quiet a full three weeks following the positive results of her pregnancy test before telling him. First she asked, "How soon do you think you'll decide about Amalgamated?"

"Oh, I don't know. There's no great hurry. It'll be several months before the take-over anyway, and the longer I hold off, the sweeter the other offers become. And something better yet could come along."

"Oh."

"Why do you look so downcast?"

"I'm not," she said with a sniff. "I've never been happier, as a matter of fact. My next painting job will be the nursery. We'll need it by the end of October."

His eyes lit up with surprise and delight. "Well, be careful not to get the color scheme too wild," he said, and kissed her.

"Only, I wanted to wait to tell you until after you had decided about your job."

"Oh, that . . . well, don't worry. It'll work out."

If the light in his eyes dimmed just a shade when he decided to stay with Amalgamated, Monica pretended not to notice. She made a promise to herself never to question that or any other career decision, and she kept that vow for three years, until the long hours Forrest devoted to work each day seemed to bear on the social development of Ian.

CHAPTER 5

A few days after their discussion of preschool for Ian, Forrest said, "Since you have a fellowship at the university this year, I suppose you could put Ian in their day care center."

He did not say, "I think you're right, Ian needs to play with other kids," or even "I'm not sure you're right, but if you're worried about Ian, we ought to give preschool a try." Instead he phrased the statement as though it were a surrender to her whim. And when she asked what brought on his suggestion, he said, slightly annoyed, "It's what you wanted, isn't it?"

"I . . . I think it's a chance we ought to give Ian."

Her remark stood with neither compliance nor argument. She puzzled over his attitude, then decided it must stem from his own upbringing. He had spent much of his childhood without either of his parents—even his mother, who doted on him when she was near, took long trips abroad with the professor, leaving him in the care of a housekeeper. It must have been hard for Forrest to realize that, for Ian, being away at least part of each day, among other children who would play with him and become his friends, would be a positive force in his life. . . .

At the end of May, she received an official-looking card from the University Center for Child Development, requesting that she set up an interview by mid-June. And bring Ian.

She felt confident the day they first entered the center together. Outside they passed a vast playground with every imaginable toy from treehouse to trampoline. She was reminded Ian did not even possess a swing set. The yard was filled with children, laughing and calling to one another, frolicking in the sandbox and climbing on the jungle gym. She counted quickly: six adults, stationed at strategic points, watching the children at play. She was impressed. Ian paid them no mind, but clutched her hand tighter as they opened the big front doors.

The classroom for Ian's age group was big and airy, well stocked with teaching tools that looked as new as the fresh coat of paint on the walls. As she talked with the teacher, Erica Thomas, Ian walked about exploring first each wall, then one area, then another. After a while Erica stopped, walked over to Ian, knelt down to his

level, and explained she wanted him to sit down in a chair
and she would give him toys to play with. She was tall
and slender, with a mop of brown Raggedy Ann curls and
fashionably big eyeglasses. She wore a peach-colored
smock and a look of enthusiasm to match.

Ian obeyed her and sat before a small table. She placed
a box in front of him with a dozen rectangular blocks,
each a different size and color, inside.

"Do as you like with these," she told him. But when he
raised his hands to touch them she noticed his mirror.
"Let me hold this for you, so you can use both your
hands," she said. Monica held her breath. Ian drew away
and tucked the mirror behind him.

Erica looked at Monica and smiled across a look of
puzzlement.

"He always holds it," Monica said.

She turned back to him. "All right, Ian. How about
putting your mirror right up here at the edge of the table?
I'll go away so you can be sure I won't take it."

Reluctantly, he did as she advised, holding his hand
over it until she was well away. She walked back to sit
with Monica and watch, and Ian began. He took the
shiny enameled blocks one at a time and examined each
carefully, holding it close to his face, rubbing its surface
with his forefinger, placing it next to his ear. When the
box was empty he began to rub his hands all over the
blocks as a medium might rub a Ouija board. Then he
picked up two of them and compared them for size.

"Those are the largest ones," Erica whispered. Monica
had no idea what any of this meant.

Ian then began to stack them tower fashion, comparing
each for size before adding it to the pile. He made no mistakes. When it was done he picked up his mirror and

placed his hands in his lap. He began to swing his legs and look at something across the room.

Erica narrowed her eyes and shook her head. Suddenly Ian took in a breath and sliced through the pile with his arm, knocking blocks all over the floor. Monica half rose, but Erica signaled her down. She walked over to him and insisted in a perfectly even voice that he pick up the blocks and put them back into the box. At first he looked as though he hadn't understood, but as she began to put them back inside, he followed suit. "Good, Ian, very good," she told him. Monica's heart was thumping. He was so responsive to her, more than she would have dared to hope. She thought at once of the lack of stimulation at home. Oh, poor Ian, how bored you must be!

Next the teacher brought out a box of twenty-four colored spools, each the same size; again, mixed up. There were six colors, with four spools of each color. Again, she instructed him to do as he wished. He looked at her until she was across the room again, placed his mirror at the edge of the table, and began to examine the texture of a few of the spools, then emptied them all out in the center, one at a time, with the flat sides down. "He realizes they will roll off; that's good reasoning for his age," Erica whispered.

This exercise he did even more quickly than the first. Soon he was stacking the spools according to color, and after he had done all six, uniformly lined up alongside one another, he looked at the group sideways, then raised up and looked down into each hole. He then worked until the spools were stacked perfectly straight, checking back through the hole after moving one then another by fractions. When done, he seemed to have gotten a new idea, and picked up one stack and placed it atop the one next to it. After he had made three stacks into one, without mishap, Erica stopped him, glancing at her watch. It was almost time for the children to come in from outside play, and she wanted to try a couple of other games.

"Wonderful, Ian," she said, then began putting the spools into the box. Again, he obediently followed suit. Monica was amazed at his cooperativeness, and could not help thinking, why didn't we do this for him long before now? Had he responded to the note of authority in Erica's voice, or even her looks? Whatever, it was definitely reassuring to see him behave in so normal a manner.

Erica was asking Ian if he was good at puzzles. He of course said nothing. Monica almost intervened but decided to keep her mouth shut. He had several puzzles at home, but she had stopped buying them for him because he would put them together once, then discard them. Before today she had attached no significance to the fact that he seemed to work them easily. She had always given him puzzles suitable for his age group.

The puzzle Erica now emptied out in front of him seemed more complicated, as there were many more pieces, smaller. Again, Ian waited until Erica was across the room before he relinquished the mirror. Then he went about his usual way of putting puzzles together, looking at each piece and fingering its texture and configuration, then comparing it to the puzzle board. He completed the puzzle in less than five minutes, only twice misjudging a piece for its proper place.

Erica crossed her arms and said to Monica, "Some of my five-year-olds can't do that puzzle." Then: "Very good, Ian. If you can do one more game for me, I'll have a special treat for you. Now, leave the puzzle on the table and walk to the yellow table in front of the fifth window from the left corner. Do you know which way left is?" (Ian looked around uncertainly.) She pointed to the corner. As he still seemed uncertain, she repeated the instruction, this time drawing close to his face. Monica could sense his fatigue. They had been there nearly an hour.

Ian walked to the corner and looked up at the windows, then walked down to the fifth one. The tables against the windows were in series of four: green, red, blue, then yellow. The yellow table under the fifth window was the second yellow table from the left. When he reached it he turned round in her direction, then looked in his hand, to assure himself the mirror had not been lost.

Monica had already explained he did not talk, so when Erica congratulated him and asked if he liked granola, she didn't hesitate for his unspoken reply before handing him a paper-cupful.

He had never eaten any before, and as he was picky about food, Monica half expected him to push it away. Instead he took it and looked at it. He then sat down on the floor and emptied it out. Again, Monica half rose, but Erica stopped her, and placed a finger on her lips. They watched as Ian sorted the cereal, placing the piles of nuts, raisins, and date pieces side by side. He seemed at a loss as to what to do with the less defined ingredients. He finally placed them in a pile together, then began to rub them with his fist as if to grind them into the carpet or make them disappear. Monica cleared her throat nervously. At last he rose and skipped up and down the length of the row, his eyes downward, pivoted, then skipped back. Suddenly he stopped and laughed.

Erica pulled out a pen and jotted down some notes with the impersonal air of a hospital technician after a blood count. Monica was dying to be assured he had shown well on the tests. She shifted in her chair. Ian had gone back to skipping up and down the walls, stopping now and then to examine something.

Finally the teacher sighed and said, "He has problems focusing his attention on me, seems not to be hearing or understanding me at times. Have you had his hearing tested extensively?"

Monica had not, though she explained they had a speech pathologist examine him at eighteen months of age and she had found nothing amiss in his ability to form sounds. But her diagnosis was hindered by his lack of co-operativeness. Monica agreed to make an appointment with the specialist whose name Erica now jotted down on a piece of paper. She asked if Ian always carried the mirror.

"Absolutely, even to bed."

"Well . . . maybe we'll be able to work him out of that eventually. Have you any idea why he prefers it, rather than a teddy bear or something else a little more . . . cuddly?"

Cuddly? "No. He has had an attachment to it for more than a year. He likes to catch the sun rays with it. That's about all I can tell you."

"The thing is, we don't ordinarily allow children to bring toys to class. It creates chaos. He could bring it for the first few days, until he feels comfortable without it." She still said nothing of the tests. "Is he potty-trained?"

"Yes."

"Does he have many accidents? Was it difficult training him?"

"No. I don't believe he had any difficulty to speak of. We had a woman who looks after him train him. I tried it, but both Ian and I got too nervous. I was too impatient. But Dixie—the woman—had all the time in the world. And I think he understood readily enough. In fact, I think he was eager to learn because he didn't like dirty diapers."

Erica placed the tip of the pen at the end of her bow-shaped mouth for a moment, then said, "Well, I'm not certain of the reason behind his failure to talk. If he doesn't hear well, that would explain it very simply. If he does, then it's probably as you explained when we first talked—too many adults anticipating his needs. I noticed as we sat here there were many times you tried to speak up for him. . . . That's often the case with late talkers. Particularly when there is no peer pressure on them . . . siblings or playmates." She sighed.

"Maybe I should talk down to him more," Monica mused. "I speak to him in the same way I speak to other adults. So does his father."

"If you mean the use of big words, that doesn't usually cause a problem. In fact, it often pays in the long run, I think, as opposed to talking baby talk to a child." She leaned back and raised her eyebrows. "He shows an intuitive aptitude for math; in fact, I'm quite amazed."

"Intuitive?"

"What he does when given a group of objects, without instruction. He can count; how high of course I don't know yet; he knows colors; he sorts and categorizes, stacks—even granola—" she ended, and smiled. "He understands the concept of positive to negative, as shown by his approach to the puzzle. Have you noticed these traits at home? Does he seem to calculate things before approaching them?"

Monica thought for a moment. "He is always good at judging distance. When he pushes a toy around the room he seems able to judge how far to go toward the edge of a chair before he turns to avoid hitting it. And, oh yes, in learning to walk. He took Dixie's hand and made her walk with him for three or four weeks. He never tried a step by himself until he was sure. At the end of that period, he walked. He never took a false step or fell the first time he crossed the room. He didn't do it trial and error like most kids. In fact, I sometimes believe he takes the same approach to speech, though I'm not certain."

Erica nodded, ran a hand through her curls, then asked Monica a number of routine questions. Finally she said, "We can take Ian when the new academic term begins in September, though he'll be just shy of three. We'll be mailing you instructions in advance, and he'll have to have a doctor's report and so forth. Over the summer, do have his hearing tested.

"If everything is all right in that respect, we'll know where to begin to try to draw him out. We believe in developing each child's individual capabilities here. Every child has special gifts."

This last summary sounded a bit like a canned speech; nonetheless, Monica felt very positive toward the school and the teacher. As they left, Erica got down on Ian's level again and smiled at him. "We look forward to having you, Ian, and we hope you'll be very successful here at the center. May I shake your hand?"

He winced and pulled away.

During the drive home, Monica's mind kept returning to the teacher's remark, "We hope you'll be *successful* here." It seemed more appropriate to someone starting a new job than a child beginning preschool. She could not remember the word *successful* being applied to a child when she was growing up. A kid was expected to be a kid. It was all right if he had his odd ways; if he carried strange things around in his pockets, or ate only pork and beans, made faces at people, or didn't talk till he was six. He or she would "outgrow it in time."

On the other hand, sometimes a kid didn't outgrow a

problem, and it was nice that so much was now known about what to expect of a child at a certain age, even if the expectations were a bit overblown these days. Life had been so uncomplicated when she was a kid. You weren't expected back then to be able to count or make your letters before you went to school. If you could, that was nice, but no one attached much significance to it.

Nowadays it seemed society had stepped up the pace of children to match that of adults. She did not read books on child rearing because she didn't have the time, but frequently she got a message from articles in the newspapers or magazines in the doctor's waiting room that was not there when she was growing up: how to distinguish a child who is super bright and how to channel his or her abilities; how to teach your child to read by the time he is three; how to potty-train in one day; how to recognize learning disabilities.

Monica wondered suddenly whether kids these days had any fun, if there was ever a time for fun anymore. . . . Her sister Jane's kids, all four of them, spent every summer with a tutor in one subject or another, always struggling for good marks in school, while Jane herself had grown up quite differently. She was more interested in boys than books, and her grades were never higher than average and often fell below. Yet she never had her summers burdened with tutors and make-up courses. Summers were for picnics, Girl Scout camp, slumber parties, and dipping into the warm, inviting waters of the bay.

Forrest eagerly awaited news of Ian's test results, even though he still had not said he was in favor of preschool. With the revelation of each new detail, he grew more excited. When Monica had told him all, he grabbed Ian by the arms and swung him in the air. "Just wait till I tell your grandfather about you!"

Forrest's exuberance surprised Ian and he dropped his mirror. He screamed in terror and would not be comforted until Forrest retrieved it from behind a table leg. Luckily, because of its tortoise-shell frame, it had not broken. Ian clutched it tightly and left the room. Soon they heard him rocking in his crib.

Monica began to load the dishwasher. "You never give up, trying to impress your father, do you?"

He lowered his newspaper and corrected her. "I gave up long ago. I'm hoping Ian can."

She felt a twinge of sorrow for him; he seldom spoke of his father and when he did his remark was usually coated with a layer of resentment. True, she was not on good terms with her mother, but she could still talk of the good times; it wasn't as though her mother had never cared for her. It was just that some things could not be forgiven.

With Forrest it was different. After losing his wife, Professor Maguire apparently became more and more involved in the chemical research work he was doing at the time and, for all intents and purposes, abandoned Forrest altogether. True, he adored his wife. Forrest had told Monica that before he was born the two of them were inseparable. However, she died of cancer, not childbirth, so he couldn't blame his son for the loss of her. Maybe it was just hard looking at Forrest, seeing him grow to resemble her more and more.

Monica could see the child in the picture, trying to please, trying to make up for something he could not understand. And she could see the father: his smile gone, the forbidding look she remembered so well, saying without words to Forrest: you will never do.

Would Ian please his grandfather? Monica didn't think

so, and she hoped Forrest wouldn't place too much importance on the prospect. It seemed a heavy piece of baggage for a boy of three to have to carry into manhood.

CHAPTER 6

Three months after Ian's entry into the University Center for Child Development, trouble began. Over the summer Monica had the complete battery of hearing tests done, which proved his hearing perfect. At the teacher's suggestion, she went around pointing out objects and saying their names clearly so that he would be sure to understand. "Table." "Chair." "Plate." "Fork." "Cabinet." By mid-September she had heard what sounded like a few new mumbled expressions from him. Though still aloof, and strangely hard to get close to, he seemed a little happier, although she didn't know whether that was fact or wishful thinking on her part. Forrest, when he was at home, noticed nothing different about Ian.

One November eve when dark came early and traffic snarls made the freeway look like a Christmas tree overloaded with red and white lights, she arrived late at the center and hurriedly wrapped Ian in his coat and tightened his hood around his ears.

"Oh, I'm so glad I caught you." It was Erica, behind. Monica shifted to face her. "I was wondering if we could have a little chat tomorrow, maybe around two o'clock?" She was smiling, but somehow it wasn't convincing.

"Of course. Anything wrong?" Regular conferences were not scheduled until early December.

"Oh, just a few matters we feel need to be cleared up." She smiled again and looked down at Ian. "Well, good night, Ian. See you tomorrow." As he ignored her, she looked up again at Monica and smiled.

Next day at two o'clock they sat together in the same spot where months earlier Ian's prospects at the center seemed so bright. Erica folded her hands and began. "He continues to spend most of his day crying, and we can't seem to comfort him. I've tried holding him, carrying him around with me, but he pulls away and wants to be alone.

"He's disconcerted by the playground, and frightened of the sliding board and the jungle gym. One day he climbed all the way to the top and panicked, and it took three of us to get him down without his hurting himself. He won't take off his shoes and socks to play in the sandbox. He screams whenever we try to get him to do that, as though he's terrified.

"He seems, in fact, frightened of everything, especially the other children. I think they make him nervous; if he's approached by another child he screams and pushes him or her away. Well, in fact . . . yesterday he knocked a little boy down and busted his lip when the child asked to see that mirror. Now, you know we have broken a rule in letting him continue to bring it to school. . . .

"Anyhow, we took Ian inside and sat him down in a chair—most of the time, isolation is the best form of discipline for a child of his age—but I have never seen him more content. He sat in the chair, rocking back and forth, staring straight ahead into nothing. When we asked him to get up and rejoin the group he put his arm out and turned away. He was in that chair for more than two hours, until lunchtime.

"And," she continued with a sigh, her every phrase hung to the previous like the link of a chain, "he often refuses to eat at all, and never tries anything except bread and butter and canned fruit. If a crumb or some liquid should spill on his arm, he goes berserk and disrupts the whole lunchtime. I've been helping him eat, but I can't continue . . . it's not fair to the other . . ." Her voice trailed off and she stared at Monica in perplexity. She ran a hand through her Raggedy Ann curls and leaned back, as though exhausted.

"I guess most of this is my fault," Monica began weakly. Since the conference began, she'd felt a knot forming in her chest and growing a little bigger with each statement. "I keep thinking every day I'll make him change. But I never do.

"I know he is in charge of the situation far better than I am; I think he's smart enough to manipulate me. But . . . on the other hand . . . if I really toughen up with him, it's worse."

"How do you mean?" It was more a statement than a question.

"He just withdraws completely." She looked down dazedly. She had not realized how near the surface her own worries were, nor how faithfully she'd kept them in check over the months.

"Listen," said Erica, and her voice now was soft and unremonstrative, "I think Ian needs the kind of help I'm not equipped or trained to give him here. I was curious to learn whether his relation with you was something like you just described.

"I don't know whether it is this place, or me, or the other teachers, or just too much stimulation for a child

who has been so isolated in the past. But I think we're
doing him more harm than good. And frankly I go home
at night and worry a lot about that. If something causes
him to withdraw from people, we may be complicating
the problem."

Monica looked up. "Are you asking that he leave?"

"No . . . only . . . if he stays with us I want to be sure
we're doing right by him. I must insist on some psycho-
logical testing. There are two doctors on the staff at the
university; one of them has worked with a child in our
program before." She leaned forward and folded her
hands again. "If we could just figure out how to get inside his head, get him to open up to us . . . I've discussed
it with the other teachers. They fully concur. I wouldn't
have come to you on the strength of my experience alone.
I want you to know that."

"Yes," Monica said. She needed a breath of air. "I appreciate your thoughtfulness. I'll discuss it with Ian's father and get back with you tomorrow."

"Fine," Erica said, and smiled her reassurance and concern.

The children, sleeping on cots at the opposite end of
the big room, had begun to awaken. Monica found Ian
among the mélange of blankets and stocking feet, awake
but looking thoughtfully at the ceiling, and helped him on
with his shoes. She hugged him tightly. He held her
shoulders and looked around at the floor as she picked
him up.

On the way home a soft, shimmering rain began and
Ian watched the wipers scan the windshield back and
forth as Monica considered Erica's suggestions. She was
angry, although she was not sure why. The center sup-
posedly treated a child as an individual, respected for his
"gifts," as Erica had put it. Yet it seemed now they were

imposing something quite different upon Ian . . . something almost insidious . . . forcing him to conform to the others. Monica had been honest about his behavior from the beginning. Erica had told her nothing of their expectations for a complete transformation within the first three months.

Forrest was incensed at the report. "You let that teacher lead you right into an ultimatum. Since when do the people we hire to care for our kid tell us how to look after him? Psychological testing! She's the one who needs a shrink."

His reaction, so swift and strong, checked her own anger. "Don't you think we might just look into it? What if she's right? I mean, I don't like it either but if there's any chance Ian needs help, we surely ought to get it now while he's young."

"There is nothing wrong with Ian except that he isn't interested in the crowd. Can't you see that? The others bore him. What would their little games and sing-alongs mean to him? He'll be designing rockets when they're playing high school football. Tell that teacher—whatever her name is—to go to hell. Find another school."

His whole attitude was reminiscent of that of his father: arrogant, pompous. This, more than anything, set Monica off. "You don't just 'find another school,' like you pick up a loaf of bread at the grocery store. The good schools keep long waiting lists.

"Besides, getting used to a new place would be twice as hard on Ian, although I'm sure you wouldn't understand that. You haven't driven him to school day after day, never sure whether he'll go berserk when he reaches the doorstep. You never pick him up at night, not knowing what state he'll be in. At least he's just about through the period of adjustment at the center. We can't keep batting him around like a tennis ball."

"Don't say 'we.' You're the one who insisted on putting him in preschool."

Their voices were angry whispers, like frosty wind through brittle tree branches. They stopped then and looked from the kitchen to the den. Ian was running up and down nervously, making soft murmuring noises, lightly fingering the walls.

Finally she shrugged and said, "If something really is wrong in his development, what happens at the next place, and the next? Why not see if we can resolve the problem—if there is one—now?

"I think we ought to be grateful his teacher was honest with us."

"She's only worried that he'll disrupt the class if she doesn't get rid of him. That's understandable, but also the extent of her concern," he pointed out, then paused before adding, "Look, if you really feel that strongly, go ahead and call a shrink."

"Well, that lets you off the hook, doesn't it?"

He walked out. She felt low and unclean for the argument. She looked toward Ian, who had stopped to climb up onto the sofa and rock. He looked very small there, just next to the big upholstered arm, and very much alone.

Had he understood the argument?

CHAPTER 7

She arranged an appointment for January 15 with Dr. Hugh Michaels, the child psychologist from the university. He listened to Monica's brief description of Ian's problems over the phone, then requested she meet with him prior to his interview with Ian. After looking over the form she completed while waiting outside his office, he asked, "When Ian is with children outside of school—I see here that's rather infrequent—how does he react?"

"He ignores them, unless they show an interest in something that belongs to him, like his mirror. Then he gets furious and screams."

"Um-hum." He looked over the form again. He had a long, thin face and brown hair parted down the side. He was young, probably in his mid-thirties, and Monica realized she'd carried around the image of doctors as elderly fellows or ladies with gray hair and thick eyeglasses all her life. But then, she had never seen a psychologist. Dr. Michaels had a kind smile to relieve his severe features, and a way of looking at you when you talked that conveyed his concern with everything you said, putting you at ease. Children probably liked it.

"I notice you moved within the past couple of years. Did he seem to adjust easily as you remember? Any unusual crying, or moodiness?"

"No . . . not that I recall. In fact, it was because of Ian

that we moved. We lived in a condominium, up on the seventh floor, and I was frightened he'd fall."

"Fall?"

"He kept trying to climb up on the balcony wall. It was fairly high, about even with my chest, so he couldn't see what was beyond it. One day he managed to get all the way to the ledge. I caught him just in time."

"Was he looking for something—a toy perhaps?"

"No."

"I see. Had you warned him of climbing up there?"

"Over and over. But still he'd try. When I caught him, that last time, he'd risen to his feet and was about to take a step, or it looked as though he was."

"Do you recall if he was looking down at his feet?"

"No. Up. I remember his arms were raised. In fact, I'll never forget . . ."

"I see"—jotting down a note—"so you grabbed and pulled him to safety. How did he react to that?"

"React? Well . . . it was complicated. My husband came in about that time. It frightened both of us pretty badly. Forrest picked him up and took him back to the ledge, and made him look down toward the street below, so he'd understand the danger. But I was convinced a condominium was no place to raise a child anyhow. I locked the door to the balcony—you see, we hadn't done that before because it was large, and a good place for him to get sunshine; there was nowhere else nearby for him to play outside—and left it until we were able to sell the unit and move."

"But you didn't say how Ian reacted."

"He screamed, I think. I don't know . . . it was such a horrible thing . . . I can't remember exactly how he behaved afterward."

"Did he ever try to unlock the door, and get out again?"

"No." You're thinking Ian tried to commit suicide. . . .

"Has he exhibited evidence of trying to hurt himself since then or at any time previous to that?"

"No." She waved a hand. "If anything, Ian is overly cautious, distrustful of others, or at least he seems to be. I'm sure you understand how frustrating it becomes when you cannot communicate with your child through words. You spend a lot of time speculating about his feelings."

"Indeed you do." He was making quick scribbles now. What was he writing down? Finally he asked, "How does he spend his time at home? What does he like to do?"

"He plays alone. He is observant, analytical. He'll spend a very long time examining new things . . . feeling their textures. He seems to like to watch things that move. If I'm using the Mixmaster or the blender, he's right there watching it work, as soon as he hears the noise."

"Um-hum. And what about your husband? Does Ian like to watch him tinker with the car or work in the yard?"

"No. My husband works at his office most of the time, and isn't much on fixing things."

"What about toys? Aside from the mirror he carries around, what does he play with?"

"Almost anything that spins. You've seen the clear bubble with colored balls inside that connects to a playpen or crib? He has had one of those since shortly after he was born and he still has it, attached to his crib."

"Oh? And what does he do with it?"

"Spins it. Over and over, for long periods of time. He seems mesmerized by it almost. Forrest thinks he's going to be a physicist. His own father is one, among other things, and it looks like Ian is absorbed in the law of centrifugal force."

He raised an eyebrow and puckered his lips. "I see." He jotted another note, then looked at her and asked a number of quick questions: Does he cling to you? (Not unless he's frightened, or when I'm about to leave him at the center.) Is he a good eater? (He is picky, but his appetite is good.) Does he favor any particular stuffed toys, like a bear or a rabbit? (No.) How about sleeping habits? (If he can't sleep, he stays awake and rocks in his crib. He doesn't bother us.)

A pause. A thoughtful look. "Has he ever slept with you?"

"No. I've had plenty of people warn me against letting that get started. When Ian was a couple of weeks old we moved him from the bassinet beside our bed into his nursery crib, and he has slept there ever since. He likes his crib."

"Is your schedule fairly consistent—mealtime, bedtime, and so forth?"

"Yes."

"Does Ian see his father on any regular basis—every night, every morning before work, say?"

"No. Forrest is gone when Ian gets up in the morning, and often still at work when he goes to bed. Sometimes they don't see each other for three or four days at a time."

"How about weekends?"

"Again, my husband often works. When he is at home, he needs time to relax. He's under a lot of stress, and Ian is not easy to deal with since he won't—or can't—talk. In fact, I think his unwillingness to talk is at the root of most of our problems. Sometimes I get exasperated with him because I don't think he wants to try."

"Um-hum. And aside from that, would you say you

have a fairly congenial atmosphere when the three of you are at home?"

"Yes. Forrest and I rarely quarrel. If we do, it isn't in front of Ian as a rule."

"How about discipline?"

"Probably not very good. I think I could force him into things he ought to be doing, like eating more of a variety of foods and so forth, feeding himself. But I . . . well, I raise my voice sometimes, and that's about the extent of discipline. I've never struck him. Neither has Forrest."

"Um-hum. You've written down here that he has frequent temper tantrums. What seems to bring these on, and how do you handle them?"

"Usually the tantrums are brought on when Ian is denied something he's after, or when he loses it and can't find it. Like his mirror. Or if he spills his food onto his clothes, or his arm, that seems to upset him. In fact, that's one reason we've been slow in teaching him to feed himself anything beyond finger foods. I guess we've taken the easy—peaceful—way out.

"In other words, the way we handle the tantrum is to resolve the problem that brought it on. We don't punish him for losing control."

He nodded silently, for which she was thankful. If he had said "um-hum" one more time, she would have gone through the . . .

"Anything else that comes to mind about his behavior that you think might be helpful in evaluating him?"

She shook her head. "I'm sure there must be more, but right now that's all I can think of."

He flipped a page of the form back again. "I see you were twenty-nine when Ian was born. Any particular reason for waiting so long to begin your family?"

"I—we—weren't ready till then, or a year or so earlier."

"I notice here, you didn't breast-feed."

She resented the inference. "I did not choose to. I was not a breast-fed baby, and I turned out healthy."

"Yes, well, some of these questions are aimed at getting a kind of consensus, to give us a general idea of what to expect in the way of behavior under certain conditions."

Yes. To categorize and pigeonhole.

His calmness and lack of comment were becoming ludicrous. She shifted in her chair. Finally he said, "All right. I think we have a beginning. Next thing is to meet with Ian . . ." He smiled. His brown eyes crinkled like Santa Claus's.

While at work that afternoon, she thought again of his reference to breast-feeding. It probably should not have irritated her. Actually she was neither for nor against it in principle; she just didn't care to bother with it. And this fact led to some unforgettable moments of awkwardness the first time Ian was brought to her in the hospital room.

She'd been nervous beforehand, and glanced time and again at the clock beside her bed. She knew nothing about babies; had never even changed a diaper, and seldom held an infant in her arms. Now that her own child was about to be given into her care, she felt painfully inadequate. What if she hurt him somehow? What if he wouldn't take the milk? What if she dropped the bottle on the floor? She thumbed through a magazine, not seeing any of it.

Finally the nurse appeared at the door, and with a check of her ID bracelet against Ian's, she thrust him forward into Monica's arms. As though one became a mother for the first time every day. As though there were nothing to it. She was out the door before Monica realized she hadn't brought the bottle. In a panic, Monica yelled for her.

She returned and poked her head in. "Oh, I just came on duty. I thought he was on the breast."

"Well, he isn't. Bring the bottle right away, please."

While the nurse was gone—an interminably long period, it seemed—Monica could not seem to get Ian positioned right in her arms, and it wasn't long before he sensed her clumsiness and screwed up his face to bawl.

"There, there now, sweetheart," she cooed, looking first toward the door, then down at Ian. She shifted him from one side to the other, then laid his blanketed form against her shoulder. When finally the nurse returned with the bottle, Ian's face was blood red. His screaming had not ceased. Monica was so unstrung that she handed him back and said, "You feed him. I'll do it next time." The nurse whisked him away, and closed the door behind.

She would always remember a sense of failure overtaking her then, thinking she ought to have breast-fed Ian after all, even while comforting herself that in just a few hours there would be another feeding . . . another chance with her son. Silly to let it get her down, when he wouldn't even remember it. . . .

CHAPTER 8

Dr. Michaels conducted several tests which he identified to Ian as "games," while Monica sat by. Ian seemed to do well on a few, and fail miserably on others. Over and over she found herself at the point of begging Ian, please, won't you just . . . . More than once the doctor took Ian's face in his hands and coaxed him, "Look at me, Ian." Ian would do so quickly, then blink and look off to the side.

Finally he said, "I think I might conduct some further tests elsewhere—perhaps at the center—where Ian is accustomed to his surroundings. I seem to have trouble focusing his attention here. After that, I'll phone you and we'll make a date for a joint consultation—you and your husband."

When he called, several weeks later, he said, "I've finished my tests, but if you don't mind I'd like to go over a few more questions with you now, if you have a moment."

"Of course." She propped the receiver on her shoulder and wiped her hands with a rag soaked in turpentine. No, she had not suffered maternal rubella or measles. No, Ian had not suffered any early infections or high fever. No, there was nothing to indicate any neurological damage at birth. The pediatrician could confirm that. (She could have sworn she answered all those questions on the form.)

"All right, how about a meeting next Monday?" he suggested.

She sat down in front of her easel, and thought over his questions again. There was something else which had not occurred to her until this moment.

Just before she learned she was pregnant, she got her first break with illustration. She had attended an East Texas folk festival, which included a fiddling contest entered by every old-timer between Nacogdoches and the state line. Her object was to take photographs at the festival and do some oils from them. While there, she met a news photographer from the Houston *Chronicle* who was covering the festival for the Sunday magazine. They began to talk, and he was keenly interested in her plans. She thought little of it at the time but a few weeks after that festival he called her. Next year they wanted to do an advance on the folk festival, and if her oils were good, they would reproduce them for the magazine. She could hardly believe it.

She pulled out her photos and set to work, only to put off the project when her morning sickness began. In the following week her pregnancy was confirmed, and the deadline for finishing the portfolio of twelve paintings would coincide almost exactly with her child's birth.

Never more conscious of time slipping away, she forced herself to settle down to the day-to-day routine at her easel. Yet often as not, she gazed dizzily at the sight in front of her. She spent part of the morning in bed with a wet cloth on her forehead and part of it rooted in front of the toilet. Not until late afternoon would she have the strength or the heart to face working, and she barely got started before it was time to put dinner on. Forrest would return from a demanding day, tired himself, and look at her washed-out face. "How was your day?" he'd ask, his

eyes averted, and when she told him she tried to work but
didn't get much done, he would fall silent, not saying that
she didn't have to do that portfolio, that he could provide
the money they needed, that the baby was more important, that *he* was more important. Still, she got his message. She made up her mind to keep going and to finish in
time, before the baby came, without making a fuss or pro-
voking a confrontation. It wasn't the money, but Forrest
wouldn't understand that. She could do it all. She was
doing it, wasn't she? Having the baby as Forrest wanted,
managing her work, getting along better and better as the
months went by, workday expanding to three, then four,
then six or seven hours.

But near the end it was close, and she threw herself
into a flurry of work not only to finish what she had
started but to have time to go back and make the changes
necessary, for she still felt she had not quite captured the
feeling she was after. Pathos. Humor. Vulnerability. Life.
Her art professor's words crept across her consciousness like a finger of fog rolling out, then whispered
back: You can't do it. You've lost it. . . .

Still, by now her strokes were more confident; she was
into the channel and swimming hard, and the drive (or
the being driven) was what caused her to go too far that
mid-October when the weather suddenly turned cool and
rainy. When she felt the sniffles coming on, she sloughed
them off like any small aggravation, an obstacle in her
path (she had dealt with many, it seemed), keeping the
tissues nearby, blowing her nose, drinking lots of juice,
and thinking all the time, half consciously, that the cold
or whatever would go away.

Yet it had not. She awoke one morning and sat straight
up in bed with excitement. Had she dreamed? The pictures were so much on her mind. Perhaps in sleep the an-

swer had worked its way up. She blew her nose, pulled on a robe, and went straight to her easel. The foot-stomping, brow-sweating energy of the old-timers—all the magic of the festival that she feared lost—had returned. She could smell the sweat, the chewing tobacco, the corn whiskey; feel the red dust, rising; hear the calls; and fiddling songs went up her spine like the bow on the strings. She threw on the lights in the studio and glanced at the props and photos that had lain by for all these months. Suddenly all of it was real, alive. . . .

Forrest was leaving early for an out-of-town trip. "You feel warm," he said as he kissed her goodbye.

"I'm wearing a heavy robe. I'll change in a few minutes."

The next time she looked up it was five o'clock in the afternoon and darkness was falling. She'd gone over six of the twelve paintings and was filled with joy for the vitality she now found in them. To each she affixed her double *M*.

She walked from the studio, a little dizzily, and felt her forehead. It was warm. Forrest was right. Only now her whole body was warm. She called her obstetrician for an appointment the following morning and went to bed. Just before she dozed off she wondered if the fever had awakened her that morning, and whether it was the cataclysmic force that brought her creative energies together to strike the needed blow. Maybe she should have insisted on seeing the doctor right away. But surely she was overreacting. . . . She fell into the deep sleep of exhaustion.

"How long has the fever gone on?" The OB's look above his bifocals was accusatory.

"I—I don't know exactly—"

"Your temp's at a hundred and one. That's a dangerous level."

"In what way?" she asked, anxiously.

"Could bring on premature labor, for one thing." He slapped his metal chart holder shut. "I want you in the hospital where I can watch you for a while. We'll do some blood and urine cultures and so forth. Call Forrest and tell him to bring your toothbrush and nightgown."

"He's out of town. I'll stop by for my things."

By the time her doctor made his evening rounds the tests were done and she was perspiring, free of fever. "You can go home in the morning if the fever stays down tonight. But I want to see you at the end of the week."

"You don't think this has hurt my baby, do you?"

"That depends upon how long you had the fever and how high it went, and exactly what caused it. Right now, I'd only be guessing. But I'd say the chance is likely the baby is fine."

By the time Forrest returned, she was well and back at work in her studio. She didn't deliberately withhold the episode from him, but she let it pass as she listened to news of his trip. Besides, he would only chastise her for letting herself get so sick and, anyhow, it was over. Even her anxiety at the hospital seemed foolish now that she was well, and on her next visit the OB reaffirmed there was little danger the baby had been damaged in any way. All the tests were normal. She tried not to dwell on it. Luckily there was little time left to worry.

On the day before Ian was born she toted the small canvases to the *Chronicle* building and set the whole features department astir with excitement. She went home, propped up her feet for what seemed the first time in months, and spent the whole evening relaxing.

Her relief following Ian's birth was complete. He regis-

tered high on the Apgar scale, and there was no mention
of any problems. The pediatrician she chose had cared for
Jane's brood before they moved to California, and with
years of experience behind him, Dr. Winters declared Ian
a healthy baby. She dismissed the prenatal fever from her
mind. . . .

Until now, more than three years later. She was about
to call Dr. Michaels and report it, but the telephone rang
just as she touched it, giving her a start.

"Oh, it's you, Mom."

Amy had spent the day shopping with Hetty Wellman.

"Was it fun?" She sighed, and sat down, the telephone
cord coiled around her arm. Fever.

"Well, I think she enjoyed it. I never know what to buy
Hetty for her birthday, she's so funny about things, so I
figured she might like to spend a day downtown, just like
we used to do when you kids were in school. Of course
she wouldn't let me buy her anything but lunch."

"Um-hum." Impossible to imagine Hetty downtown in
a dress and walking pumps. Although she lived in Houston most of the year, she never looked quite in place anywhere except at the bay, her bare arms leathery from exposure to the sun, her feet flat and crusty on the bottom
from going without shoes. Fever. . . . "Look, Mom, I've
got to—"

"Hetty spent forty-five minutes in the notions department at Woolworth's and came out with a package of yellow yarn and some crochet needles. I always thought
buying this early for an expected baby is bad luck—they
just found out about it, you know—but I wouldn't have
said that to Hetty. She's so excited about having a grandchild on the way. All she talked about."

Monica was not aware of the coming addition to the
Wellman family, but didn't say so. She needed to get off

the phone, needed to call Dr. Michaels about the fever. . . .

"I took her to the Terrace at Foley's for lunch. You know, I liked it better when it was the Azalea Terrace. They didn't hurry you so, and the food was better. And you didn't have to make your own salad."

Monica could remember, as a little girl, watching her mother Amy place a hat on her red hair and pull on her neat white gloves, bound for a day of shopping, usually for a lot of things she didn't need, and that she wouldn't know were so expensive until her husband had to pay the bill.

". . . Anyhow, Hetty proceeded to make comments under her breath about the atrocious prices on the menu. I was so afraid someone would overhear! I made a point of ordering the most expensive item, so she'd hush up and feel free to have whatever she wanted. Chicken soup. That was all she'd have. But she said it was delicious, so there wasn't much I could do. Some birthday gift, chicken soup."

"Well, that's Hetty, I guess." Was it? She could hardly remember. She glanced at the clock. Nearly five. Getting too late to call. . . .

"How's Ian?" as though on cue.

"Fine."

"Forrest told me how high he scored on the entrance tests at preschool. Ian's going to be the first genius we ever had in the family. I was bragging to Hetty all about him today."

Well, save your breath. The newest scores are still being tallied. "Mom, I've got to go. Call you later."

Of course she never called her mother. The only time they talked was when Amy called, and if Forrest answered the phone, often she spent more time talking to him than to Monica. But at least today's conversation served a purpose, gave her time to reconsider the call to Dr. Michaels. Why tell him about the prenatal fever? She had answered each of his questions honestly. If this were important, he would have asked. It probably would have been listed on the form.

She looked again at her easel. She'd begun a portrait of Ian, had sketched in the facial shape and hairline. She kept a pair of his sandals from last year nearby and a lock of his hair, plus three photos taken outside, for props. She turned off the studio light and went into the kitchen to set the oven timer, her mood low. Well, wasn't it always, this time of day? Still, the fever was on her mind. Any good mother would mention it. . . .

She decided to meet with Dr. Michaels alone, and make up an excuse about Forrest being too busy to attend. She wanted to feel the doctor out . . . to see what possibilities were derived from high fever . . . to have time to think about it. She felt somehow if she were to ask him directly it would set the wheels in motion for something she could not stop or control. If there was anything amiss, everyone—the doctor, the teacher, Forrest—would leap upon it as the cause. It might be wise for her to keep it to herself. After all, Ian was perfectly healthy at birth. No need to throw everything into a tailspin.

CHAPTER 9

Dr. Michaels seemed put out that Forrest was absent, but agreed to convey his findings to Monica. "However," he added, "since the symptoms I find in Ian may well stem directly from your husband, I'll have to insist that he sit in on all our future conferences."

She had not expected that. "And just what did you find?"

He cleared his throat. "When I am able to get Ian to focus on a test, his scores show undoubtedly that his teacher, Miss Thomas, was correct. He has an unusually high aptitude in math and in science." He lifted his brows. "Almost phenomenal. In other tests, those that measure a child's ability to understand and carry out verbal instruction, or to respond to situations which require an understanding of his relation to the things around him, or participation in a project requiring communication with me, he scores disturbingly low. Many of the tests I wanted to conduct were impossible because of his lack of cooperation. Those scores pull the average down to subnormal."

She opened her mouth to argue, but he interrupted. "Ian's ability to score can change. Six months from now he could possibly score much higher on the tests involving communication . . . that is, if . . .

"Mrs. Maguire, are you familiar with the syndrome of autism?"

"Not really," she said, but the word hit her like a stone. "Something to do with being tuned out, isn't it?"

"Yes, in a way. Let me explain. . . ." His voice became mellow and comforting. "Some years ago a psychiatrist named Leo Kanner observed a number of children who seemed able to exist in a world unto themselves, completely independent of outside stimuli; self-sufficient individuals—autonomous, in other words. That is where the term 'autism' originated. It's a difficult syndrome to diagnose at times. After all, we strive for a certain amount of autonomy, to focus in on the things which are important to us at a given time. And this is quite healthy.

"On the other hand, autism is the extreme of this faculty. The autistic person is literally locked up within himself and unable to relate to others, to cross the barrier which stands between him and the rest of the world."

He paused and leaned back in his swivel chair. "Now, there are certain behavioral symptoms by which we recognize autism in young children. I can give you some pamphlets to look at at home, but briefly, they begin quite early. Incessant crying, or a curious *lack* of crying; sleeping problems; disinterest in people and surroundings.

"Later the child may exhibit odd eating habits, an obsession with inanimate objects, such as faucets, pipes—things which are hard and cold . . ."

Ian's hand mirror.

". . . Late speech, or unusual speech patterns, such as echolalia—repeating another's word rather than responding—difficulty with toilet training, much self-stimulus such as rocking, spinning objects. Irrational fears and, conversely, lack of fear toward actual threat of danger."

Ian's nearly stepping off the balcony of the seventh floor. His fascination with lightning and thunder. His fear of climbing down, even a small space. . . .

He went on naming things. From time to time she could apply one to Ian and would feel a slow tightening in the pit of her stomach. Other times what he said did not seem to apply to Ian at all.

"Bizarre behavior; inappropriate laughter."

His game with the mirror in the sunshine; he always laughed gleefully. She could never figure out why.

"Lack of eye contact," he said next, and looked hard at her, as though he sensed her mind was wandering off, fixing on comparisons, and he wanted her fully back. "Or, more a penetrating stare that seems to be going beyond and through you, perhaps," he said. He cleared his throat again.

This is not easy for you to hand to a parent, she thought, not easy for you to peel off along with your clothing when you step into your shower tonight. . . .

"Now, in talking with Erica Thomas and with you, and watching Ian myself, I notice several of these symptoms, though I must confess he is hardly a classic case of the autistic child, if indeed he is autistic. There are a number of things that have me stumped. I'm not one to apply labels quickly."

"Nor I."

"A number of these symptoms can be explained by his home situation, perhaps. And most of them by Ian's failure to develop a strong bond with his father. It is very important that a child develop a good relationship with the parent of the same sex; if this is not accomplished, he has no measuring stick for the development of other relationships because he has no model. He has difficulty reaching out to others if he is unsure of what he is him-self; do you follow me?"

"I think so."

"I was hoping to go into that in depth today, with your husband. . . . Now, it's possible these symptoms could result from a general coldness in a child's environment, a general lack of love and warmth from his parents from the beginning. His behavior then becomes reactive . . . in other words, he decides instinctively, you don't want me; therefore I don't trust you; I have to protect myself, so I build a wall around myself."

"I have never been cold toward Ian. I was awkward and unsure when he was an infant; I remember this was distressing. But I was never cold."

Dr. Michaels looked at her thoughtfully for a few mo-ments, then said, "I didn't mean to accuse."

"I realize that." She looked down. "And of course Ian's father and I have both been involved in our careers since Ian was born. Maybe we're both at fault for not spending the time with him that we should." She was feeling more confident now. Maybe Ian's condition was something she could grasp more easily with professional help. Light bulbs were switching on. This, then, was what psycho-logical help was all about. Maybe there was something to it, regardless of what Forrest believed. . . .

He continued: "If all the reasons for Ian's behavior are environmental, then with some changes at home, some therapy and family counseling, there is probably a strong chance these troubles can be worked out.

"You see, current research indicates there must be some biochemical or genetic reason behind autism; whereas at one time it was believed environmental forces were responsible. But with Ian there was no maternal rubella or measles, or sign of neurological problems at birth, no high fever or serious infections as an infant."

She swallowed hard. "No. Nothing."

High fever. But hers was prenatal. Not on Dr. Michaels' list of possible reasons for autism. She kept her head lowered at length, thinking. Mention it anyway, she told herself, but the words wouldn't come to her lips. They were firmly entrenched somewhere deep down inside her, like the roots of a great tree. Finally she raised her head. "Ian's pediatrician assured us he was perfectly normal." Hold on to that, don't forget, and everything will be all right. "If anything is wrong in Ian's social development," she continued, her voice so low Dr. Michaels was leaning toward her slightly, "it has to be environmental. I can see all kinds of ways we might have caused him problems." She sighed. Spoke louder. "Funny that you can't see the most obvious things until someone points them out."

He smiled. "It's hard for any of us to be objective about our own children." He reached for a folder and closed it. Metal chart holders, folders, always snapped shut as though your own problems were none of your business, or maybe too horrible for you to face. . . . "Well then, let's set up a meeting when your husband can be here. Perhaps we have a beginning."

But then he paused, as though in doubt again. "Tell me one other thing. Do you have trouble getting Ian to look you directly in the eyes?"

"I . . . I don't go around forcing the issue. Sometimes he doesn't seem to be interested in looking at me, but it is usually because he's eager to get on with something else. He's very inquisitive."

"Um-hum. . . . This thing of eye contact can be confusing. There were times in the beginning of my sessions with Ian that he seemed to look at me, at least momentarily, but later, he seemed to make a concentrated effort not to, and if I forced him he seemed to be looking through me, so that I'm not quite certain."

Yes, I have felt it too, she thought, but could not say it.

"Be on the alert for that at home, and we'll talk about it again."

Are you reopening the door you just closed? "You seem to put a lot of emphasis on eye contact."

"Yes. It can be important. Well then, for now we'll base our direction on the probability that Ian's problems are stemming from his environment. I'm looking forward to meeting with your husband."

Again, she knew she ought to tell him of the fever. "Dr. Michaels, I did have . . ." she began, but could not voice the confession. He looked at her quizzically. She was sure he suspected she was not leveling with him. She rose from her chair, and let her statement take a right-angle turn. "I did have . . . a question."

"Yes?"

"I was just curious . . . is there a cure for autism?"

"No. There are behavior modification techniques, but only in rare cases has a child eventually overcome it." He looked at her expectantly again. She said nothing. He smiled his dismissal. She closed the door behind her.

She couldn't seem to get her breath. The hallway from the office of Dr. Michaels had not seemed so long before, and you had to turn left at the end and then left again to get to the center of the building and the elevators. Or was it right? She turned wrong and found herself walking at the edge of still another corridor which led to a suite with glass doors, the office of an ophthalmologist. Inside, pictures everywhere of people looking at you through various shapes and sizes of eyeglass frames. Eye contact. She stood outside the glass doors, not knowing what to do.

Probably environmental.

A receptionist inside noticed her and approached, opening the door. "May I help you?"

"What? Oh yes, I seem to have made a wrong turn." Her throat was so tight the words could hardly squeeze through.

"Perhaps I could help. What office were you looking for?"

"The . . . the elevators."

"Oh, then you turn around and go back down to the end of this hall, and when you pass suite 590, go on to . . ."

Her voice drifted off. Monica had already wandered away. Five-ninety. Eye contact. Just the other day, Ian had looked at her, when she accused him of hiding her car keys. Only a brief glance, but just the same. . . . Five-ninety. Why was she walking along the edge of the hall, instead of down the center? The carpet runner was so pretty, with a paisley design. She didn't want to touch it with her feet. Forrest rarely touched Ian, kept his distance, cold. Five-ninety.

She looked up at the doors she passed. When she finally reached 590 she didn't know what to do. Across from her there was a door marked WOMEN. She swung it open and walked in. She sat down on a bench and clutched her handbag. All she could see was Ian. Ian, running up and down the walls, watching his shadow. Ian, holding his mirror and laughing. Ian, refusing food. Ian, enthralled by the scene of a raging storm. Ian, smiling with his face upturned to the sun. Ian, wriggling from her arms, looking away. Beautiful Ian, his red curls bouncing, his lithe body always in motion, like an elfin being, flitting from

place to place as though nowhere did he truly belong. . . .

Environmental. Cold. No one fit. Not Forrest; not
Monica.

Two young women swung through the door, talking,
laughing. They glanced at Monica and passed through to
the toilets. I must get out of here, she thought, and
walked through to the hall again. She went on and on
walking, thinking of Ian, standing alone at the edge of
the playground next to the fence as the other children
played together, their laughter filling the air. Isolated, sitting in a chair, being punished for, what was it? She
couldn't quite remember. Something about, oh yes, his
mirror. Protecting his rights. Sitting in the chair, content-
edly, alone.

Autism.

To the point. Like the sting of a bee.

She was pressing the elevator button before she realized she'd found the elevators. The doors opened in front
of her and cool air wafted across her face. She entered
and pressed the "one" button. The car seemed to plunge
down the shaft taking her body but not her thoughts. Another word kept coming, kept trying to catch her up.

Fever.

The word formed in her mind in blazing letters, and
throbbed and grew larger and changed shapes and colors:
a calligrapher's nightmare. She walked from the elevator
across the lobby to the drugstore and ordered coffee that
grew cool before her and sat untouched as she gulped ice
water. Then she sat some more, as though anchored by
the chair. It was so hard to think in a straight line. This
morning she'd left her son at the center as usual. In fact,
he'd been in one of his better moods, which sent her

away, headed for Dr. Michaels with a healthy boost to her confidence.

Now, just two hours later, she struggled with a label that seemed too heavy and lopsided for his small shoulders to bear: a sum total of all his weaknesses on the one side; an almost total disregard for all his strong points on the other. She could almost believe that if she hadn't gone to see the doctor she would now be at home working, and none of this would be true.

She shook her head. Ian's symptoms could be caused by environment. Chances strong. Doctor said so. Why hadn't she mentioned the fever, given him every possible clue? But he did not say *prenatal* fever. She listened carefully for that prefix to the word, which spelled disaster for her child. He had a whole list of possibilities and that was not among them. No, he had not said that. So environment must be . . .

Fifty-fifty. Either Forrest caused Ian's problems by his apathy or she robbed her son of his chance to be a total human being before he pushed himself through her womb.

She gulped more water, forcing her thoughts to order. Maybe her worry had grown out of proportion. Now she knew. There was someone she could go to, someone who'd looked at Ian with a practiced eye since birth and seen nothing wrong in his makeup. As she rose and paid for her untasted coffee she felt as though she were in a moving picture that had been switched into reverse. She went to a pay phone and called Ian's pediatrician. If Dr. Winters was even the least bit indecisive about her dilemma, she would confess the fever to the psychologist. If not, she wouldn't mention it.

She waited for the reassuring sound of his voice. Dr. Winters was gentle, down-to-earth, grandfatherly. He listened patiently until she finished, then told her, "If it will make you feel any better, you can bring Ian in and I'll look at him. But I think by now I'd have noticed if he was autistic. I've seen several autistic children in my time, and I think those teachers and that doctor are full of nonsense.

"Tell you something. People involved in what we call 'child development' nowadays don't always practice what they preach. They say on the one hand they want to develop the child in his own fashion, but come along a child who is just a shade different, and they get nervous. There's an old saying that a little bit of knowledge is dangerous."

She sighed. "I wouldn't have worried at all if it hadn't been for that fever I had. But I just had to be sure—"

"From what I have on my chart, you developed some cold symptoms, had some fever for a short while, called your OB, and went to the hospital. But the tests showed up normal, and it looks like he was pretty thorough. Fetal monitor, ultra-sound . . .

"Take my advice. Give Ian some time to grow up. He'll talk your ears off when he's ready and he'll make friends, too."

"Thanks. You've no idea how much better I feel. I'm sorry I took so much of your time."

"You call me any time you need to talk, and don't let those rascals scare you."

She hugged the phone to her ear as the dial tone droned, unwilling to let go of this tangible proof that everything was all right. The line connected her to reality, proving that the theories and speculations of Dr. Michaels were products of exalted minds that looked down coldly and analyzed why certain little children did certain things. She hung up finally. She had not been aware how tight her grip had been on the receiver, how closely she'd pressed it against her ear.

She felt greatly relieved, almost light-headed, as she left the phone booth and drove home. The welcome feeling stayed with her all through the evening as well. Yet in the night, the doubts seized her again. She could not account for what happened that fevered night while she slept. She remembered well that she had never felt warmer than while waiting for the doctor to enter the examining room.

But what if she was wrong? What if it was too high all the day before, while she worked?

Impossible. Or was it?

Gradually, Dr. Winters' reassurances were snuffed out under the pressure of one qualifying fact: she had never learned exactly what damage a high prenatal fever might cause to an unborn fetus, having been more than satisfied to learn she'd produced a healthy baby. Also, Dr. Winters would not pick up on certain behavioral symptoms in Ian over the years. He was a pediatrician, not a psychologist. She knew her mind would simply not be put at rest until someone told her exactly what her fever might have caused. Probably something so obvious and serious that it would have been noticed immediately upon Ian's birth.

Next morning she called the patient orientation office at the clinic where her OB practiced. No need to complicate matters by identifying herself. She could be someone writing a paper on the subject of high prenatal fever.

"Anything above 100.6 degrees is clinically significant," the counselor advised, "even for a few hours."

Monica licked her lips. "Why is that?" she asked, trying to remember to sound businesslike and detached.

"Because there is much brain growth in the final weeks

of pregnancy. Now, we have a number of tests that we do if this happens. Did you want to know what they are?"

"Yes, please," weakly. The counselor named and described each test. Monica had been given all of them.

"So then, if everything shows up normal on these tests, and the baby is healthy at birth, one can assume no damage was done?"

"Not always. Usually significant brain damage will be apparent. The baby will have poor muscle tone, poor reflexes, lack of responsiveness to noise and visual stimulation, and so on. That will call for a battery of tests on the child. . . ." She named them off. None had been done to Ian. Ian was normal at birth. "Then later, after the baby is several weeks old, he will exhibit other symptoms, such as incessant crying, irritability, lack of response to his parents, and so forth. Rigidity when held. . . .

"This of course prohibits a strong bond between the child and his parents, which makes for a whole realm of behavioral problems later. Now, lots of children are just difficult for no known reason. One of my three is a good example." She laughed. One could laugh when talking to an unknown party about a paper being written, when nothing personal was at stake. . . .

"But there would be those first symptoms at birth, before this," Monica quickly persisted.

"Usually, yes." She paused. "You see, some of these behavioral symptoms are so difficult to measure or evaluate it is impossible to say whether the fever can be linked."

It all sounded a bit vague. Monica decided to chance one more question.

"Could high prenatal fever be linked to a specific illness in a child?"

"That would depend somewhat upon the cause of the fever."

Unknown. "I see. But probably by this time they've pretty well narrowed down resultant illnesses to a few—"

"No. As I say, when the cause is not diagnosed, it is impossible to say what the damage may have been."

She took in a breath. "Has high prenatal fever ever been linked to . . . oh, let's say . . . autism, for instance?"

A long pause. "No . . . I don't believe so."

Monica relaxed. Home free. But then the counselor added, "Neither can that or any other possibility be ruled out."

"Oh. Oh, I see . . ." She sat there, dumbstruck. Moments passed.

"Are you there, miss?"

"Yes."

"I know it's confusing. I'd certainly hate to be doing a paper on it. The trouble is, there are so few absolutes in this area it's hard to give firm answers. A person may never know."

CHAPTER 10

Within the week, Monica sat quietly as Dr. Michaels presented his findings to Forrest. She had weighed those hours of illness before Ian's birth against the indefinite answers of the counselor and the near-certainty of Dr. Winters that Ian had not suffered as a result, and decided she had been right all along to keep quiet about it.

Forrest looked out the window, his hands deep in his trouser pockets, not interrupting the doctor's discourse or responding if a phrase seemed to end with a question mark. The well-fitted tan suit and knitted tie, the highly polished brown Stacy-Adams shoes which he put on in confidence this morning, were being figuratively stripped off him, article by article. She had approached this meeting with a feeling of vindication: the scales of justice were about to be balanced. From now on they would share the blame for their shortcomings and be forced into recompense. Yet, as she watched her husband stand tall without flinching as the doctor accused him diplomatically of crimes just short of abandonment of his child, she felt nothing but pity. It was too much like watching Professor Maguire convey with a look: you've failed again. How many times, over the years, had Forrest withstood that punishment? There was no balance in this meeting after all.

Finally Forrest looked around and said, "I just won't buy that. I spend as much time with Ian as I can. I have to make a living, you know."

She was brought back to the present situation, irritated by his waspishness. Dr. Michaels stared at him. Stubbornly he continued: "And even if what you say was true, plenty of kids grow up with only *one* parent around, a divorced or widowed parent, and survive quite well."

"That's a different matter entirely," the doctor explained patiently. "The absence of one parent as opposed to the *presence* of a parent whose relation the child does not understand . . . . How do you suppose Ian perceives you? Does he understand what and who you are to him, what you and his mother are to each other?"

"Of course he does."

"Maybe so. But if not, you've made a stumbling block for him. He cannot begin to relate to others until he relates to you both, and especially to his father."

Forrest paused a moment, then said, "Would you like to know about my relation with *my* father? He is cold as a fence post in Siberia. I can't remember a time when he showed any affection toward me at all. He didn't kiss me . . . he rarely touched me . . . ." He turned back toward the window before continuing: "Yet I turned out all right."

"Be that as it may, somewhere along the way you overcame whatever damage he might have done. I cannot say how; an otherwise healthy child often does, to an extent, although it puts him behind and he spends a while catching up. But the point here is to help Ian, and since the signs of his inability to relate to others have begun so early, you'd be wise to solve them as quickly as possible."

"So your suggestion is that we spend more time together. Is that all?"

"At this point, I'm afraid it will take more. I want you to make an appointment with one of these agencies"—jotting down the names of three—"and let them have a look at Ian. If they discover nothing seriously wrong, they'll set up some family counseling. You'll probably need to have sessions for Ian a couple of times a week and a meeting with the therapist once a week for the two of you."

Forrest jerked around, giving Monica a start. "You guys just don't live in the real world, do you? What you are asking is full-time motherhood for both parents. When I grew up it was generally accepted and also a nice means of survival if the father worked all day while the mother stayed home with the children. Nowadays we are all expected to retire to a little cottage on a hillside, developing 'meaningful' relationships with the children. Well, maybe I'm a bit old-fashioned, but I think you're full of shit."

Dr. Michaels glanced at Monica, then back at Forrest. "Do you mind your wife pursuing her own career?"

"Not in the least, unless it comes to the point where I have to give up mine too."

Monica was gripping the arms of the chair, her anger rising. She had often suspected he took her career lightly; never until now had he been so explicit in his feelings.

Dr. Michaels leaned back in his chair, as though signaling them all to cool down, and suddenly Monica wondered what he'd do if it came to an all-out battle. Ask them to leave? Excuse himself and take a short trip to the john? How far was he willing to go with what he had started?

His voice was soft as he began: "We live in difficult times. I can't tell you how many patients I see over a period of three or four months whose problems are brought about by the same circumstances as yours. It's only fair each person have a chance to do whatever he or she wants to do with his or her life. Maybe if each of us realized this beforehand we wouldn't bring children into the world. But then we'd soon be extinct," he said, and smiled. "What I'm trying to get the two of you to do is learn how to work with a set of existing circumstances. The child is already in the world and you love him, want the best for him. But it is going to take some sacrifice, some reorganizing of your lives to accommodate him.

"I'm not saying you will have to go through therapy for the rest of your lives. Perhaps a year, maybe two. But I'm warning you that Ian is very much disturbed, and will become even more so as time goes by.

"Now"—back in control—"give it some thought, and contact one or two or all three of these agencies and just see what you are up against. The one at the head of the list is my first choice because I know several of the doctors. I know less about the others but I'm familiar enough with them to recommend you investigate them.

"If you want to talk with me further, or if you feel you can't see your way to follow my suggestion, please let me know."

As they drove home, Forrest seemed to have dismissed the content of the meeting completely from his mind. He rushed along, saying, "As soon as I drop you off, I've got to get back to the office to finish a report."

Monica felt defeated, as though nothing had been gained. What she found more disturbing was that when Forrest described the way his father treated him, he was also describing the way he treated their son. Now she realized in all probability Forrest was not aware of the damage he was doing to Ian by behaving coldly toward him or ignoring him altogether. "I turned out all right" had been his assessment. In truth, his own behavior was a frightening legacy carried from one generation down to the next.

It occurred to her then that the day might arrive when she and Forrest would call it quits. Even if Forrest did not catch the implication in Dr. Michaels' question about their relationship with each other, she did. What did Ian see between his parents? Love? Affection? Neither. In fact, he rarely saw them together at all. If they were divorced, at least it would be a configuration of life that was easy to make out, not the vague lines and curves that made up their lives now. It seemed odd, almost laugh-

able, the idea of splitting up a marriage to make it easier
for a child. Yet in their case it made sense. If Forrest were
away, maybe Ian would respond more to her. As of now,
they were three people living separate lives under the
same roof.

Still, the idea of divorce sickened and frightened her.
She hoped she could talk to her husband, and somehow
bring both of them to a new awareness, but she didn't
want to do it now, while he raced from one block to the
next. She was afraid the conversation might lead to an
argument as to the importance of her career, because
Forrest obviously felt that was at the core of all the problems. If they argued about that, then regardless of who
had the last word, the real issue would be lost. She
needed time to think, to figure how to phrase her comments diplomatically. She was about to suggest they
might talk later in the evening. But then he spoke first
and surprised her.

"What burns me up is that doctor doesn't seem to realize, if I spend part of my day in 'family therapy' or whatever they call it, I have to make up lost time at the office.
'Only a year or so,' he said. Did you catch that? Only
enough time for my entire future to go down the drain,
and Ian's along with it, because I would have to get the
company to conform to my needs. And in the meantime,
Ian sees less of me than ever if you discount the time we
all visit the shrink together.

"You can see all the doctors you want to, Monica, but
from now on count me out. I'm willing to admit I could
try a damned sight harder with Ian, and I intend to. But
I'll do it on my terms. In my own home."

It was the best news she had heard in months. She put
a hand on his shoulder and said, "So will I. We'll do it together."

When Monica spoke to Erica about their decision, the following day, she spoke with confidence and added, "I think you will see a change in Ian by the beginning of the school year in September."

Erica shook her mop of curls. "Ian is getting worse, Mrs. Maguire. Yesterday he pushed a little boy down into an ant bed."

"Oh? Did you find out why?" she challenged.

"The boy got too close to him. He simply cannot deal with other children." She paused, then headed off Monica's further protest. "Look, I know about one of those bureaus Dr. Michaels mentioned—the Family Rehabilitation League. They take children in very small groups and do therapy with them. One week during a seminar I observed classes there. I think you should look into it at least. I see it's at the top of his list. There are a lot of people on the staff at the FRL; a couple of them are university graduates. At least it would be worth a try, to take him through their clinic. And maybe one of them could work with Ian to help him along.

"It's too bad your husband doesn't . . . I'm sorry, but I have to insist on this if you plan to enroll Ian next fall. And if he were my child, I wouldn't waste a minute."

He is not your child. "I'll consider it."

"I only mean, this is early spring, and he'll have the whole summer to get his bearings. By fall we might have enough input to know what to do here at the center. Mrs. Maguire, all we want is the best for Ian." She looked at her imploringly.

Monica realized that evening for the first time that she was truly caught between two forces, neither of which she could control. She hadn't the heart to tell Forrest that Erica Thomas had swayed her again, not when he fully believed she had placed her confidence in his views. Yet neither could she dismiss what the teachers observed in Ian on a daily basis, balanced on either end with the way he looked when she left him in the morning . . . so alone and lost, even now that he seldom cried . . . and the way she found him when the center closed at night: quiet and listless. Forrest did not see these things, so how could he judge?

She also realized he was correct in his belief that the teacher's first obligation was to the class as a whole, not to Ian. Yet she was the one who faced Erica and was convinced of her sincerity. If she didn't care, there would be the simple issuance of a formal letter from the administrator's office, dismissing Ian from the center with the stroke of a pen on the signature line. Instead, she begged Ian's parents to get help. And with her own experience added to that of the other teachers, surely the concern Erica felt must not be unfounded. Surely the view of Forrest that Ian was brighter than all the other children was simplistic. Ian might be bright, but certainly he wasn't the first bright youngster to pass through the corridors of the center or through the years of experience of the teachers there.

Monica decided to tackle the list Dr. Michaels had given them. She would say nothing to Forrest, but neither would she hide her decision from him. If he suffered a bruised ego from all this, well, she couldn't help it. She was too tired and confused to argue.

By now her painting had begun to reflect a kind of frenzy: strokes on the canvas grew faster and faster, and less precise. Often she'd stop and take deep breaths, as one might do when running away from imminent danger. Worse, she had no idea what lay at the end of the path.

CHAPTER 11

The Family Rehabilitation League required a "few" completed forms, which were mailed to her the day after she called. Otherwise, they needed questionnaires completed by Ian's teacher, the attending psychologist (like all others, he must send reports of his tests, not via Monica, but on his own; secret), the specialist who conducted Ian's battery of hearing tests, and the speech pathologist he had seen at eighteen months of age. They requested from Dr. Winters a report as to his general state of health and freedom from communicable diseases, as well as records of his condition at birth.

Monica took stock as she looked through the pages and pages of blank papers with instructions at the top. It seemed somehow that this was all going a little overboard. She could stop it now. Ian had seen only one doctor, had failed to succeed at only one preschool. Should she go on with this, it might be setting wheels in motion that could not be stopped. There might be no end to the tests ahead, not to mention the expense, though if your child's mental health was at stake you were not supposed to consider that. She thought of it now only in light of the fact that Forrest would have to foot the bills for something to which he was opposed. Her paintings did not bring in the kind of money that covered even the fee of Dr. Michaels, let alone what promised to come in the months ahead. But of course Forrest would never complain about the bills, for that would reflect badly on him as a provider. He would no more hand her a weapon for use against him than she would hand one to him.

The FRL wanted a full week to mull over the reports before looking at Ian, so she dropped her papers by one morning and was assured all attendant documents had arrived. She was told she'd first see a Dr. Phillips on the following Thursday, and to bring Ian along. The organization seemed efficient and thorough. Nowhere in her report was there mention of her prenatal fever. She was not sure whether Dr. Winters would include it in his, and decided not to follow up on that point. If the word "fever" was picked up among the volumes of paper that were on file at the FRL by now, then no one could say she had tried to hide it. If it was presented in this manner, perhaps the whole issue would not be overblown.

Still, she was apprehensive as Thursday arrived and she held on to Ian's hand at the reception desk. It occurred to her suddenly that she ought to have checked to be sure everything was in order for their appointment; but then, they seemed so efficient here. . . .

Minutes later she was filled with regret. The receptionist put a check mark beside her name on the appointment list, then swiveled around to reach into a pile of folders. She pulled out a rather bulky one, and placed it on the edge of the desk. "You did receive the information in time for Dr. Phillips to read it?" Monica inquired.

"Oh yes, certainly." She flashed a cinnamon-colored smile and nodded her blond head. She glanced toward Ian, who was darting around from one corner of the room to the next. She produced a peppermint stick and pressed it into Monica's hand. "Please, have a seat."

Monica flipped through a magazine, then found a picture of two dinosaurs engaged in eating each other alive. God. She flipped another page or two and called Ian over to look at a more peaceful brontosaurus eating weeds beside a pond. She read the caption to Ian, who sat obediently beside her but began to wring his hands. Perspiration dotted his forehead. "What is it, honey? Are you frightened? Don't worry. No one will hurt you here. We're going to see a nice man who wants to ask us some questions."

The phone rang and the receptionist answered. Monica glanced up. The young woman hung up the phone and picked up the big file. She took it from the room, and soon returned empty-handed.

Monica felt a tug on her ear. Ian was after her red ball earrings. "Let go. You're hurting Mommy's ear." She forced his hand away. He leaned back and began to rock, still staring at the earring. Finally he sighed and nudged closer to the cushion behind. His feet hung just over the edge and the toes of his shoes lapped over each other. He kept glancing anxiously at the door. Soon the room became crowded. Children, obviously retarded, their eyes and limbs moving without coordination, were accompanied by worried, worn-looking parents. If the children spoke, their words were garbled. Nor could they sit still. Up and down, on the floor, into a cabinet of toys. Some of them were familiar with the room, it seemed. Monica felt uneasy. She sensed that these children frightened Ian, that he was all too aware of their difference. She saw his hand move toward the back of the couch, obscuring his mirror.

She checked her watch. Twenty-five minutes past time for their appointment. Finally she took Ian by the hand and approached the receptionist again. It was almost noon. "How much longer before—"

"It shouldn't be more than a few minutes," she assured, and offered another peppermint stick.

"No, thanks." The first was in her purse. Peppermint was not among the items Ian would eat. They sat down again. Could Dr. Phillips be sitting in his office, reading about Ian only now? Of course he could, and he is, she thought with irritation. Didn't all members of the medical profession put up a convincing front, even if they were guilty of gross disorganization? People died in hospitals from botched-up lab tests or incorrect medicine dosage and still they all walked around with this look of confidence, trust us.

Ian pointed at the door.

"Not time to go yet. It won't be long."

She had never seen him as nervous as he was this morning, and wondered if he was affected by the weeks of testing with Dr. Michaels, the probes of the teachers, the renewed efforts toward bringing him out of his shell at home. Forrest had become conscientious about making eye contact, after hearing what Dr. Michaels had to say, and often wound up forcing the issue with Ian, holding his head in his hands. Then, if he succeeded, he'd let go and call to her, "See, he certainly looked at me that time. I told you that doctor was nuts." Ian would find the nearest exit. Monica didn't want to correct Forrest for overdoing. At least he was trying, even if Ian didn't respond. It took a long time to move mountains.

Poor darling. She hugged him and kissed his cheek. He pulled free and looked at the door again, swinging his legs. She might have prevented all this by being a more conscientious mother-to-be. There were scores of books about how to bring up a healthy, well-adjusted child, so many, in fact, that she didn't know which ones were really good. Anyhow there was little time for anything but her work in those months before Ian's birth.

"Dr. Phillips will see you now." The cinnamon smile. "Ian can wait in here with me while he speaks with you. I have some toys in the cabinet." But Ian was frightened, and clung to her dress. This was going to be a problem. She knelt down. "Listen, honey, you sit over here on the couch till I come for you. Have you got your mirror? Good. Now, I'll be back in a few minutes. Would you like some toys from the cabinet? Oh, look! Some beads to string, and some puzzles."

Ian took a puzzle and sat on the couch. He clutched the mirror tightly and did not bother with removing the pieces of the puzzle. He began to rock. "He'll stay, I think," Monica told the woman. She'd picked up the phone again and waved her on, smiling. It was lucky the crowd of children had dispersed; no doubt because of the noon hour. Ian would be calmer.

Dr. Phillips was a hefty young man with light curly hair and brown eyes. He offered her a chair and went back to scanning the papers in front of him. The walls were covered with citations and certificates. Momentarily he looked up. "I see here you're an artist, and you teach."

Not exactly my point in being here today. "I have a fellowship this year."

"I admire that! Couldn't draw a straight line myself."

"Most people can't, including artists. Pardon me, but is this the first time you've seen the reports?"

"As a matter of fact it is; I must apologize. With that seminar and so forth I'm behind." He closed the folder. "Now, what seems to be the problem?"

She summoned patience. Had she not come this far, she would have walked out. She briefly explained the contents, several times referring snidely to what was in front of the doctor's nose.

"Um-hum . . . hm. . . ." He nodded, over and over, seeming to listen, but looking at the wall behind her.

"Of course I'll conduct my own tests here, then we'll put Ian into a small group of youngsters to see how he interacts, and we do have a policy here that more than one doctor observes a child. We believe that's one of the strengths of the FRL—a group of minds working together.

"I didn't get far into the other reports, but I notice Dr. Michaels suspects autism. We deal with many autistic children here, both in diagnosis and in therapy. So if the possibility exists, we ought to spot it when observing him."

"But he concluded that Ian's problems are almost certain to be caused by his environment." Which you would realize if you had read farther.

"Um-hum. . . ." He wrote something down on a card and handed it to her. "You'll need to make an appointment for testing. A technician will do a battery of tests on Ian, and after I have a chance to look over her report, I'll be at a starting point with him."

"But I understood you'd be seeing him today. I brought him along—"

"No. Not until the preliminary tests are conducted. I'll watch him from what we call our 'peek-a-boo' room, through a one-way mirror. I have found that gives me an advantage in knowing how to approach a child. Meantime I'll read this group of reports carefully—quite a hefty package."

"Quite a lot of effort was spent in getting it ready before today."

"I am sorry for that," he said, taking in a breath. "Don't be put off. We'd like to try and help Ian if we can, and we have the most highly qualified people in the city on our staff.

"Now, I'm taking a little vacation trip, getting in on the tail end of skiing season in Colorado, next week. However, I'll familiarize myself with Ian's case before I leave, and have my notations ready for the technician who assists. I'll pass along the reports to Dr. Meyer and he can be ready to observe by the time I return. . . ." You are dismissed.

She found Ian still rocking on the couch, the puzzle in his arms, his mirror clutched tightly. "He hasn't moved since you left," the receptionist told her as she wrote down another appointment for them. "Certainly is well behaved."

For fear all of her exasperation would be unleashed, she ignored the woman and took Ian's hand.

"He's a beautiful child," the woman said hesitantly.

"Thank you."

Monica featured her delving into Ian's file after they left, to find out what was the matter with him. Such a beautiful child . . . you'd never believe anything could be wrong. But then again . . . there was something about him . . . I noticed it immediately. . . .

CHAPTER 12

Again Monica considered bringing the whole thing to a halt. Ian seemed more fearful. Yet maybe that meant they were nearing the core of the problem. Maybe these people at the FRL, whose reputation had to be built on something more than what she saw today, could find out what was wrong. If the problem could be solved at home, wouldn't Ian have been more responsive to Forrest lately? She had made a point of talking to him more, even though it was difficult when he failed to speak back, yet it seemed to make no difference. Maybe she expected too much too soon.

In the weeks to come her association with the clinic reached nightmare proportion. At first she tried to excuse the early confusion. Both Dr. Michaels and Erica Thomas, and since then even Dr. Winters (during an office visit to check for ear infection), confirmed the clinic had great successes with difficult behavior problems in children.

In all Ian was observed by four staff doctors, aside from Dr. Phillips. Over a period of two and a half months, she and Ian spent an average of two days a week in the clinic, sometimes from early in the morning until late afternoon. Walking halls, waiting, walking halls, waiting, testing here, testing there with one technician after another. It seemed to Monica that much of the testing was a repeat of earlier testing, but since the tests were conducted by a different staff technician, or associate, or consultant—they had a myriad of labels for their employees—each time, she assumed the repetition was necessary to obtain the total picture. It also seemed a wise idea to perform some tests over and over again to allow for Ian's change in mood. Indeed, his temperament was not something anyone could depend upon. Some days he was cooperative. Others he was impossible. Sometimes he seemed to be trying. Other times he scarcely seemed to be inhabiting the room in which he sat. There was no doubt that, as the weeks passed and the testing continued, Ian's behavior grew more erratic. At times the staff seemed almost impatient with him. Indeed, she became impatient: with Ian, with the FRL, and with herself. More than that, she felt every day he was becoming more withdrawn, and she sensed more and more that she was losing him.

One night she lay awake for a very long time, unable to unwind and relax, to make any sense out of what was being done. It was like a painting that had been worked on too long, from too many angles: tried over and over from different ways, using this color and that, changing one detail then another, until the original object was lost somewhere in all the confusion.

It occurred to her then that she just might find Ian if she could complete the portrait she'd begun before any of this testing got in the way and messed up everything. She rose carefully, so as not to disturb Forrest, pulled on a robe, and started toward her studio. It was a feeling that obsessed her now, like the one which had driven her to finish the portfolio for the Sunday magazine just before Ian was born. The one she now associated inextricably with the fever. . . .

She closed the studio door softly behind. The portrait

of Ian waited near the easel. She propped it up in front of her. The curly hair, the pixie nose and small mouth, had been sketched in since she'd made up her mind to see Dr. Michaels alone, but she had not even looked at it again in all those weeks since. Before, she had been sure that eventually she could do the eyes, even while aware the greatest challenge lay in their elusive depth. Most of the time one found the key there. Andrew James, her art professor, had said so long ago: the pathway to the soul.

Now Dr. Michaels, with his fancy words and laboratory terms and brochures that set so much stock in eye contact, and all the weeks of technicians from the FRL holding Ian's shoulders and looking at him, turning his face forward, only to have it swing back again, down to his shoulder, had sown a field of doubt over the nature of Ian's gaze. She picked up a piece of chalk then and studied his snapshots carefully. . . . He was never quite looking on, always peering at something to the side or above; she had thought upon choosing these as props that they captured his charm and were therefore valuable to the project.

She picked up the chalk and observed the sketch for a while longer, but could not get anywhere. The unfinished face stared back blankly, defying her, denying her ability, denying her son's relation to her and to the world in which they lived. Damn the experts and all their interference. She broke the chalk. She draped a cloth over the canvas and turned out the light, then sat on the bench nearby with her knees tucked up, in the fetal position. She brought a fist to her mouth and rocked there, in the darkness.

In a moment she was aware of another sound of rocking, from Ian's room. She stopped and listened to the rhythm of it, over and over, the creak of the bedsprings and the groan of the rails, always the same, as though measured by a metronome, over and over, long-short, long-short . . . At last, charged by something she did not then understand and perhaps never would, she rose and went to his room.

"Come with me, Ian."

He seemed startled. He stopped rocking and looked at her. Momentarily. But he looked.

She went to the crib and picked him up gently. She carried him into the studio. He had checked to be sure his mirror was in hand. He gave her no argument then. It seemed to her he was almost a part of her drive, almost as though he understood and had waited for her to come, that they were going about this together, to see, to see. . . .

She placed him on a high stool several feet from the canvas and told him, "Sit quietly for a little. You can be my model."

She returned then to the canvas and picked up the chalk. She was not ready to attack the core of the problem yet. She worked on the shadows in his face, the curves and angles; she surrounded the eyes and worked toward them as an army surrounds an enemy before attack. It was like that, she sensed as she worked, filling in all the gaps before finally the last plunge, the victory. She did not know how long she worked. Ian sat looking dazedly ahead. She thought she murmured reassurances now and then, but was too wrapped up in the evolving portrait to be sure. She was aware her fingers were tiring from the tediousness, but on and on she worked, unconscious of time passing. . . .

Then there was a thud. At the same moment the sound wrenched her from her concentration, Ian jerked mightily on the stool. His mirror lay on the floor. He doubled over on the stool, his arms reaching down toward the lost treasure. She did not know how long he screamed before she reacted; surely not long; yet just as she started toward him the stool fell forward and he lay under it, still screaming, louder than before. Forrest burst through the door.

"What the hell?" he shouted, and whisked Ian up. He gave Monica the coldest look she'd ever seen and stomped out, carrying the still wailing, writhing Ian in his arms. She stood there clasping her arms around her, hearing the hurried steps down the hall. Then the crib springs as Forrest laid Ian in bed. She heard him say, "Go to sleep, son." Without comfort in his voice, or warmth or reassurance. Just "Go to sleep." In a moment he was stomping back.

She tried to explain. "I thought I could paint him . . . he was awake anyhow . . . I guess he dozed off and dropped his mirror . . . and when he . . . I didn't mean to . . ." He kept scowling at her, not understanding, and she realized she was shaking and big tears were rolling down her face.

"Do you know it's nearly four in the morning? Have you lost your mind?" He turned and left the room, banging the door behind.

She stood still for some moments, unable to move. She didn't want to see the sketch anymore, though she was not sure what had been done, how close she had come to her goal. Finally she sighed. She flung the drape over it again, turned out the light, and left the studio. Before returning to bed she stopped by Ian's room. He was not crying, but his breathing was uneven and now and then he'd hiccup and catch his breath. She stroked his back and kissed him, but could not tell if this or any of her words of comfort were helpful. He seemed to be already asleep.

Forrest lay in bed rigidly, his eyes open. He saw the
night's incident out of context with all the worry and exhaustion of the past weeks, all the coming and going and
being directed from one place to another for one test then
another, the grinding up of all emotions and the toll on
her nerves. He simply thought she decided to paint a picture of Ian, in the middle of the night.

For the first time in a long while she was aware of
needing him, of needing absolution if nothing else. She
wanted to be held and comforted, wanted to know someone's arms were stronger. Wanted to know someone
cared. She reached for his hand. He pulled it back and
turned away from her.

After that Monica found she hated the sight of the FRL
clinic, and toward the end the only impetus for continuing to bring Ian was the knowledge that soon a final conclusion would be drawn, tying all the loose and scattered
ends together. Not once, in all the weeks, would any of
the doctors or other staff members volunteer even a couple of words in speculation. They simply smiled, opened a
door, and said, "Now, Ian, that's all the games for today."

Then came the crowning blow. Ian was put into what
was supposed to be a half-hour "group observation" with
five other children. Monica was not allowed to sit with
him during this final test, but observed through the one-
way glass with Dr. Phillips. She knew what the procedure
was but assumed Ian would be interacting with children
who displayed symptoms similar to his. And that was
where the surprise came in.

With one therapist in the room holding a clipboard, six
children, including Ian, filed in before Monica's eyes.
Within the first few minutes, one child unzipped his pants
and wet the wall, spattering Ian along the front of his

shirt. Monica could not hear his screams coming from the soundproof room, but as he whirled around she could see his stricken face. She rose from her chair. Dr. Phillips put out a restraining arm. The therapist grabbed a towel and wiped Ian's shirt, and while engaged in this, another child flung a toy of some sort across the room. Another pranced around Ian, then suddenly lunged for his mirror, caught it, and ran off, holding it high above Ian's head as Ian screamed in terror, arms flailing.

Monica stormed into the room to rescue both Ian and his mirror. The therapist seemed more alarmed by her behavior than by the children's. Dr. Phillips entered behind her but she literally nudged him out of her way as she left, Ian in her arms. Passing by the receptionist's desk she said, "Tell Dr. Phillips I'll be calling him."

She drove home in a state of disbelief. She could not gauge what, if any, harm they had done. Ian, no doubt relieved to be free of the place, sat quietly in his car seat, looking out. She caught his hand but he pulled it free. She could not see his expression. She could smell urine on his clothes and thought it odd he would not be screaming and pulling at his shirt. When finally they pulled to a stop in the garage she hurried around to open his door and get a look at his face. He seemed to be concentrating hard on something she couldn't see. His look was one of penetration. She was afraid he was in shock. "Ian, Ian!" she cried, and shook his shoulders. In a moment he blinked, and sighed. She helped him out of the car.

A week passed before she was able to have a final consultation and an opportunity to speak her mind to Dr. Phillips. Each night in between Ian rocked himself into the wee hours of the morning. He wriggled out of her comforting embrace.

Forrest was outraged when she reported what had hap-

pened. "Don't you ever take Ian back to that clinic again.
I've a good mind to go there myself and tell those bas-
tards just—"

"Don't worry. I won't take Ian back, and I intend to
tell Dr. Phillips just what I think of the FRL."

"I tried to tell you to stop this foolishness before it ever
got started. It should have never gotten past your first discussion with that teacher at the center. You should have
had it out with her then and there.

"But you had to go on and on, not trusting my judgment—"

"I know. I know. And I can see that now," she said
meekly.

"Well, I'm glad you're finally beginning to show some
sense," he said, snapped his briefcase shut, and left for
work.

She had told him of the experience to get the sheer
weight of it off her shoulders, and it seemed a good idea
in view of the fact she finally had come full circle. From
now on she would not waver from the suggestions of her
husband. She had learned her lesson. She felt what she
had put Ian through was unforgivable; yet she longed for
forgiveness, and compassion. The pity was that Forrest
gave her no chance to fully explain herself. Just now
when she felt she had spanned the distance between
them, she found the door literally closed in her face. She
heard the motor of his car in the garage. She almost ran
out to catch him, to demand more time to explain. But
then she thought, oh hell, what's the use? She took two
antacid tablets. Her stomach had been in knots for two
months, and she'd lost ten pounds.

When she faced Dr. Phillips, he listened quietly to her
complaints, then said, "Autism is not an attractive specta-

cle. In group observation and therapy we try to teach by cause and effect what behavior is acceptable and what is not. The therapist had the situation in hand. It was upsetting that you stormed in as you did." A pause, for expression of remorse. None coming. "Of course, I can understand your feelings of apprehension."

"So that's your conclusion . . . Ian is autistic?"

"Three of the doctors who have observed Ian believe so unequivocally. Two of us are uncertain. Dr. Meyer and I both believe we have made eye contact and have communicated with him at a very elementary level. We know that the boy is brilliant in certain aspects. The question remains: is he able, or will he ever be able, to communicate with others at a level where he can share his gifts, integrate into society, and function?

"Believe me, Mrs. Maguire, you may not sanction our methods, and I think you have misinterpreted a few of them, but there was a key in what happened here last week. Ian's reaction was, as you just now described, to withdraw more into himself, but to show no significant fear beyond the initial experience. In other words, no cognizance of his relation to others around him.

"That would seem to weigh in favor of the opinions of the other doctors."

"But you still aren't absolutely sure?"

"No. Quite frankly, this is one of the most confounding cases I have ever seen. My own conclusion is that he is borderline."

"Does that mean he can be cured?"

"No. It only helps us in recommending therapy. I would suggest private therapy for Ian at first, maybe two or three times a week. Perhaps later . . .

"I have seen autistic children exhibit far more bizarre behavior than Ian. I've seen them more involved in self-stimulation than Ian. Of course, there is the rocking, and the frequent hand wringing."

"He wasn't doing as much of that before he came here."

"Nonetheless, he exhibits six or seven out of thirteen symptoms of autism. I have seldom seen a child more subject to irrational fears. This is another reason I suggest private therapy. We want to avoid driving him further inward. But I would certainly urge you and your husband to participate in therapy, whether or not you work with us here.

"Again, I'm sorry for the ordeal we put him—and you—through, with the group. I don't believe he'll remember it, however, so I wouldn't worry over it."

"I hope he won't. I certainly will. And what if you're wrong, and he isn't autistic?"

"One day he'll begin to blossom. And since we can discover no biochemical or genetic factor, that may happen."

Dr. Winters didn't say what he knew about the fever; or what he knew made no difference. Which?

". . . But I urge you not to build any false hopes. Believe it or not, I have kept close watch on Ian's behavior here, with the exception of the week I was away. I've been in consultation regularly with the other doctors. There is no doubt in my mind that Ian is psychotic. At this point I see little hope, and the fact is that we must deal with the situation as we see it now, regardless of what may or may not come to pass in the future."

She rose. Psychotic. She wasn't even certain what the term meant. Her anger, however, was placated by the comforting thought there was still hope Ian might not be autistic, that his problems could be worked out. It seemed enough to go on for now. Maybe the past two and a half months had not been wasted, after all.

"On the other hand, the tests already concluded hardly scratch the surface of what is available nowadays. There are centers for testing in Austin, institutions out of state, all kinds of research and new methods being discovered all the time. You could literally spend months—"

"Don't you believe that more testing at this point would be ludicrous, possibly harmful?"

"That's up to you. I only want you to know you are not bound to accept our findings here."

Driving away, she felt better and better. If that many doctors could not agree, then it seemed more certain than ever there was nothing seriously wrong with Ian. She could not make any commitments for Forrest, but as for herself she would put the past behind her and make a more dedicated effort to help Ian "blossom," as the doctor aptly termed it.

She was full of ideas when she reached the center that evening and cornered Erica. "At the FRL, they could not arrive at a conclusion, except that Ian has trouble relating," she hedged. "His father and I have decided against therapy. It was a mistake to believe we could keep placing him in abnormal situations—with doctors, technicians, and so forth—and expect him to emerge normal. What Ian needs is more time with his parents and the chance to make friends a few at a time."

Erica opened her mouth but Monica interrupted. "I know you've been concerned that Ian finds a large classroom situation overwhelming. I think I have an answer for that. I'm going to bring him here during the week, but on weekends I'm going to help him develop friendships with children in the neighborhood."

Trying to remove Erica's stoic expression, she added, "I'm going to fill the freezer with popsicles," then smiled. Erica folded her arms and leaned back, drawing in a breath. Monica wondered if she answered to the administrator, and the idea of therapy was an ultimatum that stood between Ian and the letter of dismissal. Monica persisted: "This summer we're going out to California to visit my sister. She has four kids who swim, play baseball, and go camping." Actually the idea had only just occurred to her.

There was a brief pause. "All that's well and good," said Erica, with a half attempt at smiling. "But in any case, by September—"

"Ian will have begun to improve. And if not, you won't have to bother with him any further."

As soon as Monica got home she grabbed the dictionary and looked up "psychotic." "Fundamental mental derangement characterized by defective or lost contact with reality." She'd been afraid to ask Dr. Phillips its meaning, afraid it might be something more awful, and so she'd hung on to the context in which he placed it, not wanting to destroy hope and not wanting to give in to a label. Psychosis, psychotic. It didn't seem incurable, from the definition. And certainly the conclusion that Ian was not in touch with reality was a viable one . . . not irreversible . . . but viable for now.

Yet the term continued to nag at the edge of her consciousness even after she closed the dictionary, and she soon realized it was not the term itself, but its connotation. Psychotic . . . psychopath.

Dangerous.

Dangerous to self. Dangerous to others.

No. She wouldn't keep doing this to herself. She closed it out.

CHAPTER 13

That night Forrest said, "Today we got a memo about the family picnic at the end of June. I thought we'd go, and take Ian. I even put my name down to help charcoal the hamburgers."

"Great!" Monica hollered from the kitchen. "And I thought we might spend a day at Astroworld, and maybe at the Sea-Arama in Galveston. . . ."

By the end of the evening they'd actually sat together—for the first time in months—and made a list of places to see, just like her family used to do before leaving on vacation. She had not realized how warm that could make her feel inside, or how deep a longing she had for a normal family existence, not only for Ian but for herself.

Later, as she switched off the bedside lamp and moved close to Forrest, it seemed a very long time ago she'd thought their relationships to each other and to their child were hopelessly lost.

On the first of May, Forrest was offered an assignment on the Trans-Ocean project in the North Sea. Monica soon realized that while he put on a pretty good show of weighing this career move against the importance of being with Ian, he had really made up his mind to go to Britain as quickly as the chance presented itself. Because it was a brief stay, the company would not make financial arrangements for Monica and Ian to accompany Forrest.

"You're going, aren't you? There was never any real question," she said at last.

He paused a moment, then said, "What am I to do?" He leaned across the table on which they shared a drink. "If I don't go, I can say goodbye to the chance for promotion, and if I do that, what about Ian's future . . . not to mention ours?

"It's only three months. I'll make it up—"

"It's the whole summer. I promised by this fall—"

"Promised who? What?"

She lowered her head.

"The center again. Why the hell do you keep—"

"Because, damn it, if he can't succeed there, then will he succeed somewhere else?" she said, then stopped abruptly. She had used the word "succeed." She wanted to take it back. She took a breath. "Look, why can't you face the fact he is having developmental problems, and that you may be part of the cause?" If not all of it.

"Because I don't believe he is, just because he's different and isn't growing in a straight line like the rest of them. He's bright, and it's hard to be bright. You expect him to be like other kids. They bore him."

Oh, how like your father you are, how pompous and conceited. Either that, or you are using this as a screen, to keep from giving up anything for him. She started to argue, but took a sip of her drink instead.

She was not being fully honest either, not telling him of the possibility she had wounded the unborn child that was Ian. She capitulated. It was the usual wind-up to their arguments. "Go on," she said. "We'll find some way to work around it."

"Look, Monica . . . you know how miserable I've been since Amalgamated took over. The London office is small; the work there is important. They don't send just anybody

over there. If I don't take a whack at this, I doubt I'll ever
have another opportunity.

"One thing about big corporations, they do have to
move people into top management, but they sure as hell
don't move up uncooperative employees. If this project
works out as it's supposed to, everyone who worked on it
will have a bright new feather in his cap. If I say no,
they'll pick someone else. And I know I can do it; I'm capable. That's why I have to work so hard. For chances
like this."

After he said that she really did feel compliant, and
patted his hand. "All right; I'm sure you should go."

His eyes brightened. "And I'll get to come home at
least once, maybe twice, and we'll make the most of the
time I'm here. I wouldn't ask if it weren't for just the summer, because I know Ian is growing up and I need to be
with him. I don't need a shrink to tell me that.

"And I would be in a far better frame of mind at home
if I were happier at work, and I haven't been happy for a
long time."

He reminded Monica of herself, all the times she'd
piled up assurances in front of him when she wasn't sure
he approved of her decision, when she felt he didn't support her. "Yes, that's important," she said. Another pat.

That night, lying awake while Forrest, no doubt
relieved, slept soundly, she wondered why, of all summers, did this have to be the one Amalgamated chose to
recognize Forrest Maguire? She wasn't sure whether she
resented Amalgamated or Forrest for scuttling their summer plans. But she was determined to keep her feelings to
herself. She didn't want to be the kind of wife who tears a
man to pieces with guilt as he tries to volley future with
present, because that was how her mother manipulated
her father. Not by direct confrontation, but little by little,

inch by inch, wanting things today that could have been put off, charge accounts zooming out of reason, savings accounts eroding like soil on a bare incline.

She remembered the time, some years ago, when her father was given the chance to buy into the company he worked for, but had to say no because he lacked the money. After that there was a gradual change in her father, an ever more wistful look on his face, a difference in the way he held his shoulders. She did not see it then, being far too young, and he never derided Amy in the presence of their children. But later, several years after his death, she tried to paint his portrait for Jane's birthday. She found the oils had captured the shoulders, face, and eyes of a broken man. She was crushed by what her own work had unmasked and wished she had never touched paintbrush to canvas. She put it away, unfinished.

After that she realized her mother was to blame for much more than spending her college money. Her unrealistic view of life had cost Jack Stokely his spirit, and she could almost hear her mother's ever-insistent appeal: "I didn't know it was so expensive."

Monica could not make up to her father what her mother had done. She could, however, be supportive of Forrest, cooperate with him in whatever he tried to accomplish. She could avoid a second generation of mistakes.

Even though she knew many of her plans for Ian did not hinge on Forrest, she felt defeated because there was no doubt that Ian would benefit most from the presence of his father. As she mulled this thought over, her mother called and asked, "How's Ian?"

"Ian is not very well," she said flatly, and then added, "He's having trouble in school because he can't relate to other kids, and he can't do that because we haven't taught him how, and on top of it all Forrest is being shipped off to London for three months, which blows our summer to hell."

"Oh," she said faintly.

"I'm sorry. I didn't mean to spout off at you."

"It's all right, dear. You know how much I care about my grandson, regardless of the fact I rarely see him," she said gently. "Now tell me, exactly what do you mean by 'relate'? Ian's not even four years old."

"Oh, haven't you heard? Nowadays children are supposed to be social butterflies by the time they give up the pacifier," she said. She couldn't keep the sharp edge off her voice.

"Hm . . ." Amy said slowly. This had always been the signal she wanted to think a minute. By long habit, Monica held the phone and kept quiet. Finally Amy said, "You know, there were five years between you and Jane. You almost grew up alone. And if you'll think back, you didn't make friends easily either. You never had more than one or two kids around you, but I never thought that was strange. That was just 'you.'"

"Well, I've been thinking of inviting the neighborhood kids over. There are a couple of kids across the street. Ian might find one pal among—"

"Monica, I just had a brainstorm. I talked with Hetty Wellman yesterday, and she's going to be down at the bay this summer. Her grandson is staying with her—he's about five or so. I'll bet she'd be tickled to death for you and Ian to come down just like we used to when you and Jane were growing up."

"Mother, I haven't been down there since I got married eleven years ago. She probably doesn't even remember me."

"Nonsense. She thinks of you and Jane as next to family. I could call her if you like."

The last sentence rang a bell somewhere in the back of Monica's mind. "No, just give me her number, and I can phone her sometime. . . ."

Amy recited it, then said, "I really hope you'll call her. From the way you sound today, it seems to me like a good idea for both of you. And please let me know if I can be of any help."

Monica hung up the phone and thought of her mother sitting there at her little desk, her faded red hair braided in back, her light freckled skin still good, in spite of the years. Sometimes she almost wished they could . . . .

She shook her head and went back to work. At first she had no intention of calling Hetty, and was amazed her mother even suggested it. The friendship Amy retained with Hetty had nothing to do with Monica. If Hetty had any feeling toward her at all, it was probably resentment for the way she and Forrest had snubbed the whole family since their wedding party at the bay.

Yet she mused through the afternoon. Early memories began coming to her with sharpening clarity, like photos developing in a darkroom: Swimming in the warm murky bay water. She had always felt safe there because the waves were never high like they were at the beaches of Galveston, and you could go out three or four times as far into the water before you worried about an undertow. And there was Hetty, always up on the lawn, watching, ready to sound the whistle should you get out too far. . . . Hetty and her mother chatting over coffee. If you hung around very long they'd stop talking and shoo you away. Her father sitting with Hetty's husband, Bert, on the bench rocker out front, sipping Pabst Blue Ribbon beer and talking softly. Bert survived her father by several years, but they were both gone now. . . . The smell of crab gumbo, cooking in a kettle on Hetty's old stove. Ice-cold Orange Crush in brown bottles on the Fourth of July. . . .

The bay had been a part of growing up for Jane and Monica, a place they took for granted. With their mother they would rise early two or three mornings a week in the summer, have the car loaded with swimsuits, the ice chest, and enough food to serve lunch to themselves and Hetty and her three boys, and be on the road by seven. Jane was both lovely and lazy, and slept all the way there. Monica always approached the Wellman place excitedly, and it always amazed her that you never saw the water till the end of the trip. Then, a couple of right turns down narrow gravel roads and you were coasting the alley along the back fence line of the small houses that formed the community of Baynook. In between the houses you could catch glimpses of gentle surf, lapping at spindly piers. Suddenly, the air was pungent with salt and the breeze was a little stiffer than before.

They would arrive before eight in the morning, and by eleven, Hetty would be on the front yard blowing her whistle, summoning them from their morning swim. One shrill note brought all the kids in from the water, splattering up the pier. As a child, Monica believed Hetty's total authority was embodied in that whistle.

After lunch they took a nap, then stayed in the water till five. Bert would have arrived from his Houston job and Jack would follow shortly after. They shared supper and spent the rest of the evening lazily, talking and watching the night gather and fill with stars above the bay. There was nothing significant about any one day, but altogether it formed the memory of pleasant, carefree childhood summers.

Monica backed away from her easel. She now understood the basis for Amy's suggestion. It had less to do with being around old family friends than with "normalcy" for Ian and the chance to just be a kid. She retrieved Hetty's number and quickly dialed.

CHAPTER 14

And so they had come.

Ian fell asleep shortly after Monica exited the Gulf Freeway, and even the last few abrupt turns, the crush of shell under the little sports car as they neared the Wellman place, did not awaken him.

No one seemed to be about. The sign which announced "B. Wellman" still hung from the cyclone fence, but Monica would have found it anyway because it seemed unchanged. The simple square cottage, white wood with maroon shutters, rose on brick pilings from the well-kept lawn. The bathhouse stood nearby; its white cotton curtain, serving as a door during the summer season, billowed out in the breeze. All of this she remembered as clearly as yesterday. And then Hetty herself came from the bathhouse, toting a basket of clothes. Hetty was small, smaller than Amy, but her straight posture added height. Her hair was now completely gray, but she wore it the same as always, pulled into a twist in back. She was dressed in a pink sleeveless blouse, white shorts that reached nearly to her knees, and a pair of blue canvas shoes. She still wore rimless eyeglasses. Also, her whistle: hanging from a black lanyard around her neck and flashing just above her waistline.

Seeing Monica, she left the basket on the back porch and came toward the car, smiling. The place called "the bay" since childhood had never seemed so welcome, and all the years between dissolved. Monica held out her arms.

"I hope I didn't scare Ian," Hetty told her later. They were seated on the wide front patio, facing the bay, under an awning Monica did not remember any more than the wide patio. Some things had changed. The breeze whipped around, blowing Ian's curls as he skipped along the fence.

Hetty's voice was naturally low, and had a mournful tone that most people employ at funeral homes and in hospitals. This tone became more defined when she felt uncertain about something, as she now did.

"Ian usually screams when he's first awakened if he doesn't recognize his surroundings," Monica assured her.

"Well, I shouldn't have poked my head through the window like that. Especially after what you told me over the phone."

Monica had told her little of Ian's problems, partly because she was trying very hard not to emphasize the negative side of his behavior, and partly because, upon the news that the two of them wanted to spend part of the summer here, Monica could hardly get a word in because of Hetty's excitement. Before she realized, she was agreeing to come down every Friday evening and stay till Sunday. Hetty was thinking ahead as she spoke. "We have a crib if Ian wants to sleep in it. Clark just gave it up for a big bed, and we won't need it again till the new baby comes at the end of the summer."

She was looking toward Ian now. "He's a handsome little fella. Those pictures Amy has shown me don't do him justice." She narrowed her eyes and continued to observe him as he skipped along the fence. Finally she said, "You know, after we talked I got to thinking about Carson—he was the brightest one in our three—and he never made friends easily till he grew up. I'd forgotten till you called how that used to worry me, that he spent so much of his time reading books and so little time playing. But Bert always said he'd outgrow it, and he did." She sat back. "Well, neither of you look like you get out in the sun very much."

"We don't. I still burn very easily, and freckle worse. And we rarely go to the neighborhood pool because Ian hates it."

"He may like the bay water better. Most children do. Give Buzz a little time with him. He's good with kids in the water."

She thought of Buzz, the young blond boy, cutting around in the motorboat, or splashing bay water like a porpoise, during a swim. Daring, teasing, dunking people. And later, in his Navy uniform . . . .

Hetty was talking again, assessing. It was a part of the duty you paid to older people, that you should listen and pretend to agree/understand/obey, or whatever else was appropriate. "You know, Amy and I were thrilled you decided to spend some time down here this summer. She said you were a little hesitant at first."

Monica shifted. "Well, it has been a long time, and I thought—"

Hetty's voice cut in, low but insistent. "Now, Jack and

Amy and Bert and I were friends from the time those fellas met in the Navy, before World War II. By the time we married we were so inseparable we had a double wedding. . . ."

She seemed to have rehearsed this speech, as though to reassure Monica that she and Ian were welcome. The fact Monica had heard it all before, from Amy, made no difference.

She continued: "It almost seemed we were tied together some way, you know, when Amy and I got pregnant at the same time, not once but twice. Five years apart! With Jane and Buzz, it seemed like a coincidence, but when it happened again, with you and Carson, we just couldn't believe it. Then of course Amy had to have her hysterectomy just a year after you were born. . . .

"Anyhow, the four of us went through so much together, and we looked upon you kids almost as sisters and brothers to one another. I didn't tell Amy, but I think when you decided to come here this summer, she almost felt like you were . . . accepting her again."

Monica recognized the arbitrator's hook. She ignored it and said, "It's good to be back. So many things are the same now as I remember from long ago."

Hetty took a long time before replying, and when she did her voice had grown soft and weak. "Oh, it's less lively now. All the kids are grown, so none of the families come down here anymore except on weekends. A lot of the original folks have moved away. Some of them have died. . . ." She paused again.

"When I lost Bert—" she began, but the phrase just hung there. Monica didn't want to look at her. She didn't know how to comfort a grieving widow; she would have thought after the length of time Bert had been dead . . .

"I didn't think I'd ever—" Hetty went on haltingly,

then apparently giving up, brought a hanky to her nose and said, "Excuse me, Monica. I just remembered something on the stove." She was gone without a backward glance.

Ian had spent a good half hour skipping up and down the fence line, all the way around the house. Now, as though he were not quite sure of himself, he began to step away from the fence, then go quickly back, touch it, then go a little farther, then back, aiming toward the center of the lawn. Finally he took six or seven steps, and stopped to look out at the bay. He closed his eyes and inclined his head upward.

"There, I knew you'd like the bay," Monica said from her chair. "And wait till you go in. The water is warm, and shallow."

He ignored her. He skipped back toward the fence and started up and down again, pausing now and again to catch the sunlight in his mirror, and often looking up at the sky. In a way that Monica could not quite fathom, he seemed in his natural element at times like these, and never looked to her more beautiful. His red curls rustled in the breeze. He placed his feet together and stood very still. He closed his eyes and lifted his face again, as though to better appreciate the feel of the air upon it. She wished just for a moment they could leave him alone to reside in his own little world. He seemed so happy there. She felt instinctively that if—no, when—they forced him to overcome the barrier between himself and others, something of his ethereal quality would be gone forever. All his life she had seen this special part of him, yet had never been able to capture it on canvas.

Now the doctors and teachers had another word for it. Psychotic. A stiff, unnatural word that sent shivers up her spine. As much as the past few months seemed a waste and a mistake, they had at least taught her that if she could not break open Ian's shell now, while he was still young, he might be an emotional cripple for life.

Yet it seemed to her that Ian's predicament epitomized all the compromise imposed by life. Would that part of him that she saw now, today, have to die in order for the rest of him to live? Was his world a place that each of us began with, but lost much earlier than he did so that it went unremembered? And if so, why did he cling to it? Or what made the rest of us let it go and forget it?

Hetty was detained in the house, from the sound of things, trying to humor Clark, who'd awakened cranky from his nap. This was good. Hetty no doubt continued to believe that Ian's reaction to her resulted from being awakened, just as Monica told her. As a matter of fact, it was exactly when his eyes met Hetty's that Ian had begun to scream.

She leaned back. A sense of calm overtook her that she seldom felt at home. Nothing ever seemed to disturb this peaceful inlet. She ought to do some sketching here. . . .

The door swung open, and Hetty came out with tall glasses of iced tea. Clark followed her sleepily out the door. He was a bit taller than Ian, and looked older than five. His hair was almost platinum, clipped short, and he had already acquired a deep tan. He looked much like the Wellman boys as youngsters. Monica still didn't know which one of them he belonged to.

It was but a moment later the first mishap occurred. Unaware of Clark's approach, Ian flashed his mirror to catch the sun. Clark was amazed by this trick. "Hey, lemme see that." He grabbed for the mirror. Ian swung it behind him and burst into screams. But Clark was quick. He snatched it from Ian and held it beyond Ian's reach, while Ian continued to grab and scream. Monica was across the yard in seconds, intervening in her usual way, explaining to Clark the mirror was Ian's own special toy, and retrieving it for him. Ian stopped yelling and stood back warily. Monica looked at him. "I'm sure Clark didn't mean to take your toy. Why don't you show him how it works?"

He turned his face toward the bay. She shrugged. "Listen, Clark, we just got here, and Ian's not quite used to the place. Maybe in a little while—"

The boy smirked. "It was just a dumb mirror. My mom has lots of them. She'll give me as many as I want. She gives me presents all the time."

"Of course," she said, and rose. "Maybe afterwhile Ian will feel more like playing."

"My dad sent me an 'lectric train. Maybe Ian could look at it. But he can't tear it up. My dad said don't let it get tore up or he wouldn't send another."

Monica paid no attention to Clark's queer phraseology at the time. She told him that would be nice, and she was sure Ian would love to see it. He would more likely ignore the train, but she didn't worry about that. As always, she was too relieved to see a confrontation behind her. She turned to rejoin Hetty.

Hetty sat silently for a few moments, her hand cupped around her chin, as though making up her mind about something. Monica, who had learned by now to expect the worst, braced herself for an observation about Ian's strange obsession. She sipped her tea, for something to be doing, and thought with regret: This was supposed to be a clean slate for Ian. First day, and already a strike against him. . . .

Hetty said at length, "Some of that child's habits are deplorable . . . though I suppose it's to be expected."

"Well, Ian's had that mirror since—"

"Goodness, I didn't mean that. I was talking about Clark's bullying," she said, then added almost defensively, "Ian wasn't doing any more than sticking up for his rights. That's a healthy sign. You ought to be thankful he's that way."

Monica remembered he'd been placed in isolation at school because of this very behavior. And he'd sat alone for a very long time as though thankful to be free of the other children. . . .

CHAPTER 15

Ian returned to the fence. In new places, he always looked for the borders, and having found this place to be surrounded on all sides by a fence, he felt safe at first, to the degree he felt safe anywhere. He had circled the white house and noticed that, while it was not round and perfect like his ball home, it was at least exactly square. He could take the same number of steps from one end of each side to the beginning of the next. There were the same number of windows on each side and a door exactly in the center of two sides, with gates centered in the fence across from each door. There would be a view of the sky from each of the windows, he decided, for no other houses were close enough to block the view and the

windows were tall and close enough to the floor (since
the floor was raised up off the ground) so that he might
be able to look out from the inside of the house and see
high up. He did not know whether he would be taken inside, but he wanted to know everything he could learn
about the inside, just in case.

He worried at first that the house might fall, while he
was trapped in it, so he circled around again to be sure
the ground was level underneath, so that if the house fell,
there would be no holes for it to disappear into. He
touched each short pile of bricks under the house to see if
any would sway. He found a stick and hit each of them as
hard as he could. They felt very strong. He did not know
why things fell, and he had wondered about it for a long
while, since he first began to study the clear bubble in his
crib.

He then checked the distance from the house to each
side of the fence and found it to be the same. That meant
a square inside a square, which seemed right to his way of
thinking. He then went back to the place where he could
be with his ball home. He loved the warmth it sent him
when there was nothing in the way to block him from it;
it encircled his whole body yet it did not make him feel
trapped as he felt when one of the others tried to hold
him with their arms. This feeling of closeness with his
home was never more strong than he found it here at the
bay. At the new house where he stayed with Monica, he
could not see the sky from any of the windows inside because they were all too high except in the room where
Monica painted. He was not allowed in there. And if he
could get high enough to see out, there was a fence or another house in the way.

In the yard behind, he could see his ball between the
treetops. He had not liked the trees at first because they

blocked him from his home and part of its warmth as well. But then he found his ball played games with him, winking at him sometimes between the treetops, and he laughed and skipped along, looking up now and then to see it wink, then hide, then wink again.

He thought, briefly, this place called the bay would bring new hope for him, that he could think here and get answers to questions so long puzzling him. Even the one called Hetty who looked at him so hard when they first came had not said anything bad about him, so probably she wasn't a doctor or a teacher.

But then there was Clark. He hadn't understood Clark would be one of them the same size as himself, because Hetty said they were the same age, and he knew that size and age were not always the same. It was one more of the endless confusions of the way they talked. He did not trust any of the others now; he had learned better; and he especially feared the ones who were his size. They could not be handled like the larger ones, couldn't be made to understand through screams. There were many of them at school, and he found them cruel and vicious, knowing he was different and punishing him for it. They would push at him sometimes, and shout in his ears, and sometimes they would come at him in groups of five or six and make circles around him, shouting words until the teachers made them stop. But then while the teachers tried to help, he knew they really did not like him. He would overhear them talking about his mirror, saying that it caused trouble among the "children," as they were called, though they all had separate names, and Mrs. Maguire ought to make him leave it at home. He did not know who Mrs. Maguire was for a long time, until one day a teacher looked at Monica and called her that. He counted up. That was three names for one person.

When he first began school, he thought the teachers were kind, because they let him do as he liked without being bothered. But as time went on he realized the teachers played a special part in laying the trap to keep him from getting home.

The special doctors stayed in buildings with long halls and many doors. They would bring him into rooms and have him do things to make them happy. Sometimes he did not feel like doing what they wanted him to, especially when he had done it before. It was a while before he understood why he was taken to these doctors. They never looked at his throat or in his ears, or listened to his heartbeat with a necklace; nor was he ever seen by them the times his ears or his throat hurt. At last he began to see a pattern; the sky had patterns, so he understood them. Only when he could make patterns of what the others did could he understand anything at all.

The teachers talked among themselves about what these doctors said. They also talked to Monica. Monica talked to Forrest. So they were all connected and working together to trick him. He did not know why, and he spent many hours wondering. They studied him as they studied the television. Did they wish to find out things about his world? And if they knew about his world, what would they do? He could not tell them things; words would not come right. Did his failure to talk to them cause them to try to find out by looking inside his head? Was that why they tried to fix his eyes on theirs, and look through them like windows?

Before the doctors had joined the group against him he tried very hard to talk to the others, to make them understand his feelings. Now he no longer tried, and if a word came out with sound, it was by accident and almost never the way it had sounded inside his head. Maybe not talk-

ing was one defense against them. Maybe not looking into
their eyes was another. For if they could find out about
his world by studying him, maybe it meant they were
going to try and destroy it. He had listened to them plan
ways to hurt each other on the television. And sometimes
they blew up things and destroyed them. They studied
the television. They studied him. Maybe there was a pattern. He had to be very cautious, although he was not
sure he was right about their plans.

This place called the bay could be another of their
tricks. Clark had already grabbed his mirror. What if
there were more children that he had not yet seen, waiting? On the last day he went to see the doctors, five children had appeared suddenly, children he had not seen
before. And one grabbed his mirror, while another spat-
tered him with pee. Then Monica came and took him
away. His whole body seemed to reek with the smell of
the pee, and he held his breath for as long as he could,
until she bathed him in the tub. He did not dare take in a
deep breath to scream.

Monica confused him. Sometimes she helped him. But
then sometimes she tricked him. She could not be depended upon. Today she rescued his mirror from Clark.
But he could not guess what she might do next. Maybe
she meant to leave him here. He watched her pack his
clothes at her house, but she never said they would be
staying here.

He was glad the cottage was small and full of windows.
He would not be afraid to go inside and find her car keys.
He was sure he could choose a hiding place and find his
way out again.

He noticed the crib after looking through her handbag, and was possessed of a sudden need to rest. He often
felt this; he would be thinking very hard, when all at once

his head would begin to ache and he would forget all else and sleep. Often it was a sleep as deep as that following the great heat inside his ball home. First he would hide the keys. He still must keep Monica from leaving him there; he could become imprisoned by the crib, for he could not climb down from it. His toes would not reach the floor and he could not ever be sure of the distance to the bottom, for it changed so often. Things on the ground could never be trusted to stay the same.

He had seen Hetty carry a basket of towels from the house to the little room outside with the curtain in front. He went in there and placed the keys among the towels. He knew he could not always use that as the place for hiding the keys; other places would have to be found should they stay here or come here again, for the others would guess.

Afterward he returned to the crib and climbed in. His spinning bubble was not belted to its rails; it still lay in a heap at the top of a full sack beside Monica's handbag. No matter. He did not want to think anymore, and sometimes even the bubble seemed to control him, because once he started it spinning, he could not stop thinking. At times his thoughts seemed to spin inside his head as fast as the balls in the bubble, and he would become so upset he would beat it with his fists and kick it. But soon he would realize the danger and stop. He could not break the bubble because the others might not get him another. And surely if they guessed how important it was to his efforts at getting back to his home, they would take this one away.

He wanted only to rest now. He lay down. He slept. Everything he knew of both worlds was lost in oblivion.

CHAPTER 16

Ian had been out of sight for some time, while Clark stayed within view, playing with trucks at the edge of the patio. Monica had risen to check on Ian, but Hetty stopped her. "Keep your seat. I heard the back door slam a few minutes ago, so he's inside. And if he goes out again, the back gate is locked, so he can't get out in the alley. Let him wander around and get used to the place. He can't hurt anything. All my things with sentimental value are kept up high, and have been since Clark came to us."

"It isn't like him to go off alone in an unfamiliar place, though."

Hetty chuckled. Her laugh was as low as her speaking voice, and seemed to bubble up from way down inside. "Now I know what they mean by the term 'anxious mother.' You haven't relaxed since you got here, child."

Being referred to as "child" was oddly comforting. It was like Hetty of the old days, bossing all the kids around one minute, catching them in a quick hug the next. Oh, how nice it would be to go back in time. . . .

Hetty was on the subject of Clark. He did not belong to Buzz, the eldest, as Monica had supposed. Nor was he the son of Carson, who was Monica's age.

"If you'd talk to your mother more often, you would

know all about it. Lord knows, I cried on her shoulder enough."

"Why?"

"Well . . ." she began, her voice a shade lower, "Clark's mother came to work for Carson when Clark was a year old. Before you knew it, June had dumped her husband overboard and set her cap for Carson. All this was going on shortly after I lost Bert, so I wasn't told much about it till they became engaged.

"It's funny, but when your kids grow up, it's like going in reverse. They start to think they ought to be protecting you from upsets. But anyhow, I had a feeling what was to come, though I waited for them to tell me. And sure enough, here came June, wearing a diamond as big as an ice cube, and letting me know I was about to have my first daughter-in-law and grandson all in one whack. My opinion was not asked." Her voice was so low Monica could scarcely hear. She kept glancing toward Clark, to assure herself he couldn't overhear.

"You've certainly taken Clark under your wing."

She smiled and cocked her head. "I'm crazy about the rascal, even if I don't care a hoot for his mother. Besides, Carson is his legal guardian now, and that makes him as much my responsibility as any natural grandchild."

Clark approached and asked for help in reattaching a wheel to the axle of a toy truck. Hetty worked with it patiently while Clark stood by watching. Monica left just long enough to check the back yard, but Ian was apparently in the cottage.

She returned to sit again with Hetty. It was interesting she had compared Ian with Carson, and said she had once worried about him. Monica could remember him now, that summer he appeared in eyeglasses with black frames. As glasses were considered about as attractive as braces on teeth when she was growing up, she was even less inclined to be friendly with him than otherwise. He'd always been quiet and bookish; not fun, like Buzz. It was hard to fit him into the picture of a torrid affair with a married secretary.

Once while sales manager at Bradford Oil Tool, Forrest had a narrow escape of a similar kind. But Forrest brought it to a halt. He also told Monica all about it: the offers of the new woman on the staff to stay and work late, the habit of standing above and behind him while he sat, leaning over just close enough to pillow her breast against his shoulder. The compliments, then the blatant moves. He didn't say she drove him wild with desire. He wouldn't admit that. Instead he told Monica, "You know how conservative Bradford is. I'm not getting sacked over some broad with big boobs." He didn't say, "You're my wife, and I'd rather have you any day of the week," as she would have liked to hear. But at least he kept his priorities in line.

Hetty was continuing: "Carson is the go-getter in the family. He and June belong to a yacht club up on Lake Conroe—the bay house isn't good enough for them anymore—and in the summertime they spend nearly every weekend up there entertaining customers, and leave Clark here. Not that I mind. He's good company.

"But sometimes I feel like turning Carson and June both over my knee for neglecting him."

"Where is Clark's real father?"

"He travels all over the place for Western Telegraph. Clark seldom hears from him, as far as I know. He ought to be horsewhipped too. Young people today—

"But don't let me get started on that. Carson's responsible for the boy now, and he ought to spend more time with him. He stays too busy with his job, and June stays busy on the tennis court and at the bridge table, 'struttin' around and puttin' on airs,' as we said in my day.

"If it weren't for Buzz and Peggy, Clark wouldn't have any attention at all."

Monica felt uncomfortable and let the conversation die. Maybe Carson had his own good reasons, just as Forrest did. Maybe as the middle child he just tried harder to make it in the world, outside the family. In the years Monica spent so much time at the bay, it was Buzz who shone brightest, had personality, confidence. Aaron was the baby, and therefore got the lion's share of attention. Maybe Carson, caught in between, was still trying to measure up.

She looked across at Clark, now seated alone on the porch stoop that used to be all there was, before they poured the patio. She felt a bit sorry for him. So his blond hair and healthy tan were not signs of Wellman lineage but mere coincidence. And now his new hope for a play-mate had evaporated. She was about to go in and check on Ian, but Hetty was not finished.

"You know, children have a real power over their parents when they grow up. They can hurt them in so many ways. Aaron has hurt me worse than Carson. He and his girlfriend live together in an apartment off-campus, and he makes no secret of it. If Bert were alive he'd disown him for that, not to mention cutting off his tuition money, and Aaron knows it. But he knows that I wouldn't. He just does as he pleases, knowing I disapprove. He wasn't raised that way. At least he minds his p's and q's pretty well when he's down here . . . which is seldom.

"Listen, Monica, I know you are tired of listening to me go on, but I want to say something now and I won't say any more. You really ought to try and make Amy a part of your life. You have no idea how it hurts her, that you never call, never invite her over. And Jane living so far away. I don't know what it is, because she never told me, but she's a widow like me, and I know how lonely she is. When you lose your husband, if your kids don't come around . . . well . . . if not for Buzz I just . . ." Her voice trailed off. She leaned back and folded her hands. Her gold wedding band was worn nearly through. The enlarged knuckles and prominent veins of her hands were further testimony of age. Somehow these outward signs of all she had weathered were more touching than all the words she spoke of her life. But then, the situation of Amy's loneliness was none of her business.

"Did Mother ask you to tell me how she felt?" she asked at length.

"No. But I just felt it my duty, even if you consider me an interfering old fool. I *am* old. Too old to miss out on a chance to make something right when I know it's wrong. Whatever it is you hold against Amy, remember that she was the best kind of mother to you and Jane. She never thought of anything other than your happiness."

"Is that what she was thinking of when she spent all my tuition for the Virginia Art Institute? I'm sure she never mentioned the university was not my first choice."

Hetty considered a moment, then said, "I can remember from way back, Amy always wanted to have a nice place for you and Jane to bring your friends, a place you could be proud of. She never had much, growing up."

"Yes, I've heard all that before. The trouble was, she went a little overboard. My father had to foot her bills . . . so there went my college plans, down the drain.

"And . . ." she continued, but hesitated because this still hurt and was not easy to talk about, ". . . I used to blame him, until after he died and I realized that what he couldn't change he simply endured without complaint.

"But then it was too late to tell him I understood and forgave him. If he'd just been more honest with me, or if Mother had had the guts to refuse to let him share the blame. . . ."

Hetty observed her for a moment, then said, "Jack simply stood beside Amy, regardless of her faults, and loved all the good in her. If not, they couldn't have stood as one. And that's what marriage is all about . . . or used to be, in our day."

There was a long pause, as they both realized nothing would be gained by arguing philosophies on marriage. Then a smile played on Hetty's lips and she confided, "I'll tell you something I never told Amy. Bert would not go to your house. He always said we were plain folks, and he didn't feel comfortable there. He'd rather the four of you come to our place."

"I'd forgotten till now . . . Mother used to worry that you never came. I was thinking just this afternoon about all the years you had us here. You sure went all out on hospitality."

"Well, there are lots of ways to reciprocate hospitality, or any other kindness."

Monica thought she referred to all the expensive gifts her mother used to buy the Wellmans for one occasion or another. Silver trays; monogrammed towels; expensive table linens; none of which the Wellmans probably ever took from the box. "Then you have something of an idea of my mother's extravagance."

"Sure I do, though I wasn't thinking of that. Of course, there are far worse traits in a person than extravagance."

Monica did not want to talk of this anymore. She stood up. "I've got to check on Ian."

CHAPTER 17

Monica was surprised to find Ian in the crib, sound
asleep. She could never make any sense of his sleeping
patterns. Sometimes she'd hear him rocking in his crib, off
and on, into the early hours of the morning. Next day he
would not nap at all, or even seem tired. Other times he'd
sleep soundly at night and then sleep three or four hours
in the middle of the next day. The psychologists added
"erratic sleeping habits" to their list of Ian's symptoms,
but Dr. Winters had always assured her there was nothing to worry about, that a child simply went to sleep
when he was tired. He wasn't trained to ignore the dic-
tates of his normal body functions like an adult.

The real puzzle today was that Ian went alone inside a
strange house, found a crib, and climbed into it. She
shook her head and slid a finger along his soft cheek. She
leaned over and gave him a silent kiss, then sat down on
the bed nearby. The old bedsprings creaked beneath her
weight, but this did not seem to disturb her sleeping
child.

She had become nervous and uneasy during her talk
with Hetty because she sensed a conspiracy afoot between Hetty and her mother to "win Monica over." She
could imagine them discussing the strategy over the telephone. Was that on Amy's mind when she suggested the
Wellman place for the summer? But Monica didn't think

so. Amy's reaction to the outpouring of her daughter's problems had been too spontaneous. She was, for all her faults, compassionate. And from the looks of Ian now, she had been right. What was it about this place that made one feel so at peace?

For her it had to be the sense of continuity she found. Of course, none of this would have meaning for Ian now. She had no idea why he had taken a liking to the bay, but if that were the case, then it would be worth the whole summer of putting up with Hetty's overt meddling.

Monica sat for a long while, lost in her own thoughts. Finally she realized the afternoon was drawing to a close. The room was cast in shadows. She could hear Hetty in the kitchen. She tucked a light blanket around Ian's legs and went to help.

Hetty was adding potatoes and carrots to a pot roast simmering on the stove. The aroma made Monica's stomach turn over in hunger. "I don't need any help right now, though you can set the table in the dining room afterwhile. Same old knives, forks, and plates and iced-tea goblets we've had around here for years. . . .

"Let's see, it's four-thirty now. That ought to put me right on time. I always have dinner ready when Buzz and Peggy get here at six. Those two love it here. Never miss a weekend. You sit down."

And don't get in the way. Monica looked around her. The floors were as spotless as the counters and the porcelain kitchen table where she sat. The old gas stove shone from its ancient burners to the aluminum oven door handle. As children they abided by strict rules about the house. If you dirtied a dish, you washed it and put it away. You didn't dare walk through with sand on your feet, or carelessly throw a wet towel in a corner. Wet towels were left in the bathhouse. Dirty clothes were put in a basket in the bottom of the hall closet. (This was still true, Monica learned today. When the basket was full, Hetty carried it to the bathhouse and emptied it into her washing machine.) Out of a sudden urge to tidy herself, Monica unfastened her tortoise barrette, pulled her hair tighter, and refastened the barrette.

Hetty was looking at her. "Is Ian a finicky eater?"

"Oh, don't bother about fixing for him. I brought some things he likes."

She pursed her lips. "You shouldn't let him get away with that. He ought to be eating whatever you set before him by now. Carson used to do me that way and I liked to have never broken him of it."

Monica had once held out a day and a half with Ian, and, finally realizing he wasn't about to eat the rice and gravy any more than he had the cream of wheat she offered him that morning or the dinner of the night before, she gave in. She believed from the glower on his face he was prepared to starve, but she could hear the moans inside his stomach, and couldn't bear it. Forrest had said, "He knows what he wants and will wait until he gets it; it's a sign of strength and independence."

"Maybe so," she had replied, not wishing an argument to erupt. There were many problems with Ian that seemed at the time not worth making an issue of. While she realized the error now, she didn't want to discuss it with Hetty. She shifted the conversation back to Carson. "It's nice that Buzz has time to fill in for Carson. Hard for me to feature him as the settled-down type, though. I mean, he used to seem so full of mischief when we were kids."

As the oldest, Buzz was naturally the first to be taught to drive the motorboat, and once he was given that new badge of maturity he spent most of his time reminding

everyone of his manhood. But then she had one more
memory of Buzz, her last. It was a little more poignant. "I
guess the last time I saw Buzz he was in his Navy dress
whites."

Hetty nodded. "Buzz sowed his wild oats, but Bert always said the Navy would make Buzz grow up, and he
was right. Came out with a level head on his shoulders."

"He waited a while before he married, didn't he? I
remember Mom and Dad going to the wedding, I think."

"He waited until he found the right girl," Hetty said,
then paused before continuing: "First time Peggy ever
walked in with Buzz I knew she was the one for him. You
can say what you want to about daughters-in-law never
being good enough, but Bert and I took Peggy as one of
our own and we made no bones about telling Buzz what
we felt from the beginning."

In which order? "That's really nice."

"I can't wait for you to meet her. Sweetest, prettiest little thing. Not gaudy or show-off, just simple and natural.
Good disposition." She picked up a cloth and began to
dry dishes. "And now they have their own little one coming. They had nearly given up when Peggy finally got
pregnant. And it means a lot to Buzz, carrying on the
Wellman name now that Bert is gone." She inclined her
head, looked hard at the plate in her hand, and dried it
some more.

"I gather they have their hopes pinned on a boy."

"Well, I guess they do. Seems instinctive for a man to
want a son."

And also a man's mother to want a grandson.

"But—" and this she drew out, "the most important
thing is a healthy child. If this one's a girl, they can try
again for a boy if they've a mind to. Although Peggy *is*
thirty-six, and with her history of endometriosis. . . . The

truth is, we can't help speculating. All boys on Buzz's side, and Peggy the only girl on her side, with a brother and all boys for cousins."

You've checked that out. "Looks like a cinch."

"We'll see. . . . I've been making all the baby things yellow, just in case. I've crocheted and tatted and smocked till my old fingers are nearly worn out. Thirty years of cleaning shrimp hasn't helped them much." She laughed. "That reminds me, we're reviving the big Fourth of July celebration this summer, first time since Bert died. Will Forrest be home at all, since it's a holiday?"

Monica laughed. "Not in England. I doubt he'll be home at all before September. At first they told him he could expect one trip, maybe two. But travel is so expensive. Now I think they're reneging. I'm trying not to count on a visit."

Hetty shook her head. "I just don't think it's right, the way those big companies separate employees from their families. They take unfair advantage of a man who wants to get ahead, and don't give a hoot about his family life."

She admitted that was true, but said, "The Trans-Ocean project is a great opportunity for Forrest, and with big companies you have to grab your chance when and where it comes."

"It still seems to me a man ought not be separated from his family on holidays. When Bert was alive we always made a big fuss of the Fourth. If it wasn't for Buzz, I wouldn't go to the trouble this summer, but he's just like his father. He loves this place, and takes good care of it. In fact, it was Buzz and Peggy who got me coming back after I lost Bert. First couple of years I just couldn't face it. Everywhere I looked, another reminder, a knickknack he made for me, or something he bought for our anniver-

sary or my birthday or . . . Anyhow, finally Buzz said,
'We'll take everything that you don't want to see and
store it.' But I told him no, we'd leave it, that this was the
family place and until I could face all of it I wouldn't try
to face any of it and it would probably be worse, seeing
the empty spaces where things were. Even that old brown
coffee mug he always used. . . ."

Tears sprang to her eyes. Monica felt uncomfortable,
as though she were intruding on something private. She
didn't know what to say. Hetty brushed her eyes and continued: "Anyhow, that's what upsets me nowadays. The
importance of the family seems to be going by the way-
side. At least Buzz understands that, even if his brothers
don't."

Later, as Monica walked around the big table to set the
places, she caught herself almost agreeing with Hetty.
There had been a summer evening once, when she was
nine or so. Bert, small and quiet, unobtrusive with his soft
voice and pipe, walked her and Jane and the boys out on
the front lawn. There was no awning then, or patio, just
the two steps down and then grass under the open sky.
The moon cast a carpet of lights on the rippling bay
water. Bert took his pipe and pointed out the stars. He
knew several of their names, and this impressed Monica.
It seemed nights were always that beautiful on the bay,
nothing unusual about it, but Bert could always see and
admire the small things. Like her own father, Jack, Bert
had always been a presence with his family. She could see
now that he valued the things money could not buy and
she wished somehow that she and Forrest could live life
in the same uncomplicated way. It wasn't money or material things they valued, but achievement, some need to
prove their abilities, to feel a sense of accomplishment
and to justify each day. . . . She realized this drive led

them into difficulties, both between themselves and with Ian, and she almost wished it did not exist.

On the other hand, in Hetty's generation—she had never realized this until now—she could not have been free to be herself, to paint, and to work seriously at it. She would not have wanted to give that up, not for any price. She did have the right to be a person unto herself, and not just the hub of the family wheel.

It seemed to Monica that her generation of women had the most difficult road in front of them. Her mother's generation had roles as clear-cut as paper dolls. There was no question of striving for something called self-awareness and fulfillment. They'd never heard of the terms. They were born, grew up, got married, had kids, grew old, and died, without ever questioning whether that was enough. And twenty years from now a whole transition would have taken place. Most women would grow up toward filling a career instead of a nursery. No one would question people for not having a family or for leaving their kids in day care centers.

Monica and all the women her age were caught somewhere in between. They had to pave the way while suffering the guilt feelings left over from the previous generation. It was like being torn into two pieces. And the old roles cut out for fathers were of no help either. Regardless of how "liberated" they pretended to be, most men were just like Forrest. They deeply resented their wives' insistence on doing something their own mothers never dreamed of. They would not say much most of the time, but when under pressure their true feelings would emerge. Certainly it was true of Forrest. She stopped suddenly, a fork poised in her hand. Why did she go along with that attitude in Forrest?

Because, after all these years of marriage, it was more

complicated than that. Through her wish to accommodate
her husband, she had brought a child into the world, and
that child had to be supported and looked after. She
counted the places, then remembered the heavy goblets
and went back for them. She thought she heard the faint
sound of Ian's rocking, and was seized with guilt.

CHAPTER 18

Shortly after six Buzz and Peggy arrived. Monica knew
that Peggy had been to the doctor earlier and that Hetty
was eager for a full report. Hetty was clearly worried over
the child Peggy carried. When she spoke on the subject,
her voice grew lower and more doleful, as though she expected problems. Amy had often referred to Hetty as "intuitive," and Monica was reminded of that now. Something had been said about cesarean section. That was not
natural, and therefore dangerous. "In my day . . ." she
began. Her mouth worked into a tight line. Monica did
not try to reason with her, for it seemed futile. Hetty did
not accept change easily, not in her surroundings, not in
her thinking, not even when the change was for the better. And Monica felt herself in a strange position. She was
here because she found solace in the unchanging way of
life at the bay. Yet she also found herself impatient with
Hetty's old-fashioned ways at times. Best not to become

involved. She did not want to be there when Peggy and Buzz first walked in. Let them get their family business tended to before she showed her face. After all, she was an interloper. She wasn't sure just then how truly welcome she and Ian were, how much they were disrupting the current routine of Hetty's life. It was a bad time of day for her, this time just before flowering darkness and switching on of lights, a time when whatever seemed wrong with life grew out of proportion. She did not know why. The house now smelled of dinner from one end to the other. It should have presaged a happy, carefree evening renewing old acquaintances around a big table, but somehow it did not. She found herself dreading the sight of Buzz Wellman again, though she knew there was no sound reason why. What happened between them was such a silly thing and so long ago, she hadn't even thought of it again until she came here. No doubt he'd forgotten it altogether.

She heard the shuffle of feet, the banging door, the cluck of voices, and the attempts of the boy Clark to dominate Buzz's attention. Good. She could putter a little before emerging to meet them. There was little natural light from the windows. She pulled the chain, and the naked bulb which hung in the center of the room became a glowing ball of white. Ian's eyes widened, then narrowed. He rocked some more.

"Ready to get up?"

He pulled himself to the rail and stood. He let her take him from the crib. As though by force, he unfastened his gaze from the bulb and looked at the floor as she swung him down. She was more than conscious now of his body movements toward her; the doctors had made such an issue of it over the past few months. He did not cling to her even as she hugged him, but simply let himself be held until he was safely down. Sometimes she was unable to take this rejection in stride, and wanted to shake him, force him to hug back. But most of the time she just tried to behave as though that were normal (in the hope it was) and that he'd outgrow it.

Ian walked toward the windows across the room and looked out. Monica could still hear the voices in the kitchen and now the front room, all going at once, it seemed. She still did not want to face the introduction. "The sun is going down," she remarked with a sigh.

He was still looking out the window, his head inclined upward.

"Afterwhile we'll go out on the front porch and see the moon and stars. They're beautiful over the bay."

She thought he repeated "moon" very softly, but wasn't sure. It was similar to a yawning sound. There was a time when she regarded this sort of exchange with pleasure, since it happened so seldom. But the doctors had convinced her there was a technical term for Ian's speech. They called it echolalia, and said it was symptomatic of autism. Now when Ian spoke, she felt paralyzed because his words simply reaffirmed the doctors' tentative diagnosis that he would never be able to communicate.

"Hetty has a big supper ready. I fixed your sandwich, but maybe you could just try a few bites of roast. All right? Come on." She took his hand and walked him toward the sound of voices.

Buzz was loosening his tie. Her first impression of him in his white-collar work clothes would soon be overlaid with the more familiar cutoffs and bare feet, but he reminded her even then of Ichabod Crane with a pug nose, blond hair, and clear eyes. He had reached his height of just over six feet when she last saw him, more than fifteen years ago, but she noticed now he was little more filled

out. Still he had a lanky, boyish look about him. He talked
like a sputtering engine, in short, abrupt sentences. There
was nothing smooth about him.

His mouth fell open when he saw her and he said,
"Well, look what the wind blew in, Mom. The squirt
finally grew up. Hi, Monica." He clutched her shoulders
with one arm and pecked her cheek. It was as though the
whole room came suddenly to life. Before she recovered
he was kneeling down. "And this is Ian. Gimme a fist,
boy." He thrust a long hand forward. Ian recoiled and
nudged closer to Monica's legs.

She laughed. "He's a little shy." And you come on a little strong. She put an arm around Ian's shoulder as Buzz
maneuvered Peggy forward to meet her. She was tiny,
scarcely reaching Buzz's rib cage, and exactly as Hetty
described: good skin with little makeup, a high-collared
maternity smock and light brown hair that brushed the
shoulders of it, too long for her slight build. She reminded Monica of one of those sweet-looking girls that
go through the beauty treatment across the pages of
McCall's. They'd send her out the other end with a short
pixie haircut and fluttering eyelashes, melon-colored lip-
stick and blushing cheeks.

Clark was hanging on to Buzz, trying to get a promise
for a boat ride in the morning. "Yeah, we'll go out tomorrow. After I get somebody to help me down at the
launch."

"I'll help you, Uncle Buzz, lemme, huh?"

"Yer about big enough, squirt." He tweaked his nose.
"Hey, Peggy, where's my cutoffs?"

"Eat first, while dinner's hot. You can change later."
Hetty's voice cut through the dining room with the same
authority as the call of her whistle. She had served the
pot roast with hot corn on the cob, green salad, and rolls,

and had filled a small plate and set it alongside Ian's sandwich: her subtle way of saying, just let me show you how to do it. Ian, however, resisted her urging and ate a few bites of the sandwich, then made a guttural sound, pointing to his peaches. Monica picked up a spoon and began to feed him.

Clark, already on the defensive from the confrontation about Ian's mirror, took in an exaggerated breath and said, "Look, Gram, he can't even feed hisself."

"Pipe down, squirt," Buzz said with his mouth full. "He'll learn when he gets ready." He finished chewing and gulped down half a glass of milk. Hetty quickly refilled his glass.

Ian took no notice of Clark's remark, but Monica was grateful to Buzz for what he said in reply. She felt she ought to like Clark, ought to at least view his smart crack as typical of his age. But she had never liked children the way people were supposed to. Clark was beginning to seem more an obstacle in Ian's path than a help. Perhaps Ian's experience at the center helped shape her attitude. Often when she picked him up in the evening, one or two children would come to her and say, "Ian never says anything. He sure is dumb," or "Ian got in trouble today. He pushed Roger on the ground." She had become defensive against children in general, and now she felt defensive against Clark. I've got to stop this, she told herself.

Buzz was continuing. "I'll bet I can teach Ian to swim. You like the water, boy?"

Ian was fiddling with the crumbs on his plate. "He doesn't like the swimming pool," Monica intervened. "He has never been to the beach."

"No wonder he hasn't taken to the water. Swimming pools are cold. The bay water is warm. I hope you brought his trunks. We'll have a try at it in the morning."

Peggy spoke up. "Buzz used to teach swimming three evenings a week at the YMCA."

"Buzz was a champion swimmer in high school. We still have all his trophies at home in his old room," said Hetty.

"Yeah, and track too," said Clark proudly. "I seen his shoes."

"I didn't know that," said Monica, not knowing what else to say.

Buzz shrugged. There was an edge of softness in his voice. "There isn't much you can do with a row of swimming trophies and a worn-out pair of track shoes."

"You can set them up, and be proud of them," said Hetty, her chest rising.

"Just somethin' else to gather dust," said Buzz, then he changed the subject. Had the bragging embarrassed him, or reminded him that the more intellectual, serious-minded Carson had made more of a name for himself in the world of business where men measure each other? She was not sure why, but sensed it was the latter.

Shortly Hetty said, "More pot roast, Buzz? Potatoes, carrots?" She was reaching for the bowl.

Buzz leaned back, chewing on a toothpick. "No, Mom, I'm finished."

"But you always have two helpings. What's the matter? Didn't I get the roast done enough tonight? You know, sometimes that old oven—"

"No, Mom, I'm just not hungry," he said, then looked at Monica. "Does Amy do you this way when you go to her house?"

"I . . . I don't see very much of Mother."

"Buzz had a big lunch today," Peggy softly intervened.

"Oh?" Hetty's eyebrows shot up, and she leaned back, making a comic display of trying to seem casual. "Not one of those two- or three-hour drinking lunches, I hope?"

Buzz laughed. "No such luck. One of the guys cooked up a mess of barbecue and brought it to work. I'm a sucker for that stuff; love it."

"Well, that's nice. I'll bet it wasn't as good as your dad's used to be. Anyhow . . . Monica, Buzz likes his work. They're always doing something nice like that, and they always throw a party on everybody's birthday. It's liking your work that really counts, I think. Bert always enjoyed getting up every morning, bright and early—"

"What's yer old man doin' in England?" Buzz cut in.

Monica explained about the project. Buzz knew of it; he worked for one of the larger independent oil companies. "I saw somethin' the other day about a crew of ours going up to Aberdeen."

"But not you, I hope?" Hetty looked up.

"Nah, I just push papers around. What's for dessert?"

"Homemade ice cream. Out in the— Oh, Lord, I just remembered those clothes I carried to the bathhouse to wash. I came back to the porch to check on the freezer and forgot what I was doing. Fiddlesticks. You kids clear the table while I go out there and get them started drying." She rose.

"Aw, Mom, they'll wait till morning," said Buzz. "Sit down, fer heaven's sake."

"No, they'll sour," she said as the door swung open. As soon as she was out of earshot Buzz said, "She can find more work to do than anyone I ever saw. She's gonna kill herself one of these days if she doesn't slow down."

Peggy patted his arm. "Leave her alone, honey. Keeping busy is good for her." She looked across at Monica. "Mom gets so down about Dad being gone if she has time on her hands. Buzz can't realize that."

"Don't get pushy, woman," he told her playfully, and gave her cheek a pinch.

"Oh, stop it, silly," she laughed. It seemed Hetty was right about one thing: Buzz and Peggy were well suited.

Buzz was spooning out peach ice cream when Hetty appeared at the door, holding Monica's keys in front of her. "I found these in the laundry basket. Are they yours, Monica? I don't recognize them."

"What? Oh, dear." She took them. "Ian, you know better—" Then she broke off and explained that Ian often hid her car keys for some unfathomable reason. "This is an extra set, in fact. He hid the others this morning." She looked at Ian again, who observed her detachedly. "Here, I'll just put them on the shelf up here where they can't be reached. That'll fix you."

"Smart kid," said Buzz. "He knows how to keep you from leaving without him."

"It isn't that. Half the time he hides them when we're getting ready to go somewhere together, and he knows it. I think he just wants attention."

Yet this did not seem to be the case. He was busy removing the peaches from the ice cream and placing them in a row on his napkin. This done, he then put the spoon down again and looked closely at the display.

CHAPTER 19

Later in the evening when she put Ian to bed, Monica had an idea. "Would you like to sleep with me?"

Ian moved back and leaned against the rails next to the wall, and focused on the white bulb. Then he put his hands together between his knees and rocked. He looked so vulnerable there, in his footed pajamas. She wondered if he had been afraid she would leave him after all, as Buzz suggested. Maybe he was always afraid of that . . . but why? She had never left him without explaining exactly where she would go and when she would return. She'd never tricked him, leaving him with a sitter and slipping out, like some people did to their kids. There was no reason why he should fear being abandoned. And yet he seemed to fear something. She shrugged and turned down the bed, but not without the term "irrational fears" tripping like a ghost across her mind.

It was nearly ten o'clock, unusual for Ian to be awake so late. She could feel his eyes following her movements. When she was all set, she reached for the chain and pulled. She lay down. The moonlight behind her threw shadows along the bedcovers so that they resembled a snow-covered mountain range stretching out between her and her son. Soon she heard him sigh and curl up to sleep.

She wished she had insisted he get into bed with her. She yearned for his closeness. If there was nothing organically wrong with Ian, and surely there wasn't, then who had been the first to become estranged? Who had rejected whom, at least in his mind?

I have treated Ian coldly without intending to, she decided. Maybe if just once I had gone to him in the only place he seems to feel safe—his crib—and pulled him out and into bed with me, had let him sleep next to the warmth of my own body, maybe it would have made the difference. . . .

But no, I listened to others who said, best to let him tough it out in his own room. Even Dr. Winters went along with that. But suppose I had only obeyed instinct instead of logic. Maybe Ian isn't yet asleep. . . .

She rose and went to the crib, and kissed his forehead. His eyes opened. "Come on and sleep with Mom, Ian. Okay? Please, Mommy would like for you to sleep with me."

He closed his eyes again. She wasn't sure whether it was rejection or if he was more asleep than awake. She got back in bed alone, now fully awake herself. She thought over the day now drawing to a close. In some ways it had been a success . . . there was that word again . . . because Ian had felt comfortable here immediately. Probably she ought to keep a journal of this summer, logging in his daily progress. June 4, did this and did that, didn't eat Hetty's food but did use good manners at the table; no tantrums; clung to me once; no sleeping problem, and found his way well in a strange place.

Reactions to people: rejected Clark, question mark on Hetty, no interaction with Peggy at all, a bit frightened of Buzz.

Buzz. He *was* somehow different than she expected. Hard to pin it down. More dependent? No. More . . . more conformed. Yes, that was it. Certainly there was

never a son who had more pleased his parents. In every
way poor Forrest had failed, Buzz had succeeded. Yet it
seemed as though Hetty and Bert were behind, or maybe
in front of, every decision he made. Like a road map. If
Professor Maguire—why did this analogy come to her?—if
he had produced a road map for his son, Forrest would
have followed it willingly, in order to please. But the professor produced no guidelines, only the mild, subtle criti-
cism when expectations were not met.

It seemed that Buzz, on the other hand, won total ac-
ceptance. His parents said, "Do this," and when he did,
they smiled and praised him. Everyone seemed pleased
about the results. Or were they? She thought of the
dinner-table conversation. Hetty was pushy, interfering.
Grasping. Had she become that way since Bert's death
because she was afraid of being alone, afraid of having
her family come apart beneath her watchful eyes? Was
she frightened of making a life for herself or, worse, of
letting anything happen within her power of control that
would have disappointed her dead husband?

One thing at least was obvious: Hetty wasn't as certain
of Buzz as she pretended, earlier in the afternoon. She
was asking herself all the time: could he still go away,
still sow a few more wild oats?

Monica's mind drifted back to her ninth-grade prom,
the occasion of one of her first dates. Except that the date
for the evening had taken her out the previous weekend
and, finding his clumsy advances unwelcome, curiously
took sick two nights before the big ball, leaving her
stranded for what seemed then the biggest evening of her
life.

Watching tears stream from Monica's eyes, Amy
thought for a bit, picked up the phone, and dialed Hetty's
number. Within minutes Buzz, home on leave from the

Navy, was dispatched to be her escort. Monica was embarrassed by Amy's gesture but she was also in a lurch. All she could imagine was the tall, gaunt Buzz arriving at her door in a pair of swimming trunks. It was the only way she'd ever seen him dressed.

However, he arrived at the door with an orchid in the crook of his arm, dashing in his dress whites. Even if he was five years older (she had suffered pangs at the thought of being escorted to the ball by someone in the league of a fond uncle), the uniform and his attractiveness in it made the difference. A bit lackadaisical beforehand, she became nervous and giddy. She had told none of her friends about her change of plans.

Her new powder-blue chiffon dress draped like a tent from the waist down over yards of petticoats. Her strapless bra (the first she'd ever owned) was stuffed with extra cotton because she didn't quite fill out the rhinestone-studded bodice of the dress. She wore very high springolaters and long white satin gloves.

Buzz opened the door of the shiny Wellman sedan, took great care to be sure her dress was folded up out of harm's way, then smacked the door closed and went around to the driver's seat. She stayed on her side of the automobile, ever more nervous when the leather seat bobbed under his weight as he slid in. She looked out the window as they drove away, and felt like Cinderella. Little did it matter she and Buzz had nothing to talk about aside from reassuring each other of the directions to the Sylvan Beach Pavilion. The night seemed full of promise anyway. During the slumber party at a girlfriend's house, the grand finale to the evening, she would have more to say than anyone else. Usually that was not the case.

All went well for the first hour or so. Buzz wasn't a bad dancer, though he didn't hold her very close or whisper anything in her ear as a real date might. The strong silent type was fashionable. She could see the glances of awe as they whirled around the floor. As the hour drew close to nine, he began glancing at his watch with regularity. Finally, between dances, he excused himself and was gone for what seemed a long while. When he returned he said they'd have to leave.

He escorted her home, a humiliating blow for someone who was expecting the witching hour to be midnight. She didn't have the nerve to ask him why the evening was cut short. Maybe it was something she'd done, or said. Maybe her breath smelled. She let herself in the house. He stayed at the door long enough for that. Her parents were watching television and looked up, surprised. She asked her mother to call and say she'd gotten ill and couldn't come to the slumber party. After that call, she overheard Amy calling Hetty. A couple of days later, Hetty reported: Buzz had another date at ten o'clock.

And that was the last time she saw him, although she still went to the bay for several summers, knowing he was stationed somewhere far away and she wouldn't have to face him. Until tonight. She wondered again if he even remembered that evening. Not likely. And she was probably right in her speculations about him. He may have been dashing in his Navy getup, may have a cabinetful of trophies in sport, but where was he now?

She sighed and turned over. Finally she slept.

CHAPTER 20

Monica was awakened the following morning by the feel of a soft breeze through the open window. The house was silent. The hands of the clock were at just past five. She did not quite know what to do with herself, this early. The walls were thin; too much noise would awaken the household. She pulled on a robe and got up, conscious of the noisy springs under her. Ian slept soundly, his arms tucked under his stomach. She noticed his mirror, precariously lodged between his outstretched foot and the crib rail, and placed it near his hand. If he should not see it immediately upon waking, he would begin the day with a session of frantic screams. She pulled his flannel blanket over him and padded softly to the kitchen. She put coffee in the percolator and started it brewing. Hetty might not like her interfering with the kitchen routine, but that was a chance worth taking. One thing Monica needed in the morning was good, strong black coffee, and she wasn't waiting an hour or more to get it.

She went back for her clothes then, and doubled around to the bathhouse for a morning shower. She pulled the light chain and closed the cotton curtain across the door. The old gate valves groaned when she turned them, but the water was soon steaming hot. She pulled on a shower cap and stepped in on the concrete floor. For ten minutes her body feasted on the hot needles of water.

Showers at home never seemed quite so refreshing. When she was done she reached out for the towel, draped across the washing machine nearby, and glanced instinctively at the thin curtain across the doorway. The soft breeze disturbed it little. She remembered the day when she was eleven or so that she was showering and, as there was no washing machine then, left her towel and clothes in a chair in the corner a step away. As she crossed to reach for her towel the breeze lifted out the curtain and outside stood Carson in his glasses and swim trunks. As embarrassed by what he had seen as she was, he darted away quickly, and kept his head in a book the rest of the day. She never told anyone of it, and certainly never discussed it with him. She smiled at the memory now. How modest she had been, even before there was anything to be modest about. Until coming back to the bay, she was unaware of how much of her life was rooted here. Through all her years of marriage she'd hardly ever thought of the place or of any of the Wellmans. She wondered now how she could so deftly have buried her association with it, never missing it or feeling a sense of loss when Forrest declined to accept the Wellmans as friends. Hetty and Bert had worked so hard to make a success of the wedding party held in their honor at the bay. But a sudden rain spoiled the picnic on the lawn, and twenty people wound up sitting cramped in the dining room, pretending it was just as much fun. As they drove back to Houston, Forrest observed, "God, what a bore. I couldn't see wasting my time down there, could you?"

"No . . . guess I've outgrown it."

Funny, how easily she dismissed the bay from her life in the interest of impressing her husband-to-be.

She could smell the coffee when she got back into the house. Every inch of her skin felt alive and fresh. There was something invigorating about the air down here. It took her twice as long to begin to wake up at home. By daybreak she was outside alone on the covered patio, sipping her coffee and enjoying the solitude. The sun crested the water line like a great orange ball rising, reaching higher and higher, sending a plume of rays that hit the water and fractured into blinking dots on the rippling surface. Presently she heard the high pitch of a sea gull's call, and then from out of nowhere the great bird appeared, its wings spread in a graceful decline as it neared the end of the Wellman pier and landed swiftly on the flat end of a tall vertical piling. It perched there, wings folded in, silhouetted against the pink sky, for one moment, two, then rose once again, peeling off into the glimmering light and disappearing.

Monica realized she had never fully appreciated the bay as a child. Often they were up and about this time of morning, should they stay overnight, attaching raw chicken backs to the crab lines along the pier. Had she ever looked up and appreciated the morning sky? Surely not. Why did you have to grow much older to appreciate simple beauty?

She remembered now that Bert's wooden bench rocker was not far from where the corner of the enlarged patio now reached. Yes, and there was a good shade tree behind it—she didn't know what kind. Bert often sat there quietly of a morning, having his coffee and cigarette. She remembered looking up from the pier and seeing him, alone on his bench. She felt now that she understood the calmness he must have enjoyed; one morning there must have provided a hundred reasons for keeping this place, year after year, sinking time and money into it.

She emptied her cup and rested her head back against the chaise; closed her eyes. She had slept fitfully the night before, and now in spite of the coffee and the bracing shower she might have slept again. But then the door swung out and Buzz came through, shirtless, in cutoffs; his hair, washed and combed, giving his otherwise dowdy appearance a nice, natural polish. He smelled of Old Spice aftershave.

"So you're the early riser—good coffee." He sat down on a porch stair, yawned and stretched.

"It's nice out here, this time of morning. I wish I could wake up to this every day."

"I know it. After a week of fighting the Houston traffic, it does me good to spend a coupla days down here."

She could see the outline of his body, the big swimmer's shoulders, the sunken chest slumped over, almost touching the knees of his long legs. He would look more and more like Bert as he grew older. Like the other boys, he had Hetty's light hair, but aside from that he was like his dad, only taller. "Whatever happened to that old rocker your dad used to sit on out here?"

He laughed. His voice was a bit softer than last night, but he still spat out his sentences like a dog barking. "Ya remember that old relic? It finally rotted, and we got rid of it. That first summer we came back after Dad died we . . . He wouldn't have let us take it away while he was around. Sat on it till the day before he died.

"But Carson was worried that Clark might climb on it and get hurt. Carson also poured the patio and put the awning up, or rather had it done."

"That was thoughtful of him."

"Yeah, but it was too expensive, and we really didn't need it, Mom said, and she was right." He took a long drag off his cigarette and squinted at the sun. He held a cigarette between his thumb and index finger, his other fingers fanned out. That, she recalled, was Bert's mannerism.

"Well, I'm glad Carson didn't make too many changes. It does me good to come down here and see so much left the same."

"You do some painting, don'tcha? You come down here to paint?"

"Not exactly, but I may do some. I brought my sketch pad."

He took another drag off his cigarette and sat there a few moments, without facing her. "I remember when we were kids, you used to sit around and draw on a tablet. I used to think you were nuts."

She laughed. "I'm surprised you noticed."

"You reminded me of Carson and his books. I thought you were both crazy. So then he grew up and became editor of his college yearbook, got in the Key Club, and finally wound up in the printing business. And you wound up an artist. I guess neither of you were as crazy as I thought."

"Oh, I'm not very good, not yet. I've had some notice, but I have a long way to go yet. I still haven't really developed my style, not to my satisfaction anyhow."

"What kinda stuff do you paint?"

"Oh, unless I'm commissioned for something special, just anything that captures my interest."

"Like what, for instance?"

She thought for a moment. Buzz obviously knew nothing about art. She wanted to explain in terms he could understand, which was odd, because she usually didn't care to do that for people. "Like what we're seeing this morning. The sun on the water out there, and the pier slicing through it like an aisle leading out into a kind of oblivion, a place you could move toward but never reach

. . . if I could somehow manage to get that on canvas, maybe with the boat tied there near the end where it usually stays, as a kind of link with what was within reach and what was beyond . . ." She shrugged. "You see, I can't tell you exactly what I mean, so maybe I could transfer my feelings to canvas."

He looked at her direct; he seemed to understand. "Is that why you paint? Because what you think comes out better that way?"

"Yes. That and . . . well, because when I'm involved in a painting, nothing else matters. Nothing else exists."

He smiled and looked away again. "Wish I could escape like that."

From what?

"Gimme yer cup. I'll bring us a refill," he said, then added, "I'll have the boat tied up there later this morning, if I can get someone to help me at the launch a few miles down the road; and it'll stay there for the rest of the summer." The door slammed shut behind him.

His remark came as an unexpected kindness. However, painting was hardly her reason for being here now. This summer she must concentrate all her energies on Ian, and not get sidetracked; that was crucial to his well-being. When Buzz returned she explained this to him.

"Don't worry. I'll keep the boys busy," he said. "Just wait till I get Ian into the water."

He had an easygoing manner that Ian needed to experience. Yet she featured him throwing Ian over the pier like he used to with the others. "I didn't come here to use you as a glorified baby-sitter," she quickly opposed. "And I don't know how Ian will take to the water. He doesn't know how to swim at all. At his preschool they pull out the sprinklers now and then and let the kids play. He hates it. Goes berserk. I don't know why. So don't expect much of him. He's a funny kid about some things." She wanted to tell Buzz not to push him, but didn't know how to without hurting his feelings.

"Aw, you worry too much. Baby him. He needs somebody to show him how much fun it can be, and after that you won't be able to get him out of the water. Kids have a natural affinity for water. It's grown-ups that scare 'em to death. I found that out by teachin' swimming at the Y."

Later she thought she ought to have been more explicit about Ian, but then she would have been using the words of the teachers and the doctors and she was here, this summer, to refute them all. Lately she found herself observing everything he did in their terms. What once had seemed a promise of special aptitude now had been labeled a "symptom" of something frighteningly abnormal. The doctors and teachers had spread an infection through the whole fabric of her family life, and she was here to cure it.

Ian would surely benefit from something as wholesome as summers at the bay, just as she did as a child, not to mention the presence of someone like Buzz, willing to take time with him and get him used to things that should not bring fear but delight. She realized that Forrest had robbed all of them of something invaluable: a loving, nurturing environment. And she had let it happen, and closed herself inside a private cocoon, never thinking what effect it might have on their child. What she told Buzz about her feelings when it came to painting was truer than she guessed before. And his responses were surprisingly perceptive.

At nine o'clock, breakfast done, she and Ian and Clark were led merrily down to the pier by Buzz: a Pied Piper in swim trunks, singing some Navy song in a flat, booming

voice. They left Peggy and Hetty sitting on the patio with
their coffee. Peggy seemed more fragile than last evening,
her skin more translucent. There were dark patches beneath her eyes; she wasn't sleeping comfortably now. At
breakfast she had mentioned that, because of the size of
the baby, the doctor had decided to do a cesarean section
in August. Hetty looked down at her plate and murmured
something about its being bad business to take a child before its time. Buzz remained silent during the exchange;
Peggy seemed to be trying to say the magic word that
would mollify; this seemed part of her nature. She was no
doubt aware of the praises paid her by Hetty when her
back was turned, and did not want to alienate her
mother-in-law now.

Walking down the pier, Monica had some misgivings
about the day ahead. Since arriving on Friday evening
she had tried to anticipate things, to avoid throwing Ian
into a fit of panic. Now she felt as though she were about
to lose control. He was entering Buzz Wellman's territory,
and Buzz would be taking charge. She was experiencing
what she often did: a cleft between what she wanted Ian
to become and what she knew him just then to be. While
she wanted to help him, she also wanted to protect him
from the judgment of others, and to protect herself as
well. She wanted him to change, but did not want to
force him into the pain of changing.

There was an immediate confrontation on the pier
when Buzz knelt down to help Ian remove his socks and
sandals. The boy grabbed his hands and shouted, "No!"

"He's a sissy," Clark piped up. "Why's he wearin'
socks?"

Monica glared. "He is not. He hasn't ever been to the
bay, and he doesn't know what to expect." Her voice,
begun like a pistol shot, now drifted into a monotone of

forced patience. "Why don't you be his friend and show him how you jump in the water? After all, you are a little older, and you know how to do so many wonderful things." You brat.

Clark responded to the appeal. "Okay, Ian, watch me." He pushed off his thongs and leaped from the pier feet first, sending a spray of water up on all of them. Ian stepped backward, his mouth opened to scream. But then, to her surprise, he began to touch the water along his arms. He looked at his arms in wonder, then at his legs and feet. Then he pointed out toward the bay and mumbled softly, "Wa."

Monica's heart took a leap.

"That's it, sonny," said Buzz, ignorant of the fact a miracle had just occurred. "Here, get these shoes and socks off so you can go in too."

Ian allowed Buzz to remove his sandals. "Hold on, buddy, lemme get in the water and then I'll help you in. Easy now."

Monica could not contain herself. She reached out to hug Ian. She had not seen him look this happy in such a long time. Eager to get into the water, he wriggled from her embrace.

Once in the water, which was scarcely higher than his swim trunks that near the beach, he wriggled free of Buzz and put his hands against the surface. The mirror appeared suddenly—he had an uncanny way of holding it in an almost invisible fashion—and Ian began to angle it this way and that, to catch the sun's reflection. He played in this manner for a long while, and Buzz did not bother him. "Let him get used to the place. He can learn to swim after he feels comfortable." He looked up at Monica teasingly. "See, 'Mama;' I toldja you worry too much."

Monica was too astonished to reply. He continued in

the same vein. "You just gonna park yerself up on the pier and roast in the sun, or come into the water?"

She moved away. She'd had her ankles attacked from the water before, and welcomed it. But that was half a lifetime ago. She'd grown up, even if he hadn't. "Keep your hands to yourself," she said, dabbing on sun lotion. "You seem to be doing so well I may just go up to the patio and be lazy with Hetty and Peggy."

"Suit yourself. Gimme a few days in the water with Ian and I'll show you a kid with no fears. It'll take more than Mom's whistle to get him out of the water."

Oh, if only you could.

And so the three of them played in the water for a long while, Ian by himself, flicking his mirror and going nearer the beach where the water was more shallow. He seemed to enjoy pulling his feet up from the murky water and looking at them. She remembered the muddy suction at the bottom of the bay from childhood. The suction must have fascinated him. With Ian, you never knew exactly. But it didn't matter. She could envision Ian learning to swim, and eventually joining Buzz and Clark in their game of catch-the-ball, which they played farther down the pier.

All at once she remembered the painting of Ian. Seeing his cheerful face now, she thought, I will bring the sketch of him here. Here I can finish it. Here will be his beginning. Buzz's self-confidence was strong as the smell of salt in the air, and Monica had begun to feed upon it.

CHAPTER 21

On Monday morning at the center, she chatted briefly with Erica about the water incident, adding that later in the day when they took a boat ride, Ian had not been disturbed by the whirr of the motor as she would have expected, but sat in her lap and watched Buzz Wellman as he steered the boat, his face a study in fascinated delight.

Erica smiled, a tight, constricted smile that matched her guarded expression of hope, and Monica felt a little crestfallen. Ian was already behaving in his normal way, hanging back on the playground near the fence, entertaining himself with his mirror. By now the other children did not bother with him; they did not think he liked them, according to Erica. Monica could see how hard it must be for her to reconcile what she had just been told with the little lost child on the playground now.

Driving home, Monica found herself doubtful again, drawn by the magnetic force of the looks and voices of experience. Regardless of what Erica said, her message was clear: this is not going to work, not without therapy. Well, then, she would keep Ian's progress to herself and contained in her letters to Forrest, and let the changes become all too clear to the teachers as the summer progressed. For there would be changes.

Forget Dr. Michaels and his prophecy. Forget the damned brochures stacked up on the dresser at home. She

was determined to trust her own instincts this time. She
went to work in her studio and closed everything out
until five o'clock, the end of her workday.

In the days to follow she got into a routine, working
hard during the week and anticipating only her spending
weekends at the bay. Letters from Forrest were short but
frequent, and she answered them at night after Ian was
asleep. She told him of her painting, not because he cared
to read about it, but because she was determined he accept it as part of her life. She also told of Ian's progress at
the bay. She would say she missed him, though her hand
would pause before this phrase, as though the physical
part of her which daily sought after truth on canvas could
not form dishonest words. She never said Ian missed him,
though. That would have been an outright lie and she
knew Forrest would know it. She felt comfortable in
the routine of their lives and gathered that Forrest was
finding his new post with Amalgamated more challenging
and satisfying than even he had dreamed. Often he would
say, "Wish you could be here with me," but she knew he
did not mean it. She spent many a night lying in bed, listening to the sound of Ian's rocking down the hall, wondering why she felt no sense of loss at her husband's
absence. The truth, she finally decided, was that she simply wanted to be alone. It was unsettling that the es-
trangement from Forrest before he left had been more
acute than she realized. Maybe, then, this forced separa-
tion was good for them both. When he came home in September, maybe they could build something new and better. For she did love him. And there were moments when
she did miss him. Sometimes she remembered how close
they once were—it seemed so long ago now, but at
one time they were happy with each other. Then she
would think that when he got back, when she had Ian

straightened out, then things would be better than ever between them and they would all be happy.

Finally her thoughts would come to the inevitable dead end: would things be better?

One evening the mail brought a nice check from the sale of one of her paintings in a Dallas gallery, and along with it a letter from a greeting-card company in New York requesting she do a nostalgia theme from the thirties, twelve designs in all, for a collection the following spring. If she was interested, they'd forward the quips for the cards, already completed by a writer she had worked with before. They wanted the cars, the fashion, the whole aura of the late thirties, a look they referred to as "ambience," which she regarded as "stuck-up." If she agreed, a small advance would be forthcoming. . . .

Excited, she picked up the stack of old *Life* and *Post* magazines—she had collected samples of magazine illustrations from every decade between 1900 and 1950. She marked a few pages for consideration. Then another thought occurred to her. Forrest's family album had many photos of the Maguires through the 1930's, when they were a dashing, childless couple, documenting their travels around the world with captions in the Spencerian script of Forrest's mother. "Ambience" was there, all right: Mrs. Maguire appeared in turban hats; padded shoulders; white gloves; big fur collars; dark pumps on tiny feet. The only noticeable features about Professor Maguire were his happy face and his business suit. They posed in front of long-nosed cars, spindly airplanes, posh hotel entrances, and exalted university halls.

She took the album to bed with her, and before she turned out the light she had not only several pages of ideas scribbled out, but a new question about the relationship between Forrest and his father. Did the professor want a child? Forrest was born during the war, and the professor served somewhere in the Pacific. Did his wife insist on becoming pregnant in case he was lost forever to her, a casualty of the war? If that were true, there might have been built-in resentment from the start. And there were no other children to follow Forrest, though his mother lived for twelve years after his birth. . . .

Monica settled on the pillows. She probably would never know the answer, and wondered now if the question haunted Forrest. She saw her husband as lost and abandoned again, and was filled with guilt for her failure to miss him this summer. She ought to have insisted on joining him in London, hang the atrocious expense. Maybe he wanted her to, but hated to ask. Maybe he would have suggested it, if not for her plans for Ian.

As the early weeks of summer slipped by, Ian seemed more and more attached to Buzz. He often followed him around, observing him with the quiet interest he usually reserved for objects that caught his attention. He seemed to be trying to figure out what made him work. He did not hug him or reach for his hand, or even indicate by a point and a grunt that he wished to ride his back as Clark did. He simply stayed near and watched. Frequently Buzz showed him how an object worked—he was heard to give lengthy but simple explanations on how the short-wave radio picked up its signals and transmitted them, and how the clock on the dresser worked. The latter was interesting to Monica. Ian had hidden his father's watch several times and she'd always managed to retrieve it from his hiding places while Forrest stormed around in search of it. She ought to have had sense enough to explain time to him. But she'd assumed it was the shiny case that fascinated him and, besides, she was eager to replace it in order to prevent a father-son confrontation. Peace-maker. She found herself playing that role a lot when Forrest was at home.

Once, while Monica was outdoors painting and Ian was in the garage with Buzz as he tinkered with the wiring of the electrical system in the boat, she was surprised to look up and see Buzz coming toward her, Ian following close behind. "Ya know what that kid did?"

Oh, no. "What?"

"I was foolin' around with the screws behind the dash, and he was watching, see, and I was talking about what I was doin'. Came time to use a little hex wrench and when I reached for it he had it in his hand."

"Wow! Did he give it to you?" Was he participating?

"Nah. Honest to God, I think he was about to use it himself. He knew exactly what I was doing. But I scared him when I grabbed for it, and he dropped it and backed off."

Well . . . even that was a good sign. She smiled at Buzz. "I don't know how I'll ever repay you for the time you take with Ian. It's just what he needs."

He flicked a pebble out toward the water and watched it splash. "It's nothin'. I got nowhere to go, and not much to do. I just can't get over how smart he is. I wish I could be around one day when he decides to talk and let go of some of that information he's storing up."

Whenever that may be. "Well, thanks."

Hetty walked out with a bowl of red apples. Buzz took one, bit into it, and tossed one to Clark. Ian couldn't catch an apple. No one ever taught him to play catch. That was part of fatherhood, and therefore a void in Ian's experience. Clark caught the apple. Ian was running and skipping back and forth, back and forth, along the fence. She hoped no one would toss an apple to him. He wouldn't catch it. It would hit the fence, and fall to the ground with a thud. Then they would all look at Ian, then at her, and Hetty would rush over and scoop it up. . . .

Buzz turned. "You workin' on that scene we talked about?"

"Yes . . . I haven't gotten very far. I wish you'd bring the boat back and tie it to the pier." She smiled.

"We'll have her fixed up by this evenin'. Won't we, squirt?"

"Don't call me squirt," Clark protested, and pushed his lip out.

"Aw, come on, you." He mussed his hair and started back toward the garage. Ian watched them and then followed. Monica went back to the painting before her. She had decided to do it for all the Wellmans, to reciprocate their generosity toward her and Ian this summer, and also help assuage her guilt for using them all to her own ends. For she told none of them of the magnitude of Ian's problems; she played on their simple, uncomplicated natures, their genuineness, knowing they'd expect nothing in return.

While she painted, Monica often observed Hetty and listened to a phrase here and there or conversation between Hetty and Peggy as they talked. They spoke of things which did not interest her. What color the nursery ought to be. Whether or not to use disposable diapers. Whether to bring the old playpen that had been used successively by Buzz, Carson, and Aaron down to the bay, or buy a new one with those safety features you read about in magazines. More often than not, Hetty suggested and Peggy complied. "That'll be just fine, Mom," or "However you feel it would work best." Now and then Hetty opened the subject of the Cesarean section, but Peggy didn't answer. It was a most effective way of drawing the subject to a close. So Peggy was crafty in her own way at giving where it didn't matter, to save clout for when it did.

In the meantime Ian was progressing in the water under the sure and patient tutelage of Buzz. He would not put his face in the water and went into a tirade if Clark splashed water in his eyes, but he was allowing Buzz to hold him on his back and walk him around in preparation for learning the back float. At first he gathered up his arms around him and hunched up his legs, but after a while Buzz had him with both arms out and legs spread-eagled.

Monica was forever amazed at Buzz and his patience with Ian. Neither she nor Forrest was slow and steady and methodical like him. They became easily frustrated while trying to teach Ian something which came naturally to most kids, and their behavior frightened him. Buzz, on the other hand, went over things again and again, as if time had no meaning (indeed, down at the bay, it did not seem to). He was a natural teacher, she felt, sensitive to a child's learning pace, and she often wondered why he wasted his time at some office job that amounted to nothing. He ought to have gone to college and got a degree in education instead of spending all that time in the Navy, after the fashion of Bert, then settling into a humdrum life. When he and Peggy and Hetty talked at the dinner table they spoke of company pensions and retirement plans, group insurance and how much of the maternity bill it would cover. That was how they lived: carefully, conservatively, holding on to what was safe. . . .

Like Forrest, Buzz was employed by a big firm that gobbled up the individuality of people like a hen gobbles its feed. Yet this was right for Buzz. Its solidarity and dependability were what he probably clung to in life. She ought to keep her mouth shut about his becoming something more. Becoming something more, or trying to, did not always bring happiness. Just look at Forrest. . . .

One Friday evening Buzz and Peggy arrived with some interesting news. Buzz, unusually quiet, loosened his tie and unbuttoned his collar, then doubled back to the Frigidaire for a beer as Peggy explained that her mother would be coming to spend a few weeks with them around the time the baby was due.

Hetty tried to hide her ruffled feathers. Her back, always perfectly straight, stretched a bit more taut as she cut up tomatoes for salad. "She doesn't need to come all the way up here from Florida, and spend all that money. I can help look after—"

Peggy turned a cheerful face on Monica, then said to Hetty, "I know that, but Mama wants to come. She has never been here for a long visit, and this is going to be her first grandchild. I just couldn't tell her no."

"But I was going to come every day," Hetty said, then paused. "Where you going to put her? That house of yours is not much bigger than this one."

"We'll manage. There's a hideaway bed in the living room," Peggy said. Buzz returned, sat down at the kitchen table with his beer, and pretended to read the paper. The taut muscles in his face gave him away.

Monica knew in ways that none of them did how big a mistake this would be, though certainly Buzz had an inkling. She could hardly keep silent, though she was determined to, remembering how she felt at Ian's birth, how tired she became of people stopping by to offer free advice and inspect, then to argue over who he most looked like. If the visitor was a member of Monica's family, the child bore a marked resemblance to her. If anyone from the Maguire family stopped in (seldom did they, and Professor Maguire was out of the country until Ian was two years old), Ian was surely the spitting image of his dad. More than once she was tempted to be rude. Often she reminded them, trying to keep the edge off her voice, that Ian looked like Ian. Sometimes, if she was busy at her easel, she would not bother to answer the doorbell.

And for her and Forrest it was difficult enough just getting used to having a child around. Like Peggy and Buzz, they had been married several years, were accustomed to the spontaneity that went with it. Before Ian came Forrest could call at four o'clock and say, "Meet me for dinner at six-thirty. We'll catch a movie afterward." Or, should someone higher up at the office invite them over for drinks, Forrest could accept without hesitation. Weekend trips could be planned a night in advance; longer vacations were taken with ease. They both said, before Ian arrived, that their life style needn't change. They'd waited until they could afford a child. They'd hire a baby-sitter.

Yet it was not that simple. They didn't trust anyone but Dixie, and anyhow, Ian cried so much that Monica was reluctant to leave him. What if something were really wrong, resulting in an emergency? You couldn't have dinner, then hop from one nightclub to another till two in the morning without checking back home to let the sitter know where you were. And if you stayed out very late, you had no time to sleep before the first cry in the morning summoned you to your feet.

They were at dinner now, and since there was a gap in the sketchy conversation of the evening, Monica asked Peggy, "Are you going to breast-feed?"

Peggy seemed a little embarrassed. Her eyes widened. "Yes. For as long as I can. Maybe even a year."

Though Peggy's modesty had suffered a slight blow,

the exchange saved the evening. Hetty approved. She had
apparently been instrumental in this decision. She smiled
and said, "Breast-fed all three of my boys, and it was the
best thing I could do for them. All three are healthy as a
team of horses."

Buzz was looking down at his plate. So she'd embarrassed him by her question too. I've invaded his privacy,
she thought, then it occurred to her: The simple matter of
bringing a child into the world causes an invasion of privacy. Everybody participates. Everybody has advice. The
world becomes a glass bowl from which there is no escape. Thankfully the conversation came to an abrupt end.
Clark spilled his milk, the glass emptied into Ian's lap,
and Ian pulled his first screaming fit at the Wellman
table. Everyone scurried around to clean it up, and everyone obviously appreciated the diversion, failing to notice
the oddity of Ian's behavior. Or perhaps the Wellmans
did not consider it odd.

CHAPTER 22

As talk of the coming child began to occupy more and
more of Hetty's and Peggy's time, Monica found it natural to seek out Buzz. She was growing eager for compan-
ionship. Forrest had been away nearly a month; she grew
tired of sketching, since it had become a weekend voca-

tion as well as a week's work, and more often went down to the pier with Buzz and the boys. True, Ian still had nothing to do with Clark, and Clark had long since given up on Ian as a playmate, but Monica remembered what Dr. Michaels had said about a child forming a bond with the parent of the same sex before reaching out to others. If Buzz could be for Ian what his own father could not, then maybe Ian's lack of interest in other kids did not matter so much right now.

She looked forward more and more to the early-morning chats with Buzz out on the patio. They were comfortable with each other, talking sometimes of Ian's progress, sometimes of Forrest, sometimes about the current state of the world as they viewed it, or almost anything else. There was seldom an awkward pause. Buzz learned more about her work because he was eager to have her talk about it. She told him of the habits and life styles of the great illustrators she'd studied, and of her years at the university, and about her teacher, Andrew James. All of this seemed to interest him. His eyes were wide and clear, and locked to hers as he listened. When he heard about the 1930's greeting-card line, he brought her a small stack of family snapshots, and tossed them onto her lap as she dried her freshly washed hair.

"But these are special, aren't they? What if I spilled paint on them? I'd feel awful."

He laughed. "I reckon we can trust you with 'em."

There was almost no light; it was very early yet. He went to the edge of the patio and lit up a cigarette. The tip of it swung down as he released it and relaxed his arm. She felt awkward. She didn't know whether he expected her to look at the pictures then, and remark on how useful they'd be, or take them home to her studio for consideration. In truth, she'd finished the series of drawings, and was ready to mail them anyway.

"I don't want to get these wet," she told him, and put them aside on the metal table. He stood there, saying nothing. She continued to dry her hair, finally dropping the towel and running a brush through the tangles. She parted it down the center, brushed it through, and looked up. To her surprise, he was watching her.

"You oughta let your hair down like that all the time," he said. "It looks nice that way." He took another drag from his cigarette and stepped off the porch. She watched him as he walked down the path toward the pier. His figure was a silhouette against the brightening sky, the glowing cigarette flitting beside him like a hovering firefly.

All through the day her mind returned to that brief exchange, and she would find herself concentrating on it, oblivious of the canvas in front of her. Buzz kept the boys to himself: took them on an errand to the store, swam and played in the water, and took them on a boat ride. She couldn't seem to bring herself to walk down the pier and join them.

Once Hetty said under her breath, "Look how he mother-hens those younguns. I never yet saw a man who needed a child worse than Buzz."

She awoke in the night to the sound of a gentle rain, so soft it did not disturb Ian's heavy sleep. She lay for a while without opening her eyes, as the breeze gradually stiffened and blew across her, damp and cool, and the wooden cottage creaked and groaned as though it were a living thing, old and pained, its breathing labored. The rain continued, like pixie feet upon the roof.

She raised up and looked at Ian. If he awoke frightened, maybe he'd come into her bed. But of course she knew that rain, storms, thunder and lightning all at once had never frightened him.

She turned over and gazed out the window, thinking again of the morning with Buzz. She had not counted on this attraction. Surely it had come on slowly and patiently, in the manner of all things at the bay; but her awareness of it this morning was abrupt. It seemed such a long time since anyone . . . another man . . . had noticed her. Nor had she really cared.

She touched her face. Her cheeks were flaming under her palms. There was danger in this kind of feeling. She was startled that one compliment could have had such an effect. And it was just that: a compliment. Why make more of it?

Buzz probably didn't. And yet . . .

She purposely kept her hair bound at the nape of her neck, the length of it trailing down her back; but as often as not when out in the boat or down at the pier, long straight tendrils became disengaged from the tortoise barrette and blew against her face. On one such day, they were on a boat ride with the children. They were a good distance out—the crest of Baynook was barely visible—when the wind picked up and Monica noticed gray clouds gathering. She motioned to Buzz; he nodded and, shifting the keel, headed for the pier. As they neared it, Hetty's figure made a stark outline on the lawn, and in moments they could hear the shrill note of the whistle. Monica looked across at Buzz. They both smiled.

Customarily, when they reached the boathouse Monica looped the rope over the piling. Then Buzz braced himself with feet wide apart inside the boat, as it smacked against the water at the pier, and handed her out first, then the boys into her arms one at a time, all the while steadying himself in the throbbing vessel. But on this day as she struggled onto the pier one of her feet slipped on the slimy wood and she fell slightly backward. She felt her elbows gripped and steadied. "All right, Monica?"

"Yes, fine." She nodded and turned toward him, not thinking why, and grasped his forearms while the wind whipped her hair across her face.

"Steady," he said, and swept it back from her eyes. She nodded again, and they looked direct into each other's eyes, both startled. She grappled safely back to the pier, then turned for the boys and pulled them up after. Buzz was still looking at her, the stiff wind blowing his hair. She caught his gaze again, then looked up quickly toward the lawn, where Hetty stood with arms on her hips.

Seeing it all? Monica asked herself that night as she lay in bed. Even the intuitive Hetty could make little of her son helping a family friend as she stumbled. What happened down there was like coming upon an undertow: one did not see it; only a person near it could feel its pull, sometimes too late.

At last she slept, but awoke the next morning in a fog born of troubled dreams and wondering whether the attraction were one-sided. The feeling that passes between a man and woman for each other at the same time is seldom mistaken; yet, maybe she was living out some childhood fantasy. She had had plenty in those days when Buzz called her "squirt" and ignored her in favor of her sister Jane.

She fixed coffee to clear her head and took it out on the patio. She sat there nervously, wondering if he'd join her and thinking: If I wanted you now, Buzz Wellman, could I have you? You were always a flirt. Are you flirting now, just to see how I'll react?

And why should I give a damn? If I were looking for a

man I would be smarter to hang around the yacht club instead of the bay. But then I'm not looking. I just can't seem to stop thinking about you. This is basic, animal basic. I like the way it feels when you hold my elbows. I'd like to know more about how it feels to feel more of you. I like the way you look in the morning. I like the way I feel when you notice the way I look. But why? Who are you? What have you done that I should get so excited about you?

She laid her head back, closed her eyes, and told herself she was being foolish. Yet it was not long before her instincts took over and she began to speculate on Buzz's next move. She felt reasonably sure that if the attraction was mutual, he would not come out on the patio this morning. As was the case on the morning she first became aware of some spark between them, because he wasn't the type to hand out compliments, he would disappear and keep his distance for a suitable time. If, on the other hand, he came out and spoke with her in the usual comfortable way, it would mean what she suspected was off the mark. Then she could forget it by herself and nothing need ever be said. She finished her coffee and wanted more, but did not want to go in to get it. She grew more nervous, felt more foolish. She half wished he would not come; half listened for the door to swing open and for him to appear.

A few minutes later, he did. He began with talk of a new solution he'd read of for the growing problem of some seaweed strain in the lakes surrounding Houston.

Her ears were burning; she didn't want to hear of this. "Do you remember," she interrupted, "all those years ago when you were in the Navy and our mothers made you escort me to the school dance?" Where had it come from; how long had the opening of this subject lain in wait?

He glanced her way, then looked back toward the
water. "Yeah. Those two used to be cookin' up something
all the time. I never was much of a dancer. My feet are
too big." He paused. "Anyhow, I'll bet you didn't know,
yer mom and mine had other plans . . . big plans for Jane
and me."

Oh. . . . "No . . . no, I didn't." Not exactly, anyhow.

"Yeah, but Jane didn't like me. Fact is, I didn't like her
either. She was too snooty, and no fun." He looked
around at her then. "Know what?"

Say it. "What?"

"This summer I've noticed somethin' different about
you."

"Oh?" She cleared her throat to mask the sudden leap
in her voice.

"You used to be the one ready for fun, always laughin'
and ready to play out on the pier and in the water. Now
you never smile anymore. You've gotten all serious since
you grew up."

"Have I?" Not much better. Oh, I hate this. . . .

"Yesterday in the boat was the first time I saw a smile
on your face since you came down here."

So that was why you seemed so interested. Slow down,
Monica. "You're exaggerating. But I guess people find
less humor in things as time goes on . . . at least most
people. You used to tease an awful lot. You don't anymore, at least not as much." She wanted to say "flirt," instead of "tease," but couldn't bring herself.

"I guess yer right." He lit up a cigarette and leaned
against the door.

"You used to think you were pretty big stuff."

He laughed. "Not anymore. First lesson, since you
brought up the subject: I remember the night of your

dance as well as you do, maybe better. I had to keep what was supposed to be a hot date later on."

"So I heard."

"But she wasn't so hot."

"Oh? You didn't like her?"

"Wasn't that. She failed to live up to her sordid reputation."

"Oh." She started to laugh, more out of release than anything else, and in a moment he was laughing too. Sordid reputation!

"But that was not how I told it back on the base."

Could the sound of their giggling be heard inside the house? Was anyone astir?

Finally he said, "Truth is, I was a real chump. I should've finished out the party with you."

So much for wild oats. "Oh well, it didn't matter so much. You weren't obligated to—"

"I wasn't talking about obligations. I meant—"

A silly, forked end to the conversation, when suddenly the door thumped against Buzz's back and Peggy appeared, holding a mug of coffee. "Oh, excuse me. I thought I heard talking out here. Couldn't sleep." Still in her robe, her belly round as a beachball, she came out, yawned and stretched, and sat down close to Buzz. She lifted her face to the breeze and closed her eyes, her mouth turned into a smile.

Buzz nuzzled next to her and said, "The kid knockin' around?"

"Oh, you better believe it . . . and it's my back too. I just can't get comfortable anywhere."

"Toldja he'd be a tough rascal." He smiled and pecked her on the cheek. They were so natural together. Monica looked away.

CHAPTER 23

Driving home that Sunday, Monica went over his words again and again. He didn't mean "obligation," but something else. What? That he ought to have known the other girl wouldn't come through? Or did he mean . . . and she drew this out in her mind as one rolls liqueur around the tongue, savoring it before letting it slide down . . . did he mean he made the wrong choice altogether, should have recognized the fact Monica Stokely was something special, and hung on to her until one day when . . .

She'd already turned in the drive before she noticed lights on in the house. Prowlers? Her foot rammed the brake. The tires squealed. Then the door swung open and Forrest appeared, waving. Thank God, she sighed. She glanced at Ian, hunched down in his car seat asleep. She turned off the motor, opened the door, and flew into her husband's arms. His cheeks wore a healthy flush; he smelled of cigarette smoke, leather, whiskey, and overall the faint, wood-spicy fragrance of Taproot cologne. Her first reaction was one of surprised pleasure, and she would remind herself of this through the coming week, but after that, wish to forget it because it added to her confusion.

"I meant to call, but I left the Wellman number in London, and when I got here to the airport it wasn't in the directory. I've missed you." He squeezed her long and tightly, then started for Ian.

She reached for Forrest's arm, but too late. He'd forgotten already how grumpy Ian was when awakened. At the feel of his father's arms around him he opened his eyes slightly and looked up. Puzzlement, then fear sprang into his eyes. He threw his fists and screamed. All color left the face of Forrest as he coaxed, "It's me, Ian, Daddy."

Monica stepped forward. "Daddy's home, Ian. Isn't it wonderful?" She felt like a drama coach backstage during a play, frantically trying to feed a student the lines he didn't know, before the audience guessed.

"No!" He flung his head from side to side. "Bay?" He looked around both ways. She had never seen him more disoriented.

"No, we're home, honey. Come, let's go in the house."

"Bay!" He hugged his arms around him and looked away.

She tried again. "We'll go to the bay again soon, but now Daddy's home and we'll have him all to ourselves for a while." In spite of the continued screams and entreaty "Bay!" she managed to get him into her arms and inside, explaining over her shoulder to the befuddled Forrest, "Children forget. He just needs time. It has been five weeks, you know," all limp excuses. Truthfully she was as puzzled as Forrest.

Passing through the den she noticed a stack of boxes in one corner, some of them wrapped in bright plaid, a couple marked "Harrod's," but she ignored them and kept going until she reached Ian's bathroom and turned on the faucet. Forrest was still behind her, like a hopeful puppy. To Ian she said, "Let's get bathed, then we'll give Daddy a big good-night kiss." Though the words sounded phony even to her and made no impression on Ian, they served their purpose on Forrest. He turned to the den. She heard the freezer door open, the clink of ice in a glass.

Ian was looking straight ahead. "Bay!" he fretted, wringing his hands.

"No, we're home now." She reached for the soap, wondering at the continued confusion. But then she realized their departure from the bay had been unusual. Normally Buzz helped them into the car and, lately, carried Ian and helped him into his safety seat. Tonight Monica hurried off while Buzz was in the house. Ian was keenly aware of any change in routine (another item in the doctor's brochure). This, plus opening his eyes from sleep to find Forrest, must have combined to upset him. She was tired herself by this time, but tried to be patient and reassuring. She was amazed at the attachment Ian was forming to Buzz, closer than even she had guessed. Or maybe that had nothing to do with his behavior. She didn't know. It was good, it was bad, the doctors would approve, the teachers would feel encouraged. Or not. Whatever, she was too tired to worry about it.

She quickly bathed him, sliding the soft rag over his body, rinsing him and patting him dry with a towel. When he was ready for bed she carried him to the crib and sat him down in it. Immediately he began to rock. "I'll get Daddy to come in for a kiss. Ian . . . can't you smile for him? Give him a kiss? Poor Daddy has missed you so. . . ." Still he rocked, staring ahead. She kissed his forehead and left the room to get Forrest. When they returned together, Ian was lying on his stomach, eyes closed.

"He's exhausted," she whispered, relieved at putting off any further confrontation, and conscious of a throbbing in her head.

Forrest gently stroked Ian's cheek, which caused him to flinch once, but brought no further movement. He scrutinized him silently at length, then remarked, "He's taller, thinner than when I left. He's looking more like you, Monica." He leaned over the crib and kissed his hair, then looked at him again. The gesture was touching. A timid appeal, or a surrender? She didn't know. Had he waited too long? "Come," she said. "He'll be different tomorrow."

She wondered if her voice betrayed the emptiness of its promise.

CHAPTER 24

Ian waited until he could no longer hear footsteps down the hall. Then he rose again and began to rock. He needed to hear the comforting rhythm, to see and feel the safeness of the bordering rails.

He began to measure their strengths and his defenses. He did not understand why the one called Forrest and Daddy had returned. Maybe they discovered Buzz was not one of them, and sent him away. But where had they sent him? Was Forrest going to stay now, and replace Buzz? He hoped not, with all his might. He felt Buzz was somehow of his world, although he had no way of knowing how he got here in the other world. Often he wanted to ask him if he came through a long tunnel, and did it hurt all the way? And was there a time when his ball home became so hot that he almost choked, and couldn't breathe, and fell asleep without meaning to? But of course he could never put sound with all of those words in his mind and make them come from his mouth. And also, he wasn't sure that would be the thing to do because he wasn't sure of Buzz, not completely.

He had thought and thought, and experimented and tested his belief that the others were grouped against him in case he was wrong, as his time at the bay sometimes made him feel. Yet as far as he could understand, there was only one reason for grouping together instead of following reason and matching one to one. That was to hurt another, as he had heard on the television. He had taken his blocks and held one in each hand at the same time. They felt equal. Then he put another in one hand, so that there were two. The two blocks were heavier than the one. He tried to put still another but three would not fit in his hand, so he tried another way. He took the tape in Monica's kitchen drawer and put it around three blocks. Then he lifted the group and compared it with the one block again. It was heavier than the two. He went all the way up to five compared to one. The theory proved out again and again. Once he was satisfied of this he could see it in different ways. He understood at last why the bigger ones picked up the smaller ones, instead of the other way around. He knew why Monica and Buzz and sometimes Forrest lifted him up so easily. They were heavier and therefore stronger. And if that was true, and the doctors and teachers and others grouped together, their strength against him would be more than he could even calculate. He shuddered with fear.

But they had not yet tried to use their weight and

strength to hurt him. Maybe that would come later in their plan. Just now they seemed more interested in studying him, and he could still use his two defenses: the one not to talk, which was natural to him, and the other, which he had learned for himself, of not letting them see inside his head. He had to look away from them rather than close his eyes because then he could not see at all, and could not know what might be about to happen, and that was more frightening than anything.

He had thought long and hard about this defense, for they could trick him by their use of words and this was like two strengths against one defense. He hoped to bring himself equal by turning his eyes away and, when they held his head and would not let him look away, by concentrating very hard on blanking out his thoughts so they would not see them. He found this difficult to do; sometimes his head would ache afterward; and he would only use this method if he could not look away.

But as he studied them, which he often did when they were not aware, he found the power in their eyes was greater than in his because what they said and did, even to each other, did not always match with their eyes and so their eyes must not be windows to the secrets in their heads where words stayed. His must be, or why would they try so hard to make him look at them? He still remembered, also, that the first of the others that he saw had faces cut off under the eyes. It seemed their strengths against him were so much more than his defenses against them.

And now Buzz may have been sent away. He rocked and fretted and wrung his hands. He had lived his days at the bay in a state of calm, knowing that after he arrived with Monica, but before dark, Buzz would come and would be with him until he had slept two nights and one afternoon. Then Monica would bring him back to this house, and five days would pass when he would be taken to the day school, and have to defend himself against the children, before Monica would put the bags into the car again and return with him to the bay. He had not understood this pattern at first, until it was repeated several times.

For as long as he could remember he had concerned himself with the passage of time, because among the first things he had seen at the end of his journey to this world was a large white circle with black spots and lines on it that he later came to realize was a clock. Coming from the dark warmth of his ball home into the bright lights and the cold had been the final shock of his painful journey. He cried out in pain and shivered with cold. They laid their hands upon him and passed him from one to another and washed away the coating which he wore outside his skin, and he felt the more exposed and frightened. He looked for borders that he had come to know so well, but could not find them, nor could he hear the rhythmical beat that sustained him. Even the tunnel in which he had come had disappeared.

He looked and looked above the heads of his captors, but he could find nothing which seemed to be of his world. At last his glance fell on the white circle with black dots. He did not know what it was. He felt himself being wrapped tightly in something warm but scratchy, and then, exhausted, he fell asleep. When he next awoke he was in a different space, in a small cage. There were still the ones with faces cut off under the eyes. They took him from his cage and fed him from what he later came to know as a bottle. From where they sat to give him the milk that soothed his stomach, he could again see a white circle with black dots. He noticed they, too, often looked at the circle. And when they took him to Monica, she would turn him this way and that, and look at a little white circle nearby. Later, he became aware of the importance of time passing in the world of the others. If he could understand how fast time passed, he might then be able to figure out whether he was sent here for a certain number of times that the sky was light and the sky was dark, before he would return to his natural home.

He had heard them speak of days and weeks and months and years, and at certain times they had songs and cake with candles, and now and again they asked him to blow out the candles (he never would) and called it his birthday. But none of this meant anything to him until Buzz explained it. He had begun with the clock on the dresser in the front room of the bay house. Many times Ian had taken the small clock with a band around it that Forrest wore and hidden it until a time he could study it. But one of them must have taken it away, because it was never there for long.

By the time he began coming to the bay he had decided they wanted to keep the secret of time from him, and it became then something more important than ever for him to know. While Monica was outside drawing pictures, he took Buzz into the room and pointed to the clock. Buzz tried to help him form the word with his mouth, which he would not do, then asked if he wanted to know how the clock worked. Ian laughed in joy, for this seemed to prove Buzz was not one of the others.

He showed him how the pointers called "hands" moved around in a circle and marked the minutes and hours, and he understood. But it seemed to him then that if the clock hands returned to the same hours and minutes over and over, then each new set of minutes and hours was a repeat of the cycle before, and if that was true then all his

greatest fears were reality: time did not pass, only repeated. He would never get back if time were the key.
Somewhere in his memory there was a theory to answer
this problem, but the clock was not it. He thought on this
at length, and when five days had passed at the day
school and he and Buzz were at the bay again, he tried
another idea. He had seen Monica look at a calendar of
numbers in the kitchen, near the telephone. Sometimes
while talking on the telephone she would scribble words
on it. He had heard her talk about "days" and "o'clocks."
From listening and watching he had learned the numbers
up to 31. He also understood where the numbers after
that came from. But that was of less concern to him.

As soon as Monica was busy with her drawing, he took
Buzz to a calendar in the cottage. Buzz showed him how
it worked. He told him the word at the top of each page.
But he did this too quickly for him to grasp the meaning
or even sometimes the whole word. But when he said,
"September," Ian stopped his hand from turning the
page. He knew that he had heard that word before when
the others spoke of him, but could not remember why it
was important. And since he did not know the calendar
meant placing things in time, he did not know where in
time he was and how far away September would be. But
he did know it was important because in his mind something fell into place. He released Buzz's hand. Maybe he
would tell more. Buzz then explained the seasons of the
year, pointing out pictures of how each one looked, and
told of the changes in the trees and in the flowers, and in
hot and cold. Ian had seen pictures like this before, but
did not know they were related to time. Buzz told how
the snow fell from the sky in winter. He had never seen
that happen, but the picture was beautiful and he felt a
sense of fullness inside his chest because this beauty came

from his world. Buzz told him how the warmth made the grass grow during the summer, and told of the changes in the winds and the rains. Then it all made sense. Buzz knew these things without having to read them from books, like Monica. Ian watched his face as he spoke of them, and could see that he understood the beauty of the sky and the wondrous things it sent down. But it seemed to him the others did not understand the good things that came. They never sent anything to the sky in return, nothing that stayed, and this proved sky and ground did not match up. The others did not seem to care, but maybe Buzz did.

Lately he had overheard the teachers and doctors and Monica say that he would soon be four years old. Now he thought he understood what they meant. It seemed to him one day—one number on the calendar—was a very long period. Five days at school were so long he had trouble keeping track of how many more had to pass until they started for the bay. But he did this by thinking hard. Sometimes he thought so hard he could not hear what the teacher was telling him until she pushed his shoulder. Or, if he was sitting, lifted him up. Then he'd realize she had been talking to him while he was thinking, but would not know what she said. This did not seem to please her, but no matter; thinking of this and other things, mostly theories, was his only way of keeping the fears at school from seizing and controlling him: the pushing, screaming, laughing children who bothered him and tried to get his mirror.

If five days were that long, then, as Buzz said, there were "about" 30 days in one month, and 12 months in a year. That was more time than he could count. It seemed like forever. This made him nervous and a little sad, but then maybe the number of years did not matter.

Ian understood that when a problem was to be worked
out, one part must be solved before another could be
reached. The working of picture puzzles taught him this.
He felt excited by the new information Buzz revealed,
and he would think on it, often while spinning the bubble, until his head would ache. If he could come close
enough to the solution, maybe Buzz would help him find
the way to the end.

But if he and Ian had come from the same place, then
why was Buzz able to match words with sounds like the
others? It was another puzzle, but he had soon come to
depend upon periods at the bay for allowing him time to
figure things out. Once he got away from Clark, he had
little to interrupt his thoughts, and he found the bay a
place of quiet and peace. Not like the school, where he
was hounded and ordered about all day long, and mocked
and tricked and dared and whispered about. Not like at
home, where he could not be sure who would be about,
and when they would come and go. At the bay there were
logical patterns.

And most of all, there was the water. Not the cold
water of big pools where the others liked to go, surrounded by hard hot concrete that would burn your feet.
It was when Buzz helped him in the other kind of waters,
the natural warm waters that had fallen from the sky to
remain and level the ugly, uneven places in the ground,
that Ian began to believe Buzz was special. He had
worried at first that if his sandals were taken away, his
feet would burn underneath as they did around the big
pools which he hated. But then, upon the feel of the
warm water on his arms he had forgotten his feet; he
knew he was close to a place where he belonged, and was
eager to explore it. Again, he hesitated. He was all too
aware of the danger the ground under the water might

not be even, that it might be farther away than he could tell from the surface. But he took a chance, something he almost never did, and let Buzz show him the surface underneath was as even as that on top of the water, and that it would not change or give way under his feet. He felt the mild suction, and noted that the ground was soft, and formed a cup around each foot to steady it. Not like in the big pools where the bottom was hard and rough, and where you could never tell how deep the water might be, but friendly and warm and welcoming. In his joy, he laughed and clapped his hands.

From the first, the waters of the bay seemed his natural place, just as he suspected. The water was warm and silky around his body, like the coating he wore before he journeyed here and they stripped it away, and with help from Buzz he learned that this giving of his body to the friendly waters brought him an equal exchange, and he became lighter than the water and could rest on its surface. Experiments with sand and water at school had shown him this, but he had not understood it to relate to him until his first morning at the bay.

So much began to make sense to him that morning, about how little the others understood or appreciated the sky and its patterns and beauty. They continued to spoil the ground by disturbing its levels, even as the sky sent water down to fill in the great holes they made.

He recalled watching, when he stayed at the condominium with the balcony ledge, a large hole being dug in the ground across the way. Day after day the digging went on with noisy, ugly machinery that leaned down and grabbed it with hideous teeth, throwing it aside and digging again. Before Monica said they must move from there, the others working on the hole had begun to bring huge sticks and put them into the hole. This was a long and complicated process, which he had watched for many days. He was ever more puzzled about what they did, more and more disturbed by the endless, jarring noises that began in the morning even before he left his crib and went to watch. Sometimes he would cry all day, his head ached so, but they would not understand.

At last, before they packed all the things into boxes and moved, he overheard Forrest, who was there that day, say to Monica that it was good things had turned out as they had. The building across would be much like the one where they lived, and the view would be spoiled. So it was to be a building like the one where they stayed that would fill up the big hole. Before that he had not realized Forrest lived somewhere in the building where he stayed with Monica. But then, many of the others lived in the building.

The view Forrest spoke of had been one of irregular intervals of roads that went up and down like hills. Here and there were tops of green trees. He thought Forrest was right: the view before had been more pleasing than what was to come. Yet Forrest had said he would miss something called the "skyline." What, he wondered, was a skyline? There were no lines in the sky, except those made sometimes by the shape of the clouds, and those lines would not be changed by a building. He never found out what a skyline was.

Why did the others go on ruining the place that was theirs? He spent many hours wondering about this, and at last began to wonder whether, like the water sent from the sky, he had been sent with a purpose. Perhaps they could not understand the message sent by the water, and he had been sent to explain. But then, if that were so, he would be able to speak as they did. Not only to understand and think their words, but to match them with sounds. Surely, then, his journey here must have been a mistake. Once more, his deductions led to the same conclusion.

He had come to feel so happy at the bay that, except for Buzz, he might have grown careless and made a mistake of his own. One morning he thought he saw his ball resting on the water's surface, just as he himself had done. He was certain it awaited him there. He held out his mirror and caught its brilliance. He knew it was very far away and that he could not walk there; then he realized that was the key to it all. He might walk as far toward his ball as he could, then, when he tired, he could lie down and let himself be carried on the water itself, until at last he reached his home.

He began while Buzz helped Clark work his arms and legs above the water, and as the splashing continued he looked toward the bay cottage and saw Monica leaning toward her white board, brushing color on it, her face hidden by a large straw bonnet. He had gone some distance, and finding the water slow to walk through, was about to lie down upon its surface, when he heard the shouting of Buzz. He came after him, and explained that far out the water became very deep and that big fish lived in it and would eat him.

He thought at first it was a trick, and all his faith in Buzz was lost. But later, surely in understanding of this broken trust between them, Buzz took him in the boat far out into the water and sank a rope into its depths to prove the truth in what he said. Then he told Ian something he would not forget: "You don't want to come out here; you could not get back from here if you did." And Ian believed then Buzz knew his destination, not only because of what he said, but also because he noticed from the boat that as they moved across the water's surface toward the ball, they got no nearer to it although they went very far indeed, so far that the bay cottage behind them was no longer in sight. He knew then he had been fooled by the resting place of his ball home, that it had not come to the water's surface after all, and did not await him there. And maybe, he thought that night while the others were asleep, the ball did not come because, like him, it could not get back. So it was up to him to solve the problem of getting back. Still, Buzz seemed to be helping him, and most important, he never tried to trick him into looking into his eyes.

His own eyes felt heavy now as Monica and Forrest played soft music in the den, and his head ached. He had heard Monica say the word "tomorrow" to Forrest. She often used that word, "tomorrow," yet it was another of the illogical words in their language, one which he had heard used enough to know it did not really exist, was like something they called "pretend." Only they did not seem to understand that. His mind was uneasy now as he thought of the word again. The word that was always spoken but that never became real. He yawned and lay down upon the bed again, clutching his mirror. Presently, no longer able to stop himself, he drifted into slumber.

CHAPTER 25

Monica sipped a gin and tonic, and watched Forrest's face as he told of his work in London. He had begun with a list of questions about Ian, avoiding her eyes (might they mirror Ian's violent rejection?), and showing that he had paid attention and given considerable thought to what Monica reported of Ian in her letters; maybe, she considered, more than she had given to what she had written down and seldom read over before folding the paper and slipping it into the envelope. Then he buckled up that subject, as he might have done his suitcase before leaving London, with a closing remark: "This week we'll do everything together, the three of us—have picnics, go to Astroworld, the zoo, anything Ian wants."

As though anyone knew what Ian wanted. She winced slightly at the thought her work schedule would be interrupted by his unexpected appearance, and covered it by sipping again at her drink. As he talked of London she felt guilty for her resentment, and wondered if guilt were the only thing left of her feelings for him. Guilt would come like a second thought, disguised as love, and move her to feel a warmth toward him she had not felt spontaneously. It was a bit like a dog chasing its tail. But then, she had felt glad to see him as soon as he appeared. . . .

"Looks like the chief's taken a fancy to me, as the British say," he remarked at last. "Not that I'm so bright . . ."

Oh, not indeed?

". . . it's just that you can't beat the practical experience of working for a small company." He paused. "You know how hard it is to get noticed at a company like Amalgamated. I'm convinced if I hadn't taken this overseas job"—lifting his brow and drawing in a breath—"I would have been forever lost among the multitudes. . . ."

Oh, how easily that superior note creeps into your voice.

"But over there it's different. That's the place where it's all happening. There are only fifty in the crew, and everyone is looking at *us*. It's the most important project on Amalgamated's books right now, and the executive jet lands at least once a week with bigwigs like Millikin and Snead and Draper."

He winked at her. "And it's my ideas they are listening to. Guys with more seniority are being overlooked. The chief consults with me before he meets the jet."

She smiled, knowing all this rationalizing was necessary to deflect his guilt about her and Ian. "I guess that doesn't make you popular among the ranks."

He looked surprised. "Popular? Who the hell cares? I didn't give up my whole summer with you and Ian to win a popularity contest." He grinned. "Incidentally, the chief and I had lunch the other day and we got to talking about our families. You know, he has spent practically his whole working life traveling around, so he understands how it feels to be kept away from your family. In fact, he got me this leave I'm on now.

"Anyhow, he has a grandson a lot like Ian. The kid was five years old before he talked, and you know what? His IQ is at the genius level."

She looked up. "Really?"

"He was a mechanical whiz, spent all his time taking

things apart and putting them back together, or making things. But he wouldn't say a word until he was five. Then, bingo. He decided to communicate. **He'd** been through all those tests, just like Ian, and zero—nothing. Then one day he just turned on like a radio. And within weeks his vocabulary was something like third- or fourth-grade level, so they knew he'd been doing a hell of a lot of listening."

"Amazing." But was he affectionate, or cold? "What about his social behavior?"

He shrugged. "I don't know, didn't ask."

You wouldn't. "Well, I wish Ian would turn on for us. He has done a whole lot better at the bay," she said, then chose her words carefully. "You know, part of Ian's problem stems from our lack of patience—I'm convinced of that. With Buzz Wellman he's really beginning to blossom. Buzz never loses patience or raises his voice. His whole demeanor is calm and easygoing. I think that's why he is so good with Ian. Well, with kids in general, for that matter. But he gives Ian his full attention when they're together." More than you ever did.

"Yeah? Well, that's fine," he said, then his look took on just a shade of condescension. "Be careful you don't get him bored down there, though."

"What do you mean?" As though I didn't know.

"He ought to be playing with some good developmental toys. Harrod's has everything and I found another good shop in Scotland—see those boxes over there? I brought several things back for him, a gyroscope for one. I'll show them to him when he gets used to me being home, and after I'm gone, you take some time and see if you can get him interested in working with some of them."

She was put off. He sounded just like his father. She

could feature him sauntering into a London shop, telling the clerk with all due modesty that he had a genius for a son, and asking to see their assortment of mind-bending games. "There are other things, like learning to relate to other people. He has to do that first," she said.

"He'll do that in his own time. Other kids bore him. That kid at the bay, the one you mention in your letters. Does Ian play with him?"

"No . . . but—"

"I didn't think so. Look, Monica, Ian is not the kind of average kid who is going to grow up and just get by. If we work with him—I know, I'm as guilty as you for failing him there—but if we work with him, channel his talents in the right direction, there's just no telling where he can go when he grows up."

Yes. Right into the protective enclaves of some stuffy university, just like your father, where he can dispense with the worry of having to deal with the rest of the world. "Maybe you're right," she said patiently, "but you ought to be thankful he has someone looking out after him right now who's willing to work at his pace, and dispel a few of those irrational fears we've seen in him. You remember how he used to go berserk around the swimming pool at the condominium? You ought to see him in the water at the bay now. He floats on his back. The swim teacher we hired last summer couldn't even get him out of his sandals and socks at the pool, much less into the water.

"And you can thank Buzz for that improvement."

He stared at her for a few moments. Maybe she'd told more than she intended. But the old feeling of scorn for the Wellmans and their kind came to his rescue. Couldn't be anything more than just a friendly baby-sitting arrangement, not with a joker like Buzz Wellman. "Sure,

I'm grateful to Buzz for helping him. He doesn't have the demands on his time that I do, nor the pressures. . . ."

She had sensed from the time she turned into the drive and saw him waving that something more than just a summer break had brought him home. Through their long conversation, he seemed to be paving the way for a surprise, because whenever a pause occurred he did not sit next to her and snuggle up. He seemed instead uneasy, preoccupied. He freshened their drinks and fell into a lengthy silence. She regarded him as he leaned back and rested his eyes. It occurred to her he must be exhausted. There was a seven-hour time difference between Houston and London, and he'd spent much of this day aboard a plane. She was too fuzzy from the drink to calculate how many hours he'd been up and what time it was over there. He was wearing a new wristwatch—quite an expensive one from the looks of it. Diamond chips marked the four major points on the clockface. (God, hope Ian doesn't snatch that, she thought.) She didn't recognize the suit he was wearing, or the shoes, or even the belt. She'd noticed a new trench coat thrown over his baggage in the bedroom, and his first remark to her when they began to talk was that the weather was brisk and cool in London. If they were there now, he'd be stoking up a fire in the fireplace. For some reason, she didn't take a clue from that. She speculated instead that he might be seeing someone else.

Yet Forrest was a stickler for doing the sensible and right thing. He'd fended off one secretary's advances that she knew of, and to the best of her knowledge, he had never been unfaithful to her. There was something about his pride and self-respect, almost reaching the extreme, that held him back from casual flings and, indeed, added to his coolness toward her; something stringent in his personality that she supposed rubbed off from his father.

She was about to ask him a question when his eyes opened and he asked, "How would you like to move to London for a year or so?"

She sat back, stunned. "I—I don't know. It's quite a surprise. When?"

"In the fall, if it happens. It isn't certain yet, and I do have to rush by the office while I'm home just to talk to a couple of people here—it won't take long. But the chief's near retirement and he'd like to move back to the States for his last couple of years. He wants me to handle his job over there." He paused. "Of course, if you don't like the idea I wouldn't absolutely have to do it. . . ."

Oh, please, spare me the front. "Let's wait and see. Silly to make a decision now."

"Yes, that's what I think too. When the question is really put forward . . . officially . . . I'll have to be ready with an answer, though."

She considered him. "Is your position so precarious?" Always she had trouble comprehending the enormity of job decisions. "Must you behave as though the rug is about to be pulled out from under you? I mean, what if you didn't make it with Amalgamated? You could always dance to another fiddler, or better still, buy your own fiddle."

"Maybe so. I've thought of going out on my own. But it takes capital and a lot of it today. In the meantime, we have to live on something. . . .

"If I'd done it years ago, before we had Ian, before we had a mortgage, maybe I could have. But now I don't know. I think I'm better off sticking with Amalgamated. If I play things right, I'll do fine. A lot of corporate officers have come from the ranks of the engineers."

She didn't argue. As always, she would say nothing that could be interpreted as standing in his way, and it was for more than one reason: she did not want to be like her mother, shelving her father's dreams among new dresses and furniture and kitchen floors that could not wait. Moreover, she did not want to give Forrest a tool that could be used against her later. She didn't want him to look up one day and say she had ruined his life by holding him back, and she be forced to admit it was true. Then it would all be over. Then, living together would be intolerable, because he wouldn't forgive her and she would not forgive herself.

She understood also why he wouldn't leave Amalgamated and strike out on his own. It was fundamental to his nature to seek approval among his peers. He had a constant need to be reassured that he was smart, capable. Buying his own store license would be like entering a world of the unknown and living there for a long time before realizing the fruits of his efforts. He could not wait it out. He could also not work for another, smaller firm. He would always wonder if someday it would be scrutinized by the acquisitive eye of a bigger conglomerate; perhaps his own efforts would cause that result. It had happened before.

She wondered idly if he made chief engineer of his division at Amalgamated, whether his father would write a letter of congratulations or maybe even call. He was looking at her now, his eyes wide, as though he sought at least her approval and support. It was the thing about him that surfaced now and again, that reminded her of why she'd fallen in love with him and what she still loved about him, or at least wanted to love.

She held out her arms. "Welcome home, honey. I've missed you." It was only half true, but necessary if she were to hold on to him until she was more sure of her feelings. And when Ian was well, she would be more sure about a lot of things. Right now she was more numb than anything else.

CHAPTER 26

In the following week she was to find herself thankful that Forrest would be gone before the Wellmans' Fourth of July celebration. She had not always been enthusiastic about the approach of the holiday, but now as she watched Forrest failing daily with Ian and causing them all pain and pressure in the process, she longed for all the things that made up the pattern of life at the bay.

To his credit, Forrest tried harder than ever. He attempted to teach Ian to ride a tricycle, but Ian would have none of it, and screamed until he was allowed to get off. He spent much of his time either in the throes of a tantrum or sulking in his crib, the only word escaping his lips: "bay." Wherever they went, Ian wanted Forrest to get out of the car, and would yell, "No!" and push at him. He was not accustomed to riding in the big four-door sedan in the first place, and when Forrest approached the driver's seat, the fury began. If Monica could get him calmed down, he would wind up spent; lethargic for the rest of the day. Everything from picnics to kite flying proved disastrous. Ian had never behaved worse, and as the week wore on Monica knew Forrest was out of patience, though he controlled it admirably, far better than usual. He never yelled at Ian or sent him to his room, and Monica wondered whether his determination to make the week perfect worked against them all. His nervousness was evident, even while he never openly expressed it. Half the time she wanted to shake Ian's teeth out of his head, and the other half she found herself biting her tongue to keep from reminding Forrest you couldn't make up for nearly four years of apathy in one week. She hardly thought of Buzz except in relation to Ian. During the day her nerves remained poised as a soldier's in battle; at night she was so spent she thought only of the relief of slumber. The lovemaking between her and Forrest was especially strained and taut, clamoring and out of rhythm.

On the night before Amalgamated's company picnic Forrest suggested, "I think part of my trouble with Ian is that you are always there, getting between us, trying to settle our differences. I know you mean well, but . . . I was thinking—"

"Yes?"

"When I stopped by the office this morning, some of the guys were ribbing me about going to London to get out of pitching hamburgers over the hot grill. I told them I'd be glad to live up to my promises. Furthermore, I told them my son would be with me.

"The problem is that, if you are there, Ian is going to go wherever you go, and probably won't have anything to do with me."

And that will show you up badly, won't it?

"So why don't you stay home tomorrow, and once we

get past the initial screaming in the car, I'll bet Ian will
straighten out and have a good time."

She wasn't so sure, but decided to comply with his
wishes.

The next morning she closed the car door on Ian's side
and turned to go back in the house. He was already
yelling as Forrest started the car, and she didn't want to
hear. As the day wore on, she tried to assure herself that
Ian was getting along fine, having fun—after all, they
would have returned early if not, surely—that this might
be the turning point in his relationship with Forrest.

When she heard the car in the driveway, just before
dark, she fled to the door and opened it. Ian lay sleeping.
Forrest said nothing as he pulled him out, and at first she
couldn't tell whether he was being quiet to avoid disturbing Ian or was upset over the day. They both smelled of
charcoal. Forrest's clothes were rank with perspiration;
Ian's, with urine: not a good sign. She changed Ian into
pajamas without waking him, while Forrest showered.
Then they shared a drink in the den.

"How'd it go?" she asked.

He leaned back, looked at the ceiling, and sighed.
"Lousy."

Oh, shit. "What happened?"

"He screamed from the time we left, off and on, all day
long. It was as hot as the devil's sauna bath around those
grills. I tried to get him to go over near the swings with
the other kids. He was wringing with sweat. But no, he
just clung to my pants leg and bawled. I tried to introduce him to people, impossible! He kept yelling, and
pushing people away. After a while they were beginning
to look at us a little funny."

Oh, so you finally noticed there's a problem? She could
envision Ian's face, his whimpering voice, his fright. He

must have thought he'd been taken to an outdoor clinic. All those unfamiliar people, coming near him, smiling, trying to take his hand. Why had she not thought of that?

"Finally I got fed up. There I was trying to deal with about a hundred and fifty hamburgers and him too."

"Didn't anyone offer help, so you could leave?"

"Of course they did. A couple of guys offered to take over. But Ian's my kid and my problem, too. When I finished with the meat I yanked him up and took him to the car."

Oh, no. . . . "And—"

"I left him there the rest of the day. And I think he got the point. When I got back a couple of hours later he was sleeping peacefully, and has been ever since."

You son of a bitch. "Did it ever occur to you it might be over a hundred degrees in that car?"

"Of course it did. I rolled the windows nearly halfway down—I didn't want him to try and jump out because he might have hurt himself—and besides, the car was parked in the shade. It wasn't that hot." Then a hard look. "He'll survive."

"Obviously." She turned away and took a long drink.

"I realized today half his problem is that you baby him too much, let him bully you. If you'd be a little tougher, you'd see an improvement. I'll bet tomorrow he's a different kid."

And he was. He didn't once cry. He didn't bother anyone. He didn't eat. He often sat in the corner of the den, rocking. Forrest returned to the office and stayed nearly all day. She could just see him explaining away Ian's behavior, no doubt insinuating she was at fault, and bragging about the way he straightened him out.

By the following day Ian was more himself again, less nervous than he had been since the night Forrest arrived.

Forrest mistook his behavior for compliance. He often passed her by and said, "See, hasn't he behaved better today than the whole time I've been here?"

She didn't reply. She was busy counting the minutes till he left.

On the night before his plane departed, Forrest tried, as he had in the beginning, to interest Ian in the new educational toys he'd brought from London. Ian reached for the gyroscope, but as soon as Forrest began to explain it to him, he drew away. Forrest coaxed; Ian balked. Monica watched helplessly; she could see her husband's hands begin to tremble, could recognize his effort at control, even while he told Ian, "We'll put this away and try another." Ian wrung his hands and swallowed. His eyes were wide. He was sitting on his feet, rocking back and forth on his knees.

It was worse with the other toys, many of which were designed for older children and, regardless of Ian's gifts, were far above his learning ability. She sat down on the floor nearby and tried to translate Forrest's instructions into a language Ian would understand, but it proved useless. Forrest, now exasperated by what he took to be Ian's sulkiness, grabbed him suddenly by the shoulders and said, "Look at me! Pay attention!" Ian drew his head aside, against his shoulder. He was trembling. Again: "Look at me, I said, don't you look away!" And all at once Forrest was shaking Ian violently, demanding that he look. "Pay attention. You're just undisciplined, that's all, spoiled. Look at me!"

When Ian finally obeyed and looked quickly toward Forrest through half-open lids, Monica felt her heart contract. His eyes were like that of a frightened animal, pursued relentlessly by a predator he could neither understand nor anticipate. Forrest, at last aware he'd overstepped himself, finally let Ian go. He sighed and walked from the room, then quickly returned, taking the toys with him. "I'll return these," he said, and left again.

Ian looked about him, moved quickly to a wall, and began to rock himself. His eyes were fixed on a window across the room. Why doesn't he cry? she wondered, grabbing him to her. His forehead was damp; his arms were limp. He made no move to push her away, yet did not return the embrace. He simply lay at her chest like a rag doll, spent. Soon Forrest came back in and tried to take Ian in his arms. He seemed near tears. Ian pressed his back against her chest. She waved Forrest away. She thought: You are doing to him what I do to you, thinking, acting in error. Then you try to make it up out of guilt. But it won't work with a child; Ian doesn't understand there was a yesterday and there will be a tomorrow when . . . maybe . . . things will be better. Today is all he cares about; all he knows is wrapped up in this moment.

After a while she spoke to him gently and took him for his bath. He did not seem upset; except for the tensing of his muscles and the trembling of his body, all too obvious as she stroked him with a cloth, he was frighteningly calm. She took him to his crib, laid him down, and rubbed his back. In a while she left the room, assuming him to be asleep and thinking: What are we doing to him, oh God, what are we doing to him?

Halfway down the hall she heard the rocking begin against the crib rail.

She and Forrest did not speak again until they lay rigidly side by side in the darkness of the bedroom. "I shouldn't have gone away," he began. She had not expected this, and was suddenly afraid he might insist they return with him to London. Every inch of her recoiled at this idea;

her only hope for Ian was to get him back to the bay and see if Buzz could undo the damage he suffered this week. She swallowed hard.

"Don't blame yourself. When you come home in the fall, we'll have time to work it out. Your only mistake was in expecting too much of this week. Don't worry."

"Maybe it will be better if we all go together to London for a couple of years. They say moving away from home draws a family closer. Friends of mine who were in the Army while I was living off deferments have told me what good it did them to get away with their wives. Maybe if we went away, we'd be forced to depend on each other more, to work with Ian more. . . ."

"He is worse, Monica, worse than I thought."

At last, the light shines. "Well, he certainly doesn't need badgering." Oh hell, that's it, Monica, beat a man when he's down. "I'm sorry. That wasn't fair."

He said nothing. She bit her lip, to keep the tears from coming. She knew what would be there if she could see his face: the look of the lost boy, tagging along with an indifferent father, wonder in his eyes at why he should be put away from the one who ought to draw him close.

She gathered his hand in hers and held it tightly. Finally he said, "You're right. I shouldn't have pushed. I'll leave the toys and maybe in a week or two he'll have forgotten tonight. . . ."

Damn the toys. "Yes . . . all right."

She wondered in the night what Forrest would do if Ian really were hopelessly ill . . . psychotic, or autistic, or whatever else one could call his group of symptoms. What kind of metamorphosis would take place in her husband? Would he be able to include in his list of priorities himself and his son? Could he go back to the office and admit the truth to his buddies?

She winced and turned over. Perhaps there was nothing wrong that couldn't be straightened out with time. Hadn't this summer proven that? Maybe Ian's upset at his father's sudden appearance was a good sign, rather than bad. Maybe she ought to call Dr. Michaels and ask him. But no, she'd made up her mind not to listen to experts anymore. Yet something else bothered her about the week.

She and Forrest had spoken once, briefly, about the effect on her career of moving to London. She had of course brought up the subject, prepared for his casual dismissal. While she felt that she could probably paint anywhere, and might find living abroad enriching to her work, she wanted an acknowledgment from Forrest. Even if he'd mentioned the possibility of a studio room for her when they spoke of housing, it would have been enough to satisfy her. But until she brought her thoughts out into the open, nothing was said.

She began timidly, "I know there must be hundreds of galleries in the London area alone."

He was reading the paper, sipping breakfast coffee. "I suppose," he said. "There is a great deal to see. I've been there for weeks and haven't even seen the inside of Westminster Abbey, though I pass it by every day."

She cleared her throat. "That isn't what I mean. I was speaking of markets for my work."

He looked at her above the newspaper. His expression said: Oh, that. "I guess you'll have some time to paint, but those two years are going to be crucial in my job situation. You're going to have to socialize with the corporate wives because, like it or not, that is important."

"You mean, afternoon teas, bridge games, and all that," she said coldly.

"Yes. I would hope you'd want to help me in whatever way you can. All three of us would benefit." He looked back at his paper.

You've got me, and you know it.

She cleared the table and left the room in a fit of frustration. There was nothing she could say. If the proceeds from her paintings equaled his earnings or even came near, she'd have plenty to say. If she hadn't always been determined to support him in his pursuits, she could have told him to cram his career with Amalgamated or hire someone to impress the other wives. But the truth was that her income was still minimal, and probably would be for some years, until she'd made a name for herself. Try explaining that to someone who equates success with money and prestige. And he knew . . . how well he knew and how well he used . . . her deep-rooted feelings about filling the role of helpmate.

Even if they had quarreled he'd have won; they both knew it, so what was the point? She now lay awake thinking about marriage and what a damnable trap it was. If she left him, then pursuing her career would be an unaffordable luxury. She'd have to find a job and she was not trained for anything other than teaching art . . . and she couldn't support herself and her child on that. And even if she found some position that paid enough, when would she paint? At night, the only time she'd have left for Ian?

She recognized a dead end when she saw one. She'd go on to London or wherever Forrest needed to go, because, hard as it was to face, he provided her the means of getting on in her career. She'd go on and on, and find a time during the day and a place, not saying much about it, just doing it quietly as she always had.

She punched her pillow and closed her eyes. What it really came down to was, simply, that she wanted Forrest to tell her he thought the pursuit of her career was as important as the pursuit of his and that he supported her in it as much as she supported him. Sadly, these were the very words he could never bring himself to say because they would diminish his view of himself.

When they left Forrest at the airport on the morning of July 3, the car was packed and ready to go to the bay. For most of the drive south along the Gulf Freeway, Monica thought of nothing but Forrest. As he departed, carrying his British-looking trench coat over one arm, he looked defeated and forlorn, his last efforts at winning Ian turning to dust as the boy refused his parting embrace and ignored his promises about how wonderful things would be when he came home again. Never had she felt so empty as she watched him walk down the corridor toward the gate, and so guilty for her own failure to make him feel at home during his visit. She was torn in so many directions that she no longer felt like the parts of her made up a whole. It seemed every role she played was another mask to wear. For her husband she played the loving and supportive helpmate; for the teachers at the center she radiated confidence that she was performing the necessary miracles in her son's progress this summer; for the gallery owner, who called now and then to check on her progress and share some exciting detail about her opening, she gave assurance that all her work for the fall exhibit would be finished on time. Even for Ian she had to pretend: that she saw progress every day; that she was sure she had done nothing in the past which sealed his fate even before he was born. There was no one to whom she could turn for understanding. She had no close friends. Not even her mother was her friend.

If Ian had isolated himself, it was little different from the way she had turned inward. But, unlike her son, she was now restless within the walls she'd built, and wanted, for the first time she could remember, someone to listen and sympathize.

CHAPTER 27

Ian could tell by now they were going to the bay, and he sighed with some relief and relaxed. Forrest left on the big plane. Before he walked away Ian thought maybe he would not come back, that maybe since he had been able to keep him off and to win that now familiar battle of the eyes, they had seen the effort to overpower him through this teacher was hopeless, and sent him away. But then, he said something about coming back, and now Ian was confused. Why would he come back? Would it mean they would be put against each other again, and again, until finally he was forced to give in? If that were so, he would have to be strong against him, that was all. But he was frightened. He wondered if Forrest was a doctor instead of a teacher, or both? He'd come this time with toys and games, and wanted him to play with them. But if he wanted to see if he could play with them, like the other doctors, why did he tell him, "I know you can do this

one," then get mad when he could not? The other doctors did not do that. Forrest must have something special
to do, but what? He hoped Forrest took the games and
toys away with him. He would not play with any of them,
even those that were interesting, for they might be tricks.

Over and over he thought of Forrest; he could make no
pattern of his place called "work" or why he came sometimes to Monica's house. Forrest didn't seem to do anything in order. Long ago, when first he began at the center, he noticed the children were brought in the mornings
by people called a name and another name such as
"Mom" or "Mother." Sometimes they were brought by
people called a name and another name such as "Dad" or
"Daddy." He did not know where they were brought
from, or where they returned at night. Once it occurred
to him that the children, being his own size, had come
from the same place as he had come from, and had been
changed through the power and strength of the big ones
who came for them. But then he decided that could not
be right. The children seemed to want to be with the people who came for them. They wanted to touch them and
hold their arms around their necks. Also, there were many
children at the center and many more at the doctors'
places, and if they had all come from his sky home then
surely he would have seen other balls fall from cracks in
the sky. As many times as he had watched the great show
of thunder and lightning, he had never seen another ball
fall through. The only explanation he could reason was
that the words "mommy" and "daddy" meant more than
one thing. The one called Monica and the other called
Forrest were assigned to him, each with a separate responsibility of teaching. They had nothing more to do
with him, and they had nothing more to do with each
other.

He had always believed this, and the day that Forrest

took him to the park proved it. All the big ones were in twos, except for Forrest. He must have had a special lesson to teach that day, but what? It had been so hot by the big fires, and Forrest kept pushing him away, pointing toward where the other ones of his size were playing. But he could not go there, for they would be like the others at school, and gang up on him. He could not guess what they might do. It was safer to stay near Forrest, but it was so hot he was frightened. His skin felt as if it were on fire. And many of the larger ones came by and tried to touch him and take his hand, like the doctors. And they talked to Forrest about him.

He desperately wanted to go away from there, and when Forrest finally took him to the car he thought they would leave the park and go back to where Monica stayed. But Forrest tricked him and left him there. He said this would "teach you a lesson." Was this lesson the reason for bringing him to the park? He wasn't sure. He didn't think so. He watched Forrest walk away, and banged on the window and screamed, but he wouldn't come back. He wouldn't even turn around and look.

At first the car was very hot and he thought it would be like the great heat inside his ball home. The seats burned his legs. The metal on the doors burned his hands. He screamed again and again and tried to get out, but he could not hold on to the hot door handle to open it. He thought of squeezing through the opening above the window, but then he might fall, and that would be worse than staying in the car because he did not know how far it was or what lay at the bottom. He screamed again and again, hoping Forrest would hear him and return.

At last the car began to get cooler and he stopped to catch his breath. He was thirsty but there was nothing to drink. He had to pee but there was no place to go. Finally he could stand it no longer. He wet his pants. He hated the smell. It was almost as bad as the day he was peed on by the other one of his size. He took big gulps of air through his mouth and held his nose shut, until at last he fell asleep. It was a deep sleep, like the one after the great heat in his ball home, and he did not awaken until he was in his crib.

Why did Forrest do that to him? All the next day he wondered if Forrest would do something else to him, or say something that would make him understand. But he did not come around that day. He did not come till the day after that. And that was when he tried to make Ian play with the toys.

He hoped now that the plane was gone, something would happen to keep Forrest from coming back again, for he was not sure he could match him again. His shoulders ached from being crushed in his grip. His whole body ached, though not so much as his shoulders. Through the night he had continually awakened, hurting. He had been careful to make little noise, in case they might overhear and come back to his crib. At last he had been shown the strength of big arms and hands, and he would remember the pain for a long time.

The air near the bay was different from anywhere else. It had a different smell than the air at home, and a different feel: cool, moist. He liked the feel. It was something like the feel inside his ball home. He rubbed his fingers along one arm. He always did this when they neared the bay. Sometimes he felt her watching him, and would stop.

He thought again of Forrest being on the big plane, and wondered how far it would take him. Long ago he had believed that it was by the use of a plane he would get back to where he belonged. He had seen them flying on the television, and noted that they went through the clouds very high and fast. The only confusing part was that they continued horizontal and did not turn up and go inside an opening in the sky. Therefore, they must not be the way for him. But then, as he began to realize the others were trying to prevent him from getting back, and that the planes were for the others to ride in—he had never been in one—it seemed clear planes were only for the others. Planes would not go up into the place where he belonged. It was the same with rockets. They went to that place called "outer space" where there are no borders. They also came back to the ground.

He sighed. It all led to the same problem: if he were to get back, he had to get first to his ball, awaiting him. As far as he could figure, there was no other way. And for all his theories, he felt no closer to the answer than the first time he ever spun the clear bubble with balls or flicked the mirror to catch the brilliance of the light glowing from his home.

CHAPTER 28

Hetty met them at the gate with hugs and kisses. She got in Ian's face and told him hello and, as always, ignored his shimmying away. She told him Clark just couldn't wait for him to get back so they could play. It was ironic the way adults covered for children. By now Clark not only realized Ian wanted nothing to do with him; he was also jealous of the attention Ian was receiving from Buzz.

Monica began her own cover-up and told Hetty all the things they had done over the past week, omitting the mention of how miserable they were while doing them.

Preparations for the big Fourth celebration were well underway. This year the family next door was in charge of the fireworks display. Several families of Baynook rotated the responsibility, because the display was more spectacular when organized in one place, and no one family had to bother with the work any more often than every five years or so. When Hetty spoke of reviving the celebration she was amazed to learn Ian had never seen a fireworks display.

It's just one more thing I've never done for him, Monica caught herself thinking. I should have realized how important fireworks would be for a child, how it would thrill him and ignite his imagination. But then, the pressure trap seemed to be closing on her again. She was sure her parents never worried about her "experiencing" things when she was Ian's age. She saw fireworks because they spent each Fourth at the bay, and her family was at the bay because they were best friends of the Wellmans, and it was the natural order of things they should spend holidays together. She could put the question to Hetty now: how many "experiences" did you "plan" for your children that you felt were a necessary part of their upbringing? Her answer would probably be a stare of bewilderment.

No matter. Monica was glad all over again they were here. Inside, the kitchen counters were lined with groceries. Packages of hot-dog buns filled nearly half the space on one side of the sink, surely enough to feed thirty or forty people, with seconds. The Frigidaire was crammed with weiners, foil-wrapped cheddar cheese, and big white onions. There would be baked beans and potato salad to accompany the traditional hot dogs, and Hetty was already cooking the chili in her big electric roaster. The smell of it made Monica, who'd not yet eaten that day, want to open the lid and dive in. Ian, on the other hand, winced and hurried out the door, his hand over his nose. Buzz and Peggy were due to arrive in time for dinner as usual, which tonight would consist of sandwiches, potato chips, and cookies, in order that all space and energy be directed toward tomorrow's feast. Monica spent the afternoon grating cheese and chopping onions, fighting off tears in spite of the matchstick Hetty insisted she put between her teeth. Ian stayed outside, content as always to be rushing up and down the edge of the patio, his eyes on the mirror as it reflected the sun.

As she worked Monica thought how long ago it seemed she'd felt a slight stirring for Buzz. The week with Forrest put a large barrier around all her feelings. She still felt numb, suspended, and now, exhausted. Her back ached as she stood above the sink.

"I don't know," Hetty clucked, passing through to stir the chili. "I haven't had this big a crowd down here since Bert died, not on any day of the summer. To tell you the truth, it makes me nervous. I'm always afraid someone will wind up getting hurt. Seems we've been lucky all these years, that nothing serious ever happened. And this year, there'll be hard liquor as well as beer. Buzz still toes the line, but he won't let me interfere with the plans of his brothers." Her voice grew lower and morose as she talked. "I don't say anything, as long as they don't get rowdy. But I don't like it. Every time they come down here they bring hard liquor, and there's just something about the Fourth that makes people go a little crazy. . . . Bert wouldn't have stood for it, and they know that." She poked her long neck above the roaster and took a deep whiff as she stirred.

"Don't worry, Hetty. What can happen?"

"I don't know . . . nothing, I suppose. Still . . ."

She drew back and replaced the lid, removed her glasses and wiped off the steam.

The morning of the Fourth began with the bright sunshine of promise, which brought a smile to Hetty's lips as she stood on the covered patio sipping coffee. She seemed more relaxed this morning, as though the passing of night dispelled some of her misgivings about the day. She might well relax for much of this day. Most of the work had been done the previous evening, and the rest would have to wait till late this afternoon near the time everyone began arriving. She'd told Monica as they cleaned the kitchen last night: "Honey, you just don't know how much I appreciate your help today. Peggy just isn't up to helping, and June wouldn't lift a hand if her life depended on it. Carson spoils her so. . . ."

Monica watched her now from the chaise, the light catching her sharp features in bas-relief against the sky. Her gray hair was pulled into that timeless twist at the back of her head, so accustomed to the pins in their places that by now there must have been grooves in Hetty's scalp. She knew she might never again catch a glimpse of the woman as she looked that day, at that particular moment, and softly stole inside, swooped up her camera, focused the lens, and released the shutter before Hetty noticed she'd left her chair.

Startled, she looked around. "Well, I'll say, I never thought you'd be interested in a picture of an ugly old biddy like me. Whatcha gonna do with it? Put it in the garden to scare off the crows?" Then she laughed, and disappeared into the house, muttering about something she just remembered wasn't done in the kitchen.

Monica could tell that Hetty was pleased. For just that swift moment when the click of the camera reached her ear and realization struck, she basked in the flash of limelight. She might wonder to herself time and again how that picture turned out, but modesty would forbid her to ask. If it was a good shot, Monica would do a portrait from it, maybe a pen-and-ink.

She had tried the same method with Ian, making many photos of him over the past year or so, and tacking them upon the board in front of her, yet nothing ever seemed transferable onto canvas and she would realize still one more photo had not captured him. She still had not been able to finish the portrait, even in this place he seemed to find so natural to himself. Andrew James said long ago that the eyes were the key; that was where one found the vulnerability which was the port of entry to the soul. She hated the reminder, for it was Ian's eyes she was not able to paint. At first she blamed it on the doctors and the weight they placed on their eye contact theory, yet it was Forrest who made matters worse when he returned. Casually dismissing the theory as a "piece of shit," he nonetheless reverted to it as the agonizing week wore on, as though finally admitting that the doctors and teachers *were* on the right track.

She'd already wondered how Forrest would cope with the certainty of an imperfect child. Had he suspected that Ian was seriously ill long before any teacher or doctor suggested it? Were all his proclamations about Ian's genius an escape from reality, a daily reassurance to himself that he'd not produced someone he couldn't accept? Was that why he never took time with his son? Was he running from Ian now?

She felt the weight of the summer on her shoulders again, the need to talk to someone, even while unsure how much she would say. Buzz, of course, was the only person she knew who would be sympathetic. She was now more certain than ever that Ian was making progress at the bay; the past week had been a measuring stick. She also felt she had to work it out alone for the most part, or else be left with no choice but to mention the fever and thus invite more confusion, more uncertainty, and perhaps, more guilt.

But with all the goings-on over the holiday, she was not apt to be able to talk to Buzz at length. And it might well be that even he would not fully understand. It might change the way he dealt with Ian, might make him self-conscious . . . might undo all he'd done so far.

I'm just upset by last week, she told herself. What I need to do is relax down here and get it all back in perspective.

Peggy had come out the door as Hetty hurried in, and now sat on a chaise. Even though she looked especially tired, she had offered to help make the sandwiches for last night's supper, but neither Buzz nor Hetty would let her complete the sentence before they chimed in a loud "No, ma'am." Buzz asked her if she'd already forgotten the doctor's warning to be careful these last few weeks.

Monica, never quite sure what to say to Peggy, for they had so little in common, searched for a way to break the silence this morning. She thanked her for bringing Ian a toy windmill. It was an unexpected gesture, and thoughtful especially in view of the fact she must have been doing very little shopping these days. Ian had shown no thrill, until she explained how it spun in the breeze. After that, she could not get it from his hands. He seemed almost as enamored of it as he was his mirror. He had already devised a way to hold the mirror in the same hand as the slender pole attached to the plastic windmill. Monica watched him now, skipping about the periphery of the yard, letting the wheel catch the breeze and whirl into a red and golden circle. He would one day, many years hence, regard this place with the same fondness as she did. Or would he?

Peggy leaned forward abruptly and clasped her distended abdomen with a surprised "Oh!" Then she chuckled, and added, "He kept me up all night with this kicking. Wish he'd behave." Her voice held a gentle, cajoling tone. On an impulse, Monica raised her camera, but then Peggy shifted and called, "Clark, Ian, come here! Feel the baby kick."

Clark was at her side at once. She pulled his head to her abdomen. "Listen, can you hear? Give me your hand. Feel it?"

Clark nodded in a knowing way. "My mom has told me all about babies living in their mommies." Then he listened again. "Does that mean the baby wants to come out? Why doesn't he come out?"

"Ah! There it is again. Well, Clark, at least I think it means he's a healthy rascal."

He again. But it did at least seem out of step with characteristic modesty for Peggy to share the experience with Clark. Or maybe not. . . . Ian was still involved in his windmill. Monica went to him and led him toward Peggy. Maybe feeling the baby kick would help him relate to others. At first he pulled away, but then she gently persuaded him to come back, assuring him she was not going to take his toys away.

Reluctantly, his head went down by degrees; he let her

rest it against Peggy's stomach. Two or three moments passed. Nothing. He looked up, puzzled. Then, suddenly, "Ah—there it is, over here!" Peggy pulled his head forward, to the other side. This time he felt the kick. Monica watched his eyes widen as the kicking continued. He looked up once, not at Peggy but out into space, his eyes narrowed as though trying to figure something out. Then he laid his head against her stomach again and listened.

"It's the baby in there," Monica told him. "A brand-new little baby is coming for Peggy." She did not add Buzz's name, for fear it would confuse him. "Isn't it wonderful?"

Clark pushed forward again. "I wanna hear some more."

Ian looked up abruptly and pushed him on the chest. Clark lost his balance and fell. "Hey, you—"

Monica was there at once, helping him up, apologizing. Ian remained with his ear fixed to Peggy's stomach for quite a long time. At last, she gently tried to push him away. "There, I think that's all. Go along now . . ."

Ian ignored her, though her voice became more insistent. Finally Monica, embarrassed, forced him away. "That's enough," she said firmly. Ian looked bemused. He ran to the edge of the yard and pivoted, then skipped up and down. Now and then he looked back, as though to assure himself the stomach was still there. Then he stuck the pole of the windmill in the fence and went off with his mirror.

Monica turned to Peggy. "I—I'm sorry—"

Peggy stopped her. "It's all right. He was fascinated." She smiled and leaned back again.

"Well, it was kind of you to share that moment with him," Monica said. "He hasn't the faintest idea about babies, and I don't plan to have another."

"Oh, why not?"

"I just don't want to have more than one." When you're not sure your first child is healthy, you don't want to risk another. When you don't feel certain your marriage will last, you don't want anything to further complicate its demise. I don't want to compound my mistakes, Peggy. Even Forrest doesn't speak of having other children, though he did right after Ian was born. Kids are for people like you and Buzz, not Forrest and me. . . .

Peggy was silent momentarily. Then she said anxiously, "The kicking is a sure sign the baby's healthy, isn't it? He keeps me awake nights, so often. That, and the back pain." Monica was surprised at her worry. Whenever conversation turned toward that subject at the dinner table or elsewhere, she always seemed confident regardless of Hetty's misgivings. In a moment she added, "Dr. Peavey says the heartbeat isn't very strong, but that I shouldn't be concerned.

"Oh, but I am." She was leaning forward again, speaking softly but hurriedly. There were little circles beneath her eyes. "Of course, I haven't said anything to Buzz."

Whyever not? Why choose me to tell? "I'm sure the baby's fine. Your doctor would have told you if not. They can discover so much before birth nowadays," she said, then added, "Even determine its sex."

"Oh, I'd never want to have them do that to me." She leaned back.

"I notice you always refer to the baby as 'he.'"

"I know. From the first, my instincts told me it was a boy. Buzz feels it too."

"You're probably right. I was certain about Ian too. I think that first instinct is the one that counts, before everybody begins speculating about how you're carrying it and so forth, and you get confused. But you can't always rely on instinct." She was pursuing a point now, perhaps cruelly, but here was an opening to find answers to several questions she had mulled over. "What if it's a girl? Will you be disappointed?"

"No . . ." she said faintly. "But then I'll have another. If I do it soon enough, the endometriosis won't have a chance to get started again. That's what the doctor said. In fact, Buzz wants several children, so I'll have to get pregnant again soon. I wouldn't chance it past the age of forty."

The inflections in Peggy's voice told more than the words. As she'd suspected, the Wellmans were pressuring Peggy, or perhaps Hetty was pressuring Buzz, who was in turn bringing it to bear on Peggy, maybe even unconsciously. How senseless. The sun played on Peggy's once again placid face. She was a little pathetic in this role. Strange she wouldn't have mentioned her worries about health to Buzz. Of course, Forrest was told nothing of the fever which might inflict damage on Ian's health, but that was different. Buzz was different. More understanding than a lot of men, and more concerned with his family than Forrest. He was conservative, however; having "sowed his wild oats" while younger, he was probably doubly conservative when it came to the wife he finally chose. Did that trait build up a false modesty between them? Would a woman like Peggy be able to tap the deep well of compassion existent in her own husband? If not, what a waste.

Oh, Peggy, I would give anything if Forrest gave a fraction of the care Buzz does, especially when it comes to Ian. "Well, if you get a nasty letter from the Zero Population Growth advocates, tell them your third can count for my second."

Hetty was at the door then, looking for Buzz. "I think

he's out back, cleaning up some extra chairs," Peggy told her.

"Anything I can help with?" Monica asked.

"No. It's the American flag. I just thought of it—imagine a Fourth without that flag hanging on the back porch. Bert would have never . . . but anyhow, I can't find it."

Buzz was rounding the corner. "It's in the closet where you keep the laundry basket, don'tcha remember, Mom? On the top shelf. Never mind, I'll get it. You can't reach that high anyway."

"Can you find the bracket for it, and hang it on the back porch post where Bert used to—"

"Yeah, Mom."

"But since Carson had the porch painted, I don't know if that hole where the nail used to go in would still . . ."

Their voices drifted off as they went into the house. Peggy leaned back and said, "I'm sure glad Mom thought of that now, before it's too late. We'd never stop hearing about . . . I mean, she just wouldn't forgive herself."

It seemed to Monica that, for Hetty, observing old rituals and keeping things as they were served as amulets to help assure that the continuity of life at the bay would not be disrupted. And for her, their importance was near equal to nailing the shutters fast against an impending storm.

CHAPTER 29

Sometime in the early afternoon Monica became aware that Clark was busy with an activity of importance, at least to him. Now and again she would look sideways from her easel to see him sprint across the patio carrying something. He'd begun by pulling the newest lawn chaise to a place near the edge of the patio, and as the sun's rays glanced at different angles he'd move the chair slightly, to be sure the awning was providing as much shade as possible. All the other chairs had been moved far away from it, to isolate it, and grouped out on the sunny lawn.

Next she noticed him move a heavy wrought-iron table from across the porch. This was quite a task for a small boy with his lithe frame. He'd move a little, stop and figure, then move some more. The noise of metal grating across concrete was excruciating. "Can I help you?" she called. He shook his head. She winced at the noise as he continued, but said nothing.

After the table was in place, he disappeared inside the house for a while and Monica forgot about him, becoming absorbed in her work. She was making a second attempt at the painting she and Buzz had discussed their first morning at the bay, and was not very far along. Now the summer was half gone, she felt she better get to it.

When Clark finally returned, he bore a folded patchwork quilt that Monica recognized. Ordinarily it lay folded at the foot of the bed where Hetty slept. The quilt with its wedding ring design had special meaning for Hetty, having been passed down to her and Bert from his mother when they married. If Hetty knew her family heirloom, and one with special sentimental value, was being unfolded and draped over a lawn chair outside, she'd probably have a fit. Monica looked at Clark. "Say, what are you doing?"

"I'm fixing this chair for my mommy," he told her without a backward glance. She felt a sudden twinge of pity for the child she had never quite been able to like. While she would take no honors for mothering, from what she'd heard, June Wellman all but abandoned her son to his step-grandmother. And yet here he was, preparing a throne as though for a queen coming to visit. Over the past twenty-four hours, Clark asked Hetty again and again, "Are you sure my mommy is coming to the party?" Hetty assured him calmly, patiently, over and over again, that she was. The exchange did not seem significant to Monica then. But now she linked it with Clark's many references over the summer about what his mother did for him, what she said to him, what she bought for him, and she was ashamed of herself for having blamed him for belittling Ian.

Nor could she escape a little self-pity, that she should not have that sort of adoration from her own son. Well, maybe someday . . . maybe someday Ian would grab her and hug her neck and say, "I love you, Mommy," and move close to her out of some need other than protection or conveyance. Maybe someday he'd do all the things she had seen other children do, pay her the homage others paid their parents naturally, even though she'd not be as deserving as some.

She crossed the patio and went quickly to find Hetty

inside. She wanted to tell her of the quilt before she discovered its whereabouts on her own. Hetty would no doubt speak sharply to Clark before she considered what he was doing and how important it was to him. She might be able to convince Hetty to leave the quilt alone. Surely the thing could be cleaned if it got soiled.

Hetty was drying a tumbler in the kitchen. "I know he has it. I loaned it to him," she said, then raised the tumbler to the light to check for water marks.

Relieved, Monica said, "Oh, that's wonderful. I was afraid you'd—well, anyhow, that's fine." She started out the door, then on impulse she grabbed Hetty and hugged her tightly.

"What was that for?"

"Everything."

Little time had passed before Clark was adding a pillow in an embroidered case and, as a final touch, toward the late afternoon when Ian was sleeping and Hetty began warming the chili and removing the weiners from the plastic packs, he pulled a stool up to the crowded counter and made his mother a peanut butter and jelly sandwich. "My mom doesn't like hot dogs," he said with gravity. Monica and Hetty shared a smile behind him as he went carefully about it. Not a bad job for a five-year-old. He then obtained a table knife from Hetty, who watched anxiously but said nothing, and cut the sandwich into halves, then, after a thoughtful pause, into quarters, put it on a plate, grabbed two paper towels and folded them neatly, and started out the door. Monica, busy unwrapping buns, called to him. "Clark, it will be a while before your mom gets here. Here, let's put some plastic wrap over her sandwich so the bread won't dry out." Grape jelly had oozed from all edges of the quarters.

"All right." He handed her the plate and folded his

arms behind him, eyeing her closely. She sealed the
edges of plastic over the plate and handed it back. He
took it out, then hurried back to fill a big goblet with ice
and red Kool-Aid. As though fearful he wouldn't have
time to get all his work done, he stole a glance at Hetty
and reminded her he was excused from taking a nap. Then
he raced out with the goblet, slowing to a walk when
Hetty cautioned him about spilling it. Buzz was at the
back door when he reached it, and opened it wide. "Careful down those steps, squirt," he told him.

It's a conspiracy, Monica thought, like a surprise birthday party. Not for the benefit of June, but rather for the
boy who was not really a Wellman except by default.

She became more curious about June, whom she had
heretofore dismissed lightly. Would she appreciate the
effort on her child's part? Would she praise him, sit upon
the throne with him at her knee? Oh, please let her have
that much sense. . . . Yet, from what had been said of
June, it seemed unlikely. Then again, Hetty may have
painted an unfair picture of June, may have seen her op-
portunistic side and overlooked a better, more loving one.

Ian awoke at four-thirty, quiet and docile. Buzz suggested going next door to survey the piles of fireworks
lined up for the big display. Clark followed right behind
Buzz, but Ian clung to his mother and would not go until
Buzz picked him up.

Monica stood on the Wellman side and marveled at
Buzz's knowledge of fireworks. She found herself in-
trigued by the array of colors, sizes, and shapes. When
Buzz began by saying, "These all make different shapes
and colors in the sky," Ian had listened and looked carefully, as though trying very hard to understand what, for
some reason, was important to him.

"See those down here at this end? Roman candles.

Those long narrow cylinders are designed to shoot flaming balls. The bigger ones are supposed to make more sparks than the small ones, though you can't always depend on that. And here, these are skyrockets, the little round ones. That little pencil-like projection at the end is stuck in the ground, the fuse is lit, and it shoots way up and makes snowflake shapes of all colors. Beautiful. These here are thunder rainbows. And down here, giant missiles —the ones that look like rockets ready to launch. And look here, these things about the size of salt boxes, see, Clark, hexagon-shaped? Those are not used till the end of the display. They each have seven firing tubes that make big bright flowers in the air. And there are a lot of little ones down here—comets, smoke bombs, pinwheels. Some of these things go about seventy feet up into the air; others go as far as a thousand feet."

Monica continued to stare at the pile as they returned down the alley between the houses and walked up the Wellman side of the fence. The display occupied a good six feet by three feet of the lawn, and was well organized. Indeed, it looked as though the neighbors bought out a whole fireworks stand, lock, stock, and barrel.

She heard Clark ask Buzz if he could help light the fireworks. "Nope, yer still not big enough. Even a grown-up doesn't get any closer than at the other end of one of those long torches they use to light the fuses." Monica thought of all the years at the bay without accidents or mishaps, then she thought of Hetty's worries of the day before and of the booze and beer which would be served. Oh well, the danger would be next door, not here. . . .

"Can you say 'fireworks,' Ian?" Buzz asked.

Ian turned away.

"Aw, come on. *Fire-works*." He spat it out clearly.

"Fie . . ."

"Good boy!"

Ian narrowed his eyes and looked at the unlit fireworks again. In wonder? Appraisal? "It's going to be just beautiful," she assured him.

Now Buzz was handing each of the boys a box of sparklers. While Ian looked his over one by one, end to end, and twirled one between his fingers and stroked it up and down from flint end to handle, Clark was overcome with excitement and insisted that Buzz light his immediately. The hissing noise began. Soon there was one white flickering glow, then another. Ian watched intently as Clark flashed the sparklers about and, though Clark offered him one to hold, Ian drew back and shook his head. He seemed to be growing nervous. He'd begun to wring his hands, off and on. He went to the edge of the yard and skipped back and forth, now and then glancing up toward the sky. It must have been difficult, Monica thought, for him to relate what Buzz told him to what he saw on the ground next door. She'd heard Buzz telling the boys the display would last an hour or better, and from the size of the outlay, there was no doubt he was right. Was it all so elaborate when she was a child? She couldn't remember. But surely, since Ian was preoccupied with the sky, the display would be thrilling for him.

Yet there was little time to wonder. She was in charge of covering the long picnic tables with paper cloths, then placing paper plates and plastic ware, napkins and paper cups just where Hetty designated, then helping Hetty bring out the heavy receptacles of food from the kitchen.

Around five o'clock Clark stationed himself at the back fence, awaiting the sight of his parents' car. First Aaron and his girlfriend Alyson arrived, bringing another couple along. The four of them were already clad in bathing suits. Soon Aaron and his slightly balding but young-looking buddy produced three coolers of beer, which they placed alongside the tables of food. Afterward they went after something else, while the girls, keeping to themselves, hardly speaking to Hetty and oblivious to Monica and Peggy, walked down the pier in their flashy bikinis, their long straight hair gleaming swaths down their backs between their tan shoulders. Alyson was blond, like Aaron; the other girl was brown-haired, like her boyfriend. With their golden-tan bodies they looked like two sets of Barbie and Ken dolls. Aaron had (upon Hetty's direction) spoken to Monica, displaying a vague remembrance that she doubted was real, and that made her feel uncomfortable. She could have taken him down a notch or two by saying she remembered him in diapers.

The boys now headed for the pier, following the girls. The girls spread their multicolored beach towels down near the end and fell upon them, eager to catch the rays of sunshine, fast mellowing. Shading her eyes, Hetty looked out at them. Spoon in one hand, she observed, "Will you look at those bathing suits?" (A point with the spoon.) "I'll bet there isn't an eighth of a yard of material to them." Then she sighed and murmured something about young people today leaving nothing to the imagination.

CHAPTER 30

As the sun began a brilliant and slow descent, coloring the sky pink and lavender, she looked toward the cottage. Aaron and his friend were plugging in stereo speakers from electrical extension cords just at the edge of the patio. Ian watched with great interest as they ran cords from the plug inside the front room and out along the patio, now and then looking away to peek at the sun, then looking back. In the process the boys threw on the cottage ceiling lights, casting an artificial-looking spot on the room through the windows. Its old furniture, chenille-covered beds, wall prints, and large square television set, its hanging light bulbs, all lay exposed suddenly, like an aging damsel caught in her underwear, all the ugly bulges and folds of age at once a spectacle to be leered at. It was somehow depressing, seeing it this way, although this time of day always made everything seem sad and lost. . . .

She busied herself rearranging the table to make room for olives and pickles, nuts and relish. Clark was staying at the back fence, not giving up hope, though time was passing by and still Carson and June had not appeared. Hetty, either sensing his worry and getting him involved so he'd forget it momentarily, or not sensing his feelings and thoughtlessly tearing him away from his chosen station, made him come to their aid by opening the front door for each of her emergences. She was wearing a pink apron with pinafore sleeves that looked like it came from the 1940's era, starched and pressed, and because of its outdated look, making her appear aged and tired. She looked all at once frightened, as though she realized she could not control what the evening would bring, not without Bert, and it seemed to Monica then that the whistle she wore so religiously was a sadly inadequate source of power now that he was gone: like a great watchdog, old and toothless, his hearing dulled, his howl a mere querulous whimper.

She nodded toward the coolers and said, "Is that *all* beer?"

"I think so," Monica said.

"Humph. When Bert was alive we'd take one cooler for twice as many people, and still have part of it left over."

Times have changed. The world did not stop where you decided to get off. Kids are wilder. Adults are wilder. Everything moves faster, and faster. "Try not to worry. I'm sure it'll go well." Her voice was not as cheerful as she intended.

"At least Buzz is here," Hetty said for the first of many times that evening.

Every time she started back in to pick up a new platter or pot, Clark begged to be excused. "Is zat all, Gram? Can I go back now?"

"Not quite. Don't you worry. If I hear your dad's—your mother's car—I'll come a-runnin'."

Clark looked impatient, and settled himself at the edge of the steps, now and then rising to make a run for the back fence, then hurrying back to his involuntary post.

Hetty was silent as she went about her work. Monica was certain the prospect of loud music annoyed her as much as the coolers of beer, though she never said. Periodically she'd catch a glimpse of Buzz, looking after one thing or another, here, there, everywhere, like an efficient host. There were some ten years between Aaron and Buzz, with Carson halfway between. They obviously weren't close as brothers nowadays, each of them loosely representing a different generation in fact, and certainly in behavior. Thankfully, the boys didn't start the music just then, but turned out the front-room lights and went to join the girls again on the darkening pier. Soon all of them were in the bay, splashing, laughing, calling to one another. From the pier came, too, the shrill notes of radio music: reason for the temporary abandonment of the more elaborate sound system hooked up at the cottage. They must be planning a dance on the patio later in the evening. She thought of the school dance so long ago, when she was twirled somewhat awkwardly around the floor by Buzz. The dancing tonight would not be like that.

Monica took a bubbling pot of baked beans from the arms of Hetty, who looked at her through steamy glasses and asked, "What could be holding up Carson?" She shook her head, wiped her lenses, and looked across at the throne prepared for June. The Kool-Aid, now watery with melted ice, threatened to overflow the top of the sweating goblet. The sandwich was there, wrapped in its protective plastic. What if Carson and June didn't show up? Monica listened anxiously for the sound of tires to cross the shell drive but heard nothing except the few notes of music that echoed from the pier, like the sounds of a rock concert played far away and becoming dreamlike in the long transit.

Hetty excused Clark from his post and Monica placed the last pot—simmering chili—on the table. The smell of it evoked again her memory of Fourth celebrations long

past. She followed Hetty into the kitchen, and glanced at
Ian, who was skipping along the fence beside the fireworks, keeping his eyes on them, up and down, up and
down. . . .

"Looks like Aaron and his friends plan to make quite a
night of it," Hetty stated with a casualness which her
raised eyebrows contradicted. "While Bert was alive they
weren't so smarty-pants. He wouldn't have stood for all
that down on the pier. He'd have been down there by
now, to see what was going on." Then she turned toward
the sink and opened the taps full. Over her shoulder she
added, "At least I'm glad Buzz is here. I can depend on
him."

It was past seven before Carson and June arrived,
bringing two other couples along—business associates.
Even the noise of the burgeoning party next door, min-
gled with the rock music coming louder and louder from
the pier, could not obliterate Clark's excited cries: "It's
my mommy! She's here! Mommy, Mommy, Mommy!"
Monica sighed with some relief that finally the drama
which had been unfolding all day would have its climax.
As she came through the back gate, June received the
hugs and kisses and clinging, all the outpouring of affection saved up for her on this day. It was hard to tell how
eagerly she accepted her son's offering. She stepped gingerly to avoid tripping over Clark's arms and legs, which
all seemed to be coming on her at once. She was tall and
slender, with swingy brown hair and a deep Coppertone
commercial tan. Her bright sundress was cut low in the
back and high in the front. Her yellow sandals were the
bottom line of a chic ensemble. Her long nails were
highly enameled, her fingers flashing with rings as she
began to fend off Clark's adoring hugs. "Yes, darling, just

let Mommy get across the yard. Stop pulling on my dress. Yes, I'm coming. Don't hold my hand so tight."

Hetty came to the screen door and said, "In two years I haven't seen her in the same dress twice."

When June reached the porch, she greeted Monica with a wide smile that displayed good, straight, very white teeth. Her brown eyes were fringed with long, thick lashes. She was a knockout all right. No wonder Carson . . . Monica felt suddenly dowdy in her shorts and espadrilles. She hadn't expected anyone to be so dressed up. She introduced herself. June looked a little confused at first, then said, in a nasal midwestern accent, long on the *i*'s, "Oh yes, Carson, look who's here! I—uh, you remember—uh—"

"Monica Maguire," Hetty helped her.

"Of course! Carson, darling, your childhood playmate." Anything but. Monica smiled. "Hi, Carson."

Carson held a case of liquor under one arm. He looked as though he took care of himself, in his blue golf shirt and good-fitting slacks. He pumped Monica's hand. "How are you? Did Mom say your husband is overseas? That's great. Here, let me introduce Patty and Jim Sinclair, Ed and Shirley Tanner." (Nods and smiles.) Carson had exchanged his horn-rimmed glasses for the new look: rimless, slightly tinted lenses. In the growing shadows, she could not see his eyes behind them. He looked like someone in a mask. "You'll excuse us while we get something wet down. We've had a long day and a long drive on top of it." He looked past her. "June, ask Mom if there's plenty of ice."

Hetty emerged then and switched on the hanging porch light. Monica had never liked its yellow bulb. It seemed almost as garish as red, but that was something better left unsaid. She noticed then that Ian stood at the edge of the porch, quietly watching. Clark had not given up. As they all trooped around the edge of the house he continued to vie for his mother's attention, cutting between the chitchat of her and her friends, which they spliced back together, little bothered. Monica reached out to Ian. "Come on, let's go around. It's almost time to eat." He seemed more guarded than usual, and refused her hand, though he followed a couple of steps behind. She was curious as to what would happen when—and if—Clark managed to get June to her throne.

As they rounded the corner, June was saying in a voice laced with saccharin, "Oh, but, Clark dear, this quilt is much too hot, and this pillow—really, I'll suffocate. What? Oh well, isn't that a nice sandwich. But I think I'll just put it here under the table and, whoops—"

The goblet of Kool-Aid now lay on its side, its contents spilled over the edge of the table, dripping down onto the sandwich. Now the voice was decidedly truculent. "Oh God, my shoes are soaked. Clark, run to the kitchen and get a towel to clean up this mess. Hurry, Mommy's shoes will be ruined. . . ." And as the door banged behind him, "Oh, shit!"

One of their women guests brought a stack of napkins from the table to help with the mess, and Carson was handing June a cocktail in a tall glass. "Thanks, honey. I can use this. Thanks, Patty. Kids! They're always up to something. Honestly, sometimes it's all I can do to keep my temper. . . ."

As the others pulled their chairs around, June handed the quilt and pillow to Carson and said, "Here, do something with this junk, will you?"

"Hell, that's Mother's pride and joy. I hope it didn't get messed up."

"Tell her we'll have it cleaned." She glared up at him,

then dabbed at her shoes. "I know Clark means well, but . . . if I were at home in my jeans and tennies, this would never happen."

"Ain't it the truth," someone said, and they all laughed.

Monica stood by and watched as their glasses clinked with ice and they leaned forward in earnest conversation. She knew the routine, though she could not hear the words from where she stood. Is that what Forrest and I used to look like, hobnobbing with customers? she wondered.

When Clark returned with a big towel June waved him away and said, "Go and play with the little boy over there"—pointing toward Ian—"and let Mommy visit. We'll have lots of time to be together later. What? Oh, I don't know. We'll probably get home late. We have a party to go to after this one. You spend the night with Gram, okay?"

Clark ambled off, his chest high, looking about for something to do, Monica knew, to make himself look very busy and important. "Come over here," she called. "You and Ian and I will have hot dogs together. We can sit over near the fence." Mother-rescuer. Wouldn't Forrest be surprised? She, who had scarcely ever felt an honest-to-goodness emotion toward any child save her own, suddenly envisioned herself as future Scout leader, room mother, car-pool driver. But just as quickly another vision of herself as mother of a child whose life would never be so ordinary flitted through her mind like a scrap of paper across a windswept lawn, lost and unredeemable.

The party was divided into camps now. Even Peggy and Buzz and Hetty had grouped themselves in lawn chairs near the edge of the yard. The assemblage down at the pier's end were toweling off, gathering their things to come up for supper. The Wellman pier had no lights strung up and down its length, but other piers within the crescent of Baynook were so equipped, and as streams of bulbs began to glow, reflecting in the water below, the bay looked like an exclusive yacht club, awaiting expensive crafts to motor into the harbor. She'd overcome her feeling of depression she suffered earlier, in between light and darkness. She walked to the table and filled plates for Ian and Clark, and gave each a Coke, thinking again of Orange Crush in brown bottles. There was no reason to think Ian would eat a hot dog; he never had before. But tonight she fixed him one hopefully, putting only cheese and mustard with the weiner because she was certain he would not accept chili.

"I want everything," Clark said abruptly, and grabbed his plate from her hands. He added a few extra touches to the hot dog and topped it with a spoonful of baked beans. Monica grimaced. Ian might have strange eating habits, but they made more sense than that. She led them to the back porch and sat down with them under the yellow bulb. The American flag fluttered slightly in the soft breeze. She'd helped herself to one of the beers in the cooler. She had no desire for food as yet, having nibbled on grated cheese earlier, and decided to wait till the boys had eaten and the crowd now forming around the table had dispersed. Hetty could be heard already busy in the kitchen again, no doubt enjoying her own party least of anyone.

Monica had asked her once why the people next door, in charge of fireworks this year for everyone, did not come over and eat with them. "It's a rule we observe around here. Each to his own for food. We share only the fireworks. If we try to combine the whole party, it gets too big. We learned that a long time ago. Besides, different families have their own tastes in eating . . . and drinking." So there would be fewer than twenty at the Wellman place tonight, but surely there was enough food for fifty. Monica took a long swig of cold beer. It wasn't Orange Crush, but it wasn't half bad at that.

Clark was whipping through his hot dog, enjoying himself immensely as chili and mustard and cheese oozed out each end. When Ian rejected everything on his plate, Clark thrust out a hand and offered him part of his conglomeration. Ian slapped angrily at his hand, knocking the contents of Clark's plate out onto the ground and sending Clark tearfully away. "Oh, blast!" Monica jumped up. "Clark, I'll make you another. Ian, really!"

Ian then noticed a drop of chili on his forearm. He was on his feet at once, screaming at the top of his lungs, holding his arm away and wriggling backward as though in an effort to extricate the contaminated limb from his body. Unnerved as usual by the speed of things once they started to go wrong, Monica slapped a napkin on his wrist, wiped it off, and told him sternly, "Sit here. I'll fix you a peanut butter sandwich. Next time someone offers you— Oh, never mind."

Peggy was at the table fixing Clark a new plate, and speaking softly. "Maybe Ian doesn't like having food pushed at him. Let him get his own. He knows what he likes."

"He's mean. I don't like him," Clark whimpered. "Why does he always come here?"

Monica bit her lip and doubled back to the kitchen. Grabbing the peanut butter, she told Hetty, "Look, I think we ought to go. Ian's not in a very good mood. Maybe he doesn't feel well."

"Don't be silly," said Hetty. "He'll miss the fireworks. Besides, you did half the work for this party. Just relax

now. You worry too much over that child. Let him alone
and he'll find out how to get along."

Monica acquiesced after a moment or two. It was too
late to start home in Fourth of July traffic anyhow. She
slapped the sandwich together and went out to find Ian.
By now he was back at the fence, skipping up and down
and eyeing the fireworks. The windmill which had held
his interest so briefly still rose from the fence post, whirling on and on. She sat down on the ground nearby and
called him to eat. He devoured the sandwich. Small wonder. It was after eight o'clock and he hadn't eaten since
noon. She sipped her beer and tried to relax.

He finished eating and held up the white paper plate
before him, examining it carefully. It seemed almost to
glow against the darkness. "Moon," he murmured to himself, then placed his open palm against it and began to
hum. She'd never heard him hum before. What would the
doctors think of that? A step forward, or back? Communication or self-stimulation? They'd never be able to
speculate, for she had no intention of telling them. He
didn't seem to be aware of his own melody. It was haunting, sad. He was such a beautiful child; and no more so
than at times like these when he became totally absorbed
in something others scarcely noticed. What did he see?

"I love you," she said quickly, pulling him close. He
wriggled away and returned to the fence. In the dark she
could see little more than the toy windmill which caught
the spotlight from the side of the house and spun it into its
own whirling motion of red and gold. Ian himself, some
two feet below, was but a shadow on parade. . . .

CHAPTER 31

Later she heard the music from the big speakers. It was not loud, not yet. She fixed a hot dog for herself. Buzz passed her at the table, helping himself to seconds.

"You doin' all right?" He didn't look at her.

"Sure. Great party."

"Yeah. Where's Ian?"

"On the other side, playing." The buns were now crusty, having sat too long. The potato chips were limp. Nothing would taste good. Even the cheese was hard and waxy. "Remember Orange Crush?" she asked.

"Sure. They don't make it anymore, do they?"

"I don't think so. At least, not in brown bottles. I think the brown bottles were what made it taste so good."

"Yeah. Well, I guess I've got enough here to make me good and miserable. Can I get you a beer, Coke?"

"No, thanks."

"Sorry we don't have Orange Crush." He winked, and walked away.

She looked across to where Carson and June sat with their friends. Clark perched at the base of his mother's chair, quietly, as though just being near her, feeling her physical presence, were sustenance enough. Now and then he'd lean against her legs. Absently, she'd pat his back and go on talking.

Monica noticed as she ate that Buzz still seemed to be

overseeing the evening. He didn't mix with Carson's group, who must have been getting into their fourth or fifth round of cocktails by now. Aaron, Alyson, and their friends had taken two six-packs of beer and gone back down for a boat ride. They seemed to have forgotten their music; or maybe Aaron warned them of his mother's old-fashioned ways and continued to ease the trappings of his generation gently upon her.

Buzz watched as the boat cut foamy swaths across the bay. He looked very much the way she remembered Bert: straight and thin, prominent rib cage, folded arms, cigarette dangling from his mouth. The two of them had a kinship with this place, shared by no one else, not even Hetty. Father and son. She could not feature Forrest ever forming that kind of unwritten, unspoken bond with Ian. Perhaps she was wrong; certainly it was unfair to speculate while Ian was so young. Yet the Wellmans were so different, so steeped in tradition, at least down to and including Buzz.

She wondered what would happen upon Hetty's death. Would the place be doled out in equal thirds among the boys? If so, would all the differences which surely ran among the boys, basic to their natures, suddenly surface, egged on by their wives, making them enemies? It was a painful thought, a situation which ought to be avoided. Perhaps Hetty would leave it all to Buzz, and give something else to the others. Surely if she did not, Buzz would wind up on the bottom rung, a loser by default. He would not fight over a parcel of property like a vicious animal fights for his territory, for that would destroy its very appeal, the essence which made it survive unchanged through the passage of time. Once spread over by the venom of greed, it would lose its meaning for someone who loved it, become distasteful. And love it

Buzz did; she was certain of that, like a farmer loves his
land. A phrase from the marriage vow crossed her mind:
what God hath joined, let not man put asunder. Silly, but
somehow it seemed to fit.

The boat motor whirred to a stop; the group emerged
one by one, laughing, onto the pier. Buzz took one more
drag off his cigarette, his fingers fanned out, then he
turned around and headed toward the house.

Full night had come.

The moon hung peacefully against the black void as
though pasted there. Next door several from the group of
neighbors and their friends huddled around the fireworks at the edge of the yard, one of them having toted
an electric light with a cage front so they could better see
the selection before them. In the Wellman cottage someone turned up the music a few decibels higher and flung
on the lights in the front room again. Now the cottage in-
nards looked even worse by contrast, like a Bourbon
Street dive. The sight of it saddened Monica and she
looked away.

Clark was standing as close to the outlay of fireworks as
the fence would permit. All the others had begun to
gather in a group next to the patio. Ian, prancing around
the edge of the yard, appeared to note these changes,
then returned to his prancing, holding the windmill again.
He seemed to have forgotten the fireworks about to burst
forth, or maybe didn't understand what was about to happen, and now concentrated his attention on the crossbar
at the top of the chain link fence on the other side of the
yard. Up and down he went, watching it, pivoting, up
and down, windmill spinning above him, a drum major
with his baton strutting up and down in front of a march-
ing band. . . .

She was about to go near him as the display began, instinct telling her he might be frightened by the loud noises, but then all too soon the first POP split the air, signaling the start, quickly followed by another POP, then still another, POP, SPUTTER, until within seconds the sky was a glorious shower of yellow, pink, white, purple, each color rising like a meteor to take its place in the glowing spectacle. Monica stood motionless, transfixed by what she saw. Even the displays she recalled as a child were not to compare with this, for if they were, surely she would have remembered. The whole sky was bathed in colored lights and the bay below was a mirror that reflected and duplicated the brilliance, doubling its powerful splendor. POP, POP, SPUTTER, POP, THUD, PING, POP-POP, it continued, louder and louder, it seemed, like the reports of cannon on a battlefield, while fireworks burst again and again as though one might go higher and still higher and outrun the others before splitting and scattering like glitter and dripping down like watercolors flung against a board. Several moments passed before she thought of Ian again, then she looked across the yard and saw him.

His body was rigid, head up, mouth gaping, arms riveted to his sides as first one, then another and another burst of color illuminated him. He looked grotesque, like a figure struck by lightning and welded in place. She ran to him, realizing only then his screams of terror had been muffled by the loud music and popping noises. She called to him as she ran.

When she reached him she grabbed both his arms and forced him to face her, hoping to explain, and her own words were drowned out by the noise and she was like someone dumb trying to make sounds that wouldn't come. He glanced at her for one bleak moment, his eyes flames of distrust, accusal; she would never forget that look. Then he broke from her grip and began to run, down the yard toward the pier, and she to follow, calling after him still. She had not known him capable of running with such speed; he was halfway down the long pier before she reached the first cross member, and she fled after him, the wood a slick surface under the espadrilles. She thought he'd jump into the water, and kept running and calling to him, stubbing her toes on the uneven boards, groping for balance. Yet when he reached the end he stood looking above, his arms wide, and when she drew to him she could see his mouth forming, "No! No!"

She clutched him, but he pulled loose and looked up toward the yard again, his face aglow from the lights washing over him and changing in chroma with each new noisy burst above. He looked back at the sky, then at the yard again, and she looked with him. Everyone's eyes were cast upward, as though expecting an outer-space craft to appear. No one would see them on the pier, and if they chanced to see they wouldn't understand, would think she and Ian had run to the boathouse for a better view of the spectacle. Oh, God. Her hands were on Ian again but he wriggled free with all his strength. She might have been his enemy rather than his rescuer. He knocked her elbow up against her chin and her teeth clamped down hard on her tongue. She grabbed her cheeks in pain as he tore off again, up the pier, a zigzagging, glowing form. Somebody look down, somebody see, please. . . .

Back up the yard she struggled, this time following his steps to the fence by the fireworks; he shoved his body to it, his arms flailing, his voice calling again, "No, no, no!" But the people smiled at him puzzledly. She called for help, sprinting by the others watching the display, but no one seemed to hear and she didn't reach for anyone because that would mean stopping and Ian might be anywhere by the time she gathered help.

He then ran down to the edge of the back fence and smashed himself against the closed gate. She could understand by his actions he intended to get into the other yard and stop the fireworks but she couldn't understand why. If only she could calm him down and explain. "Go in the house," she called. Her voice was more audible on this side of the yard, but he ignored her and his own powerful screams eclipsed her words. He ran more and more, like a frightened pony, up and down the back fence. From everywhere the colored lights now shone, illuminating his contorted figure like electric shocks, and he ran and ran some more and couldn't be stopped. She was breathless, her throat constricted, heart pumping, but grab him as she might she could not hold him, and his stamina far outlasted hers. She stopped and heaved, and let him run. As long as he could not get out the gate, the fastener far too high for him to reach, he could not get into the street or across into the yard next door. And he would run himself out, then stop.

At last he headed for the bathhouse and plunged through the curtain. She followed him in and pulled the light chain, thinking at last it was over. He huddled in a corner by the washing machine, his hands over his head, screaming, screaming, could no one else hear? She tried to comfort him, to explain, but she couldn't get her voice above his and he wouldn't let her near him. His strength was unimaginable as he forced her away, and quickly ran out again and looked up into the sky, circling round and round with his arms in the air, imploring it to stop. He ran more, and this time back to the front lawn above the bay, looking up all the time as though in disbelief, then doubled back, still eluding her reaching arms, to the fence by the road, screaming still.

"Go into the house," she kept calling, her own voice now raspy, but he seemed oblivious of her presence. Still she repeated, "Go into the house, into the house," and at last he turned and went through the back door, though she did not know whether by some inner signal or in answer to her command. Once inside, he ran the length of the hall, back and forth, as though in a cage, then into the big front room he fled and ran headlong into June, who was just coming through the door, spilling the drink from her hand and very nearly knocking her down. "What is this, you little—"

"Find Buzz!" Monica shouted to her and rushed out the door. Ian had doubled back, passing her by, and she caught him just at his shirt edge but still he could not be held, would not stop his screams, and she wished for anyone to come, but no one did, and the music, surely louder than ever, seemed to vibrate the very house as Ian hurled himself from room to room, arms waving above, then back up and down the length of the hall and outside again, trying to affirm the lights and the noise were still present, she knew; oh, God, please make them stop the things, turn them off, how many will they set? she wondered. How long will this go on? She called for Buzz herself, but no answer came, and each time another burst of color rent the sky she saw the terror repeated in Ian's eyes, and knew she herself had somehow betrayed him. At last he bolted back toward the house, the back door slamming behind him, and ran the length of the hall and, this time, right into the outstretched arms of Buzz.

He shouted, "No, no, no, no," as Buzz held him, and beat his fists against the face of the man who had befriended him, wriggling in his arms.

"It's all right. Look at me, Ian, look at me," he kept saying, but this seemed to make the boy all the more determined to flee. Monica rushed toward the record changer to turn off the music, and flung the arm off the record, scratching it across like a zipper tongue. By this time Ian had wriggled free again and fled down the hall, outside on the front lawn, Buzz quickly following. Monica stood at the door and folded her fist against her teeth as she watched her son race around, pounding against the fence by the fireworks, his body lit up, evading Buzz as he had evaded her, and she didn't know how to end it, didn't know how to stop the display in the sky. Hetty and Peggy, Carson and Aaron and all their friends were now standing by like a crowd of onwatchers after a freeway accident, gazing with morbid curiosity, the fireworks display forgotten in the face of a newer, more spectacular show.

Buzz signaled Monica to the end of the fence and, at last, they came from either end and closed in until both were upon him at once, crouching over him on the ground, fending off kicks and fists, and still the screaming went on, his face blood red from his own incredible straining.

In the end Buzz pinned his arms back and put a leg over both his, like a caretaker quieting a delirious patient in a psychiatric ward. He held his face with one hand and demanded, "Look here. Listen to me. Stop screaming!" Monica, not knowing why but moved by some instinctive force, slapped Ian full across the face. The smack was like the touch of a torch to her palm. Ian flung her a glance, his eyes monster wide for an instant, then glanced at Buzz again before he fell limp, his head, drenched with sweat, relaxing on the ground.

CHAPTER 32

The sky was ink black and still now.

Buzz had carried the semiconscious Ian into the house and laid him inside the crib. Both of them stood at length, holding the rail with all four hands, staring down at the stricken figure. Monica had never been so frightened, but anger surfaced above that. She thought of the screams that no one heard; the running that no one saw.

Where the hell were you and everybody else? She bit her lip. "I've never been so helpless. It was like a nightmare. I couldn't stop him, and no one . . ." Her voice drifted off. She gripped the rail harder.

"I saw Ian going down the pier, and you behind him. But I thought he just wanted to get somewhere to see better. I know how he darts around and I thought you were following to be sure he didn't fall off the pier. I never realized . . .

"The rest were like me. With all the noise and commotion, they just didn't understand."

Because most of them were half looped.

"I . . . I'm sorry."

"It wasn't your fault." This was a programmed reply. She didn't have the energy to say more, and certainly the blame did not rest with him.

Hetty was standing by now. "Don'tcha think we ought to get a doctor? There's one in Kemah if he's at home—"

Buzz reached into the crib and stroked Ian's forehead. Monica, who so far had not been able to let go the rail, thought it a kind, gentle thing to do. Something that she should have done. "What do you think, Monica? I could go into Kemah and check."

Her mind was going numb. She stood still gazing at her child as they awaited an answer. Then Ian opened his eyes. She touched his damp hair and said, "It's all right, Ian, Mommy's here." He rose slowly, confusedly, and sat back against the rail with his eyes fixed at a point across the room. He glanced down at the mirror in his hand, then back across the room again. "He'll be all right, I think," she said. "I should have known. Sometimes loud noises and—well, just leave me alone with him." Buzz and Hetty went back outside.

He had begun to rock. She leaned down over the crib and tried to pull him against her, but he wriggled free and in a moment his moist body, slightly trembling, fell back to rocking. She waved a hand in front of his eyes. They flickered. He pushed her hand down. She tried talking to him, tried to explain the fireworks would not have hurt him, but he ignored her words. At last he lay down and pulled his knees up against his stomach. She tugged at the chain on the ceiling light and left her hand on it, in case he should be frightened by the sudden darkness. He made no sound, no movement. She went back to him and followed his gaze. He seemed to be looking out the window, into the darkness. "See, it's all over now. Everything is all right." She glanced at the clock. Ten-thirty. The first fuse had been lit around nine o'clock. She heard music now from what seemed a great distance, soft and muted. Ian continued to stare out the window. She went to him and stroked his back until his eyes closed.

She began to hum a lullaby and tears smarted behind

her eyes. Not so far away, in the kitchen, she heard voices
and stopped to listen. June was telling Hetty, "That kid's
a real weirdo. He nearly knocked me down, and he
spilled my drink all over the front of my dress. Now I'll
have to stop by the house and change. We'll be late to the
Harrison party." She paused. "Do you think we ought to
let Clark play with him?"

Had it been someone else, Hetty might not have been
so inclined to speak in Ian's behalf. However, June's
opinion on most matters was immediately suspect. "The
child was frightened, that's all. Nothing wrong with him
that a little time and patience wouldn't cure . . . not that
you would know anything about that."

Monica heard the taps open, and the click of high heels
across the kitchen floor. A door slammed. She resumed
her humming, and thought all at once of a child who'd
been in her class at school when she was very young,
six or seven. She could not recall his name. He was
taller than the rest, and his head was too large for his
body. He had a hooked nose and little beady eyes and a
strange, off-center smile. His hair was blond, nearly
white. Everyone feared him. Behind his back they made
jokes about him, sang rhymes with ugly words that she
could not remember. What had been his name? His
mother had come to the school now and then to bring
something he'd forgotten, and would lean over his shoulders and kiss him. Monica was revolted and wondered
how a mother could love so horrible a creature.

She laid her head against the rail and let the tears
come. What had become of him? What had become of all
the youngsters, all through school, who were different,
out of place, feared because they were not understood
and called cruel names to make them go away? Were
they now geniuses, working in science laboratories, or

heading big corporations like the one for which Forrest worked? Or were they locked away, isolated from the rest of the world, convinced of their difference, refusing to cast themselves into the mold the world imposed upon them?

Weirdo . . .

She looked at Ian again. Please, God . . .

At last she rose and left the room, satisfied that Ian was asleep. She heard the parting phrases of Carson and his friends. She waited until they'd gone around the side of the house and through the back gate, and heard the thud of the car doors closing and the crunch of tires on the drive. Then she went out on the patio. Aaron and his group had taken their radio and a lantern flashlight, and gone back down to the pier. She looked toward the remains of the fireworks, but could see nothing. Apparently everything had been cleaned up. Perhaps the entire evening had been a horrid nightmare.

She sat down on a lawn chair, next to Hetty. The breeze was cool on her face and neck, but her legs felt sticky against the cushion. She felt very much alone. She thought of Forrest, so far away, working. Always, when trouble came, he was away. Damn him.

She heard the clink of ice in a glass. "Here, you look like you need this." It was Buzz. She looked up into his smiling, if uncertain, face. "I'll say one thing for my brother Carson. He buys good bourbon. And he left half a bottle behind."

"He also left Clark behind," Hetty added.

Monica took a sip of the drink and closed her eyes. She was exhausted, yet every nerve was taut, every muscle poised in readiness to spring into action should the nightmare start again. She tried to remember anything which could have caused Ian's alarm over so harmless an event as a fireworks display, but the only thing she could imagine was the isolation which had been imposed on him through most of his lifetime. To him perhaps the noise, the bursting colors, had been more stimulation than he was ready for, and if so, that was her fault.

Buzz and Hetty were chatting softly about the subject. Buzz remembered being put on a kiddie train in an amusement park as a kid, and screaming bloody murder until they took him off. He recalled it was the noise of the engine that scared him. But he was too young to know how to say so.

"But as soon as we realized, Bert took you right off," Hetty quickly reminded him.

Buzz lit up a cigarette and they all sat silently again. Peggy had gone to bed right after Clark. The party next door had adjourned to the interior of the house. The moon was the only light above the bay water again, more beautiful in its simplicity than all the fireworks which obliterated it. Fireworks. She thought some more, and it occurred to her maybe that French doctor she'd read about was right. He swore the bright lights and cold probes suffered by a baby at birth in the delivery room were harmful to its emotional health. When she first read his statement, she thought him a nut. Maybe, though, he was smarter than she thought. Maybe the trauma of bright lights at Ian's birth had affected him in some bizarre way unknown to any of them. Maybe she ought to contact someone about it, ask questions, get material on the possible effects of after-birth shock and how to deal with them.

She was too tired to think, but her mind wouldn't stop.

Maybe the fever. . . . No. Remember what Dr. Winters said. And even the counselor at the OB clinic said significant brain damage would probably be indicated at birth.

Probably . . .

She finished her drink. Buzz offered to fetch a refill. She handed him her glass and looked up at the expression on his face which said, *I am here*. Hetty told him to poke his head inside the door of Ian's room, to be sure he was all right. The door yawned open, then quietly closed. Monica shut her eyes and let the cares pull away like water from the shore at ebb tide.

CHAPTER 33

Ian had never been more afraid. Even his efforts at pretending sleep just now had tried him more than ever before. Keeping his body still when in his head were still the burstings and explosions had been an act of supreme will. He lay there, tensely conscious of the beginnings of pain all through his arms and legs and shoulders, and waited until the house was completely quiet. Even long after Monica left, he heard a door open and close, and knew the approach of someone. He kept his eyes tightly shut. He waited some more. He heard the clinking of glass and ice together from the kitchen, then heard the door open and shut again. At last he rose, and began to rock.

If he kept his eyes open, the explosions would stop inside his head. But he still would not know if the others had succeeded. Never able to outguess them because their methods and aims had no pattern, he would not have suspected they would go to the ends they had on this night. Not destroy his home . . . maybe, even, the whole sky. His home did not have time to move away as it did when thunder and lightning and rain came. This time he saw them aim for it and smash it to bits with their weapons.

What was there now? If only he could climb out of the crib. He looked down, and was seized with dizziness. He lay back and swallowed, and rocked some more.

Were they afraid that, if they did not destroy his home, he would somehow get back? And if so, why? Had he done something lately that showed them he was close to the answer, without knowing it himself? He thought and thought, but no answer came.

If only he could get to the window and find out if they had succeeded.

Maybe it was something about time passing. He thought back to the day Buzz showed him the calendar. He had wondered about September then, but forgot it when Buzz went on to tell about other things that seemed more important. But just now it occurred to him that Monica spoke to the teachers about September, and also to Forrest. Maybe that was how it all fit into place. Maybe September would be soon, and the others must carry out their plans for him by the time that page was on top of the others on the calendar. Yes. That seemed right. Time did matter. The others measured all things by time. If only he could see the calendar again and find September.

He was a prisoner of his crib. Why could he not overcome the fear, just this once?

He was breathing very hard now. He would have to figure a way, but how? Now he was alone. Now he knew that, even as he had believed in Buzz and trusted him, it was clear Buzz was one of the others. He had been a part of the destruction of the sky. He had held him down and made him look into his eyes, while Monica struck him on the face. He felt a tear slip from his eye, for now, without Buzz, there was no one.

He rocked, and wrung his hands.

If he was right about September, why had they acted tonight? This could not be September because Forrest was not back. Maybe this was only a testing of their weapons, and not real. Maybe the real attack on his sky was to be practiced and practiced.

If this was true, he had to gather all his strength and organize his thoughts. He could never be sure when someone would turn the calendar page and September would appear. And what then? Did they plan destruction of his world because they could not learn from him its secrets? Or did they keep him here because they feared he would warn those of his kind? For warn them he would; he was certain in his place he would be understood, that the language would be what he carried inside his head and not what came out when mixed with sound. In his world all was peaceful and consistent, and warm and soft. If they planned to destroy his world and feared only that he would warn those of his kind, then their studies of him might be to find out how he could get back so that they could use the same means to get there. Yes, that seemed right. His home was far away. Surely it would be easier to destroy it if they could come close to it.

September . . . September. How long till September?

For whatever time was left him he must be very careful. He must be quiet and do as they told him as much as he could, in order to trick them into believing he had given up any plan to get back.

He lay down flat on his back and looked up. Everything depended upon his hope that tonight had been practice, that nothing would really happen until September. But how could he know? They were not people of patterns, like him. Their movements and actions were erratic. He rose and gripped the rails. He shoved a foot down between them and tried to touch the dark space under the crib.

He could feel nothing. He imagined himself leaving the crib and falling endlessly through space with no borders. He let go the rails. He swallowed hard and moved back toward the wall. He rocked. What was out there? Perhaps everything he knew was gone. His breathing was shallow. He whimpered.

No one heard.

CHAPTER 34

Eleven o'clock. By now Monica sat alone on the patio, sipping her third bourbon and soda and looking out at the beautiful moon, a confirmation that the horrors of this night were but the product of a child's imagination. The sky, the bay, the whole dark cloak of night in front of her had never seemed so beautiful. Even the stars seemed brighter than usual.

She half rose to go in and awaken Ian, and bring him

out to see. But then, coming outside might only frighten him more, and he'd already been through so much. He surely needed the deep sleep he fell into tonight. She shouldn't disturb it. There would be other nights like this.

Finally, sometime after midnight, she stole into the room where Ian slept. He looked peaceful, his buttocks hiked up as though nothing had ever happened, his hands folded under him, clutching, she knew, his mirror. She almost smiled, then felt a lump rise in her throat. She stroked his cheek. It felt dank. He hadn't even had a bath.

She lay gingerly across the chenille spread on the nearby bed, trying not to make the springs groan. Impossible. Ian lay undisturbed, however. As soon as her body relaxed, she slept too. Her dreams were as bizarre as the evening had been. She and Buzz were out in the boat with Ian, in the throes of a sudden squall. The boat pitched around, waves crashing over it with avalanche force. And all at once she realized they were not in the peaceful bay but in the turbulent North Sea. She kept thinking, we'll never get out of here, there's no way to go, no way to shore. She was pitched by the wind up toward the starboard, with Aaron and his three friends. All of them were shoved up against one another like sardines in a tin, while at the other end, Ian sat alone, his arms gripping the bench to steady himself. He had, instead of a frightened look, a peaceful, almost impish grin across his face. From somewhere in the distance she could hear June's voice saying, "You did this, Ian, you did it. Let's throw him over. Throw him over." And, as though in answer to the entreaty, the others turned to Ian and began to move toward him, their faces set, their voices chanting, "Throw him over, throw him over." Fighting the wind, her shoes slipping under her feet, she held them back with both arms, and said, "No, you can't touch him be-

cause he isn't the same," and they oozed back like bone-
less bodies. She found her way, step by step, through the
smashing waves which threatened with each moment to
capsize the craft, to the other end. It was a most lengthy
journey, although even in the dream she was aware he
was but a few steps away. At times she could not see his
face for the water washing over it. When she finally approached him she grabbed his arms and looked into his
face, to try and speak to him over the noise of the
waves and wind. But it was his face no longer. It was the
face of the boy in her childhood classroom whose name
she could not remember. He flashed her an off-center
smile.

Abruptly she awoke. She sat straight up in the bed.

The day was dawning. Her whole body ached. The
pieces of her dream clashed together like cymbals in her
head, then tumbled into place, each detail becoming
clear. When she reached the point that Ian was no longer
Ian, she looked over at him quickly in his crib, for assurance. He lay on his back now, arms and feet outspread,
his light blanket wrapped around one leg and bunched
against the railing. She was not sure, but thought he had
awakened and rocked intermittently through the hours
she had slept. But then again, maybe it was another
dream running simultaneously with the first, or coming
before or after. She put her hands over her eyes and tried
to clear her head; even while wide awake, she was in a
state of total exhaustion.

Her skin felt gummy and she had a dull headache. She
wanted nothing more at that moment than a hot shower
and some strong coffee. She carefully rose from the bed,
aware again of the noisy springs—surely they could be
heard throughout the cottage—and grabbed a fresh pair
of shorts and a shirt and underwear from her bags in the

corner. She tiptoed into the quiet kitchen to put on the coffee. She pulled the light chain. There was no sign whatever of all the dishevelment of yesterday and last night. Everything had been put away. From the looks of the counters, floor, stove, and cabinets, Hetty spent the better part of the night scrubbing down the kitchen like a sailor scrubs down a deck.

The breeze felt cool and welcome against her as she left the house and headed for the shower. She stood under it for a full five minutes and just let it soak her hair and body. The water had never felt so good; nor had the soap, gliding smoothly over her limbs. Finally, the whole bathhouse steamy, she reached through the shower curtain and grabbed her towel. She could never do this without glancing toward the opening of the bathhouse where the light curtain fluttered.

Nothing, surely nothing, could be so refreshing as this ritual. Had she the opportunity, she would do it every day; it would be addictive for her, like jogging to others more energetic. The house remained silent as she carried her coffee to the patio and sat down to dry her hair. A gray morning, this one; there would probably be no sun to brighten it. The sky above the still water was just a shade lighter than the bay itself. The hulk of a tanker sat out there far away, like a great beached whale, the only interruption to the horizontal line dividing water and sky.

She looked up and threw her hair back. There seemed to be movement at the end of the pier, partly concealed by the boathouse. She narrowed her eyes. Someone was down there at the end, pacing. Now she could make out the long legs in cutoffs. Buzz.

She fluffed her hair and watched him briefly, considering. He usually had coffee on the patio with her. Why was he down there alone? He might blame himself for what happened on the previous night. He had taken such delight in showing Clark and Ian all the fireworks before they were catapulted into action. She threw the towel down, parted her hair and combed through it, then walked down the pier toward him. Again she was aware of the coolness of the breeze, of the good feeling of clean hair and skin as she walked. He saw her halfway down, and smiled. "You feelin' better this morning?"

"Considerably."

He shoved his hands in his pockets and looked out at the bay. She thought of his sudden appearance at the door when Ian was in a panic last night, his arms outstretched toward her child. She told him about the bizarre dream. Curiously, he played no part in it past the fact that she knew he was there. Even more curious, this seemed to bother him.

"It fits sure 'nough; I wasn't much help last night either."

She stared at him; she wouldn't have expected him to take her dream and connect it with reality, not a person like Buzz. "Listen, you don't owe me any apologies. I'm grateful for what you did." Then she remembered something else. "I slapped him; right across the face. I never thought I'd do a thing like that. Oh, now I wonder how much damage I did to him last night. Poor little—"

He slipped an arm around her shoulders and pulled her close. "You followed yer instincts. He was hysterical. Sometimes a slap is exactly the right thing. Brings a person to his senses."

He kept holding her, looking out at the bay. The water sloshed around the pilings. She felt uncomfortable suddenly, but would not move away. She had to speak, to break the awkwardness. "Anyhow, thanks for what you did. If not for you, I don't know . . ."

He didn't answer or complete the sentence for her. Had

he called Forrest a bastard for abandoning his family, she would have been put on the defensive and could have pulled away from him and begun to explain that was not right, that Forrest had needs too. But he didn't. Why did he not let her go? Why did she not pull away? But she could not. This moment held more comfort than she had known in months, years. Now was the time to tell him about Ian, the whole struggle of the doctors and teachers, the label being bandied about and whispered on the breaths of the "experts," all of it. "Maybe it was a mistake, coming down here," she began. She was referring to the whole summer, but when he interrupted her, she realized he hadn't understood.

"No," he said. "I'm glad you did. Don't go now."

He clutched her more tightly, and she remained stockstill, afraid to think, afraid even to take a breath. He should have taken his arm away, if not earlier, surely now. She ought to pull free of his clutch. Yet neither did as they should because, somehow, they could not seem to fight the pull. It was then she felt his chest swell as though in resignation, or decision, and they looked at each other. He took her face in one hand and kissed her, first gently, then harder, both hands pressing against her cheeks.

When it was over she stared at him and felt a flood of realization that what she only half allowed herself to suspect was true. But in the same instant his expression said: I shouldn't have. He released her, clumsily, like you might shimmy out of a sweater you find scratchy against your skin. "I'm sorry. I had no right." He looked out at the bay again.

She did not dare speak. She turned around and took quick, jerky steps up the length of the pier, her thoughts no more in line than her feet.

CHAPTER 35

Back in the bedroom across from where Ian slept, she stretched out on the end of the bed and tried to put things in order, but they wouldn't come. Whatever people said about modern marriage and changing partners, of bed hopping and all the rest, what happened just then was no casual exchange. Her ears were pounding with excitement, her breath shallow and uneven. What's happening to me? she wondered. And it frightened her that she was not in control any longer and, further, had no wish to be.

Oh no, this wasn't right.

She grasped the end of the footboard with both hands and took in gulps of air. Only a kiss, a source of needed comfort. Yet, more than that, because it came from Buzz. With someone else it might have had little or no meaning, a moment stolen in the kitchen during a cocktail party when everyone was heady with liquor, that would later be forgotten, dismissed.

But with Buzz, a moment off guard would be costly; an irreparable tear in the closely woven fabric of his morals. He was not like the other men who'd thrown off the strictures long ago. He'd been busy for years putting them back together. Maturing.

Poor Buzz. She turned on her back. A soft breeze through the window cooled her face. She felt better.

She'd have to get away, that was the only solution, the obvious climax to the summer whose purpose had somehow been changed to one of fulfilling her own needs, rather than Ian's. She did not want to be strong against the halting advances of Buzz, did not want to dissuade him, and that was the dangerous part. She knew she might not be able to; knew she would probably not even try. Yes, get away. Leave today and do not return. She heard the crib groan and Ian arise, and was soon lulled into sleep by his rhythmic rocking.

She awoke at eleven, feeling drugged. Someone, Hetty no doubt, had pulled the spread up from the footboard and draped it across her. Ian was gone from his crib. His pajamas lay in a clump in the center. Out on the patio she found them all. Ian was spinning the wheels of an overturned wagon, bursting now and then into gales of laughter when Clark applied a stick like a brake to the motion. Hetty noticed Monica's look of astonishment. "See there, what did I tell you? Those two will get along." She folded her hands and looked on with satisfaction, then leaned forward to adjust a couple of hairpins in the back of her head.

Monica walked over to Ian and took him in her arms. "You had a fright last night. Okay now?"

He pulled away and began to skip up and down the fence, catching the sun with his mirror. Monica told Hetty, "I was up earlier, then . . . then, went back to bed." She looked for a change in Hetty's expression. There was none. "I thought we were in for a poor day, but I guess not," she added, yawning.

"Oh, sometimes that old sun is just tardy about showing up. You know what Ian did when I got him out of the crib? He tore out straight for the yard, looked up, and started flashing that mirror around. And laugh—and clap his hands—you've never seen anything like it. Oh, was that child happy! I had a time getting him back inside to get him dressed."

"Thanks, Hetty. I'm amazed he'd let anybody but me get that near him in the morning. Usually he's—"

"Fiddlesticks. He knows I'll take care of him. He's not nearly as shy of me as he used to be. Time Forrest gets back in September, he'll be a different child altogether."

Ian looked quickly toward them, paused, then returned to his playing. Monica sat down, too exhausted to argue or even speculate. Besides, Hetty might be right. Now, in light of Ian's improvement, how could Monica explain why they wouldn't be coming to the bay anymore? She almost wished Ian hadn't bounced back so quickly from his ordeal of the previous evening. As a matter of fact, it almost seemed to have had a positive effect on him.

Buzz was coming up the pier now, toting a plastic sack full of beer cans and trash left on the boat by Aaron and his party. "I ought to skin Aaron alive for leavin' such a mess," said Hetty. "I'm still washing beach towels this morning. I'll bet you he doesn't leave that kind of mess for Alyson's mother to clean up when he stays at her house. If Bert could see . . . But then, at least nothing serious happened last night and I'm thankful for that. For some reason, I couldn't fight off my worry. I'm kinda glad it's all over for another year."

"Oh dear, I've slept through all the cleaning up," Monica exclaimed.

"It's all right, hon. You did more than your share of the work yesterday, and after what happened last night, you needed the rest. I cleaned up a little last night before I went to bed, and Peggy helped me this morning."

"Where is Peggy now?"

"Taking a nap. She really tires easily these days. Buzz

says she dozes off right after supper nearly every night. Poor little thing. I'll be glad when that baby comes." She sighed. "But I still don't believe they ought to do one of those Cesarean sections and take it before its time. I'm not so big and I delivered one ten-pound baby—Carson."

"Ten pounds?"

"Lacking an ounce or two. Time he came, I needed a wheelbarrow to carry my stomach around. I was in labor fourteen hours with him."

She was proud of this, proud of having done it all on her own. Ian had come in sixteen hours, the last five or six excruciating labor, but Monica didn't mention it now. Hetty continued: "Well, I'll say one thing. At least she's not going in for any of that natural childbirth business where the father stands by and helps deliver the baby. Buzz ruled that out even before they knew it would be a 'C' section. That's a bunch of malarkey." She shut her mouth then, and Monica knew what was on her mind.

"Forrest wasn't there either, in the delivery room," she assured her, and let the subject drop. Actually they had considered natural childbirth, but neither of them had time to attend the classes beforehand. Later she was a little sorry. She had never spoken of her regret because she was afraid it might make him feel inadequate. That, if anything, was the strongest bond between them and the only one she truly understood: build up Forrest, at all costs.

She spent the afternoon indecisive about her plans, taking care to avoid Buzz and not daring to look direct into Peggy's sweet, trusting face. Hetty insisted they all stay for dinner before driving back and Monica thought, as they sat down at the table, now is the time to tell them I won't be coming back. But then her determination dissolved as she listened to Hetty brag about Ian's behavior throughout the day. It was clear she took great pride in what had been accomplished. Finally she said, "I think last night was a big turning point for Ian, because it showed him how concerned we were when we realized what a state he was in.

"Why, by this time next year he'll probably be right here among us watching when the fireworks go off. Maybe we'll take our turn, though I think it's really supposed to be handled by the Gantleys next year. Well, anyhow, next year it'll be better.

"You'll know there's nothing to be afraid of, won't you?" she asked him.

He looked up, but did not smile.

"Don't push so fast, Mom," said Buzz. "He may not be quite ready for this subject."

Monica used the cue. "I'm getting a little behind in my studio. I may not be able to come back for a few weeks, until I get caught up. My work has to be done by early fall, and I lost a full week while Forrest was here."

She knew that Buzz was watching her from across the table. Hetty said, "Well, don't wait too long. Before you know it, the summer will be over."

"Yes . . . I'll be in touch." She excused herself and went to pack their bags. While endeavoring to make more room in Ian's case for the clothes Hetty had washed that morning, she was surprised to find two objects that did not belong: the small, windup clock from the big front room, and a picture calendar she'd seen on a wall near the television. She sat back on her heels. Ian, of course. But what would he want with these? What if this were the beginning of a new pattern for him, a whole new string of problems?

She wasn't sure whether to confront him, or just replace

the items and let him discover them missing, and watch his reaction. She decided on the latter.

She looked around to catch Ian watching her. He made no move to stop her or object. His look gave her the eerie feeling it was she who'd committed the misdemeanor and he had caught her in the act.

Monica involved herself totally in work for the next three weeks and did not go to the bay. She had in fact spoken honestly: she was behind in her work and somehow the Fourth of July marked a turning point because she realized she had but a few weeks left to complete two thirds of her portfolio. On weekends she asked Dixie to care for Ian, so that she could spend Saturdays and Sundays in her studio.

Ian seemed different. Just how, she could not say. He seemed more watchful, less involved in his own little world, though he was wakeful through much of the night, rocking and spinning the bubble. To Dixie he reacted first with a look of puzzlement, then a kind of resignation. In fact, that was the confusing aspect of his behavior: part puzzlement, part languidness, and yet all the while, watchfulness. Erica Thomas was (thankfully) on vacation, and though the substitute may have been taking notes on Ian's behavior at school to pass on to Erica, she didn't bother Monica. Dr. Michaels called once, but she made up an excuse for his secretary. "I'm just leaving. I'll call him this evening." She didn't return the call.

She thought Ian might fear another fireworks display, or maybe was only befuddled by the change in routine. She explained to him that her work kept them home and he responded with his usual detachment.

Most puzzling of all through this period: he was more cooperative. He seemed to be trying to reach forth, even while he stayed within himself. She would have been delighted if this were the only change in his behavior, but with all the other changes, she could only shake her head and wonder because none of it was quite . . . quite. She decided much of what she observed was brought on by her own imagination, her reaction to the dreadful night of the Fourth. Paranoia.

Letters from Forrest (now less frequent) became more and more slanted toward the prospect of moving to London: "Housing is atrocious here, but the chief has given me some tips and I think we can make do. We can lease a fairly nice home not too far from the office, and there is a good school nearby for Ian."

Another letter: "I think Ian will have a good life here. It's safer than in Houston—very low crime rate by comparison—and when he is old enough he could walk to school or catch the bus, and you wouldn't have to worry about anything happening to him."

On and on he wrote, as though everything about Ian were perfectly normal, that at five he'd be ready for kindergarten, and even without the ability to adjust to life in his own back yard, he'd do fine in another country, a different culture, among a different kind of people, though not a great deal different. Maybe distance allowed Forrest to fool himself. She could never tell exactly what he was thinking, even when he was near.

His smoothing over everything as though it didn't exist grated on her nerves, and his failure to even mention what might happen to her own career made her angry. Now and then he made mention of certain social clubs for wives of Americans living abroad. She hated social clubs and he knew it. She was tempted to double-check and be sure the letters were addressed to her. Often as not she crumpled them and threw them in the trash.

CHAPTER 36

Near the end of July, Peggy's child was born, some two to three weeks earlier than the doctor's planned Cesarean section. Peggy went into labor one night, and delivered a boy weighing less than five pounds in the wee hours of the following morning. The labor, lasting between four and five hours, was difficult in itself, and made no easier by the fact that Peggy was frightened. When Hetty called to relay the news to Monica, she added, "The poor child suffered so. The baby just isn't strong. It's his lungs. But they're watching him closely, and if he makes it through the next twenty-four hours . . . It's such a sight. They've got him hooked up to all those tubes and machines, you know, and he's jaundiced—yellow as an Eagle pencil."

Monica spoke to her encouragingly. Nearly five pounds. She'd known babies to survive at less than four. And jaundice was common. Yet, in her own mind she saw the poor gnarled infant attached to all the machinery and wondered if a baby remembered such an ordeal. Surely not. She remembered the fear in Peggy's face too, that morning when they chatted about the baby, the instinctive fear that everything was not right.

"Let me jot down her room number," she said finally, and after saying goodbye called a florist and ordered flowers. She realized suddenly that she'd be expected to

visit Peggy at the hospital. Or would she? The flowers
would have to suffice.

She had not left the telephone bench before the phone
rang again, startling her. She grabbed the receiver. Buzz,
on the other end, was without his usual cockiness. His
voice sounded nasal and faraway. It was the first time he
had ever called her on the telephone. "Just wanted you to
know. Little Bert's here."

Little Bert, of course. Number what? Three? Four? "So
I heard. Your mother called. Congratulations. You sound
tired."

"Yeah. Been up since six yesterday morning. I—" he
said, then paused.

"Buzz, I know it has been rough. I'm sure he'll be—"

"I've hardly seen him," he interrupted. He paused
again; his uncertainty was so unlike him. Buzz should
have been the proud father of a healthy son. Offering ci-
gars. Spouting off about how big and tough the kid was.
How he'd have him swimming by next summer. None of
this seemed right, not like something that would happen
to a Wellman. She wanted to comfort him, but didn't
know how.

"Buzz, are you still at the hospital?"

"Yeah."

She hesitated, and phrased her suggestion very carefully so that he would not mistake her idea. "Let me fix
you something to eat. I'll have it ready when you get
here. If you had something in your stomach you could go
home and rest more easily. . . ." She let her voice trail
off, not sure how he'd react.

Long pause. "No . . . I couldn't . . . do that."

Did you misinterpret my meaning after all? Why did
you call me? "All right. But do stop for something to eat,

then go straight home and rest. You'll feel better for it. Hetty will be there, won't she?"

"Yeah. Mom, and Peggy's mother, both of them are here."

Oh, I see. "Well then, go on home and rest. I'll be thinking of . . . all of you."

He hung up. She felt so badly for him. He had helped her so much, and now, when he needed help, possibly without even knowing he needed it, she could not provide it. Had he never kissed her, she could have helped him more today, as she wanted to, as a friend. Now her hands were tied. It seemed so senseless. She went back to her studio and picked up the brush. She kept seeing him there, in the phone booth, his eyes heavy from lack of sleep, his heart aching because in his mind he had failed, and there was no one to tell it to.

After a full week both Peggy and the child were released from the hospital. They wouldn't be coming to the bay for a while, explained Hetty. They needed to be near the medical center. "I'm going down myself this weekend, with Clark. Won't you and Ian come?"

"Oh, I don't know, I—"

"Please. June and Carson left to go scuba diving for a week, and Clark's happiest down at the bay. It's gonna be lonely down there for me."

"All right then, sure."

As they turned onto the shell drive and saw Hetty waiting at the fence, her whistle catching the sun and making a beam against her pink shirt, Monica knew she'd done the right thing. She did not look forward to the weekend, but realized she owed Hetty more than a favor, even if imposing on her hospitality was a strange way of paying it. She knew the talk would center on the baby and Peggy's ordeal and all other subjects uppermost in Hetty's mind, none of which Monica cared to hear about. She braced herself to listen attentively and sympathetically.

It was well she did. From the time they unloaded the car Hetty talked fast and nervously, and called Peggy several times a day to check on the baby and offer a bead or two from her lengthy string of advice. "You worry too much," Monica told her once. "They wouldn't have sent . . . Bert . . . home if he were in any danger, would they?" Without meaning to, she often paused before saying the name. Somehow it just didn't seem to connect in the long line of Wellmans.

"I suppose not," she said with a sigh, but kept up her round of calls just the same. After one such conversation with Peggy, Hetty looked across at Monica guiltily, then said, "It might surprise you to know that when you and your sister Jane were born, I did exactly the same thing. And the two of you were healthy as could be. Guess I'm just a natural worrier." Then she leaned back and said, "I know I'll be accused of interfering. Half the time when I call it's Peggy's mother who answers." She laughed. "I think it just eats up Roberta to have to report what's going on over there. She was a private duty nurse for thirty-five years, you know." Then she drew up her shoulders. "But she'll only be here a little while, and if Peggy needs help after she's gone, I'm the one who'll have to go in there and fill her shoes. It's only fair to Peggy that I know exactly what's going on, so I won't walk in cold turkey."

Early Sunday morning it began to rain—the first time since early June—and through the day the showers pelted harder and harder. Lightning pierced the sky and thunder rumbled. Around three o'clock, Hetty turned on the shortwave radio to get the weather forecast. It was the fourth time that day she had done so. The report was punctuated by a frustrating amount of static. Part of the Gulf Freeway was under water now and rain was predicted through the night. "Maybe you and Ian ought to stay over till tomorrow," she urged.

"Oh, I couldn't," Monica said quickly. Ian seemed to be growing more and more excited and energetic as the storm continued, probably from being pent up in the small cottage. He flitted from room to room, looking out the windows, in the process cutting through the center of Clark's toys and games which lined the floors, and bringing on one angry protest after another. Monica, losing patience, wondered how long it would be before Ian lost his fascination for thunder and lightning. It seemed he had always been this way and she still had no idea why.

She'd hoped to wait out the rain before leaving, but it was apparent now she'd been unwise. She had no idea what they might run into on the return trip, and her journey would be especially tricky in her little sports car. Could her nerves have held out, she might have stayed. But she'd had all she could tolerate of dealing with Ian and listening to Hetty.

"If I didn't have to drive back to Houston myself in the morning, to keep a doctor's appointment, I'd have you take my sedan," Hetty told her, frowning. "Your little car wasn't built for driving through this kind of weather. I wish you'd change your mind. I just don't feel right about—"

"No, really I can't." She threw their things together and loaded the car. Ian was given graham crackers to occupy him for at least part of the trip home. By three-thirty she had everything ready and packed. She came back, under the protection of an umbrella, for her handbag and keys. Ian was waiting by the door. She searched her bag. The keys were not there. "Oh, damn." She looked at Ian. "Did you take Mommy's keys?" He looked away. Experience had taught her that losing patience at these times was self-defeating. He would become panicky and unable to show her where the keys were. If she kept calm, sometimes he would eventually lead her to them. She took him by the shoulders and explained. "You and Mommy have to go back home before the rain gets worse. Now, did you take Mommy's keys and put them away somewhere? Tell me, and when I find them we will go. We'll come back to see Hetty and Clark another day. Soon. Now, where are my keys?"

He lifted the chenille bedspread and pulled out the keys. She let out a long breath. "All right. Let's go." She picked him up and bade Hetty goodbye, then raised the umbrella again and made her way to the car. Ian wouldn't hold on to her neck, and wriggled around as he continued to watch the weather as best he could. It was impossible to keep him dry. It was like toting a big smacking fish across the yard.

They headed down the shell road in a blinding downpour, punctuated every few moments by more lightning. Each crack of thunder brought Ian to the edge of his car seat. He craned his neck to see the lightning. Well, at least he'll be occupied, she thought.

She clutched the wheel tightly and concentrated only on the road, now and again switching lanes to avoid low, water-filled places, and a couple of times to bypass cars which were stalled, their red taillights blinking to ward off collision from behind.

The drive from the bay to their house was normally an hour and a quarter in length, but past five o'clock they were just nearing the southeast end of town, with still another half hour of driving in front of them. Cars would be bumper to bumper now. The freeway ahead was a slow-moving conveyor belt of taillights. At least, however, the storm was over and the sun was breaking through. She relaxed her fingers on the wheel, only then aware of how tightly she'd gripped it. Her hands ached. Rain was still falling, but at a much slower rate now, the finale. The sky was turning violet in contrast. Normally she'd be edging into depression at this hour, but today the reverse in weather brightened her spirits.

She looked off to the left and there, as though by magic, was the most vivid rainbow she had ever seen. Each of its colors was well defined and brilliant. Her first reaction was to wish she could capture it on canvas. Then she caught herself. "Look, Ian, a rainbow! Look there, coming out of the sky. See?"

He looked. His eyes widened. For several moments he stared intently. Then, with the suddenness of an air raid, he threw out his arms and began to scream.

"What is it? Ian, control yourself. What the hell—Ian, my God!" She put a restraining arm across him, while trying to steer through the thickening stream of traffic. He was squirming and throwing his fists, kicking, and screaming at the top of his lungs, trying to free himself. If not for the car-seat belt, he would have gone through the windshield. As usual, unprepared for his sudden outburst, she soon found herself screaming back. Still, he could not be controlled. He wriggled and cried out, pitched and kicked. At last she pulled the car off to the side of the road and spanked his legs hard with her hand. She was so overwhelmed by the whole episode, coming as it did on top of a grueling and slow trip along a dangerous highway, she hit him more times than she should have. She hit him again and again, her hand prints appearing in a glow on his thighs, until at last she realized he was no longer wriggling to get out but begging her to stop. His eyes were stricken with terror. "No, no, no, no!" he cried.

She leaned back and took several gulps of air; his breathing was fast and shallow. He was holding his thighs. She put a hand to her forehead and looked around. In a car nosing slowly down the lane alongside them sat a man and woman, gaping at her and talking, their expressions frowns of indictment. God. They probably think I'm a child abuser, she thought. And maybe they are right. I'm no more in control than my child. What's happening to me? She turned to Ian and tried to make him look at her. His face was locked against his shoulder. She was seized with a desperate need to make him understand, as though a measure to keep this from happening again would somehow make up for her own loss of control. She grabbed his shoulders. "Ian, you must not do that to me while I'm driving. You could have caused us to have a wreck. We could have been killed. Don't you see?"

He looked straight ahead, limp now and lethargic. Still, she was determined to drive her point home. "That means *the end. No more.*" How explain the peril of death to a child less than four, even if he has brought himself close to it time and time again? She'd never taken him to church, never introduced the concept of God and heaven. Anyhow, she wanted to impress him with the danger, not the Sunday-school ritual which she had trouble grasping herself. "Dead means buried in the ground. Never to be anymore. That's what you could bring us to, if you don't learn to control yourself. Do you understand?" She couldn't seem to stop trying to impress him. Now and then, for part of the way home, she'd find herself telling

him something more, different words with the same meaning and sometimes even the same words.

He rode in silence. Her spirits took another reverse
turn. She finally withdrew into silence herself.

CHAPTER 37

Buried. The word echoed in Ian's head. Under the
ground. All chance for ever getting back gone forever.
All chance gone even to see the sky. She had said the
word on the day he tried to reach the sky from the balcony of the seventh floor. And now she had said it again.
More than once. And she was just as upset now as then.
She must use that word when it seemed he was getting
close to the way of escape, to frighten him into giving up.

All this day he had watched the cracks in the sky, to
see if another ball would come out; yet it had not happened. Even though the lightning and thunder lasted
longer than ever, not another ball had fallen through. He
had been more and more disappointed, for as he realized
Buzz was one of the others, and not one of his kind, he
had hoped another might come and be with him, and he
would not be alone anymore.

But then a miracle came. He would have seen it even if
she had not shown him. She called it a rainbow. That, he
felt certain, was to confuse him as to its real meaning.

The others had words for all the things familiar to him, and he accepted them in his head because they were all different parts of his home and it was all right for them to have separate names. He even understood their two names of sun and moon for his ball because it did look different from day to night. But calling the lines of color that reached all the way from the sky to the ground a "rainbow" was beyond his understanding. Rain was not colored; a bow was something groups of the children learned to make at school. What he had seen was a bridge of colors sent down for him to use as a walkway back home. But as soon as she used her force against him and hurt him, it was taken back. By the time he dared raise himself up and look again, it was gone and she was driving the car again. Would another come? He did not know. He believed now that, as time passed and September came near, those in his world were trying as hard to come for him as he was trying to get to them.

It made him feel better to know that his first and main theory was correct. There was a connection between the spinning colored balls and his home. The colors of the balls were all repeated in the bridge toward his home. The answer must lie in them. He would study them more. But how much time did he have? Since the night they used their fireworks against his home, many changes had taken place. The number of days and nights between trips to the bay had changed. Buzz had not come again. Monica watched him more closely. The others must be making plans quickly now. Their patterns always became more erratic when change was about to happen.

Maybe another bridge would be sent for him at a time when he could reach it. Meanwhile, he would study. He put a hand over his leg. The red place left by her hand felt hot, and stung. He was frightened. It seemed that here in this world he had always been frightened. Before leaving his own world he had never been frightened except for the time of the great heat.

It seemed to him now that the great heat had not lasted very long, and his own natural home provided an escape from it through peaceful sleep. Here it was different: there seemed to be no escape from his fears, nor any end to them.

CHAPTER 38

Not until they reached home and she began to unload the car did Monica notice her handbag was missing. How could she have left it? Oh yes, the keys. She'd spent the last few minutes looking for the keys, and in the process, eager to get home, she'd forgotten to go back for it. Her driver's license, credit cards, money, everything, were back at the cottage. She fought down anger at Ian. When they were in the house she called Hetty. "Keep the bag there and leave your extra house key in its usual place. I'll come down tomorrow and pick it up, and maybe stay around and do some work right there. Now that the weather has cleared it ought to be ideal."

Hetty happily agreed. She was always flattered when Monica painted at the cottage.

By Monday morning the sun shone bright, and except

for the numerous pools of water along the streets and the glistening grass and trees, there was little evidence of the flooding torrents of yesterday. She left Ian at the center, feeling a bit guilty about going to the bay without him.

Around ten o'clock she pulled into the shell alley, and when she reached the Wellman garage her heart quickened. Buzz's car was there. At the sound of her car he peeked out the garage door, wiping his hands. He looked surprised to see her, but otherwise appeared as the normal Buzz: cutoffs, barefooted and shirtless. He'd been working on the boat motor.

"Didn't Hetty tell you I was coming down?" she began hurriedly. "Left my handbag yesterday."

"I haven't talked to Mom," he confessed. "Our place is like a hen house right now, with the new baby plus Peggy's mother around. I took some vacation days to help out, but I've been informed my presence is not necessary." He spat out his words as usual, but she detected his injured feelings. He was looking through the car window at her, and now opened the door. "Come on out. You in a hurry? I've got some coffee inside; not that it tastes anything like yours, but it's drinkable."

She felt awkward, and didn't want to stay. But it was too late. He spied her gear in the back seat. "Oh, then you were gonna stay?"

"I—I just brought it along in case. But I really ought to work in my studio. It's more convenient." The lie was no more effective than the curtain at the door of the bathhouse had been.

"Don't be silly. You always said you like to paint here. I won't get in your way. I'll be out here in the garage most of the day. Somethin' wrong with the damned electrical system on the boat. Fer God's sake, it's nine years old. What we ought to do is chuck the thing and buy a new one. If I wasn't so damned attached to it . . ."

He carried her gear across the yard. It was possible he saw the opportunity to prove to her they could mend what had happened, spend a few hours in each other's company, more or less, with nothing coming of it. The whole thing might blow away what now hung like a spider web between them. And in such a nice, Wellman-like way.

When he had set her things in the back she said, "I understand . . . Bert . . . the third is doing fine now."

"That's right. He still has some trouble with those lungs, but time should take care of that, accordin' to the doctor at least. He ought to be fully healthy . . . or at least, the chances are better than before."

Why do you keep qualifying it? "That's good. I'm glad."

"I think the best thing for him would be to bring him down here, where the air's a little cleaner. But my opinions don't seem to be in demand right now." For a few moments he seemed about to say something more. Then suddenly he turned and went back to the garage. She followed him with her eyes till he was out of sight, wondering why he continued to hold back from revealing his feelings, just as he had on the telephone that day.

At last she shook her head, and tried to concentrate on her work. She was beginning the last of the paintings due the gallery in Dallas: one of the three different oils from photos she took deep in the woody trails of the Houston Arboretum. It had not gone well. In fact, she wasn't very pleased with any of the group. Lately all her work seemed stale, and she wasn't sure whether it was because of the continuing problems in her home life or the limit in her ability as an artist.

Andrew James had written recently and asked her to send some things to his gallery in San Francisco: an excellent chance of new exposure for her work. Yet she could send him nothing. He'd take no pride in her growth as an artist since he left Houston. He'd never accept anything she had done so far. . . .

Each stroke of her brush was like a stab of chastisement. I do the same things over and over again. My work shows no imagination. I do what is safe, what I know I can sell. And the great challenges are always the ones I wind up putting away: the portrait of my father, the portrait of Ian, and now the pier; experimental forms I want to try but put aside over and over again, and anything else that isn't safe. . . .

I have no courage, I—

She heard the back gate open; one moment, two, passed; she heard the wire rings on the bathhouse curtain screech across the rod. A clanking noise, a thud. Then nothing. Then the gate closing.

It had taken her a while to get focused on her work, and then to become disenchanted with herself and slide into self-pity. And now she was back where she began. She listened for sounds coming from the garage. She listened for the sound of another car in the alley and noted that, except for her and Buzz, the community of Baynook seemed to be a ghost town. Hetty had told her that only on weekends was it alive. Today proved she wasn't exaggerating. Monica thought that she should pack up and leave now. She wasn't getting anywhere. She just had stared at the unfinished picture in front of her, half the time not seeing it. If she left now it would be such a good, sweeping acknowledgment that the moment on the pier . . . one kiss . . . was not taken seriously. Here we are, Buzz, alone together and acting like buddies, no more in-

terested in each other than we were all those years ago
. . . at least no more interested in each other than you
were in me. And just to prove it, I'm leaving. Have a good
day. No, don't bother. I can carry all these things myself.
See ya. Say hi to—

The gate again. Why the hell does my pulse do triple
time whenever you come within twenty yards?

"One o'clock."

In spite of herself, she jerked.

"Whoops. Sorry, lady. I didn't mean to scare ya. You
want a hamburger?"

"What? Oh, yes. I could go and get them, if you're too
busy."

"Nah. If I stay in that garage any longer I'll go blind
from the bad lighting. There's a greasy spoon cafe down
the road. I'll be back."

He walked off, whistling. She listened for the gate to
open and shut, then for the car to start and cross the shell
and rumble off. And she continued to stare at the picture,
thinking of nothing but the return of Buzz and listening
for it. She didn't want a hamburger. She could hardly
swallow, let alone eat a hamburger. Why was she too
mesmerized to say "no, thanks"? It was like being caught
in a giant wave at Galveston Beach. It swelled higher and
higher; you could see it, feel it coming nearer and growing bigger, stronger, and then it overpowered you, en-
gulfed and took you with it, and didn't let go till at last it
broke in a surging shower of white and left you on the
shore. . . .

When she finally heard the car again, she steadied herself and thought, I can still leave. I can work through
lunch, or make a pretense of working, then get out of here
by, say, two. Two is a nice round number, a good time of
day to leave for Houston. . . .

"Nothin' doin'. Mother doesn't approve of people working through lunch around here. And she may not be with us today, but her spirit stalks the place, wearin' her whistle. Come on, we'll sit down at the end of the pier. You need a break."

The breeze caught her laugh and carried it away. "All right." *You're daring me now, just like when we were kids playing rough in the water. Buzz the ringleader, dunking people, swimming under and coming up suddenly from behind in one great lunge. Splash, spatter, glug, gotcha last! How I waited, half with fright, half eagerly, for you to choose to pick on me while Jane, bored with the game, climbed lazily up the ladder with her prissy behind (you watched that part), and sunned her lovely self on the pier, her nose upturned. . . .*

Once they were at the end of the pier and he dug into the sacks, she realized eating hamburgers in the lusty breeze would be awkward in itself. Her hair came loose from its knot and blew in her face, and the water was too high for her to put her feet over the edge, so she moved from one position to another, trying to get comfortable, keep the hair out of her eyes, and anchor down the food he was handing over.

He was watching her. A smile played at the edge of his mouth. Barefoot, he had already put his legs over the side. "Take off yer shoes and put yer feet in the water," he demanded. "Go on, you think the water's gonna bite?"

"You're right." *Don't tease. It is your teasing that gets me still.* The water slipped warm and smooth over her feet and up to her shins. *Say something. Anything. To show you're casual, at ease.* "At times like these I'm tempted to cut off my hair. It's a darned nuisance." She bit into the hamburger and several strands of hair as well.

He went on watching her. She continued to eat, pretending not to notice. Finally he said, "It's good to see you chowin' down on that hamburger. If you get any skinnier, you'll blow off the pier."

"Thanks a lot."

"I didn't mean to hurt your feelings."

"Well, if you had my problems, you wouldn't have much appetite—" she began, then remembered Buzz had a few problems of his own.

"What? You mean, Ian? Why do you make such a big deal over him anyway? You let a buncha people tell you what he ought to be doin' at his age, I'll bet. You read some books. Why, there's nothing wrong with him that time won't take care of. Just like Bert. All those women fussin' around him. I can't even go near him without somebody tells me I'm holdin' him wrong, or I need to wash my hands. This morning I decided, to hell with it."

Forrest did not want to touch and feel. He stood back and watched.

Buzz took a bite of hamburger and looked out toward the bay. His face was set, yet he seemed less determined than ever. Still she could not think of words to lend him support, or bring him up from the sudden descent in his spirits. After a while he said, "He's a cute little fella. I just wish I knew why he came into the world so puny. Maybe somethin' I—"

"Listen, you may never know. And one day when he's all grown up you'll ask yourself why you let it eat away at you." That's the way it is with Ian. That's the way I hope it is with Ian.

He smiled at her. "That's a pretty big piece of philosophy coming from you."

"It's always easier to see when you're on the outside, as you well know."

He was quiet for a while, then said, "Why'd you quit coming down here for all those years?"

"Forrest. Don't tell your mother that; she wouldn't understand. But he never could see how special it was here, and I guess I was too wrapped up in his life to bother to come without him . . . till this summer. I never realized you noticed my absence, though."

"I didn't very much, not till you came back. What's gonna happen after this summer?"

"I . . . I don't know exactly. We may move to England for a year or two."

"Oh? Is that what you want to do?"

"It doesn't seem to be a question of what I 'want to do.' Or even Forrest. It's more a matter of what Amalgamated wants us to do."

He laughed. "And all this time I thought people like Forrest and Carson went after what they wanted and got it, and the rest of us just sat around and wished for what they had.

"Not that I do. I mean, money can't buy everything."

"That's true."

He picked up a pebble from the pier and threw it into the water. His voice grew a little deeper. "I just wish to hell you hadn't come down here this summer and now that you _are_ here I wish the damned summer wouldn't ever be over with because I count the days in between seeing you, and each one seems longer than the one before."

This was a big admission for him. He was looking at her expectantly. She took in a breath and looked away. "I think of you all the time. When I ought to be thinking about Ian . . . when my mind ought to be on my work . . . I'm thinking of you and wondering if you feel the same or if I'm crazy, or just . . . foolish. . . ." Why is it so quiet? Surely even the breeze has quit blowing. Oh Lord, what do we do now that it's all out? Something happen. Anything.

Presently he moved closer. She felt his hand close over hers, warm and safe. He turned her face toward him and kissed her, and in her mind she pleaded with him not to stop this time.

He released her slowly and stood up. His fine legs were apart, like those of a sentinel. "We shouldn't have been here together today." It was like that day in the boat. The wind blew his hair.

She looked up at him, and shaded her eyes. "I know."

"You know how much I've wanted you, right from the first night."

"Yes."

"Stay with me now, for a while longer."

She nodded.

He took her arm and helped her rise. Their separate reflections in the water below moved closer, almost into one, then floated alongside them, back up the long pier toward the cottage.

CHAPTER 39

He was a gentle man, more patient and loving than she'd known a man could be, and she had to keep telling herself from the start that, however much they meant to each other, September would inevitably come, and with it the return of Forrest, the closing of the bay house, and every other possible terminating factor that could be brought to bear on two people who wanted and needed each other but had no rights to their desires.

Their days together followed one on another like the planks of the pier, reaching farther and farther out into the sea. Sometimes upon arriving on a weekday morning she'd pause to look at the quiet cottage, unassuming and plain, more a place of solace than she could ever have dreamed. And now it seemed as though the years away were but a short interlude in the fabric of her life, that they were for only one purpose: to bring her back. She shut out all thoughts of the days going by. As though all of life had turned in reverse, it was now the weekends which interrupted her time at the bay. She arrived at the gate as breathlessly as though she'd run the distance from Houston to Baynook. And when she was there with Buzz, it was much like the total involvement she had once found only in her painting: nothing else mattered; nothing else existed.

Peggy's mother stayed on; the baby made only halting progress; Buzz took more vacation—there was a lot due him; he had fifteen years at the company—and Hetty, since Clark's real father had paid him a surprise visit and taken him off to the Rockies camping, stayed at home in Houston. She knew that Buzz was going down two or three times a week, and each time had a list of chores ready for him to jot down over the phone. At first he and Monica kept to their separate rituals of working in the morning, awaiting eagerly the afternoon hours that would be theirs. Gradually, as Monica's work wound to a finish, the separate sessions became shorter; the hours together longer, spinning themselves into the late afternoon when she would rush back to get Ian from the center before closing time.

She could not get enough of Buzz, could not wait until he appeared at the edge of the cottage, signaling her to come in, the touch of his hand, the feel of his body enfolding hers. This was safety as she had never known it, never dared believe she needed until now. They did not speak of the child consigned to endless trips back and forth to the medical center, or of the other child, consigned to a world of his own making, because it was their escape into each other that gave them comfort. When they lay quietly next to each other, watching the hands of the clock ticking relentlessly by, they talked of each other.

The interest in her work he expressed at the beginning of summer was genuine. He liked to listen to her talk about what she had done and how she felt about it, where she thought her weaknesses lay, where her strengths. It seemed no one since her days in art class so long ago had cared to know these things, and she let them out in rushes, not having ever known how good it was to talk about what she so naturally kept to herself.

Once they talked of hands. She had done endless sketches of hands—one of the first features she noticed about people. Transferring hands to canvas was difficult; many artists never mastered that skill; it was like a separate talent unto its own.

Buzz held up his hands in front of him. "I've got my dad's hands."

She took one and held it, felt of it. So many times she'd watched his hands in motion: performing chores outside the cottage, steering the boat around the bay, gently holding Ian as he taught him to enjoy the water, reaching out to clasp her hands . . . "They're nice. Long, and slender for a man. Mine are too knobby, like my elbows and knees. Forrest gets provoked because usually there is paint underneath my fingernails instead of enamel on top of them."

He looked at them both at length. Finally he said, "Nothin' wrong with hands showing good, honest work."

"Forrest doesn't look upon painting as good, honest work. He wants my hands to reflect *his* good, honest work," she said lightly.

He raised up above her and smiled. Then he kissed her. This was the way all discussions ended that touched on Forrest or, now and then, Peggy. She might have complained of Forrest more, but Buzz was not the sort to minimize their wrong by diminishing their spouses. He would be taken only for what he was, and she understood this and loved him the more for it.

She wanted to make him understand just how much of a human being he was, however, how much untapped potential lay in the man who'd spent fifteen years behind a desk shuffling papers from point A to point B. She was sincere in the things she told him and meant no harm. He listened thoughtfully but did not answer.

One day she confessed her childhood longing that he choose her to pick on while playing in the bay water, rather than Jane. She watched the playful look come into his eyes.

"Get dressed."

"What?"

"Get dressed. We're goin' swimming."

"But I don't have my swimsuit."

"Take yer choice. I'll take you down there either in your shorts or your birthday suit."

"You idiot! Wait a minute. Hold on now . . . okay, okay!"

So they had gone, though she protested all the way, and in the water he seemed bent on making up for all the energies wasted on the pretty girl with the turned-up nose. Splash, spatter, glug, gotcha last! They laughed and played like children, until she was sure she'd swallowed half of the water in the bay. Then they sunned upon the pier. Later they took a long ride in the boat. This was one of the days she loved best, in a succession of days that were better than any she'd ever known in her life. For the first time, she felt she had a claim on the place she had always loved.

One morning she began her trip to the bay under an uncertain sky. By the time she turned off the freeway, the rain had begun. Slowing down, she began to think of Forrest, thoughts generally reserved for sleepless nights. For however cold she now realized he was, he was loyal. More, he had a certain disdain for catting around. It gave one an appearance of irresponsibility. And things like that mattered to him because they mattered to his peers, mattered more, even, than her opinion. Leave her he might, but carry on an illicit affair, probably not.

Her hands were tight on the wheel as she finally turned on the shell drive, heart thumping, afraid Buzz wouldn't be there because of the weather. But his car was in its usual place. She opened the door and made a dash for the back porch. The door unlocked, she rushed in and called to him.

"Oh, I was so afraid you wouldn't be here," she panted, hugging him. He was unusually silent. He helped her off with her wet clothes. His silence made her apprehensive. "Buzz, do you think anyone down here knows what's going on?"

"Nah. Not on weekdays. No one comes down regularly except on weekends."

But passersby would see her easel, and, if they were nosy, might notice two of the same cars that had been there all summer on weekends were now there during the week. "We could meet at my house." She'd told him that before.

"No, I couldn't do that."

The bay was his place. Her home belonged half to someone else, as did his with Peggy. On principle, he would not have her with him in either. He was helping her with her shoes. She raised his face in her hands. "What's the matter, is something wrong? Anything happened? The baby?"

"No. Everything is the same as it was. Nothin' new."

In the shadows of the room his face was dark, and sad. She kissed him. She knew what was needed to make everything all right, to make all the dragons flee, and leave them safe. "Make love to me."

From outside, the Wellman place seemed unchanged. The boat was tied at the end of the pier, bobbing to the swell of water beneath and tugging gently at its rope. The cottage rose above the drenched lawn, a square with eyes cut in all four directions. Only the voices inside the cottage were different. "This is wrong, not fair for either of us or for the others," said his.

"Do you mean you want it to stop?" She had a tight grip on a corner of the sheet.

"No. Doin' what I want to do just takes some getting used to, that's all," he said, but the words were faint and without conviction. Louder was the voice of guilt. A lengthy pause, then: "I don't care. I won't give you up."

Monica thought Buzz recognized the obvious ending to be September. She, who had been forced to face the com-

ing of fall for months, was now simply blotting it out for
as long as she could. Yet it seemed that day had an odd
note of finality about it and she stayed longer than usual,
not wanting to let him go, and was fifteen minutes late
picking up Ian. She wondered if the assistant teacher in
charge noticed anything in her face. She wondered the
same thing of Ian and spoke to him all the way home
with forced animation. He gazed out the window, silently.

CHAPTER 40

On a Tuesday shortly after, Monica answered the doorbell to see a huge bouquet of long-stemmed red roses hiding the face of a delivery boy. "Oh—thank you," she stam-
mered. Till that moment, she had forgotten this was her
birthday. The card was signed, "With love, from Forrest."
He always sent roses, on her birthday, on their anniver-
sary. He was punctilious about this, or rather, his secretary was advised to be. She kept the dates marked on her
calendar, so the roses came automatically, as though
punched out by computer, even now, while he was overseas. Monica could call his secretary here to tell her they'd
arrived, and ask if Forrest reminded her to send them, and
the secretary would become reticent and awkward (it
had happened once before), attempting diplomacy, to

keep from saying, "No, I did it on my own, Mrs. Maguire."

She placed the flowers in the living room, not in her studio where their odor would leave a funereal stench in the room. While cupping one to smell its fragrance—just for the sake of form, so she could write Forrest about it— she pricked her finger with a thorn. She looked at the spot of blood rising like a bubble from the flesh, and felt a sudden urge to cry. The flowers seemed to epitomize the state of their marriage from the beginning: one of empty form. Being so far from home, he might at least have taken the time to call and wish her many happy returns. But he wouldn't because he wouldn't remember anything special about the day.

A question she'd come close to asking him while he was visiting in July welled up again: what do I mean to you, Forrest? Why did you find me attractive; why did you marry me?

It seemed almost unbelievable that all these years later she would not know. She remembered, after they began to date, his telling her, "Honest, Monica, when I first met you I dreaded the moment you found out what my father was like." She had assured him at the time she did not believe in the old saw "Like father, like son." Was that simple statement what stirred his feelings for her? Not a very healthy beginning, unless something else could be built from it, something deeper and far more meaningful. Yet the only thing that seemed to have grown between them was habit.

She grew more and more angry with him as she worked through the afternoon, even while she knew she had no right in the face of what she was doing to him. Still, she had to commit infidelity to find out what she ought to have known at home: warmth and love and, most of all, a sense of need and of being needed. Oh, how snide he would be with her for her involvement with Buzz. "That joker? You're kidding me. Hard times, eh?" Never letting on how badly he was hurting from having come in second place.

She remembered then the jealousy he'd harbored against, of all people, Andrew James, before they married. She had not realized then how strange of him not to come right out with it, but to wait until he sniffed out some weakness in the man that allowed disdain. She asked herself for the hundredth time why she could not see all those years ago that she was marrying a man cut from his father's cloth. The only thing he lacked was the old man's confidence. So he waited till he had a peer opinion to back him up. Then: "To have someone tell me James was a fag. Of course, I'd always figured that. . . ."

She shrugged, her burst of anger spent. She would never confess the summer to Forrest, regardless of how many years went by. Not because she feared his wrath, but because she couldn't bear his look of disdain. She was more than ever determined to make the most of every moment left to her and Buzz. For the sake of Ian, she thought she would stay married to Forrest and somehow force him into developing a relationship with his son. These final weeks of summer might be her only chance of happiness, then, and she would take them.

The afternoon was drawing to a close. Her strokes were beginning to show her negative mood, and so she stopped. She closed the studio door and picked up her handbag and keys. She was always glad for the diversion this time of day of picking up Ian. She was long into the habit of forcing a cheerful face for him in hopes it would help to draw him out, and also fool the teachers at the center that all was going well with her son.

Buzz extended his vacation through Labor Day weekend. Monica was thrilled but asked anxiously, "You don't think it will look . . . funny?"

"Nope. I get six weeks a year, and I've done this once or twice before. And Peggy and I won't be taking any trips all this year because of the baby."

You haven't called him Bert lately. "And what about Peggy's mother?"

"Who knows? She keeps staying. Peggy won't tell her to go. She'd never tell her mother that, and anyhow, the old lady has her convinced that she's the only one who can handle the baby until they say he's all right for sure."

"They" is such a big word, thought Monica.

He paused and laughed. "Mom hardly comes over there either. She's mad enough to chew nails. But I guess you know that."

"No. I haven't talked to her."

"Well, she's always talkin' to your mom, telling her all about it, so I just figured—"

"I . . . my mother and I don't speak very often."

"Oh, why not?"

"Something that happened a long time ago. And actually it has turned out pretty convenient. At least she stays out of my business."

"Boy, there's a helluva lot to be said for that."

One day near the end of August, Peggy's mother surprised everyone by packing up and leaving. The baby was considered out of danger, and the woman had a telegram from Alabama that her brother had taken ill. Buzz explained it over the telephone. "When will I see you?" she asked him.

"I don't know. Listen, I gotta go now."

Her hand was numb as she replaced the receiver. She had known all along that time was running out for them, but somehow the way he put it, so bluntly, cruelly almost, she was stunned. Just like that. No tearful farewell, goodbye kiss, nothing to seal it, to say it mattered. Not a day together again to conclude what had begun nearly six weeks earlier at the bay.

She went around the kitchen banging cabinet doors as she prepared supper. Well, it was for the best, and what more could she have expected? Forrest was due home in a couple of weeks. In the small square compartment where Ian's change of clothing was kept at the center, she'd found a mimeographed note that morning: For all parents, conferences regarding the new school year would begin the week following Labor Day. Please sign up for a time period convenient for you. . . .

The summer was gone, lost forever. Ian was not the child she predicted he would be by this time. The center would now insist they find another place for him and, considering the results of all his tests, would "suggest" some kind of institutional therapy. And Forrest would return, ready to whisk them off to London anyway.

And Buzz. She and Buzz would not even have a chance to say goodbye. She kept going over his words, "Listen, I gotta go." Not "I'll miss you till we get something worked out," or "I didn't mean for it to happen this way, and I'll never get over you, but we both knew. . . ."

Maybe, just maybe, he had only used her after all. For all the support she felt they brought each other, maybe he was really the same old Buzz from childhood, unchanged, laughing when she was not around, playing jokes, making another date with someone else for after the ball.

She sat down. Her line of thinking was, she knew, the merest form of childishness. The only thing to suffer damage through all this was her own pride, and she could survive that. The thing to do was face facts: her husband did not care for her, though he felt an obligation toward her and toward his son. She'd reached out, first in desperation for her child's welfare and then for herself, to the hand of a man she trusted.

She looked at Ian, skipping about the den, stopping now and then to glance at the television before skipping off again. This whole summer had been plotted and planned for his benefit, yet he had gained least of all, not because he wasn't capable of changing but because she had made some big mistakes on his behalf and, as was her nature, had become more involved in herself than in his needs. Since the first time Buzz kissed her on the end of the pier, she had let worries about Ian flutter off in the breeze. It was too bad Ian could not have been blessed with a father possessing some of Buzz's better qualities. But that was life.

She remembered something Dr. Michaels had told her about a boy's failure to develop a relationship with his father, about the ways in which his emotional growth was crippled. And he had added to an insulted Forrest that in the case of divorced parents the child gets along because he is not confused about his relationship to a parent who is *there*, but *not* there. Assuming, then, that her own prenatal fever, which had haunted her for so long, had nothing to do with Ian's predicament, and that his problem was one of identification with his father, she was brought to a decision that day. It seemed so simple she could not imagine why it had not occurred to her before. Forrest could go to London if he liked, and obviously that was in the future, but he would go without her and without Ian. He had already written her of the tons of work to be done both in London and Aberdeen in the coming years, and of the tough job assignment awaiting him should "things work out." So it would be an uprooting of Ian, a move to a new and totally different world, and still, through it all, with a father who had no time for him. Maybe within the two years Forrest was gone she could turn Ian into a child who had the confidence necessary to deal with an exacting father, one who expected his son to be brilliant. One strikingly like Professor Maguire.

She would take Ian out of the center, out of preschool altogether, and hire someone—maybe Dixie, maybe someone else—to care for him. She would buy some self-help books and learn how to help him with what he needed to know before he went to kindergarten. For until he was five, or even six, she did not have to worry about how he got along with others.

She thought back, trying to remember why it had seemed so important to get him into a day care situation. Loneliness. That was it. She had sensed his loneliness. Well, being surrounded by kids hadn't helped. Maybe Ian had to find a friend in his own way, someone with as different a view of the things around him as he had. Likely, there were not many kids in the world like Ian, so maybe he would always be something of a loner.

In the final analysis, she had to admit Forrest was probably right in some ways. Surely in two years she could have him ready for the things he must face. Why the rush to pit him against other children now?

Her decision made, she felt more confident than she had in a long while. Let Forrest try to argue her out of it. She would stand firm. And truly, she didn't believe he'd fight her very hard.

Through the evening her thoughts remained objective. She had known from the beginning there was nothing of lasting value for her and Buzz Wellman; and that he felt the same and, as far as she knew, still did: the conservative family man on a busman's holiday. She was by nature a loner; she would survive the loss of a man whose caring had seemed born of no ultimate design, only honest need and loneliness. She would take the summer for what it was worth, and relinquish it all.

Yet in the night she could not fight down the tears. She had known her affair would end but she wanted him to be equally hurt by the predicament; she wanted him to care as much as she did, to miss her as much as she missed him now, to go through the rest of life having known a special kind of love that comes only once and stays with you forever, even after the hurt is over. She did not want to be dismissed by a blank, dull voice over the telephone. She wanted more than anything to be reassured what she feared was not true: that what she had given was never fully returned.

By morning she had reached another decision about what the future held. She would be the first to speak of breaking off. She did not know how she could reach Buzz in order to tell him, and that was the hell of it. They were both left dangling by a woman's sudden decision to depart with her suitcases for Alabama. Before noon, Hetty called.

"I'm going down to the bay on Wednesday, taking Clark—his father left him with me two days ago. I've already talked Peggy and Buzz into bringing little Bert down. The child is six weeks old and has never been outside the house. So why don't you and Ian come? At least let Ian have a good time for the last visit. Then he'll look forward to coming down next year. You know how bad the weather was last time."

"Oh, I don't know . . . I'd feel in the way. I—" she faltered, for this was not in her plan. Certainly she didn't want to see Buzz again, only talk to him by phone.

"Well, I wish you would come on. Call me if you change your mind."

Hetty had agreed with her so readily . . . probably didn't want the chaos of so many people in the small cottage at once, and only called out of kindness. The presence of an infant was enough confusion itself. Bottles, diapers, schedules, crying. It made dealing with others difficult and awkward.

Through the next day or so Monica stayed busy. She'd been commissioned to do an oil painting of a restored hotel in Cherokee County, to hang in the lobby. She was to work from a dozen old photographs of the original building along with color guides researched by the local librarian. She had received them in the morning mail, registered and insured. She was looking them over when the phone rang on Thursday morning. Hetty again. This time more insistent, even though her voice was low and mournful, a harbinger with downturned mouth and grieving eyes. In fact, she sounded as though something terrible had happened. Monica listened for mention of the baby. However, Hetty said only, "I want you to come on down this weekend. It would mean a lot to me. Now that I'm here . . . well, it would just mean an awful lot, that's all."

Does Buzz know you're calling me?

She almost declined again, but was afraid that might seem a bit peculiar, might lead to suspicion. "I'll be there, but I think Ian and I will just come down for a day. Peggy will need the crib anyhow and I'm not sure Ian will take to the bed so easily." *Maybe I can take Buzz aside just long enough to tell him to call me from Houston next week. Otherwise I'll keep my distance.*

"Suit yourself. I'll expect you then, on Saturday morning."

Not ten minutes after that conversation, the phone rang again. She picked up the receiver, half hoping it would be Buzz. "Long distance, London." An operator's voice. Then the voice of Forrest, low, barely audible.

"Listen, honey, the chief has had a heart attack. He died this morning."

"Oh, Forrest, I'm sorry."

"Yeah. Two years from retirement. A damned shame."

Why had he called her? It was the first time he'd called all summer long. "Did you need something done here? Are they bringing his body back?"

"Yes, but not to Houston. He's from Baltimore. I've already called the office to arrange for flowers from us, and all that." He paused.

What then? "Well, I'm awfully sorry. What can I do?"

"I don't know. I just wanted to hear your voice."

Oh hell, I can't think of anything to say.

"Monica, I don't know what's going to happen to me now."

Oh, now I see. "What do you mean?"

"I may be coming home . . . for good. Now with the chief gone, I'm not sure anymore. His position is kind of up for grabs. There's probably going to be a power play. You know how big companies are, divided into factions like political parties."

"Yes." You've been licking the wrong butt, in other words.

"Well, that's all. I'll be in touch. I just wanted you to know."

"Well . . . hang in there, darling." What else can I say?

"Yeah, that pretty well sums it up. Bye now."

Static. A click. Oh, and since you forgot to ask, Ian is fine. I am fine. You are about to throw our lives into another cartwheel. Oh, how I hope you get that job over there and don't come home. Now that I had it all worked out. . . .

The conversation stayed with her. She went over it and over it in the next couple of days. While her immediate response had been anger, she had soon felt sorry for him. Why was it that sympathy was the only feeling he could ever awaken in her anymore? If Forrest were struck a blow, she winced with pain, if not immediately, at least upon reflection. Why was it, hard as he tried, and brilliant as he was, things always seemed to go wrong for him? Why did he insist upon riding the chief's coattails up the corporate ladder, when he could have done it on his own? Why did he always believe he had to please someone in order to succeed?

His father, of course. Since Forrest could not please him, he could never believe he was good enough unless he pleased someone who filled the professor's slot. And he was passing this legacy right along to his own son. No wonder he couldn't see how badly he was handling Ian. He could not see the mistakes he was making on his own behalf.

"I wanted to hear your voice," he said on the phone. This phrase haunted her night and day. Why couldn't she have picked up on it? Said something more? She could have said, "Honey, it doesn't matter. We'll make out, whatever you decide to do. We're behind you, a hundred percent." But she hadn't. She was too involved with trying to work around him and make some sensible plan for herself and for Ian.

She wondered, as she drove down to the bay on Saturday, whether life was nothing but a series of manipulations, destiny a matter of someone else's whim. Lucky Ian. She looked across at his meditative face. No worries, no cares. As long as nobody got in his way, he was happy.

Cross him and he let you know right quick. Surely no one was more in control of his situation than Ian. Autonomous . . . autonomous. . . . Autistic. Oh no, that wasn't what she meant. She wanted to pull back the ugly train of thought, but it was gone, out of her reach, hurrying toward its own endless destination. . . .

CHAPTER 41

Monica turned down the shell drive. Hetty was not at the gate today. Her car was parked alongside Buzz's blue coupe, proving they were all here. Yet the place had an odd, deserted air about it, already showing signs that the season was drawing to a close, at least for her, for she knew she would not be coming back. Ever.

This place would accept no further claims on it from her in the future. She sat and looked at it for a while, before stepping out of the car. The breeze rustled the little puny tree near the walk between the house and bathhouse, and caught the flimsy bathhouse curtain, ballooning it out, then letting it fall, catching it still again, then letting it go. The lawn was neatly trimmed; the back porch swept clean, the windows gleaming brightly. How she loved it all.

There had been a time, long ago—she'd forgotten till now—when her parents had the chance to buy a property down the way. There was a cottage on it, smaller than the Wellman house, that needed renovation. Her mother began drawing plans to fix up the kitchen, add an extra room. In the end, of course, there was no money to buy the property or fix up the house. Not for the first time, the savings had been spent elsewhere. Her mother's catchphrase that seemed to epitomize her whole life came back to Monica now: "I didn't know it would be so expensive. . . ."

She sniffed and got out of the car. Her stomach was in knots.

About the time they were rounding the cottage, she heard the sound of a whirring motor. She could see the Wellman boat, cutting out across the water. Buzz was sailing alone. She greeted all the faces on the patio at once.

"You need some help unloading?" Hetty asked.

"No, we didn't bring much today."

"Help yourself to iced tea in the kitchen."

"In a minute." She sat down. Ian, as was his custom, left her and skipped to the fence line. Before stopping he would make his way all around it, then settle on a place at the edge of the yard, and run up and down, flashing his mirror. Peggy sat in a chaise holding the tiny new baby. There were dark patches under her eyes. Her long hair was pulled back with a blue ribbon in an apparent attempt to look cheerful. She smiled at Monica. Clark was hovering nearby like a proud uncle. "Want me to give him his bottle? It's almost time, isn't it? Can I show him my 'lectric train?"

"After a little," she said gently to the boy, then to Monica, "Would you like to hold Bert?"

She did not want to, had always felt awkward holding babies. But it seemed unkind to refuse. The past few weeks of the summer had not left her without pangs of remorse for Peggy, but she had told herself time and again that Peggy would not suffer for what she and Buzz had together because she would not know; nor was she being robbed of her husband. In the end he would come back to her and stay. In fact, she thought suddenly, reaching out her arms, it was six weeks now, time for a husband's return to the mother of his child. Maybe I was answering but one very basic need for Buzz.

Baby Bert was tinier than she expected. He was wrapped tightly in a yellow blanket. He looked like a yellow rosebud, unopened. She lifted a corner of the blanket to see his face. He didn't look six weeks old, as best she could recall from her limited experience with infants. His face was still pinched and red. She had been right. He was surely uncomfortable in her arms, yet he didn't cry. He squinted his eyes and opened his mouth slightly. His breathing sounded like a small bellows, groaning. She did not envy Peggy her place as a new mother; she would not have wanted to be in that place again.

She noticed then Ian was standing not far away, looking. Hetty saw this too. "Come here, child," she demanded, and pulled him forward so that he could have a closer look at Bert. Monica brought the yellow bundle near.

"See the baby, Ian? Isn't he tiny and sweet? Look how little his fingers are." She unfolded the baby's fist and showed him. He's getting something, she thought. Something is registering. Maybe if I can hold his interest long enough—

Suddenly, the baby cried out in a nasal whimper. "Time to eat," said Peggy, rising. But Hetty was ahead, disappearing in the house to fetch the bottle. Shortly she returned, tested the temperature of the milk on her wrist, handed the bottle to Peggy, and began to expound on her experience with Buzz, Carson, and Aaron during their respective infanthoods.

Monica watched Peggy's face. It was clear she endured this lecture only to avoid hurting Hetty's feelings. She was a good person. How inconvenient it must have been at this point, packing bags, toting all the paraphernalia required for a baby down to the bay. She wished above all things at that moment she could tell her: Peggy, I bear you no ill.

She felt hemmed in now, sorry she had come. She noticed Clark following Ian around the yard. It seemed he would never give up for good. "Hey, my mommy brought me a new truck. You wanna see it, huh? Hey, guess where I'm going next month. Astroworld! Bet you haven't been there." On and on he droned, switching from one subject to another. Ian paid him no attention, kept a few steps ahead of him all the time. Once she had resented Clark's prattling and bragging, but that was another of the things that had changed over the summer. She thought of the painting she intended to do, of the pier with the boat tied to it at dawn. It was not finished. She had not worked on it for weeks. She thought she might finish it still, as soon as she finished the Cherokee Hotel painting. Too bad, though; it would have been nice . . . fitting . . . to present it to Hetty today.

Finally, lunch. Buzz was seated with them, uncharacteristically silent. Hetty broke the tension. She raised her eyebrows. "Next weekend is Labor Day. Monica, you and Ian ought to come on down. It'll be one more chance before—"

"I don't think so. Forrest might be home by then." She glanced quickly at Buzz, whose expression held something inscrutable. She looked away. Her head was begin-

ning to ache. She put a pimiento cheese sandwich and
some potato chips on Ian's plate. He retaliated by chewing up a bite and spitting it out on the table beside his
plate. Monica punished him by denying him a brownie
for dessert, which in turn led to a stem-winder tantrum.
To keep the peace and avoid awakening the now sleeping
baby, she gave in. Ian placed the square brownie in the
center of his plate, edging all the crumbs off the dish and
onto the table. He smoothed a finger across its surface,
then smelled it. Then he turned the plate so that the
brownie was at a diamond angle, and looked at it some
more. He would not eat it.

She couldn't understand why he was behaving particularly bad on this day, and wondered whether the tension
at the table was the cause. Always before, the talk had
flowed, the bantering and kidding of Buzz bridging all
the gaps. Hetty would bring up something that happened
long ago at the bay, and they'd talk about it. Peggy
couldn't join in, but always listened with enthusiasm.
Today was different. At last chairs slid back on the linoleum floor; the table was cleared. Buzz excused himself
and mumbled something about the boat. Peggy, yawning,
headed out to the patio for a nap on the chaise.

"You go on, honey," Hetty assured her. "Monica and I
can clean up the kitchen."

Monica usually washed dishes because Hetty could dry
and replace things in the cupboard with the quick hand
of familiarity. Both young boys had disappeared. Monica
thought nothing of this at the time. She stole quietly into
the crib room to put her watch and rings in her handbag
—today she was making doubly sure not to leave anything
behind.

The crib had been outfitted with new yellow linens for
the baby who now rested there, wrapped tightly in his

blanket. He reminded her again of a tiny, delicate yellow rosebud. The bubble with bright-colored balls which Ian so loved had been left at home. In its place was a lullaby merry-go-round, suspended high above, more suitable to an infant. Monica paused to gaze upon the crib for a moment. It was changed completely, and seemed still another sign of the dwindling summer.

She no sooner reached the kitchen than Hetty said softly, "Let's round up the boys and put them down for a nap in the twin beds there in the big front room. Then you and I can have a visit to ourselves without interruptions. I need to talk to you about something."

She felt rooted to the floor. Surely her face was as red as it felt. She went off dazedly in search of Ian, wondering how Hetty had found out. Buzz was a loyal son, but surely he wouldn't . . . ? Maybe she'd driven down once, or maybe often, seeing their cars. Maybe she only suspected. Well, don't give anything away that you don't have to, she told herself.

Damn, I wish I could get to Buzz.

Absorbed in these thoughts, she'd circled the house twice before she realized she had not seen any sign of Ian. She dispatched Clark to the bed and asked if he knew where Ian was.

The boy looked up from his play. "I hadn't seen him."

Alarmed now, she shaded her eyes and looked way out on the bay. Buzz was on the pier, driving a nail into a cross member midway down. No motion at all in the water. She went around to see if Ian was near the garden hose at the side of the house. He was not there. She went to the back gate and looked up and down the shell road. No sign of him. She went out and walked into the dark garage. Still no Ian. Now she was thoroughly afraid.

"Ian!" she called to him, again and again. He did not come.

Finally she decided to try the rooms in the house again. She disregarded Hetty's look of puzzlement as she passed through the kitchen and poked her head in the crib room. And there he was, hands clutching the rails, staring through at the baby. When she drew up behind him, heart still fluttering, he jerked and looked quickly round at her. Then he turned back to gaze into the crib. He never let go the rails.

"The baby is sleeping," Monica whispered. "He will use the crib now. You can sleep in the twin bed across from Clark for nap. Won't that be fun?" She was speaking softly, coaxing him away. His hands were hooked fast to the rails. He ignored her. "Come on, silly," she said, prying both hands open and pulling him back. "You're a big boy. You need to learn to sleep in a big boy's bed. It is no higher than the sofa at home and you climb on and off that all the time." She was aware it was pure folly to reason with him in this manner, and that now was no time to try and wean him from the crib; yet she had no choice.

To her surprise, he gave no more resistance, but let her lead him into the big front room and help him into the twin bed. "Now, move over close to the wall," she told him. "See, Clark's already asleep." She rubbed his back and, seeing his eyes droop a little, rubbed some more, massaging his shoulders longer than she intended, watching his eyes narrow into slits, then open wide, narrow again, and finally close. It had been easy, she decided as she rose. I'll take him out of the crib at home this evening. I've gotten him this far; no need going back.

She paused at the door and looked down on him once more. She was tempted to lie down beside him; in fact she came very near doing it. And she would remember that moment of indecision long after this day was past. But then, Hetty awaited her in the kitchen.

CHAPTER 42

Ian sensed a change in the air and their words confirmed it. The others spoke of not coming back to the bay. Monica said Forrest would be back. And although he had not been able to keep the calendar to study and get straight in his mind what time meant and how it was measured, he was certain by instinct something was to happen to him very soon.

He pretended sleep only long enough to be sure she was gone. He needed to think but he could not think in this strange bed with no rails, no borders to make him safe. He needed to get into the crib, but they had put the baby there. He tried rocking against the wall in this bed, but he had an uncertain feeling that he would fall because the wall was not connected to the bed. He wrung his hands.

He understood the baby had lived inside Peggy, because they had spoken of the "baby" on the day she let him feel and listen to her stomach, and they had spoken again of the "baby" when they showed him the small one wrapped so tightly today. It reminded him of the animal toys Monica used to put in his crib, that took up too much space.

He wondered whether living inside one of them was like living inside his ball home. He decided not. The thumping he heard inside Peggy's stomach was not like that inside his ball home. It was hard, irregular; lacking rhythm. It was all very strange. And now she kept the baby close to her, near to where its home had been, except when it slept.

This answered many of his questions about the others. He had been right about the children at the school and in other places. They had not come from the same place as him, then changed after they arrived. Now he realized they came from inside the larger ones. This explained why the children wanted to touch and be held by their mommies and daddies. Their mommies and daddies were to them something like what his home was to him.

They started small, and grew. He did not believe he had ever been as small as the baby with Peggy, but he had come to realize he was growing because he could reach places now that he could not reach before and he took up more space in his crib. He wondered if being here made him grow; if that were true, then it was possible if he could not get back to his home in time, he might not fit into it.

Why could he not have been kept near his home? Why hurled through the long tunnel into a different world, separated from all that he knew and needed? He fretted and wrung his hands some more.

He moved his head to the edge of the bed and looked down. She said it was no higher than the sofa at home. He wondered if he got close enough to the edge, would his hand reach the floor? He moved as close as he dared, and reached. His fingertips brushed the floor. It gave him

a brief sense of security, knowing that he could touch it.
He still did not know how he could manage to gain his
thinking place, in the crib.

He tried to put his theories in order again, as he had
many times, hoping that when he had them all together
in his mind, the final key would come out the end. His
home was a round ball which belonged inside the borders
of the round, spinning sky. Like the colored balls in the
bubble, it fastened to the inside borders of the sky while
the sky was in motion.

The sky was always in motion, not like the bubble,
which spun until it simply slowed to a stop or until your
hands brought it to a stop, and then the balls inside it fell.
The only thing to stop the perfect spinning motion of the
sky was a sudden crack: thunder and lightning. Then the
ball homes inside the sky fell and were still. And once in a
while, perhaps only once in all time, one of the ball homes
fell through the crack: the one belonging to him.

When this happened, he fell from his home and made
the terrible journey that brought him here. He believed
he was thrust through a long, dark tunnel then, though
upon his arrival in the bright lights, the tunnel had disappeared. Perhaps the others destroyed it, as they destroyed
other things that had been used. He still did not know
why he fell from his home, but he did know it awaited
him now, and when he returned he would find out.

He closed his eyes now and thought of this journey
again. It was very long and painful, and ended with the
sudden bright lights. He opened his eyes. And that was
when he dropped his mirror. It made a clapping noise on
the floor.

He took in a breath to scream, but then something
stopped him. He looked down at the mirror, lying on the
floor. Suddenly many things made sense. Everything went

down: water poured from a cup, a plate knocked from a table, everything. If anything was let go, it went down instead of up.

There could be but one reason for this: a pulling force that held all things and people here in bondage to the ground. Therefore, you had to get higher than the pull to escape it; that was the answer. The reason his ball home stayed near the spinning sky was that the outside of the sky had pull as well as the inside. He had long believed this. If not, the ball would have fallen.

Could the answer be that the ground moved also? But it did not seem to move, even while having a force to pull you to it. Things moved on it, people walked and ran, cars and trucks and trains moved along its surface, and boats moved on its water just as his ball home moved around the surface of the sky. It seemed to him the earth and sky were in some ways the same, then, that they were both pulling away from each other. So it was logical to get into the pull of the sky you would have to go far enough away from the pull of the ground to overcome its strength.

The trouble was how. Would another walkway of colors ever come, and if it did, would he be in the right place, on the ground, free to go to where it was? Or would Monica trap him inside a car again and latch him into a seat, to keep him away?

Were any of his theories right? If not, why was he trapped here? Why did the others want him? What need had they of him, when they could make their own come right from themselves? His theories had to be correct. They wanted to destroy his world. Why, he could not know. There was so little time, none to waste on figuring their reasons. His forehead hurt. Perspiration popped up on his brow. There was so little time. He edged over until most of his body was off the bed and both feet touched the floor. Then he climbed carefully down, stood up, picked up his mirror, and tiptoed into the room with the crib. He heard voices from the kitchen and, off and on, water running down the sink. The baby was sleeping, right in the middle where he needed to sit. He might move it over, but if he did the rocking might disturb it and make it cry, and then the others would come. He would have to move it somewhere else while he rocked and thought.

He could not reach over the rail and the baby would not fit between two rails. He would have to get the rail down. He had seen Monica do this and also Hetty, and he knew what to do, but it was noisy; he'd always hated the screech. He licked his lips and stood still until the sound of water came again. Then he lowered the rail. He lifted the baby slightly and put it back. He had thought it would be as heavy as the animal toys, but now he realized it was much heavier. He could not take it far. He might leave it on the big bed where Monica slept, but what if it rolled off? Then it would cry, and the others would come. He hesitated. Then he thought of a place not far away where it was soft and the baby would not fall or cry. He knew once he was in the crib he would have to somehow find the courage to climb out. He'd nearly done it on the night they set explosions in his sky. Today in the light he would be able to look down and see the floor. Surely, today, he could do it. He must.

He lifted the baby out of the crib and took it to the hiding place.

CHAPTER 43

Monica plunged her hands into the dish water and began. She would not speak until Hetty had. When finally Hetty did, her remark surprised Monica.

"I want you to do me a favor."

"Oh? Well, I owe you plenty."

Hetty knitted her brow and shook her head in dismissal. "I want you to help me get Buzz straightened out."

"Oh? How do you mean?" She took a firm grip on the stem of a heavy goblet, and sponged it over and over again. Hetty turned on the rinse water.

"Well, since little Bert came into the world, he just hasn't been the same. I know it came as a blow that the boy wasn't healthy. He cried to me one night. First time since he was twelve years old. . . .

"But the trouble was, he seemed to think it was his fault somehow. He told me he was sorry. *Sorry,* mind you. As though he owed me a healthy grandson."

Didn't he? "Well, maybe he'll get over it. Bert's going to be fine, isn't he?"

"If they are careful, his chances are excellent for growing up into a fine young man. Are you done with that goblet?"

"What? Oh, yes, of course." She rinsed it off, handed it to her, picked up a plate.

"But unfortunately, that isn't all. I've had a few suspicions that something not quite right is going on with him. Oh, it was mainly my old intuition at first, and I fought it down. Something about the way he looked at me . . . just once before, when he came home on leave after his tour in Japan . . . Well, anyway . . ."

Monica swallowed, and handed Hetty the plate.

"When I got down here on Wednesday, I could see that Buzz hadn't done a fraction of the work he set out to do. Here he's been off his job for a month, and the faucet in the bathhouse isn't fixed, the back right burner on my stove is still only lighting up halfway around. He hasn't even started the work that needs doing down on the pier . . . not till today anyway . . . that's a few of the things I noticed on Wednesday. And so I can only figure he hasn't been coming down here like he said he was, after all.

"Or he *has* been coming, and using his time in a different way."

Monica closed her eyes and sighed.

"So that's where you come in."

She could not speak; she could feel the nails coming to pin her to the cross. After a long pause, during which she tried and failed several times to come up with a decent remark, Hetty said, "A long time ago, there was a family, name of Hodgkins, three houses down. Where the Millers live now. The boys were small; Aaron wasn't even here yet.

"Well, the Hodgkinses were neighborly people. She was kinda pretty, smooth skin and nice hair, pretty eyes. There weren't many houses down here then. In fact, probably no more than five or six on the whole run. Before we knew it we were spending quite a lot of time with them. He was a merchant marine, and after a while he went out on a boat.

"Now, Bert was as handy as could be around the place, just like Buzz, as you well know, and pretty soon it seemed he was going down to the Hodgkins house to fix one thing and another and staying longer and longer. Finally it dawned on me what was happening."

She paused. "I don't think I ever had anything hurt me so bad. But the last thing I wanted was for Bert to know that I knew. I just didn't want that between us for all the years we had in front of us, and I knew a man is weak in some ways, and sometimes gets off the track.

"So I went to a good friend of Bert's. Well, as a matter of fact I went to your dad, Jack. I asked him to help. I don't know what words passed between them—don't even care to know—but that was the end of the whole thing. Bert didn't spend any more time down at the Hodgkins place, and when Mr. Hodgkins came back off the boat they put the house up for sale and moved away. I never found out where, which suited me just fine."

Monica relaxed a bit. Lucky she'd kept her mouth shut. Hetty didn't know as much as she thought. Imagine her father Hetty's confidant. . . . The "giving" in that friendship was not so one-sided after all, then. Monica ran her tongue over her lips. Hetty was speaking again:

"Will you help me now, and see if you can talk some sense into Buzz?"

They were facing each other direct. Monica could sense Hetty's helplessness. And her intuition, which had gotten her through so much in the past, was only half good now. Maybe the better part lay buried in her husband's grave. She knew *what*, but not *who*.

"I—I don't know what I could say to him," she faltered. "I think it's wrong to interfere in someone else's life."

"Nonetheless I think you could persuade him. He talks to you. And it will save this from hanging between us.

You know, the world is different today than it used to be when I was young. A thing like this could go on, and eventually break up the family. People these days are interested in themselves, and that's the end of it. Lord knows, I learned that already with Carson and June. But Buzz has always been different, more willing to listen to reason, to do what was right."

More willing to follow the map you laid out for his life. And now you're afraid someone has struck a match to that map and you are left with nothing but ashes. No more son to help fill the place of a dead husband. Nothing left to hang on to for a woman who is growing old, and fast. . . .

Monica was too stunned to feel as relieved as she knew she should. Right now she felt she'd just had revealed to her the secret of the changeless way of life at the bay: Hetty had the strength of a seawall and the wisdom to match. Even now, when she was only half right, she would wind up having the last word.

Hetty slipped off her apron and adjusted a couple of hairpins in back. "I'm going down to the store to pick up some more formula—I promised Peggy. Bless her heart. She had one more disappointment when breast feeding didn't work out. I think Buzz is still down at the pier.

"Monica, won't you talk to him?"

"Yes."

"You'll never know how much I appreciate—"

"No. Please don't say that."

Hetty hesitated at the back door, as though she'd thought of something else. But then she walked out. Monica followed and walked the long way around the outside of the house, to avoid disturbing the sleeping children.

As she walked down toward the pier, her mind was becoming clear for the first time in months, like a morn-

ing draped with fog after the sun finally burns through.
She felt she could face it all now, even the fact that Buzz
had not cared for her as much as she hoped. He was a
Wellman, after all, and, like his father before him, would
welcome the chance to go back home where he belonged
after a few weeks of stolen pleasure.

He was searching through a big box of nails as she
approached. "I think we need to talk," she said. There
was no need for her conversation with Hetty to be mentioned. She would cut it clean by herself. The fact that
she did not want to say the things she had to say made no
difference. He did not want her. She had to remember
that and she would be all right.

They sat down a safe distance from each other and slid
feet into the water. It reminded her of their first time.
The sun was very bright that day. He looked out at it and
squinted. She saw this from the corner of her eye. She did
not want to look at him. Her courage was already ebbing.

"I'm sorry about what I said over the phone. Peggy
walked right in the room just then. She thought I was
talking to Bob Arnold from work."

"It's all right. I was—"

"Monica, I've made a decision."

You didn't have to. The end of summer and other circumstances did it for you. All I have to say is that I fully
concur, and we can get off this damned pier where I can't
resist you and go up and join with the others where it is
safe. Stop looking at me, for God's sake.

"I want to marry you."

Five words in the proper order can cut a swath through
family, morals, obligations, and all other items of monu-
mental importance. "Well?"

"Buzz, I—I mean, you just can't—" She couldn't get her
breath.

"Look at me and say you don't care for me, and I'll never bother you again."

She kept looking ahead, squinting at the blazing sun. "I'm sorry, but we have to give it up. We've both known from the first—"

"But you *do* care, you do love me?"

"Yes." After a fashion, yes. What a big word it seems right now.

"And there's nothing left between you and Forrest, is there?"

How thorough you are. "Only Ian." Oh, I'm not ready for this.

"That doesn't count because Forrest isn't a father to his child. Listen, Monica. If you could have anything in the world right now, what would you have?"

She considered a way to phrase it. "I would have both of us free to do as we wish, Buzz."

"Well, then—"

"But you have more to give up than I do, more to lose. I can't let you do that only to have you realize in time that you've made a mistake. You'd hate me then. At least I know that much, and have known it all along. I never meant to go so far that we couldn't get back.

"I . . . I needed you and loved you and I still do, but I can't let you do this." Please, don't press too hard. I'm not strong like Hetty. . . .

"You don't understand," he said. She looked at him. In his face were traces of anger. She had never seen them there. "I want to tell you what it was like, in the hospital, when Bert was born." He paused and took in a breath. The anger disappeared, was replaced by sorrow or remorse, she couldn't tell which. "At first, when I saw Bert, even though he was all messed up and they wouldn't let

me touch him, I felt that he was mine and I was rootin' for
him, for Peggy and for all of us.

"But then, after I watched him hooked up to all those
tubes, all jaundiced, behind the glass under the light, I
started to feel . . . detached. . . . I kept going back to
where I could see, to try and regain the feeling I had at
first. But it wouldn't come. He seemed less and less like
mine. I went back over and over again, but I couldn't feel
anything. Nothing. I went back to the waitin' room and
sat for a long time. It scared the holy shit out of me. I was
numb. . . .

"They still hadn't said anything about his chances for
survival. Finally, a nurse came up and told me if he could
make it through the next twenty-four hours, he'd have a
good chance.

"Some fella sittin' nearby that I'd never even noticed
came over, clapped a hand on my shoulder, and said,
'That's great, Pop. I'm in for my fourth grandson, so I got
an idea how you might be feeling.'

"So then I started to think about Dad, and that somehow brought me up to the point where I could feel again,
but I didn't feel the same. It was like somethin' inside me
jackknifed. I went back and looked at Bert again, and I
kept seeing my father and thinking that if Bert didn't survive, I would have somehow let my old man down. . . .

"Honest to God, I never would have told this to anyone
but you. Oh, I was rootin' for my son, but for all the
wrong reasons. It was like every other feeling, everything
I should have felt, was locked out, blocked."

Oh, Buzz, don't get tears in your eyes, please. . . .

He sniffed and looked out at the sun again. "That was
when I went to call you, right before I left the hospital. I
wanted to tell you how I was feeling, but I just couldn't

bring myself to it. So I went home and sat down and thought, and everything started to clear up for me.

"I started back, way back when I was a kid, and went through every step of my life again. And all it amounted to was bein' Bert Wellman's kid, and doin' what he wanted me to do."

He sat silently for a few moments. She didn't know what to say to him. Finally he continued: "When I was in high school he said, 'Buzz, don't go to college. Get your military duty behind you and learn a trade. That's the way to make a steady living.'

"So I did. I joined the Navy and went to drafting school. Well, I got sent to Japan for a long tour, and while I was there I met a Japanese girl. I was nuts about her, wanted to marry her. Her family didn't take to the idea too well, but they didn't block us. We wanted to marry before my tour was over, but they said that was too soon, that we ought to wait and see, that she could come to me

"Naturally, I went to my folks about it. My dad was so mad it took my mother to keep him from sockin' me. What the hell did he spend his years in the Navy fightin' the sonofabitch Japs for, to have me marry one of the slant-eyed bitches ten or fifteen years later?

"So I dropped the whole idea. I don't know. I guess I didn't really love her, and maybe I half believed he was right or I'd have fought harder. I never even wrote to her. . . . Meantime Carson told Dad to go get screwed, that he'd do what he wanted to do with his life, and Aaron didn't have to worry because Carson had already paved the way. Dad was cool toward them, tight-lipped. But he was ready to pin a ribbon on me.

"When I got out of the service, draftsmen were a dime a dozen and I found a job in purchasing, the same one I

still have except I've worked up to full-fledged purchasing
agent. One of twenty-five. Big deal.

"When Peggy came along, Mom chimed in with Dad.
'She's the girl for you. Sweet and steady, make you a
good wife, a happy home.' And they were right about
Peggy—she'd be good for any man—and we got along together and I was kinda fond of her. You couldn't help but
be. I still am, and I'm not sorry for the years we've had together.

"But fer God's sake, I never felt for any woman what I
feel for you, and I've had it up to my neck being what
someone else wants. I know the timing is all wrong, but I
never asked for it to be this way, any more than you did.
You're the only person in the world I've ever been able to
tell how I feel about things. Peggy knows how to be a
good wife, but her ideas are of the same vintage as my
folks'. She doesn't know what's inside me, and never will.

"Monica, I want to go back to school—to college. I
want to find what I want to be and become it. You said I
could once, and it was like plantin' a seed. I can't get it
out of my mind. I think of it more and more."

She was still sitting by, her feet in the water, leaning
back on her hands. She had not interrupted the avalanche
of feelings that Buzz expressed, but with every word he
said she was brought more into perspective, and again
and again she realized what her own selfishness had
created. She could not marry him and she knew it. She
had allowed her own feelings of entrapment to awaken
his, and she had done this without worry as to what damage she might cause. And now, even as he went on about
the logistics of his decision, she knew that she would have
to kill that new being that she had created inside Buzz.
She would have to tell him that he'd had too much pressure, and that his priorities were temporarily mixed up,

and that it was better to go back and fill his father's shoes because at least then he would be taking responsibility for his life. Something until now she had known nothing about. She would most of all have to avoid telling him that she would never forget him or all he had come to mean to her this summer because that might weaken them both.   .

He was silent. She was about to choose the words that would hurt him more than anything ever had, yet do it as gently as possible: I'm very sorry, Buzz Wellman, but I cannot save what I created in you; it is not healthy and cannot survive, and it is all my fault for tampering with your life in an escape of my own. And further, I have overstated myself. My paintings would not pay the grocery bill, let alone support two families while you return to school. I'm so far from being what you believe me to be. God knows, I don't deserve anyone as good as you . . . and I'd give anything to keep from hurting you by telling you all this. . . .

She opened her mouth to speak but she never got to those words. From the lawn in front of the cottage above them came the high shrill note of Hetty's whistle.

CHAPTER 44

Long after that final day of the last summer at the bay, Monica would break into a cold sweat at the sound of an ambulance siren, and in her mind live through it all again, the screech of Hetty's whistle merging with the siren sounds, there being nothing in between, no space of time when she and Buzz ran up the pier, the whistle still blowing as though Hetty could not stop it. As they reached her, standing like a sentinel dead center in the yard, Buzz shook his mother's shoulders. "What is it? What is it?"

"The baby's gone. I found Ian in the crib, and the baby gone. And Ian won't tell me where he is." She looked at Monica. "Where has Ian taken little Bert?"

Monica passed her and ran into the house, with Buzz behind. In the crib room they first saw Peggy, doubled over on the vanity bench, her blue ribbon askew, her face ashen, and Ian, cowering in the corner, screaming and wringing his hands. Then they were all looking at him, shouting in bewilderment, "Where is he? Where is the baby?" And Monica knew even as her own voice rose above the others that they had made the fatal mistake of throwing him into a panic. He would not tell because he could not. Finally, when they all realized at once the futility of what they were doing, and all except Monica had left to search again for the child, Ian opened his arms wide in supplication, and with his tear-strewn face suffused with fear, pleaded, "Let Ian go!"

She took him in her arms. He shivered and did not return her embrace. "Everything will be all right, darling, don't cry. Sh. Don't cry." She stroked his damp forehead and his cheeks, and pulled him on the bed and rocked him. His breath rose and fell. He was silent and limp. She would have to control her voice and ask him again in even tones where the baby was. But then she heard the voice of Buzz in the closet. "He's here, Mom, God in heaven, call an ambulance." Then softer, to Peggy, "I think he's breathing."

And then, in quick succession: "Oh, Buzz, face down, in there, face down . . ." from Peggy, and then from Hetty, rounding the corner, "They're on their way . . . Where did you? . . . Great Godamighty, in the laundry basket!"

Monica stayed with her child and closed her eyes and prayed until the sound of the ambulance siren approached.

Through all that happened on that day, Hetty showed the greatest strength when she said, "It was my fault. I shouldn't have insisted they bring the child so soon . . . shouldn't have left the house with the baby unattended." And she never wavered from that statement, nor would she hear any argument. Not even later that night, at the hospital, when she called Monica at home to say with a new, quivering voice, "They told us, had the baby been healthy, he wouldn't have suffocated. It's only that, with his lungs and all. . . . You know, I almost went back to check on little Bert before I left for the store. But we hadn't been in the kitchen more than a few minutes and that door between is so creaky I was afraid I'd wake him up if I . . . I should've obeyed my instincts and gone in there anyhow. In all these years, it is the first time I ever let my guard down.

"Buzz is taking it so hard. He keeps saying it's all his fault. But I held him by the shoulders and looked him in the eye, and told him I never wanted to hear him say that again. I won't have him carrying around responsibility for what I've done. Or you, either. Children have to be watched. They don't understand about hurting others. . . ."

Three days passed before Monica called her mother. When Amy answered, Monica found she could not say the words after the first breathy "Mother—" But Amy had been waiting for that sound in her daughter's voice for many years.

"I'll be right there," she said, and when she arrived at Monica's house, very soon after, she took her into her arms and let her cry as long as she needed to, as she had done when Monica was a child.

Amy, who knew as much as she will ever know—that the Wellman baby died at the bay due to some complication of his lungs—has never asked the reason for the change in Monica's feelings for her. She still does not know that Hetty once said there are far worse traits in a person than extravagance.

Two summers have now passed, and the Wellman place has been sold.

Peggy gave birth to a healthy baby girl last spring, and she and Buzz have moved away to South Texas, where he accepted a new job, and also began night classes at a small college. He called Monica one evening unexpectedly, to tell her about college, then hung up quickly. There was much she wanted to say, things she wanted to tell him that last day on the pier but wouldn't dare because he was too close. But then he was gone. The dial tone hummed in her ear, to remind her of the distance between them.

She told no one of the call and feigned surprise when Amy reported the same information, learned from Hetty.

Amy now stays with her grandson Ian five days a week, while Monica paints. She asked to do this when Monica told her Ian would not be returning to the center or to any other preschool. Monica was then prepared to give up painting altogether . . . until some other time. But Amy said, "If I could help you in that way, it would make me feel so much better about . . . everything." And so she comes. There is but one strict rule she has been asked to obey: that there be no mention of the Wellmans or the bay in front of Ian. She understands he would associate it with the tragedy that took place there, and it might frighten him. She does not know that talk of the bay might evoke memories that would haunt him more: his small wet face, his outstretched arms, and the last three words he has ever spoken: "Let Ian go!"

One day Monica put in a call to Dr. Michaels, to tell him at last of the prenatal fever that would be the missing link in his diagnosis. She thought now that pinning a label on her child might be easier than the day-by-day wondering that once seemed less painful. But when she heard the doctor's voice her hand grew clammy and she said instead, "Ian has progressed over the summer. I'm going to keep him at home with me for a while," and hung up. She could learn to live with the clinical term "autistic" by herself. Later, when it could not be put off any longer, she would allow it to others.

To Forrest, who returned in mid-September of that year, she gave the fever, like one presents a gift. The

odds were good that Ian had suffered damage, there was
no longer any getting around that, and a damaged child
was a predicament with which Forrest could not live.
More than that, she did not want to live with him through
the years as he struggled with the living reminder that
imperfection was a part of the world. She would rather
give up her dependence upon him.

She considered giving him instead the affair of the summer with Buzz, but that would have come as a powerful
blow to his fragile self-esteem. And so, with the release of
the secret she struggled with so long, she offered Forrest
his freedom and watched without surprise his reaction
grow up inside him over a period, then surface. Under-
standably, now that he knew, he just couldn't ever feel
the same about her . . . or even about Ian. Of course, if
she'd been more honest about the fever when it happened,
or even later . . . but then . . . .

Forrest is dutiful, and would have stayed if she asked.
She did not. Back in the States now, he is a rising star in a
small company in Michigan. His checks for Ian's support
come with the regularity of a clock. Now and then they
correspond. In her letters to him she builds him up and
wishes him well. It is natural by now for her to do this.
She never mentions her own work; nor does he ask about
it.

Monica has learned how to close out the past and go on
with her painting, with which she has met some success.
The rough sketch of the bay at sunrise, with the boat
roped to the pier, lies unfinished alongside the portrait of
her father, in a closet. She destroyed the sketch begun of
Ian's face some time ago and completed another, which
seems to have captured his essence. He is running alone in
a field under a bright blue sky, full of soft clouds. He has
been holding a red helium balloon, but the string has es-

caped his hand and he now runs toward its undulating tail with arms open, head uplifted. The painting is said to have a curious sense of pathos, which has become a distinction in the Monica Maguire style. It was sold in a gallery in Boston, and brought the highest price of any of her paintings to date. She is glad to have it done. She does not want to see it again, though she believes now it was her gateway to freedom in style, for afterward her style began to fuse more with herself.

She did a self-portrait in abstract after that: a small flesh-colored face, carved by dark lines, without discernible features, except the eyes. From that small face emerges a deep purple ring, and around that still another, lighter purple ring, and on and on, and round and round, lighter and lighter, shaping into a hooded robe from which the face looks out.

She crated it and sent it to Andrew James in San Francisco. He wrote of entering it in the first annual Women in Art Awards exhibit in Washington, D.C. Monica, involved in other paintings, hardly read the note before discarding it. Then, two months later, came another letter with a check enclosed. The painting had taken first place, and won $5,000. *National Art* called the painting "imaginative . . . courageously honest," and would feature it on the cover of their November issue.

Monica looked at the check for a long while and thought: I never knew painting it would be so expensive.

Sometimes Monica dreams that Ian will come into her room and climb into bed with her and say, "I love you, Mommy," and put his arms around her neck. But she does not tell anyone of this recurring dream, and continues to embrace him, thankful at least he does not pull away.

Amy sees Ian from a grandmother's view. She is patient and kind and unassuming, and does not broach the subject of what shall be done with him when he is older, of school age, when a decision about his future must be made. People did not worry about these things in her days of rearing children. As though reacting to this treatment, Ian seldom throws tantrums. He seems content or, as Monica often senses, resigned.

Monica still has a spell of depression, late in the day after Amy has gone and before the dinner hour has arrived. Sometimes she sits alone at a table until the time has passed. Sometimes she sips a glass of wine. Now and then she watches Ian skipping along the periphery of life, skirting the borders of the room, and begins to weep, for yesterday, for today, and for tomorrow. Otherwise she works near the window with good sun exposure, and while she's involved in a painting, nothing else matters. Nothing else exists.

CHAPTER 45

The September of meaning for Ian has come and gone.

While saddened by his inability to return to his natural home, he no longer believes a limit of time has been put upon him for figuring out how to get there. And though he still spends much of his time on theories, he also ob-

serves changes around him and wonders if the others
have begun to study ways to become one of his kind. He
has considered this as a possibility because the changes
began to occur when the September had begun. Could it
be that the others had only until then to force his secrets
from him and, failing, must lose their turn, like in a game
where each player has one turn? Must they now wait
until all the pages of the calendar have been turned and
all time has passed away?

There are signs that make him feel certain this new
theory is correct. The teacher named Forrest no longer
comes, nor is he spoken of. Monica no longer takes him to
the bay, where they played tricks on him, then assaulted
him all together for trying to figure out how to survive
among them until he could get away. Nor do the others
speak of the bay anymore.

They live in a new place now that is smaller and more
logical in proportion, called an apartment. The outside
part is exactly square, and he can see his ball high above
the fence which borders it. There is also a window in the
room where he sleeps, and he can see his ball from there
at night, when it glows white and sprinkles the sky with
stars. Will it await him for all of time?

The lady Monica calls "Mother," who comes for five
days, then after two in between, comes for five more, does
not try to get him to do anything. She touches him and
holds him, and she also touches and holds Monica, and
there seems to be a certain feeling between them that he
has not seen before. He senses this and, for reasons he
doesn't understand, sometimes finds himself feeling a
kind of fullness in his chest that used to come only from
flicking his mirror at his ball home.

Then there are days when the lady called "Mother"

does not come. On many of these days, Monica helps him into the car and they go for a very long drive, making one stop along the way. He waits in the car while she goes into a place where there are many different kinds of flowers. When she comes out, she is always holding a yellow flower with a long stem that she calls a "rosebud." Sometimes she brings it to her nose to smell. Sometimes she lets him smell it. It always smells the same.

They go, from there, to a place with lots of trees and grass, and stones sitting on the ground, the color of the sky when rain is about to fall. He waits in the car again while she walks among the stones to a certain one, which is among a group of small, short stones. She always goes to the same stone. She always places the rosebud in front of it, then sits on her knees with her head down. After a while she comes back to the car and they drive to a park nearby with many great trees with big trunks. She swings him in the swing for a long time and he watches his ball home wink at him from between the treetops. She rarely says anything to him while he swings and he likes this time and feels safe because everything about it is consistent. Sometimes he forgets his own thoughts, and wonders what she is thinking about.

He knows now that Monica has been the only one of the others consistent since he arrived. He could not see this until the others around her had been sent away, and with them, the confusion. He feels that, should his chance of returning come, he would not want to go without her.

He did not begin to see Monica in this new way until one day when she sat in her usual place, at the usual time, before dark, and began to cry. Not to scream like the others, but to cry: silently, sadly, as he has done. He had never seen any of the others do this before. He understands loneliness. He understands soft, helpless weeping. He has seen her cry many times now.

He feels a growing urge to touch her and make her know that she is not alone because he is here.